4—
#71

The Case of the 'Hail Mary' Celeste

Aberystwyth Noir series:

The Day Aberystwyth Stood Still
From Aberystwyth with Love
Don't Cry for Me Aberystwyth
The Unbearable Lightness of Being in Aberystwyth
Last Tango in Aberystwyth
Aberystwyth Mon Amour

The Case of the 'Hail Mary' Celeste

The Case Files of Jack Wenlock, Railway Detective

MALCOLM PRYCE

B L O O M S B U R Y

LONDON · NEW DELHI · NEW YORK · SYDNEY

First published in Great Britain 2015

Copyright © 2015 by Malcolm Pryce

The moral right of the author has been asserted

No part of this book may be used or reproduced in any manner whatsoever
without written permission from the publishers except in the case of brief
quotations embedded in critical articles or reviews

Epigraph appearing on page v from 'From a Distant View of a Provincial
Town' Copyright © John Betjeman. Reproduced by permission of The Estate
of John Betjeman

Every reasonable effort has been made to trace copyright holders of material
reproduced in this book, but if any have been inadvertently overlooked the
publishers would be glad to hear from them

Bloomsbury Publishing Plc
50 Bedford Square
London
WC1B 3DP

www.bloomsbury.com

Bloomsbury is a trademark of Bloomsbury Publishing Plc

Bloomsbury Publishing, London, New Delhi, New York and Sydney

A CIP catalogue record for this book is available from the British Library

Hardback ISBN 978 1 4088 5892 9

Trade paperback ISBN 978 1 4088 5194 4

10 9 8 7 6 5 4 3 2 1

Typeset by Hewer Text UK Ltd, Edinburgh
Printed and bound in Great Britain by CPI Group (UK) Ltd, Croydon CR0 4YY

Beside those spires so spick and span
Against an unencumbered sky
The old Great Western Railway ran
When someone different was I

—John Betjeman

Author's Note

From the case files of Jack Wenlock,
Great Western Railway Detective, 1930–1948

When King George V announced in 1917 that he was changing the name of the British royal family from Saxe-Coburg and Gotha to Windsor, a collective groan went up from the palace staff. They knew what it meant: they would have to spend the week working through the night changing the name tags on the King's pyjamas and PE kit. To the man on the Clapham omnibus the announcement was perplexing. The British people had spent the past three years valiantly fighting the Hun but had always been far too well-mannered to remind their King that he was German himself. Why change things now? The following story, taken from the case files of Jack Wenlock, suggests a solution to the puzzle.

There were twelve Gosling class special railway detectives created at the Weeping Cross Railway Servants' Orphanage between 1902 and 1914. By the time the railways were nationalised in 1948 only one was left: Jack Wenlock. This is his story.

Lightcliffe	Shot at dawn, 1917
Tumby Woodside	Stole money from dog, thrashed to death, 1921
Temple Combe	Died in the electric chair at Sing Sing, 1925
Conway Marsh	Crushed by elephant in Indochina, 1926
Kipling Coates	Lost in opium den, Shanghai, 1927
Mickle Trafford	Dragged from ship by a giant squid, 1928
Luton Hoo	Stabbed in the eye with a swordstick, 1929
Cadbury Holt	Missing, presumed eaten by a lion, 1930
Hucknall Byron	Sent to Gulag on Kolyma River, 1935
Cheadle Heath	Adulterer, blotted copybook, expelled, 1936
Amber Gate	Lost on the Hindenburg, 1937
Jack Wenlock	Fate unknown

Chapter 1

I T WAS TUESDAY the second of December 1947 when Jenny the Spiddler walked into my office: almost a month before they nationalised my mother. Some people will regard that as a fanciful turn of phrase, forgivable perhaps in someone who had worked his entire life on the railways. But I don't mean it that way. The Great Western Railway really was my mother. I was born in a specially constructed maternity engine shed at the Weeping Cross Railway Servants' Orphanage in 1914, the birth arranged in such a fashion that the first thing I saw upon opening my eyes in this world was a 4-6-0 Saint class locomotive. This was done in accordance with the ethological theories of Oskar Heinroth, who had shown that a greylag goose takes as its mother the first thing it sees on emerging from the egg, and it had been supposed that a human baby would be the same. My mother was engine number 2904 *Lady Godiva*. She had a domeless parallel boiler, raised Belpaire firebox and boiler pressure of 200 psi, although by the time I was born her boiler had been replaced with a superheated half-cone device. As for the flesh-and-blood mother who had her confinement in this engine shed, from whose loins I emerged but whose face I was specifically prevented from glimpsing, I know nothing. Every moment of my life thereafter was spent in the service of the Great Western Railway, or God's Wonderful Railway as we all knew her. I was a Gosling class detective, that fabled cadre of detectives who trod the corridors of the GWR trains in the years 1925 to 1947. There were twelve of us in all and I am the last. No official record of us now exists, with the exception of this testament. I have decided to make my case files over to the national archive, as a gift to the people of this land, with the instructions that all files remain sealed until after my death. I am in good health and expect to live a long while yet, and hope that when the hour of my death comes Princess Elizabeth will be on the throne and the dark secrets contained within these pages will have lost their power to precipitate a Jacobin revolution in England.

She came at fifteen minutes past five. The door was half panelled with the top made of opaque glass and I could make out the shape of a girl through the glass. She knocked on the wooden bit. I said come in but she didn't so I walked over to open the door. She wore a plain cream mackintosh, tightly belted, ankle socks and a pancake hat. Her hair was worn in the style made popular by Veronica Lake. I stepped aside and she walked in and sat down without being invited.

'May I take your coat?'

'Then I'd have to give you my hat, wouldn't I?'

'Not if you didn't want to.'

'I'm not sure if I would be able to get it on again, it's not a very good one.'

The pancake hat was attached to the side of her head as if someone had thrown a pie at her and it had stuck.

'It looks rather fetching to me.'

'Well, it isn't. I knitted it myself. That wasn't the problem, it was the wool. We – that's me and Aunt Agatha – unravelled it from a bed sock. That's OK too but you can still see the curl in the wool. It's very hard to get that out. The "Make Do and Mend" booklets never tell you how to do that.'

'I thought it was part of the style.'

'Shows you how much you know. Have you got any snipes?'

I took out a pack of Player's and reached it across. She took one out with slightly trembling fingers. I struck a Swan Vesta and held the flare up to the end of her cigarette. She drew in the smoke and avoided my gaze and then darted a quick look at me and away. She was trying hard to be nonchalant but you could see she wasn't used to having men light her cigarettes for her. She let out a slight choke. I lit one too and regarded her through the curling tendrils of smoke.

'I've never done this before,' she said, then added, 'I need to see a Railway Gosling.'

I smiled.

'This is where you say they don't exist.'

'I don't know if they exist – I've never seen one.'

'The people at the Anaglypta Mill told me you would deny it. They said Goslings are very shy. They said don't leave the office until he admits it.'

'How do you know you've come to the right office?'

She twisted in her chair and nodded towards a glass case in the corner containing a stuffed goose. 'I saw the goose through the glass in the door.'

'It could be from Lost Property.'

'Yes, I'm sure it could – left behind by the King of Timbuktu.'

She continued scanning the room. There wasn't much to look at. On my desk there was a telephone receiver, subscriber number Weeping Cross 723; a lamp, an ashtray, a pen and some blotting paper. A copy of Chesterton's *History*. There were two framed pictures on the walls, and above the cold fireplace hung a map of the Great Western Railway. On top of the filing cabinet there was a photo of my mother, 4-6-0 Saint class locomotive, number 2904 *Lady Godiva*. There was also a hatstand, and behind the hatstand a small bookcase containing the Boy's Own Railway Gosling annuals, volumes 1 to 10, with the exception, of course, of the 1931 edition.

'Who's that?' She pointed at my mezzotint next to the door.

'A sixteenth-century Frenchman called Salomon de Caus. They imprisoned him in an insane asylum.'

'What did he do?'

'He said that one day men would use steam to turn wheels.'

'I don't believe that will ever happen.'

'Me neither.'

'You're funny. Do you carry a gun?'

'No.'

Disappointment flickered in her eyes. 'Well, can you fight?'

I stared at her for a brief moment and then looked towards the window. The panes were filmed over with soot and cracked. One was broken. The frames began to rattle and the air quivered. From afar came the sound of singing metal: rails quivering. This was followed by a soft wail, the sort a man might emit from a distant dungeon when on the rack. The walls began to hum; the glass in the windows rattled more fiercely. The approach always seemed slow at first, then the train arrived like a wrecking ball slamming into the side of a building. There were more wails, louder, with furious snorts and coughs. Gobbets of smoke puffed through the broken light, filling the room with the stench of sulphur. Then she was gone.

4

'The 5.17 to Hereford,' I said.

'See, I knew you were a Gosling. I bet you can tell from the sound exactly what sort of train it was, can't you?'

'Yes, it's a 4-6-0 Castle class, the one with a sloping throatplate in the firebox. You can tell because even after the modifications to the blastpipe and chimney, the steam superheating still falls short. Hence the characteristic double cough in the chuffs.'

She brought the knuckle of her index finger up to her mouth, and twisted her head slightly to one side as if needing to examine me from a different angle.

'Castle class?'

I nodded.

'Sure, but which one?' She smiled impishly.

'It was number 4070 *Godstow Castle*.'

'Golly! You can tell all that just from the chuffing?'

I paused and let the slowly widening grin on my face answer her question. She burst into a smile. 'You're kidding, aren't you?'

'Of course.'

She laughed. It sounded like silver bells and was the loveliest laugh there had ever been in my office. I enjoyed the moment, although I didn't laugh. The truth was, I hadn't been kidding. It really was *Godstow Castle*. The double cough in the chuffs was a dead giveaway.

'Why did you ask if I could fight?'

'This case might be dangerous. I need a Gosling who can fight. I read all the Railway Gosling annuals when I was a little girl.'

'All of them?'

'Well, except the 1931. I know all about you. Every Gosling has fired a King class 4-6-0 from Paddington to Bristol Temple Meads.

5

The movement of the right arm with the shovel is the same as the punch to the ribs that breaks the heart of the prizefighter and makes him kiss the canvas like a sweetheart. Is that true?'

'Yes, that's true.'

'The books also say you are practised in the secret art of Chinese temple boxing, like Fu Manchu. Is that true?'

'I'm afraid that's a secret. How old are you?'

'As old as my tongue and a little older than my teeth. Guess what I do.'

'I don't think I could.'

'I work in the Anaglypta Mill, I put the bubbles in.'

'So you're a spiddler.'

'You don't have to say it like that.'

'I didn't mean to offend. How do they get the bubbles in?'

'You know I can't tell you that. I'd lose my job. I've come about my aunt Agatha, in case you are wondering.'

'I was beginning to.'

'Couldn't we . . . why don't we go to the Lyons tea shop? I could tell you there.'

'You can tell me about it here.'

She looked disappointed and frowned. 'You're no fun. Aunt Agatha saw a murder. It was in the adjacent carriage of a passing train. She was on the 4.50 to Brackhampton and fell asleep for a while. When she awoke there was another train passing them on the next line. For a while their speeds matched and they ran in parallel. Just then the blind in the adjacent compartment snapped up, and there it was: a man with his hands to the throat of a woman. He was throttling her. Then she went limp in his arms and the train speeded up and was gone.'

She gave me a look of triumph, then slipped off her chair and walked over to the wall and the picture of Oskar Heinroth. It showed a portly man in an astrakhan coat and wearing a homburg running through a wide path in a birch forest. He was being chased by a low-flying goose, and you could tell from his gait that he was not used to running and probably had not done it for many years. He seemed to be laughing.

'Who's this? Your granddad?'

'It's just a picture.'

She walked over to the bookshelf and knelt down to read the spines. 'You don't have the 1931 either.'

'No one does.'

She stood up and walked back to her chair. 'You don't seem very curious about my aunt Agatha. Don't you want to know what happened next?'

'I already know what happened next. She reported the murder to the police and they didn't believe her. They said there was no murder, no one had been reported missing, and there was no corpse. In the absence of these things it would be very difficult to conduct a murder inquiry. They told her to go home, have a cup of tea and forget all about it. They probably also pointed out that the incident took place just after she had been asleep and so the likely explanation was she was still dreaming.'

She slipped back on to the chair and took another cigarette. Her hands trembled even more as she brought the cigarette up. 'That's exactly what happened. How did you know?'

'It happens every month. We call them throttlers. Little old ladies who make up stories like that. I had ten case files cross my desk last year alone.'

'Well, that shows you are not as smart as you think you are, doesn't it? Because if that is true you must be the Gosling.'

7

I shrugged. 'If you say so. What did the murdered woman look like?'

'She was a nanny. With a perambulator and a little boy with her.'

'Your aunt saw all that?'

'Yes.'

'What did the boy do while his nanny was being strangled?'

'Is that important?'

'It could be the key that unlocks the whole case.'

'I'm not sure, I don't think she mentioned what he did. Anyway, that's not the best bit – you'll never guess what happened next.'

'What happened next?'

'Are you taking me to the Lyons tea shop?'

'I don't usually finish until 5.30.'

She looked at the clock above the door. It was 5.25. She stood up and dragged her chair over, climbed up and pulled open the hinged glass front of the clock and moved the big hand forward. Then she came back and sat on my desk. 'The best thing is this. When she came home from the police station that evening an ambulance turned up and took her away.'

'Which hospital did they take her to?'

'The ambulance was unmarked. This was a week ago. Then yesterday I received a letter from Saint Christina's Home for Lunatics, Mental Defectives and the Feeble-Minded. They had taken her there.'

'Did they tell you why?'

'No. I went to see her yesterday. They told me she was too unwell for a visit, but I could go tomorrow.' She reached into her bag and took out a tin of corned beef. 'I'll take her this. By my reckoning this is definitely covered by the terms of carriage and conveyance, which means you are duty bound to help her. Can we go to the Lyons tea shop?'

'Yes.'

Chapter 2

THERE WAS A sharp frost beginning to form as we left the office. It sparkled like powdered glass in the fog, shimmering around the streetlamps and muffling sound. As we walked across the station forecourt to the tram stop we passed a seal grey Morris 1000 parked in the place reserved for taxis. A young man sat inside wearing a trilby and a trench coat and resting a newspaper on the steering wheel. As we passed he tossed the newspaper aside and reached for the ignition key. Something about the manner in which he put away the newspaper made me think he had only been pretending to read. The tram clanged to a halt and Jenny jumped on the stairs at the back and climbed, running her hand along the curving white handrail. It wasn't really necessary to sit on the top deck, we were only going three stops, but I didn't mind. We jumped off outside the Astoria.

The Lyons tea shop was empty. Three waitresses stood and watched us walk in with an air that suggested they would have preferred the place to remain empty. We took a seat next to the window. I ordered an egg each, three slices of bread and butter and a pot of tea. Jenny asked for two glasses of dog soup, which turned out to be tap water. The waitress wrote down the order with a slight nod and then walked away. Jenny looked at me with suppressed excitement. She leaned forward and whispered. 'It's no good pretending any more, I saw it.'

'Saw what?'

'Your gun. On the tram, I saw it outlined in your pocket.' She nodded towards my jacket. I slipped my hand inside and pulled out a metal container that looked like a fat cigarette holder. It might conceivably look like the outline of a gun to someone who had never seen one. I handed it to her. 'Open it.'

She prised the hinged lid open and looked inside. It had a red velveteen lining in which rested a rectangle of something that looked like wood, but wasn't.

'What is it?'

'It's called Formica. It's a modern luxury furnishing. It's resistant to heat, abrasion and moisture and it's printed with woodlike patterns using a rotogravure printing process.'

'Looks just like wood.'

'Yes.'

'But it feels . . . all different, like . . . I don't know . . . satin.'

'The texture is very similar to satin. They use it in the sleeping cars of the Hiawatha trains on the Chicago, Milwaukee and St Paul Railroad. And on the *Queen Mary*. Although only in first class.'

'What are you going to do with it?'

The tea arrived and Jenny poured while I paused to consider the answer. How much should I tell her? Normally I tended to keep my cards close to my chest, but there was something about her. She was very pretty, of course, but there was something else. Gaiety with a bit of mischief, in a nice way. She was impish.

Her gaze met mine. 'Go on!'

'You remember that picture in my office, of the man being chased by the goose? I said it was no one special, but that wasn't

11

true. It was Oskar Heinroth. He was the man who invented the Gosling process. Or, at least, the theory behind it.'

She was about to lift the lid of the tea pot and give the leaves another stir. She stopped and her eyes sparkled.

'I suppose the theory would be rather boring for you,' I said.

'Not on your nelly! But . . . I thought the Gosling process was supposed to be top secret.'

'I'm not sure if it matters any more. The Goslings will be gone soon, I expect, once the railways are run by the common man.'

'Are you sure?'

'You'll notice they don't polish the engines any more. They are all black. In the old days we had eight men to every engine cleaning and polishing through the night. All the bright colours, shining brighter than the buttons on a sergeant major's tunic.'

'It's sad that they don't polish the engines, but this is what we fought the war for, isn't it?'

'Yes, I suppose it is.'

'All those people who died. They didn't lay down their lives so we could go back to being servants of the toffs, did they?'

'No, they didn't. And you mustn't think I dislike the common man. I happen to be one myself. I was raised in the Railway Servants' Orphanage. You probably pass it on your way to work. St Christopher's.'

'Yes, I know it.'

'Oskar Heinroth discovered something called "imprinting" which means when a greylag gosling emerges from its shell it will regard the first thing it sees as its mother, even if it's an umbrella stand.'

'But that's silly! How can a little goose think an umbrella stand is its mum? They don't look remotely similar.'

12

'That's the point. How does the goose know what his mother is supposed to look like when he comes out of the shell? He's never seen her before. He just assumes the umbrella stand is his mum.'

Jenny giggled. 'And a railway train was your mum?'

'Yes.'

'How exciting! Which one?

'2904 *Lady Godiva*. She's a 4-6-0 Saint class locomotive.'

'I was born in Aunt Agatha's front room. I expect my real mother is a postcard of Skegness. Or a half-knitted bed sock.' She looked glum at that thought and then immediately brightened as another occurred: 'Do you . . . ever see her?'

'No, I'm afraid she was withdrawn in 1933.'

A man walked in and strode past us to take a table near the other door opening on to Tanner's Row. It was the chap who had been reading the newspaper in the car outside the station. I could see now that he was quite a young man, probably not quite turning twenty. His face was thin and long and the skin smooth and boyish, marked with bright red pimples and razor nicks. The coat was well worn without being shabby and it was slightly too big, which suggested it had been handed down. His trousers were a touch too short, the bottom of the turn-up not quite resting correctly on the black leather brogue. There was a look of mild hostility in his face: it was the look of a boy wishing to pass for a man, but self-conscious about it. I was pretty sure he had been following us.

'So what does this have to do with your thingummy piece?'

'My Formica?'

'Yes.'

'Oskar Heinroth left some money, £5,000, as a prize for the Goslings. I want to win it.'

13

'What's the prize for?'

'For solving the greatest mystery in all the annals of railway lore. It happened in 1915—'

'Oh, Jack!'

'What?'

'It was a special excursion train containing twenty-three nuns travelling from Swindon to Bristol Temple Meads. The nuns disappeared. Vanished into thin air. The train arrived at Bristol without them. They searched everywhere, all over the country, but not a trace of them was found. They've never been seen since.'

'Oh . . . why, yes. The newspapers called it—'

'The "Hail Mary" Celeste.'

'You seem to know quite a bit about it.'

'Of course I do. Everyone does.'

'I thought it was just we Goslings.'

Jenny rolled her eyes as if I were being especially stupid. 'There isn't a person in the whole country who hasn't heard of the "Hail Mary" Celeste.'

'All the other Goslings tried, you see. They went off in search, but . . . they never came back.'

'How many Goslings are there?'

'There were twelve in all, born at the orphanage between 1902 and 1914. I'm the only one left.'

'Are they all dead?'

'Some are definitely dead, some are insane, some are missing and one . . . one . . .'

'Yes?'

'Cheadle Heath is still around, I occasionally see him. But he's not a Gosling now. He had to . . . he left.'

'I see.'

'He blotted our copybooks, you see.'

'Oh no!'

'Yes.'

'What did he do?'

'Actually, I would prefer not to talk about Cheadle.'

'Did none of them find a trail?'

'Some people think Cadbury Holt did. He's officially listed as "missing, presumed eaten by a lion". He went to Africa. He never came back, although Cheadle got a postcard from him. Cadbury was the editor of the missing 1931 Gosling annual, you see. Some people say he wrote about his adventures in that.'

'So is that why no one has seen it?'

'I expect so.'

'Did they print it?'

'As far as I know.'

'In that case, you should talk to the printers. Do you know who printed them?'

'A place called Master Humphrey's Clock. They don't have any copies. The chap promised to ring me if he ever gets one.'

'No, but they might have the thingybob plates. They have to keep them in case they want to print some more.'

'Thingybob plates?'

'It doesn't matter what the name is. My auntie wrote a book about ointment making so I've seen how they do it. The letters are all back to front, but you could read them with a mirror.'

Our eggs arrived and we ate in silence broken only by the click-clack of cutlery and, from outside, the hum of passing traffic. The waitress took the boy a pot of tea, but he made no attempt to drink it. Instead he took the newspaper out of his pocket and held it in a way that suggested he was observing us from behind it. He ordered no food and I suspected he must have been on expenses, but not very big ones.

'So what will you do with the money if you win the Heinroth Prize?'

'I will use it to find my mother.'

Jenny looked up from her boiled egg and studied my face. 'You mean, your real . . . I mean, your flesh and blood mother.'

'Yes.'

'Do you have any idea where she is?'

'None at all. She delivered me, and then left on the number 27 bus never to be seen again.'

'How do you know what bus she caught?'

'Because I see her in my dreams.'

'What does she look like?'

'Her face is concealed by a headscarf, but you can tell she is young, perhaps no more than eighteen, and big with child. She's scared, too. Or at least I sense she is. She always steps off the bus and stares up at the portico of the orphanage as if she has no business being there and she knows it.' I paused and thought for a while. Then I said, 'When I find her I will use the money to buy her a fitted kitchen. Do you know what they are?'

'Yes, I've seen one in a magazine. I thought it was the cat's kimono.'

'I saw one at the Daily Mail Ideal Home exhibition.'

'I've never been to London.'

'Oh you should! It's very gay. That's where I got the Formica. I want to make the kitchen out of Formica.'

'That sounds lovely. I wish I had a man who would do that for me.'

I called for the bill.

'You know what I would do if I won £5,000?' Jenny said.

I shook my head.

'I would buy a Biro!'

It was my turn to look impressed.

'I saw one in Barker & Stroud's,' she said. 'It cost fifty shillings!'

'By Jove! That sounds like rather a flash sort of pen. I should very much like to have a Biro myself.'

Jenny reached her hand across and rested it on mine. 'You can share mine.'

I walked her back to the tram stop. She wouldn't let me take her further and only allowed me that far after extracting a promise that I would go with her to visit her aunt Agatha the following evening. We arranged to meet at six outside the National Milk Bar. The parting was slightly awkward. We stood facing each other, saying how nice it had been. The thought crossed my mind that I should kiss her but that would have been extremely bold. I had never done such a thing with a client before. All the same, it felt that the hour we had just passed together had been too enjoyable to be strictly business. I was surprised to discover how quickly the time had flown. We shook hands and when the tram arrived Jenny said, 'Abyssinia.'

'I beg your pardon?'

'ABYSSINIA!'

'What about it? They've got a narrow gauge line from Addis Ababa to French Somaliland. Three foot three-eighth inches. I went on it once. I've still got the ticket.'

I stopped speaking and observed the look on her face. She

giggled and shook her head gently. Then the tram stopped with a shrill *ding*. Jenny jumped forward and kissed me on the cheek. Before I could react she had jumped aboard the tram which was already moving off with a *ding, ding, ding*. As it turned the corner she waved and shouted again, 'Abyssinia.'

'Abyssinia,' I said.

I wandered back through the deserted streets to the railway station. Lamps still glimmered on the platforms and along the track but all else in the building was in darkness. The clock of St Bede's chimed seven. I took out my key and entered the side entrance, not bothering to put on the lights, preferring to fumble my way in the dark to the wire cage lift. The hum as I ascended was soothing to my nerves. At the top, as was my habit, I paused on leaving the lift and stared through the window at the street outside. Across the way was the five-storey department store, Barker & Stroud's. The building style was ornate, the sort they called neo-gothic. For many years the striking feature had not been the unnecessary crenulations and spires but a hand-painted advertisement for Lindt, the Swiss chocolatier. It was on the end wall and gave a fine prospect to passengers arriving from the north on platform 7. The painting was still there but had faded so much over the years that you would not be aware of it if you did not know where to look. I saw it every day: the ghost of a Swiss maid in an alpine meadow, holding a pail of milk. Moreover, I knew the girl who had posed for the painting: it was Magdalena from the orphanage.

I entered my office and picked up the post that had been left just inside the door. The message boy had been late today; I did hope everything was all right. Perhaps they would be getting rid of him, too, now the common man was going to take charge of the railways. I took the small pile to the desk where I could read it under the lamp. The room was cold and I did not remove my coat. There was a note about my expenses, an inquiry concerning a stolen postal order and a note from Mr Lambert asking if I had made any progress with the mysterious death of Driver Groates. My eyes flicked to the folder lying in my in-tray. It had been there a while now, and so far I had been unable to penetrate the mystery. I had no particular desire to re-open it tonight. I suspected Mr Lambert merely enquired for form's sake so if anyone should look into the matter he could say that he had been following the case closely. There was nothing of great urgency. I cycled home to my lodgings on Devil's Curtsy, and said as I cycled, to no one in particular, 'Abyssinia!'

THE BOY'S OWN
RAILWAY GOSLING ANNUAL

Vol. VII	1931	Price: 1/-

Replies to our readers' letters

C. P. RUPERT, HEREFORD—The reaction of the Thomas Cook clerk which you describe is called Exasperation. Rest assured, he did not refuse to sell you the ticket because you are a Jew, but simply because no such ticket exists. The railway line you claim to have found on your atlas linking Penzance with New York is almost certainly a submarine telegraphic cable.

J. ELDERFLOWER, EDGBASTON—The artery to which you refer is the carotid and has nothing to do with carrots.

DEIRDRE R., STENHOUSEMUIR—Yes, conceivably, if it were a very large boa constrictor and a very small hippo.

THE CONTINUING ADVENTURES OF RAILWAY GOSLING
CADBURY HOLT – ON THE TRAIL OF THE MISSING NUNS!

An Audience with the Consul

'What I don't understand, Mr Holt,' said the consul, 'is why you don't just buy a boy from the market like anybody else.'

'It really is far less trouble for us,' added the consul's assistant, as he waved vaguely into the air with his pipe. 'And you can obtain any predilection your heart desires . . .'

'Clean, too,' said the consul. 'Fresh as you like.'

'So long as you are willing to pay,' added the pipe smoker. 'Of course you get what you pay for. It's no different to the markets back in England.'

I turned my gaze upon the pipe smoker, and fought hard to control the fury erupting within my breast. 'I advise you, sir, to withdraw these infamous insinuations.'

'My dear chap,' he said.

'No, I am not your dear chap. Withdraw your calumny or you will leave me no choice but to challenge you to a duel. These are not words I use lightly.'

'I withdraw it on his behalf,' said the consul with an air of weary resignation. 'I can't afford to lose another assistant.'

'I withdraw the remark,' said the pipe smoker. 'All the same, I consider your plan as evidence that you are in need of the services of a good brain doctor. Even if you are a Railway Gosling, which I rather doubt.'

'Yes,' said the consul. 'What sort of name is Cadbury Holt? Sounds a rum sort of name to me. More like the name of a cake. Well, you'll need more than sugar and spice in your guts if you are serious about this plan of heading off into the desert in search of nuns. Especially with this . . . this . . .' He indicated the prisoner who stood before his desk and who would act as my guide. The wretch really was the sorriest, most louse-infested rogue imaginable. He wore a grin of permanent insolence and in his eye was a leer that would shame a pickpocket at a funeral. 'We will keep his brother in jail and if you do not return within a month, or send word that you are safe, we will shoot him.'

'Try not to forget to send us word.'

'Frankly,' said the consul, taking the top off his fountain pen,

21

'I resent the fact that I will be landed with paperwork for your funeral.'

'Yes,' said the pipe smoker. 'Personally I wouldn't entrust him to look after a rhubarb patch, let alone a Christian soul.'

Chapter 3

WHEN I ARRIVED at the station next morning the light was on in my office. The door was ajar. There were two men inside. One of them was the young man who had followed Jenny and me to the Lyons tea shop. He was sitting in my chair, which I thought was slightly impertinent. He also sat rather untidily with his ankle resting lazily on one thigh. He was not exactly slouching but not sitting properly upright either. Posture is usually a good indicator of a man's character, as is the diligence with which he polishes his shoes. The other man was standing, half facing the window, and turned as I entered. He was much older and gave off an air of authority. He was relaxed without being slovenly. He had a bald head that shone with health and the hair on the sides had been fiercely trimmed with clippers; in the dim morning light I could see individual bristles glinting.

'Ah, Mr Wenlock!' he exclaimed, and then made an exaggerated arm movement to consult his wristwatch. 'Bang on nine. I knew you would be. Your clock is five minutes fast. I was going to adjust it but knowing your reputation I thought perhaps you had a reason for it.'

'I think the cleaner must have changed it.' I went over to correct it. The glass was still ajar from when Jenny had opened it.

'The cleaner, yes, I expect it was her. I hope you don't mind, she let us in. She said you wouldn't be long.'

'Not at all, she has my permission to do that.'

'Bit parky out this morning, isn't it? Looks like snow.'

'Oh yes, snow before the end of the week I'd say. May I ask you gentlemen your names?'

'Young,' said the boy. 'Mr Young.'

The older man stepped forward and offered me his hand. 'My name's Old.'

We shook. 'Pleased to meet you, Mr Old, and you, Mr Young.'

I paused and examined them both. There was an insolence in the manner of the boy that I did not greatly take to, but Goslings are not proud. Pride is a very unhelpful emotion for a detective to possess. A clear head is essential for solving mysteries, and nothing interferes with that more than the sort of rush of blood you get when someone upsets you.

'Would you gentlemen care for a cup of tea?' I asked.

'That would be splendid,' said Mr Old.

'How do you take it?'

'As it comes,' he said. 'As it comes.'

'Four sugars, milk in first but just a drop, no more,' said the young man. 'Biscuits, too, if you've got them.'

'I'll see what's there.' I left them to it. The cubby hole with the kettle and pot was at the far end of the corridor next to the washroom, from where I collected water. The cleaner had left a third of a pint bottle on the shelf, and it was so cold up here there was no danger of it going off. In summer it was a different matter. I took my time, allowing the tea to brew correctly, and returned.

'Sorry, no biscuits.' I drew up another chair to the desk and sat down. I stirred and poured the tea. Mr Old half sat on the edge of the desk.

'Would it be considered a trifle abrupt if I were to ask you gentlemen your business?'

'Are you busy?' said Mr Old. 'We could always come back.'

'No, but I am curious to know how I can assist you. Are you from the Railways Board?'

'We're from Room 42,' said Mr Young.

'I see. I'm not familiar with that place. Have you come with anything specific in mind?'

'We have someone who would like to talk to you.'

The young man gathered some letters from my in-tray and picked up the paper knife. He began to cut one open.

'I must ask you not to do that,' I said. 'My correspondence is private.'

'You shouldn't have any secrets from us,' he said without looking up. 'We're your friends.'

'That's for me to decide.'

He put down the letters and picked up the photo of my mother, 4-6-0 Saint class locomotive, number 2904 *Lady Godiva*. 'Choo-choo!' he said.

'Please be careful with that,' I said. 'It has some sentimental value for me.'

The boy continued to be unpleasant. 'Choo-choo,' he said and pretended to drop the photo. 'Choo-choo.'

'Will you excuse me for a second?' I stood up and walked out. At the end of the corridor was a cupboard where the cleaner kept her mop and bucket. Inside was a shovel. I picked it up and made my way back. We used it for shovelling snow but in former times it had seen much more glorious service. It was a Great

Western Region fireman's shovel. To the layman, a shovel is a shovel, but not to the fireman who wields it. The GWR shovel is considered to be the best, even by the men from the other companies. It has a deeper well where the blade connects to the handle and this makes it better for performing the one operation in the morning without which no train can start, namely cooking the driver's breakfast in the firebox. All shovels can be used to do this, of course, but the GWR shovel is superior because of the well where the fat from the bacon collects.

I took the shovel back into the office. Both men looked up expectantly. Although the shovels of the GWR, the LMS, the SR and the LNER all had their own peculiar characteristics, there wasn't much to choose between any of them when it came to the purpose I now had in mind for it, the act of hitting a man on the head.

'I hope you don't intend using that for a violent purpose,' said Mr Young. He stepped sideways away from me and towards the door.

'Yes, I do. But first I am going to ask you both politely to leave.'

'And what if we refuse?'

The older man snorted. 'Isn't it obvious? He's going to hit you with the shovel.'

'We'll see about that,' said the boy. He shrugged his shoulders and squared his stance.

'This strikes me as most unnecessary,' I said.

'Me too,' said the older man.

I twisted the handle so that the blade became horizontal. 'I was going to give you a cauliflower ear, but it seems that I shall have to remove your head instead.'

'I'd step out of range if I were you,' said Mr Old.

The sound of the lavatory being flushed disturbed the moment and both men pricked up their ears at this, and seemed to wait. Footsteps resounded on the linoleum, approaching the office. The door opened and a man walked in. It was Lord Apsley. He wore an Ulster overcoat and his trousers below the coat showed a very sharp crease and his Oxford shoes had been meticulously polished. I judged it to be Kiwi 'Dark Tan'.

Lord Apsley had been the proctor of the Weeping Cross Railway Servants' Orphanage throughout my time there. Three times a day we would sit at long tables eating while he sat and looked down on us all from the high table, his eyes roving over us, searching for evidence of moral slippage that would require his correction. If he didn't find it, he seemed disappointed. He had achieved renown serving in the Second Boer War, and upon his return in 1902 the War Office entrusted him an urgent task, that of reinvigorating the 'pluck' of the British people. The quality of British 'pluck' had shown itself to be sadly lacking during the First Boer War, when British arms had been humbled by brown men armed with spears. The deepest wound to our nation's pride had been incurred during the battle of Isandlwana, in which two officers received Victoria Crosses for riding away on horseback while their men fought and died where they stood. Lord Apsley had been scandalised by this and taught us that for an officer to escape on a horse while his men fought to the death was cowardice of the first stripe. Some officers were shot in the back by their own men as they attempted to flee. He also took a dim view of the twelve Victoria Crosses awarded for the defence of Rorke's Drift, since the recipients had fought like rats in a trap, unable to escape, and this could hardly be counted as an act of bravery since they had no choice in the matter. Isandlwana means 'Day of the Dead Moon' in the language of the Zulu people and this refers to the solar eclipse that occurred at half past two in the afternoon. At the orphanage they told us the sudden extinguishing of the sun in the middle of the day was God's way of firing a warning shot across the bows of Britannia, telling us to pull our socks up. So Lord Apsley devised the Railway Gosling system to serve as a moral beacon to the children of the land, and to infuse a dose of moral cod liver oil into their hearts and sinews.

Since then, another battle had consumed his life, the one against the ravages of lead. They call it the Old Soldier's Colic. It has its origins in the eating of lead soldiers as a child. And then, later, amid the loneliness and confusion of the battlefield, the soldier chews lead bullets as a comfort and reminder of the warmth and safety of the crib. With time, it turns the gums blue and gives the skin of the cheeks a gun-metal pallor, something which in Lord Apsley's case was heightened by the application of medicinal rouge.

Lord Apsley took in the scene with a quick glance, then sat down. 'Put the shovel away and sit down, Jack.' I did. He reached into his jacket and pulled out a cigarette case. He offered me one and took one himself.

The boy offered us both a light.

'Quite a pickle you find yourself in, eh, Jack?' said Apsley. 'Lifetime's loyal service to the Great Western and now, well! This government of Bolsheviks, pigeon-fanciers and cloth-cap dem-agogues are taking her into public ownership. What do you think of that?'

'I rather think they will soon end my employment. Is that right?'

'I rather think they will, Jack, I rather think they will. Another fifteen years and they will probably close the whole lot down to save money.' He held the cigarette aloft in his right hand and rested the elbow in the palm of his left, and looked thoughtful. 'The railways will now belong to the party of the working man, a chap who generally has low tastes. Railway Goslings no doubt strike him as belonging to the world of the toffs, a breed of people who are the object of his contempt. He never stops to ask whence he takes the right to steal the railways. Whence he takes the authority to appropriate the property of his betters. The authority, of course, comes from Mr Marx. The railway will be run by Jacobins.'

'I should be very sad to lose my position.'

He seemed to consider that opinion and nodded softly. 'Whose side are you on?'

'I . . .'

'Do you love England?'

'Yes, sir, very much.'

'Good man!'

He remained silent for a while. The shrill wail of steam engine joined the ticking of my clock to fill the quiet.

'Do you know what a bradawl is?'

'It's a woodworking tool, I believe.'

'Exactly right. Ever done any carpentry?'

'At the orphanage. I was rather good at it.'

'That's right, you were. Well, I've got another question. Do you know what a leucotome is?'

'I'm rather afraid you have me there, Lord Apsley.'

'Never mind, I didn't expect you to know. A leucotome is also a bradawl, the only difference being it has a fancy Latin name.' He turned his head to Mr Old. 'Is that right?'

'Greek, sir. From leukos meaning white.'

The lord nodded and continued. 'Why take a tool as old as Noah and give it a bright new name? I'll tell you. Because if a man tried to stick a bradawl in your eye I rather fancy you would give him a bunch of fives. But if that same man wore a white coat and called himself a neurological scientist and told you he was going to perform a transorbital lobotomy on you, I imagine you would be rather excited. It's the eye socket, you see. The bone is thinner than the shell of a sparrow's egg.'

'You stick it in a man's eye?'

'Above it, really. I saw it on the Pathé Animated Gazette at the flicks. You stick the leucotome between the eye and the bone of the socket. Then five sharp blows with a mallet and the sharp end pierces the bone and drives home into the brain. You bang it in for three inches and then – and this is the bit that they tell me takes seven years at medical school to learn – you sort of wiggle it about. What do you think of that?'

'I think it sounds rather unpleasant.'

'There's a lot of blood I'm told.'

'But what for?'

'To cure him. A transorbital lobotomy can cure a man of any number of ills. What the neurological scientist calls delusional states of mind. It cures the facetious man, and the chap given to a love of beastliness. There was a time when God took care of these things. But nowadays it seems God has run out of ammo and we are left to attend to such matters ourselves. With a bit of carpentry we can cure the beast in man and all the other moral termites. We can cure the man who does not love England. Do you follow?'

'Yes, Lord Apsley, I do and I can assure you I love my country.'

'I'm relieved to hear it. You received a visit from a lady yesterday. She does not love her country. Do you understand?'

'I'm not sure that I do.'

'I'm sure she seemed perfectly normal to you. But do not be deceived. The ways of the serpent are subtle. You heard Mr Churchill's speech? From Stettin in the Baltic to Trieste in the Adriatic, an iron curtain has descended across the continent. Warsaw, Prague, Budapest, Belgrade, Bucharest and Sofia. You can add Weeping Cross to that list. Russia has gone. China is on the brink. Two of the most populous nations on earth. The tide of history is sweeping by borne on a sea of yellow people. It could happen here, Jack. Is that what you want? The yellow man does not have time for the finer feelings like love or charity. There is no pity in his heart, no joy. You never hear laughter in China, Jack. We had a scripture master at the orphanage before you were born, Mr Gunner. He'd been there as a missionary, he told me about it. He said, you can travel the length and breadth of the country and never once hear a chuckle, never see a baby smile. Can you imagine such a thing? The yellow man is an unfeeling brute, and the same goes for his Tartar cousins to the north and west, the Ivans. You thought they were our friends, didn't you? For six years we fought alongside them in pursuit of a greater foe but the Ivan is not to be trusted. When he took Baghdad, Genghis Khan filled nine sacks with human ears.' He paused and addressed the boy. 'Go and fetch more milk, there's a good chap.' The boy left without a word and the lord resumed.

'My aunt was a ward sister in the British Military Hospital in Bowen Road, Hong Kong when the Japanese arrived. Christmas Day. Black Christmas they called it. Those Jap soldiers were in the hospital three days. My aunt survived those three days. Later she hanged herself. The Jap soldier fancies that his conduct is animated by a lofty code of chivalry, "bushido", but this is a nauseating hypocrisy.' Lord Apsley's voice dropped in register as he recalled these horrors. 'It could happen here, too, is that what you want?'

'No, sir.'

'Good man. They could never defeat us by force of arms, but there are other ways to bring a chap down. I saw it in the Transvaal. You undermine the stout oak of a man's heart with the woodworm of beastliness, facetiousness and the creed of Mr Marx.' He paused as another thought struck him. 'And poems that don't rhyme.'

The boy returned with the milk and poured some into the tea.

'Ever heard of Mad Jack Mytton?'

'No, sir.'

'In 1826, barely nineteen, he rode his horse up the steps into the Bedford Hotel in Leamington Spa, into the entrance lobby, continued up the grand staircase on to the balcony and then leapt, still on horseback, into the restaurant below. He studied at Cambridge and took two thousand bottles of port and three books. He had a thousand hats and seven hundred boots. He had two thousand dogs, many of whom wore livery and dined on steak and champagne. His horse lived in the manor house with him, along with the dogs. He drank eight bottles of port a day and his horse drank one and died. He won four thousand pounds at the Doncaster races and lost them all when the wind blew the money away. He attempted to cure his hiccups by setting fire to his shirt. He died in 1834 at the King's Debtors' Prison in Southwark. Tell me, Jack, was this man a great Englishman or a facetious man?'

'I really don't know, Lord Apsley.'

He stood up. 'I don't know either, and it bothers me. The man was a famous son of Shropshire. You are named after him. Did you know that?'

I was too astonished to reply and Lord Apsley continued by taking a letter from the pocket of his coat and proceeding to read from it.

'. . . *in honour of his big heart I wish my son to be named Jack. And since you have told me his surname must be a railway station I choose for him the name of those wild green and darling hills where, after a picnic of raspberry jam sandwiches and wasp-tormented tea, Jack began his journey with a gasp of joy, in the place they call Wenlock Edge. In Saxon times, Wena meant hope, and Lock meant stronghold. I wish my son's heart to be such a stronghold of hope, for with hope we can face all trials, and without it we have a foretaste of death, and I say this as one for whom all hope has run out.*'

He refolded the letter with one hand and thrust it roughly back into his coat pocket. 'These are the words of your mother. You never met her, but it still behoves you to honour her memory. Think on these things.' He strode to the door, followed by the other two, and said just before he left, 'You know where your duty lies.'

Chapter 4

F OR A WHILE I sat in my chair and trembled. At the orphanage Lord Apsley had expressly forbidden us to ask questions about our mothers. We had been given the impression that no information was available. That he could so casually slip a letter out of his pocket like that was, well, I'm not sure what it was. Was it even a real letter from my mother? Would Lord Apsley lie? He had always responded to liars with fury.

> *The sand of the desert is sodden red,*
> *Red with the wreck of a square that broke;*
> *The Gatling's jammed and the Colonel dead,*
> *And the regiment blind with dust and smoke.*
> *The river of death has brimmed his banks,*
> *And England's far, and Honour a name,*
> *But the voice of a schoolboy rallies the ranks,*
> *Play up! play up! and play the game!*

This is what we were taught. We boys were the future of England, her growing backbone, and England did not lie. 'Red with the wreck of a square that broke.' How often had we sung these words. Why did the square break? Because of the moral termites that had infested the stout oak of an English heart.

Beastliness, facetiousness and the one they would never reveal, the shame deeper than beastliness. A boy who lied would not quibble to resort to beastliness.

It's possible that you walked past the red-brick Victorian building behind the gas works many times without ever realising it was an orphanage. The sign saying St Christopher's Home for the Children of Railwaymen was hidden by the sycamore tree and we were not allowed to play in the front garden. But even if you missed the orphanage you probably patted Kipper the collecting dog. He was a Border Collie with a brass collecting tin strapped to his back. He also had a small piece of cloth on his rump, like a saddle, on which were pinned pewter brooches which you took after you put a penny in the slot. It was an honesty system, but it worked because only a cad would steal from a dog.

Only once did Kipper return with his badges gone and no money in his tin. Tumby Woodside was found to have chocolate on his mouth that he could not explain; or rather, his explanation that a gentleman had given it to him for no reason was not believed; and lying according to Lord Apsley was a darker sin than even stealing from a dog and Tumby had to be punished accordingly. I took my place in the assembly hall for the thrashing of Tumby. We flinched with each stroke of the birch but after a while we stopped and watched in silence longing for Lord Apsley to tire, but he was like a man possessed and his face as he thrashed came to wear an expression, almost of joy, like the one on the faces of the women kneeling at the foot of the cross in stained-glass windows. After it was over we all sang, 'Play up! play up! and play the game!' We did not know Tumby was dead. His body was locked overnight in the infirmary. That night Ron Dingleman,

Magdalena, Cadbury and I broke in and we each dipped a finger into the chocolate crumbs still stuck in the corner of Tumby's mouth because we longed to know of what it tasted. Some time after midnight, as I walked across the cold yard to the lavatory cubicles leaning against the kitchen wall, I saw a figure in white in the room where Tumby lay, taking the boy into his arms. I thought for a while it must be Jesus and was bitter in my envy of Tumby. But after I had finished my business and pulled the lavatory chain I saw that the noise disturbed him and he rushed to the window. I hid in the shadows until the light upstairs went out. Then I returned to the dormitory and climbed into bed.

I placed a telephone call to Weeping Cross police station and sergeant Dickson told me they had no record of the incident reported by Jenny. This was intriguing. Normally when they send a throttler home and tell her to put her feet up and have a cup of tea they dismiss the murder story but always record the report in the incident book. I pondered the story over my second cup of tea. In my experience, people only very rarely get throttled to death in a train compartment. Indeed, you are far more likely to encounter a German spy cold-bloodedly plotting the ruination of our land than witness a murder. Murderers on trains are more frequently found in novels by lady writers. I was pretty sure this wasn't a murder at all, but a crime that could under certain circumstances resemble it. A crime that is far more intriguing, known as a Fishbone.

I explained it that evening when I met Jenny. She was already standing outside the milk bar when the clock of St Bede's chimed the hour. This pleased me because a lot of chaps said their girls were always late on such occasions. We sat in a booth in the window and ordered two strawberry milkshakes.

'Have you been looking for clues, Jack?' said Jenny.

I laughed. 'Actually, I've been thinking rather than racing around like Sherlock Holmes.'

'Really? What about?'

'It is my belief that your aunt did not see a murder being enacted in the adjacent carriage.'

'Oh, you're a flat tyre!'

'Yes, I know this must come as a disappointment. But you see, it would be very unusual to see someone done in on a train like that. I've caught quite a few German spies but never a murderer.'

'Are there many German spies?'

'There used to be. There was a time when you could scarcely move for them.'

'Are they easy to spot?'

'Oh no, quite the opposite, their cunning knows no bounds. The last one I caught was five miles north of Banbury on the 10.27am Paddington to Leamington Spa stopping train. He greeted me with a warm smile that would normally have greatly charmed me. But you know what gave him away, don't you?'

'Was he eating a sausage?'

'No. It was the cowardly duelling scar.'

'I didn't realise a duelling scar was cowardly. Don't they have to charge into battle to get one?'

'Not at all. If you knew the truth you would be filled with scorn. They call it *Der Schmiss*. It's really just a peacock's tail. In England when chaps used to settle their differences with a duel, they did so with pistols and real balls of lead. Usually one or both of them would go home in a wooden box. This was the English way. No cheap theatricals. A cold foggy dawn on the heath, two loud bangs and it was all over. Not so in Germany. There the act has been debased into a spectacle in which the contestants acquire a toy upon the cheek to foster the admiration of ladies. A blemish, deliberately acquired, that one must regard as a part of the German's toilette along with his powders, potions and perfumes. There is not the slightest degree of danger involved in this type of duel. Both chaps wear chainmail breast shirts, collar protectors, nose protectors and even eye protectors. The only part not protected is the cheek. All that is required is that one drop of blood be lost.'

'Oh Lord!'

'Yes, indeed! Not only is there no danger to life, there is no likelihood that the duel will be painful. The rapiers these chaps use are sharper than a surgeon's scalpel. The wound is so clean and surgically exact that it can entirely disappear within days and so sometimes the duelling masters will sew horsehair into the wound to ensure that it is at least visible. But the problem with that is it makes the cut smart like a wasp sting and so the German is generally averse to it. When all is said and done, a German duelling scar is nothing more than a shaving nick, the type that Englishmen inflict upon themselves up and down the land every morning and never give a second's thought to.'

'What did you do to him? Did you box his ears?'

'I certainly would have liked to, but unfortunately the rascal hadn't done anything wrong as far as I could see. There is nothing in the terms of carriage that prohibits a chap with a scar from travelling. But you can be sure I kept a close eye on him, lest he be tempted to make himself disagreeable to the ladies travelling on the train.'

Jenny bent low over the straw from her milkshake and looked

up at me. 'So what did she see then if it wasn't a murder? Although I would like to make clear that I am not yet persuaded that she didn't.'

'It is my belief that your aunt saw a Fishbone.'

'A Fishbone?'

'Yes. In this crime the nanny and boy are working together as a team. The nanny pretends to have a fishbone stuck in her throat, and appeals to a stranger for help. The gentleman goes to her assistance and places his hands upon her throat to dislodge the bone. While he does that, the boy picks his pocket and hides his wallet under the baby. Seen fleetingly through a train compartment window it might indeed look like the nanny was being throttled.'

Jenny scrutinised me through half-closed eyes, as if weighing the evidence of my story. Finally she said, 'Golly.'

'Yes, it is fiendishly clever.'

'It seems a very strange thing to do. Like something you would read in a book. Would anyone really do such a thing?'

'Absolutely. I happen to know a girl who specialises in it. Her name is Magdalena. We were at the orphanage together.'

'Do you know where to find her?'

'Not easily, but I know where to find her father.'

She placed her thumb and index finger to her throat. 'Fishbone?'

'That's right. You will remember when you first came to my office I asked specifically about the behaviour of the boy during the throttling.'

'Yes, you did. So even then you suspected. That's awfully clever.'

'So are you persuaded now?'

39

She considered again. 'I'm not saying yes and not saying no. We will ask my aunt what she thinks.' She sucked the last of her milkshake and shot me a glance of mild horror as the burbling sound seemed unnaturally loud. 'Oops.'

'I shouldn't worry, I'm sure they've heard it before.'

The tower clock struck a quarter to the hour. 'We need to leave about seven,' said Jenny. 'I should have made it last like you.'

'Have another.'

'Oh no, I shouldn't.'

'I must be frank and confess that I will submit an expenses chit, so you might as well.'

'I've never met a man who had expenses before.'

'Mine are very frugal. In fact, if we have three milkshakes I shall only claim for two.'

'In that case, I won't have another.'

I reached into my inside pocket and took out a card. 'Perhaps you would be so helpful as to fill out this for me. It's just some paperwork I have to do.' I slid the card across the table, took out my fountain pen and handed it to her.

'Are you keeping tabs on me, Jack?'

'Just for my records. Name, address, next of kin.'

'Shall we call it the Case of the Missing Aunt?'

'No need to fill that bit out. I haven't decided on a suitable title yet. I expect I shall just call it Jenny the Spiddler.'

She made a mock gasp as if that were somehow quite thrilling, and began to write. 'Tell me what it's like to drive a train.'

'Oh, I haven't done that for ages.'

'You can't have forgotten.'

'No, but I'm sure you wouldn't be interested in that, it's nothing special.'

Jenny looked almost shocked. 'Jack, how could you say that? Nothing special?'

'Quite ordinary, really.'

'Yesterday, every time you talked about trains your voice went soft as if there was nothing more important to you in the world.'

'It would really bore you. But if you insist, I should say . . . I suppose it's like being inside a corned beef tin, full of soot and ash and sparks and smoke, with a din so loud you can't hear a word the other chap says. Then it's as if a giant picks you up and shakes you so hard your brains come out of your ears.'

'Oh, Jack, I had no idea it was so terrible.'

'Terrible? No, you misunderstand. It is wonderful. It's something that is so . . . that is like . . . well, I mean, imagine riding through the night on an elephant in full flight, a stampeding elephant made of iron. It would be pretty hairy, I agree, but nothing on earth can resist you. It's something you feel in your belly, that sound you hear from the bridge when a train passes underneath, that clackety-clack . . . it's not like that in the cab, there are no gaps, just endless clacketyclackclacketyclack. And you feel each one like a horse kicking you in the behind or in the stomach. Those rails are so hard, the wheels so hard . . . And when you reach eighty miles an hour, you feel each piston stroke in the ribs, and the fireman shovels with fury now, faster and faster, and the old elephant snorts and snorts and roars and your ears go deaf with the terrific din, and the whistle, Jenny, oh the whistle is like, oh like a choir of ghosts screaming in your ear, on and on you roar, wailing, chuffing and chuffing, and wailing and moaning, screaming through the wayside

41

halts, past the crossing gates, frightening the hares in the field at dawn, you see that red disc on the crossing gates and . . . and there are so many different sounds in each chuff, a boom, a roar, a wail, a moan, and then you thunder into a tunnel, oh imagine it! Those chaps sitting on the cushions, they would die of fright if they knew, if they understood what a risk it is thundering into the blackness at eighty miles an hour and no chance whatsoever if there happens to be a train already there, it's wild, you don't care, you can't, there's no point, like diving off the highest board in the world you just have to leap, and your nostrils fill with the perfume of sulphur and hot oil and coal, on and on and faster, until your whole being throbs, Jenny, throbs and you pull one more time on the whistle and . . . on—'

I banged my hand on the table and knocked over Jenny's glass. 'Oh, I'm so sorry . . .'

'No, no, it was my fault for putting it there. Here, let me . . .' She picked up her napkin and dabbed at the drops of spilled milkshake.

For a moment we did not speak. I stared at the table.

'It sounds . . . it sounds wonderful,' said Jenny.

I smiled. 'Yes, rather. You know what some men say . . .' I stopped.

'What?'

'Oh, nothing important.'

'What do they say?'

'That . . . well, I really don't think I should say.'

'Oh, don't be such a flat tyre! What do they say?'

'They say it is like the pleasure a man experiences privately with his wife.'

Jenny's eyes widened. I gave a sort of smile and picked up a spoon. Then I put it down on the table and turned it over. After a second I thought better of it and turned it back.

'Well?' said Jenny.

'Well, what?'

'Jack!'

'What?'

'I mean . . .' She paused and looked at me intensely. 'Is it?

We took the number 7 bus to Saint Christina's Home for Lunatics, Mental Defectives and the Feeble-Minded, which lies some three miles out of town in Wildernesse. The traffic was quite heavy but after we crossed Mendicant's Bridge it began to thin out and the night filled with the glitter and sparkle of the lights and flares of the factories. We drove slowly past Robinson's the boot-blacking factory, Greaves and Weatherspoon the rat catchers, the Chicory Coffee company, Quails the nicotine throat pastille manufacturers, the crepe bandage wholesaler, the firm that makes ersatz chrism from coal gas, the mothball warehouse, the creosote mixer, Coal Tar toothpaste company, a quicklime merchants, and Chumley's the biscuit works and biggest employer in Weeping Cross. We made frequent stops and the bus quickly filled up. It was the time of evening when the shifts changed. The smell of the sewage-processing works began to seep into the bus. The sewage works is quite extensive and occupies a patch of waste ground that also contains the bombed-out munitions factory and electricity works. In the middle of the waste ground, standing proud among the rubble, is a pub, the Kingfisher.

The asylum opened in 1903. The building is very grand and, looked at from a distance, beyond the wrought-iron gates, like a country house. We walked up the drive, past the gatehouse and into a reception area where we explained our business to a lady sitting at a desk. There was a strong odour of disinfectant and lavatory smells, and the noise of muffled moaning and crying from somewhere far away. The receptionist looked displeased at our request and summoned a nurse with whom she discussed the matter in whispers. The nurse then went off and returned with a doctor who tried very hard to give us the impression that he was very busy and our visit was an imposition.

'I thought I told you your aunt was sleeping,' he said to Jenny.

'That was yesterday,' she said. 'She must be awake by now.'

'Why must she?'

'Well . . . isn't she?'

'No.'

'It's really not like her to sleep for three days.'

'It's not like anyone. Do you think it's easy? We're operating at the forefront of medical science here.'

'Perhaps you can tell us what is wrong with her,' I said.

The doctor breathed in deeply in a manner suggesting that his patience was almost at an end. 'Hallucinations.'

'She never hallucinates,' said Jenny.

'Of course she does. We all do. Do you think the world is real?'

'I hope it is.'

'Perhaps you should read some Planck, then you wouldn't be so cocksure.'

'Are you saying planks aren't real?' said Jenny.

'Planks? You mean wooden ones? I suppose they are proba- bilistically true, much like Dr Schrödinger's famous cat. I suspect the question is ill-phrased and rather than asking if they are real one should ask if they are likely. And I suppose one could come to the conclusion that they probably are.'

'Planks are likely?' I said.

'Highly likely. But not inevitable.'

Jenny took out the tin of corned beef and offered it to him. 'Can you give her this?'

'I'm afraid she's not up to solids at the moment.'

'Well, perhaps when she is feeling a bit better.'

'What is the nature of the treatment you are giving her?' I asked.

'She has been artificially induced into a coma by administration of insulin via injection. The treatment is very modern.'

'She's in a coma?' said Jenny.

'We wake her once a day to have her cleaned and fed, then back she goes. We call it Depatterning.'

'How long will you do it for?' I said.

'Until she gets better, of course. How long do treatments usually last?'

'Yes,' I insisted, 'but how long will that be?'

The doctor half closed his eyes as he thought, and said, 'Oh, it could go on for years.'

'But why does she need to be in a coma?' said Jenny, starting to get upset. 'What good will that do?'

'What do you mean, what good will it do?'

'She means, how can that make her well again?'

He peered at Jenny, half squinting. 'Are you perhaps a psychiatrist?'

'No, of course I am not.'

'So why do you insist on challenging the work of some of the foremost practitioners of the art? Why the hubris?'

45

'She's not challenging, she—'

'How can putting her into a coma make her better?'

There was a pause. The doctor took another weary breath. 'It starves the brain of glucose.'

'Is that good?' said Jenny.

'I would say it is excellent, although I suppose it does all depend on the yardstick one is using. Marvellous organ the brain, you see. Really quite wonderful, and, to tell you frankly, we really have no idea what goes on up there. But we do know one thing. The old noggin uses glucose as a fuel so by cutting off the supply we get some pretty interesting effects. Starved of glucose the brain actually starts eating itself. It's an ingenious treatment, because ask yourselves, what do we store in the brain? Memories. Until now we had no way of erasing them. Now the brain does the job for us. Three months of this and she will be restored. A tabula rasa. No nasty memories left to frighten her. You can give the corned beef to the nurse. I must be going or I'll miss my bus. Good night!' The doctor walked off like a soldier doing double march.

Chapter 5

W HERE IS THE loneliest place in the world? It is
found in the heart of the signalman who leaves a
troop train waiting on the wrong line, and then in
a moment of confusion forgets about its presence and sends the
express passenger through. Silas was Magdalena's father, and
he wrecked the troop train one terrible night in 1915. It was not
always easy finding Magdalena, but Silas would know, and it
was seldom difficult to find Silas because every day he would sit
on the crown of Dandelion Hill, up by Devil's Curtsy, watching
the approach in the distance of the 5.23 Taunton to Aberdeen
sleeper.

I waited till just after five before leaving my office and making
my way through town towards the hill that overlooked the town.
Sleet was falling. You couldn't really see the flakes in the gath-
ering dusk, except beneath the streetlamps, but you could feel
the wetness of them, like the touch of a dog's nose. The traffic
was at a standstill on Mendicant's Bridge, and the lamps along
the parapet, standing proud on stalks, glimmered in the swirling
flakes. Trams trundled heavily along the centre of the road, and
rolled to a standstill, bells ringing. With their electrical conducting arm reaching up into the netting of wires slung across
the sky they looked like insects. At the crossroads a policeman
stood with arms outstretched, like a statue; the sleet melted on

him and varnished his dark blue coat, dripping off the rim of his hat. The sleet was dirty, like water from a miner's bath.

Weeping Cross is fifteen miles south of Shrewsbury on the Hereford line. They say if you look down on the town from the air it looks like the face of a man with a black eye. If that is so, then the railway station where I had my office would be the mouth and the Astoria cinema would be the nose. His right eye would be the boating lake, although since it was drained during the war it doesn't look much like an eye at the moment. The black eye is over to the west and consists of a dark smudge of factories, yards and works. The left ear is the engine sheds and railway sidings. This was the spot where in 1151 Roger Sainte-Foy-de-Montgommery brought back a fragment of the true cross from the Second Crusade. He planted it and a tree grew that had the face of Christ formed by knots in the bole, and this wept tears of medicinal gum every Easter. My lodgings are on Devil's Curtsy, the hilly ridge about where the right ear would be. This is where Silas sat.

He wrecked the train after staying up all night nursing Magdalena's baby brother Ben, who had been very poorly with scarlet fever. Just before dawn the child died. Silas walked the three miles to the railway station where he declared himself unfit for work and asked to be relieved. The request was turned down. When you look at a signal box you see a quiet place where nothing seems to be happening. But this is misleading. The signalman's domain stretches over many miles of track in all directions and he is forever moving, shunting, parking and switching trains from track to track. Parking a train temporarily on the wrong line is not uncommon. The trick is to remember where you've put it. The trains are everywhere, but you cannot see them. It is surprisingly easy to forget where you have put a train if you can't see it. Especially if you have been up all night nursing a sick child. Silas had a special train not on the official timetable, a troop train. This was commonplace during the war and made the signalman's job that much harder. It's easy to forget a train that doesn't normally pass at that particular time each day. He put the troop train on the wrong line, the 'down' line, to allow the late-running Liverpool to Newton Abbott express to pass. It was then, he later told the court, that he fell asleep for a few minutes, his mind so befuddled by the great agony of mind occasioned by the death of his son. When he woke he accepted the Taunton to Aberdeen night express sleeper forgetting that the troop train stood in its way. It was then that the fireman from the troop train appeared at the door of the signal box, in accordance with Rule 55 which stipulated that if a train was detained at a signal for longer than three minutes the driver should dispatch the fireman to the signal box to remind the signalman of his presence. The fireman asked Silas what he intended doing with the troop train and Silas replied that he had already sent it on, to which the fireman said, 'No, you haven't, I just left it not two minutes ago.'

Once you have realised your error it is already too late to do anything about it. Nothing on earth can now stop what is about to happen. But a lot of time can pass before it does. Or it can seem like a lot. Perhaps it was no more than a minute but that minute will be the longest that any man has ever known. It is like an arrow shot from a bow. It may still have many miles to cross before it hits its target, but no amount of wishing can make it return to the bow. In that window of time, Silas did three things, all of which have become part of railway legend. First, he looked at the fireman and said with a desperation that was all too apparent: 'You can't have.' This was enough for the fireman who turned tail and raced like a devil to warn his driver who no doubt was taking the welcome break to catch forty winks. Silas then stood up and walked to the window where he rubbed a little hole in the condensation. This was pointless. The die had been cast. He said, 'Lord, I've done it.' Then he turned to the boy who kept his ledger and said quietly, 'Please telephone the station master and say that I have wrecked his Aberdeen sleeper.' And then they waited, doing nothing except listen to the wind whistling around the eaves of the signal box, to the rain spattering against the panes. There was nothing to be done. All they could do was listen. After a minute or so there came from far off a deep, deep rumble. When the sound reached the men in the box, something very strange happened, but the boy swore on the Bible in court that he had seen this. Silas's hair turned white in an instant. Then the night turned as bright as if a full moon had appeared from behind a cloud and both knew, too, what this meant. The passenger train had been provided with the latest electrical lighting, but the troop train would have been composed of older rolling stock, illuminated with gas, piped to each carriage under pressure. The entire reservoir would have escaped in seconds and caught on the spilled coals of the overturned engine. Sixty people died on the sleeper and no one knows how many troops died because this was war time and such information was kept secret. But it is hardly likely that any could have survived the blaze, which raged for eighteen hours.

Silas was handed down a sentence of twelve years'

imprisonment with hard labour and his wife collapsed in court and died of a broken heart. Magdalena came to live with us at the orphanage. That's why Silas sits up on Dandelion Hill every evening to watch the passage of the 5.23 Aberdeen sleeper.

The first chef's hat of smoke appeared in the sky beyond the tower of the spire of St Bede's; it was followed by a tiny wail. From this distance, there was almost no sound, it was like watching a silent film, but you could still feel the joy of the train, like a dog returning to a place he loves. More chef hats of steam filled the sky. Each one bigger than the one before. Soon there was a trail of them strung out like washing against the sky, and the black snowflakes of soot would be fluttering down in a thousand back gardens on to real washing hanging on the line.

Silas was sitting quietly on the bench, looking out over the town. I sat down next to him. I took out of my coat pocket a tin of powdered egg and offered it to him. 'I think this might be yours,' I said. 'I found it here on the bench yesterday.'

He took the tin gratefully. I expected he would trade it for drink or cigarettes but I didn't mind.

The train wailed again and I checked my watch. 'Bang on time,' I said.

His cheeks were crimson but not with the bloom of health. He nodded. 'Three minutes late yesterday.'

I took out my flask of medicinal brandy and offered it to him. He took a drink, then tapped the newspaper lying next to him on the bench. 'We're going to get our own atomic bomb. What do you think of that?'

'I must admit, I don't really know much about it.'

'It's something to do with diverting the rays of the sun.'

51

'I suppose if everyone else has one, we'll need to get one.'

He paused to consider the possibility. 'You keeping well?'

'Yes, never better.'

'What will happen to you once the government takes over the railways?'

'I don't know.'

He sighed. Clearly he already knew what was going to happen. 'How's Magdalena?' I said.

The question brought a smile to his face. 'Oh, she's doing all right for herself, I can tell you. You'll never guess where she's got to now.' He reached into his jacket. 'Only that new holiday camp at Barmouth, Buckley's.' He pulled out a postcard and showed it to me.

'By gum!' I said.

'There's a cold tap in each room and if you want a hot cup of tea in the morning you can get a flask of hot water from the restaurant before you go to bed.'

'It's the modern world, Silas.'

'You can say that again. There's a dance hall, swimming pool with a border of rhododendron plants, and even a miniature railway to take your suitcases from the reception area to your chalet.'

'Yes, I heard about that – hauled by a 0-4-0 built by Hudswell & Clarke. I expect it must cost a packet to stay there.'

'Week's full board, complete with free entertainment and three square meals a day, cost £3 at the height of the season. A week's holiday for a week's wage.'

'It's a wonder how they do it. Is it true they have a television receiver?'

'Yes, but she hasn't been able to get a seat so far.' Silas

chuckled. 'My oh my. The roof is real asbestos, too. Who'd have thought, eh? I never in my wildest dreams imagined I'd see a daughter of mine staying somewhere like that.'

The news that Magdalena was in Barmouth pleased me a great deal, since it would provide me with an excuse to go there myself. As children, we used to make an annual summer outing to Barmouth, and for all of us, the trip was the highlight of our year. It did not surprise me, therefore, that Magdalena was there. I expected she had travelled with a gentleman who would pay for everything.

People who have read about orphanages in books may imagine that our life was harsh. I have nothing to compare it with but it never struck me as unpleasant at the time. We were seldom beaten; the masters and mistresses were generally kind. Part of the reason we were treated well, I believe, is the very fact that this was an orphanage paid for by the railwaymen out of their own pockets. For hard-up working men to make such an allowance out of their small wages shows generosity of spirit that communicated itself to all connected with the establishment. If a railway man died and his widow was not able to support all her children, one or more could apply for admission. The home was established in 1883 and was chosen for reasons that I do not know for the Railway Gosling programme which began in 1902. This was when Lord Apsley became a regular feature.

The building itself was built of red brick with a clock tower rising above the central portico of the main door. The tower ended in a spire. Only visitors used this rather grand entrance. We children entered by a door on the side of the building. On the ground floor were classrooms, cloak-, hat- and boot-rooms, a kitchen, a pantry and a dining hall, which also served as the place of assembly and religious instruction. Lavatories were outside at the back, next to the garden where we were taught to grow vegetables. On the second floor were dormitories named after the benefactors of the orphanage. My bed was in Duchess of Albany. There was also an infirmary and one floor up were the masters' rooms and a library. And above that in the garret the punishment room.

The next morning was a wild day, with sheets of rain sluicing over the platforms as if they were the edges of a weir. Some might think it hardly the best weather to travel to the coast but the journey is so lovely my heart would leap at the prospect at any time of the year. The clouds boiled in the sky, blue and black, and where they occasionally broke apart the shafts of light were too dazzling to look at it. The Cambrian Coast Express had arrived in Shrewsbury 23 minutes late, although I am sure this was no reflection on the skill of Driver Mann and Fireman Satchell. I arrived to find a gentleman from first class pressing money into the hand of Driver Mann to encourage him to make up the lost time. This is a common sight. The driver takes the money but it makes no difference to the speed of the train. There is no power on earth that would prevent a driver from making up lost time. You might as well bribe him to make his heart beat faster, or bribe a nursing mother to love her baby more. Since there is every chance that, all being well, between here and Machynlleth they would be able regain some of the time lost, the gentleman from first class would assume, no doubt, that his bribe had worked.

I was lucky enough to be invited by Driver Mann and Fireman

Satchell to join them on the footplate on the approach to Barmouth, but sat on the cushions as far as Dovey Junction. Even at a distance of some three coaches back I was able to appreciate the skill with which Driver Mann adjusted the cut-off to suit the changes in the gradient and Fireman Satchell placed his shovelfuls of coal. The crisp response from the exhaust bore testimony to this accuracy. I spent some of the time considering the strange death of Driver Groates, a case that had taunted me with its mystery for more than six weeks now. It was a conundrum that I examined in idle moments like this, much as one would a crossword puzzle. I was confident all the information necessary for a solution was contained in the bare details of the case and that sooner or later the truth would be revealed to me in a small epiphany. Sherlock Holmes would have called it a three pipe problem. The incident took place at the end of October on the Birmingham to Paignton night train, which departed Birmingham Snow Hill. Driver Groates and Fireman Stalham were on the train returning home after having brought the express from Bristol earlier that evening. Sometimes when a driver and his fireman returned home they were given another train to work but in this case they were lucky and were allowed to travel on the cushions. The train left Birmingham Snow Hill at 11.47 and at approximately 13 minutes after midnight Fireman Stalham pulled the communication cord. The guard was the first to arrive on the scene. He found Driver Groates slumped dead in the compartment, with a very severe head injury. Fireman Stalham – who was in a state of extreme distress – claimed that someone had thrown an object through the window of the compartment and this had struck Driver Groates and killed him. There was indeed some broken glass on the floor, but the window seemed to have been broken from the inside, and no trace could be found of the object said to have flown in and killed the driver. Strangest of all, the light bulb in the compartment had blood on it. Fireman Stalham walked out of the hospital in his dressing gown sometime between 3am and 4am and has not been seen since.

We reached Dovey Junction at 17 minutes past two, which meant Driver Mann and Fireman Satchell had made up 15 of the 23 minutes' delay incurred on the run from Paddington to Shrewsbury. And it was here that they were kind enough to let me join them on the footplate. There are few more dramatic stretches of railway line in the world than the run north from Dovey Junction up the Cambrian coast to Barmouth. Visitors from Norway and Switzerland, where the railways are renowned for their beauty and engineering daring, admit that they have nothing that compares with the wonder of it. Only the British could have built such a marvel, they say. In other countries the engineers would have thrown up their hands in despair at the task. For many miles the line is no more than a ledge on the sheer cliff face, so close to the sea that on windy days, when the waves break against the tracks, passengers get their feet wet and find crabs in their bags afterwards. In 1883 a whole train was washed away in a storm. All being well, I should arrive at Barmouth by tea time.

As we crossed the Barmouth Bridge a passenger pulled the communication cord. Driver Mann was halfway through telling me about the new sensation at Paddington station whereby announcements concerning train cancellations and other alterations to the timetable are communicated to passengers via a system of electrically operated loudspeakers. The system works very well, he said, although some elderly passengers had been disturbed because of what they described as the presence inside their own heads of a voice. I've seen a loudspeaker used in this manner at the Ideal Home Exhibition, and I was most impressed. I was keen to hear more but before I could ask further, the communication cord was pulled, and since we were already proceeding at Dead Slow across the bridge, we very shortly came to a standstill. We each scrambled to lean out of the cab and peer down the line. Normally the location of the coach in which the cord has been pulled is indicated by a small flag operated by a butterfly valve connected to the brakes, but in this case we had no need to consult this contrivance because the man who had pulled the cord could be plainly seen climbing out of the carriage and clambering down the bridge towards the sea.

If you have travelled this section of the railway you may think the man was in no great peril. The estuary is not deep and the bridge, built across low piles, is more of a causeway. However, on this particular afternoon the sea below him was roiling and bubbling like tar in a road-mender's cauldron, and the fierce wind blew in such gusts that the entire train shuddered beneath its onslaught. It was quite clear that the man would certainly drown if the wind tore him from the side of the bridge. Only a fool would have attempted a climb like that. A fool or a Gosling.

I handed the driver my hat and climbed down the ladder to the track. As I did, two men from the middle of the train also climbed out and jumped down to the track. I thought they were trying to help the man but it was obvious from the desperation with which he increased his pace after seeing the two men that they were his pursuers. He now climbed over the parapet and was trying to work his way down the lattice of wooden struts. It wasn't clear where he thought he was going. The two men walked in an unhurried manner along the side of the track towards him, causing him to turn and change direction, but when he saw me he stopped, hesitated, and in that moment a wave like a giant's hand reached up from the foaming waters and plucked him off the bridge and into the darkness. The two men stopped and looked briefly over the parapet and cast me a glance before walking back to the compartment from which they had come. The long wail of the man's cry followed by the splash that ended it reverberated in my mind long after the sound had ended.

THE BOY'S OWN
RAILWAY GOSLING ANNUAL

Vol. VII   1931   Price: 1/-

Replies to our readers' letters

E. C. BINGHAM, BIRKENHEAD—As currently constituted the British
Army has no need for torturers, although skilled interrogators will
always be highly sought after. We suggest you apply to a regiment of
your choice when the time comes but do not send them the drawing
of your blood-curdling invention.

D. H. AMBERLEY, BRISTOL—The prisoner is locked into a sealed
chamber and the executioner pulls a lever that drops a pellet of
potassium cyanide into a vat of sulphuric acid. This gives off hydrogen
cyanide gas, perhaps more familiar to our readers as the Prussic Acid
beloved of the lady authors of sensational murder mysteries. Strictly
speaking cyanide does not smell of bitter almonds; it is bitter almonds
that smell of hydrogen cyanide.

THE CONTINUING ADVENTURES OF RAILWAY GOSLING
CADBURY HOLT – ON THE TRAIL OF THE MISSING NUNS!

The Oasis of El Garrabadhib

We travelled in the early hours and late at night; by eleven the heat
could break a man's heart, and we spent the middle hours of the day
lying torpid and enfeebled in the shadows of our camels, waiting for

the cruel disc of the sun to begin its descent, too broken in spirit to even have the strength to curse the fate that had brought us there. Each night we gasped in wonder at those glowing snowballs in the sky, the beautiful desert stars. And then we drew in closer to our camp fire as the desert grew bitterly cold. Each night after reading the stars, Gimlee would tell me how many days were left before we reached our goal. And each time he would laugh as if party to a joke that excluded me.

By the thirteenth day of travel, I was so emaciated with hunger, so worn out with sitting in the camel's fo'c's'le, so tormented by the incessant sting and bite of the bugaracha flies, that I no longer cared whether I lived or died and wished only for my death to be speedy and accompanied by one glass of cool water. I travelled in a perpetual swoon. And then we saw it. The Oasis of El Garrabadhib. The Fabled One, the Jewel of the Desert, the ancient Jhabra crossroads from where all routes to the continent of Africa were said to start. El Garrabadhib. Not since I was a child on Christmas morning had my heart felt such an upsurge of joy as the one that visited me then. I cared not what fate lay in store for me inside these ancient city walls. All I longed for was one slice of juicy pomegranate and a sherbet from a laughing virgin girl. And lo! My simple prayers were answered. As we approached the town a horn was blown by the watcher in the tower and the sound smote the still desert air with its shrill call. The city gates opened and children on donkeys rode out towards us as the cry rang out, 'Kurjoomba! Kurjoomba!'

We followed the throng down the main thoroughfare to the dusty square. Somewhere in the seething mass of humanity, I hoped, lay the object of my quest: a man renowned in every country of the desert, in every tribe, a legend and a god to some. His name was One-eyed Jheg. A tribal elder now, but in times past he had been a fierce warrior, a freebooter and wide-roving adventurer. A man who had dined with kings and, so it was said, worked for both the British Secret Services and the French at the same time, drawing a double stipend and still to this day drawing two pensions from the post office in Casablanca. But his greatest boast was to have seen the fabled lost Kurjoomba Holy Women. They said he had been there at El Gaberdine the day the nuns raided the fort in search of their stolen sisters.

Chapter 6

THE TWO MEN were waiting for me beyond the ticket barrier at Barmouth and stepped into my path. One of them was slightly taller and had a distinctive nose. It looked like a Plasticine sausage that had been pressed into the centre of his face. He told me the Dingleman would like to talk to me and asked with forced politeness if they could pat me down for guns. I said I had no objection. I seldom carry a gun but I did have my Formica and they soon found that. It was clear neither of them was familiar with the latest scientific advances and they plainly doubted my explanation and so we agreed they would hold on to it and see what the Dingleman thought. Buckley's Camp was on the hillside at the north end of Barmouth, overlooking the town and separated from the sea by a wall of sand dunes. We all bent slightly and dashed through the rain to the waiting car. The man with the Plasticine nose didn't get in, but told me he had business to attend to in town.

Ron Dingleman was a gangster. He had also been at the orphanage. I was surprised to find him there the day I came looking for Magdalena, but I was sure it was no coincidence. He had arrived at the orphanage much later than the rest of us, when he was thirteen. Cadbury Holt was the oldest Gosling, he was born in 1902. The rest of us were born in batches between 1902 and 1914. I was born in 1911. Magdalena arrived in 1915, when we were both four. The Dingleman arrived in 1917. Children brought up in orphanages regard each other as brother and sister and are not romantically attracted. But the Dingleman arriving later, as he did, was different and he was terribly fond of Magdalena. We all were, but not in that way. The Dingleman was not, strictly speaking, eligible for the home because he was not the son of a railway man. They found him asleep in the firebox of one of the engines in the shed. A waif, half starved and bruised, who had besought the warmest bed he could find on a cold January night. He had no business being there, but the discovery inspired compassion rather than anger. Everyone who works on the railway is haunted by the memory of Benjamin Hawkins, an eleven-year-old cleaning boy who was burned to death after falling asleep in the firebox. Engines are cleaned round the clock and on a bitter cold winter's night when the desire to sleep can be overwhelming, the cosy warmth of the little metal room can be a dangerous place for a small boy. When next morning the firesetter shovelled in live coals, he was still asleep.

When they found the Dingleman he refused to speak and so, because the firebox had been made by the Dingleman & Byron foundry in Derby, he was named after it. Byron soon shortened to Ron. Subsequently, he always refused to say what his history had been prior to his appearance in the firebox. Magdalena says he told her, but she never repeated it. After he left the orphanage he became a bare-knuckle fighter and then, because there was not much of a living to be made, became a bodyguard for a local gangster, whose empire he eventually took over. He quit the ring completely after killing his opponent with a left hook.

The Dingleman had taken a VIP chalet at Buckley's. We had

to park outside the main reception building and walk along a path between rows of chalets until we reached one at the end that was three times the size of the others. The front door led directly into the lounge, which was spacious but had the hard, cold air of a village hall, the sort where Boy Scouts hold their meetings. This is one of the chief drawbacks of linoleum; it lacks the warmth of carpet, despite being very modern. There were two doors in the back wall and an assortment of modern-looking furniture, of the kind you saw in magazines but seldom in the homes of real people. There was a sofa and some chairs arranged around what I believe is called a coffee table. Three spivs sat in the chairs. The most striking item in the room was arranged along the left-hand wall and almost took it up entirely. It was an iron lung. This consisted of a fat tube of beige metal with a meter on the top like one used on weighing scales. A boy's head was visible, protruding from one end, like a junior human cannonball. He stared with quiet patience at a teddy bear pinned to the machine, just above his head. There was a pillow beneath his head placed on a shelf attached to the machine, and under this was a small occasional table spread with newspaper. The Dingleman was gently combing the nits from his son's hair on to the newspaper. He looked up at me and smiled.

'Jack,' he said, standing up and reaching out a hand for me to shake.

I shook his hand. 'Ron! Well, this is . . . I mean . . . you're in Barmouth! I'm not sure what to say.'

'Say hello, that usually does nicely.'

'Hello!'

'How are you keeping? It's been a while. I heard they are going to cashier you. That true?'

64

'I really couldn't say at the moment, but I don't view the future with any confidence.'

'They haven't told you?'

'Nothing has been said, although naturally it would be prudent to expect the worst.'

'Yes, I've always found that a good policy in life. Dirty shame if they get rid of you, though. You've worked hard for that railway.'

'I certainly have.'

'Come and meet my boy.' The Dingleman was always affable, unless you upset him. I walked over to the iron lung. His boy had a head shaped like a teardrop. His lips were small and baby like, and his eyes were clear and blue, and stared up placid and unblinking. He looked about eleven or twelve but it was difficult to judge from the head alone.

'Hyperion, this is my friend Jack Wenlock. He works for the Great Western Railway.'

'I am pleased to meet you, Mr Wenlock.'

'My boy's got ambition – tell Mr Wenlock what you want to be when you grow up.'

'I'm sure he wouldn't be interested.'

'Of course he would, wouldn't you?'

'Yes, certainly I would.'

'Well, sir, one day I intend to ascend by rocket propulsion into outer space.'

'Like Buck Rogers?'

'Yes! Once I am cured.'

'The boy can dream, eh? Space man! All I ever wanted was to be was a bookie's runner. These nits are a blessed nuisance.'

'You didn't seem to mind them when you were his age.'

'No, but I minded that metal comb the nurse had. I've still got holes in my head from that. Could use me as a tea strainer.'

I smiled at the boy. 'I bet you didn't know your dad had them, did you? It's just a phase. Wait another year or two and they'll get tired of you and move on to someone younger.'

'You are a kind man, Mr Wenlock,' said Hyperion. 'The railway company is lucky to have you.'

The Dingleman grinned with pride. He put his arm on my shoulder and guided me across the room to the sofa. We sat down. One of his men handed us each a Scotch and soda.

'Chin, chin,' said the Dingleman, raising his glass. I raised mine in return.

'So, what brings you to Barmouth, Jack? Come for a swim?'

I smiled. I strongly suspected he already knew why I was here.

'Oh I just thought—'

Before I could finish the sentence, he nudged my arm and said, 'It's all right, I already know why you are here.'

There was a knock on the door and we all looked towards the sound. The Dingleman nodded to one of the men nearest the door and he opened it. The man with the Plasticine nose entered carrying a suitcase. He placed it down on the coffee table, clicked the fasteners and opened the lid. Inside were three items. The man took them out one by one. A hat. A wallet. And some false teeth, smeared with blood. The Dingleman picked up the hat and looked inside. There appeared to be spots of blood in the lining. He put it down and examined the wallet. He tut-tutted.

'Some poor chap fell in the sea,' he said, 'came on the same train as you. Damn fool thing to do, go swimming in December.' He looked up at the man and said, 'I don't suppose you were able—'

'We were unable to save him,' he said.

The Dingleman nodded.

'Ron,' I said. 'This is . . . what have you done to this—'

'Not done anything. He fell in the sea, my boys tried to save him but the waves were too strong. Isn't that right?' He looked up at the henchman.

'Yes, they were just too strong. All we managed to save were his hat and teeth.'

'You be sure to see that his widow gets them.'

'Ron,' I said again. He raised his finger in a gesture admonishing me to silence. 'Come!' he said. 'Let's go outside and admire the lights of Barmouth.

We walked out into the cold wet night. The wind howled softly and the lights of the camp gleamed in the wetness. Ron took out a cigarette case and offered me one. We smoked.

'Times are changing, Jack,' he said.

'Yes,' I said simply. I didn't know what else to say. He was almost certainly right. Times were always changing. And people always complained about it.

'They betrayed us, you and me, they betrayed us.'

'Who did?'

'The who is a long story.'

'I don't understand.'

'Wait till you lose your job in January, then you'll understand.' He puffed his cigarette and narrowed his eyes as if in deep thought. 'Do you read the papers? I do. They don't even want to hang us any more, did you know that?'

'Yes, I'd heard.'

He sighed. 'Now they get boffins to write papers about us instead, to explain why we did what we did. To understand us.

All to do with our childhood. They wouldn't want to write papers about mine. I never told you about the time before they found me in the firebox.'

'No, you didn't.'

'Never will. Who wants to be understood? It's none of their business.' He paused and added, 'Hyperion's all I've got.'

'I heard you had a boy, but I didn't know about—'

'The polio? Two years ago. He's not really mine. Remember the Tooting Thunderbolt?'

'Who?'

'Chap I killed in the ring. Hyperion was his son. He was there, in the front row, the night it happened. I sent money to his mother. In secret. She found out and came to thank me. I liked her. She's doing time now. For helping girls who got into trouble. Know what I mean?'

'I think I do.'

'You get ten years for that. For helping people. That's what I mean, about them betraying us. Look at you. You gave them your all. Tooting Thunderbolt had a dodgy ticker. That wasn't his real name, of course. Just a stupid name for the posters. Real name was Cyril Samuels. The doctors warned him not to go in the ring. Been invalided out of the Army. Shell shock. Couldn't find work, but had to feed his boy, didn't he? So he went in the ring. Spent four years on the Western Front and came back in pieces. Do you know what Victorian pastiche is?'

'Is it a type of cake?'

'Might as well be. He wrote some poems in the trenches.'

'I hear a lot of chaps did.'

'Sent them off to the magazines. They sent them back, saying

68

they were Victorian pastiche. That was his reward for serving his country.'

'Ron, I must ask. That man whose belongings you brought in. There was blood.'

'What do you expect, falling from a train into the sea in a storm? My boys tried to save him but they couldn't. That's all you need to know.'

'All the same, I have to—'

'He was on his way to kill Magdalena.'

I was shocked by this but did not allow it to register on my face.

'I know you've come here to find her. So did he. But he fell into a trap. He'd been hired, you see, to kill her. There's not much that happens that I don't get to hear about. That postcard Magdalena sent to Silas was a red herring. I sent it. I thought, if he comes to Barmouth then it's true what they say. And he'll pay the price. Well, he came.'

'Silas thinks she's here. He's chuffed.'

'Don't give me a sermon, Jack. I played the trick on Silas to save his bloody daughter's life. You're looking for her too.'

'But not because I mean her any harm.'

'I know that. But you can help me find her.'

'Have you quarrelled?'

'No, but she's done a runner. She's in trouble. I want to help her. I can protect her, but she doesn't believe me. I can protect her but I can't find her, she's too slippery. You know what she's like, how she used to go missing from the orphanage. Cheadle used to run away too but we always found him, didn't we? Or at least Kipper did. But Magdalena, she was a will-o'-the-wisp. Even the dog couldn't find her. How did she do that?'

69

'My feeling is Kipper knew where she was, but liked her too much to betray her.'

'Really?'

'I know that sounds rather foolish, but that's how it struck me at the time.'

'That doesn't sound foolish, Jack. It makes perfect sense.'

'I don't know where she is. I heard she might be here, that's all.'

'I know. But you will find her before I do. That's what you're good at, detective stuff. All I can do is threaten people. But this time threatening won't work. She's too scared.'

'I thought she might have done a Fishbone.'

'She did. She stole a letter from some toff. Turns out he was a courier with a letter for His Majesty the King. Who says Magdalena never gets lucky?'

'She stole a letter addressed to the King?'

'Yes, to the King.'

'Then she must give it back.'

'I don't think that is on her list of priorities.'

'Surely, Ron, you know that if I retrieved a letter addressed to His Majesty, stolen on the railway, I should have no choice but to return it.'

'This letter is important to me, Jack.'

'But it belongs to the King!'

'Trust me, if you have to upset me or the King, you are better off upsetting the King.'

'What is she so scared of?'

'She's scared of being hanged.'

'For stealing a letter?'

'For reading it.'

'That sounds like quite some letter.'

'Guess who it was from.'

'I really have no idea. Letter to the King . . . could be from anyone. Was it from overseas?'

'Yes.'

'Well, that hardly narrows it down.'

'You'll never guess in a million years, and even when I tell you, you won't believe it.'

'Perhaps you might as well tell me, then.'

'It was from the nuns, the ones who went missing in 1915.'

He said it so casually that I thought at first I must have misheard. 'Ron, no . . . you must be . . . are you . . . but they are dead.'

'Are they?'

'They must be . . . mustn't they?'

'Well, if they are, they still have the capacity to write letters. Soon as she read it, she knew she was in trouble. She says they will kill anyone who knows what is in the letter. I want it.'

'But it belongs to the King! How can you ask me to give it to . . . to . . .'

'I'm not asking you to give it to me. I'm asking you to trade it. For the life of this girl.' He reached into his jacket pocket and took out a photograph and handed it to me. It was a picture of Jenny. 'You give me the letter, nothing happens to her.'

The photograph showed Jenny leaving the Lyons tea shop with me, three days ago.

'And don't pretend you don't care about her, you bought her dinner. I've never known you do that before. Didn't think you liked girls.'

I felt myself blush.

'Her name's Jenny. Sweet girl.'

'I must warn you, Ron.'

'I know, I know. I know what you are going to say. Believe me, I don't want to hurt anyone. But I'll do what it is necessary to protect Magdalena. She was going to show me the letter, but she's friendly with this chap. Sugar daddy, I suppose you'd call him. He's quite highly connected. Ever heard of Room 42?'

'Yes, but I don't know what it means.'

'Doesn't matter. She knows this chap, he's not part of Room 42 but he knows people who are. He told her, they will kill anyone who reads the letter. Told her to get out of the country. Now she's gone AWOL, in order to protect me. She doesn't want me to read it, but she doesn't understand these things like I do.'

'If you get the letter, how will it protect her?'

'I will make the King an offer he can't refuse. Her safety in return for his letter.'

'And what if you give him the letter and they still kill her?'

'Jack, are you saying the King's word is not good enough for you?'

'No, that's a fair point. If the King gives his solemn word on the matter, then—'

The Dingleman burst out laughing. 'Jack, I wouldn't give two figs for the King's word! Of course I'm not going to trust him. I'll make a copy of the letter. If the contents are so compromising that they will kill to keep them secret, then it seems to me we have a pretty good hand of cards.' He saw the expression on my face. It really was disreputable to suggest the King's word could not be trusted. He laughed again.

'Don't look so glum! Here!' He took some tickets out of his jacket pocket. 'Take the girl to see a show. Have some fun.' He slid the tickets into my breast pocket. 'Just don't forget what I told you.' He placed his arm on my shoulder and opened the door. My boys will drive you back to the station. You'll find them in all the usual places if you need to get a message to me.' We walked back into the room, the Dingleman's arm still on my shoulder. The man with the Plasticine nose handed me the case containing my Formica.

'And do yourself a favour, Jack. For your own safety, put that funny piece of wood in a container that looks less like a gun, will you?

Chapter 7

T HE FOLLOWING EVENING was a Saturday and I went to see Johnny Chattanooga and the Pasadenas with Jenny. I did not tell her the tickets came from the Dingleman; I said I had won them in a raffle at Buckley's. I had decided on the journey back from Barmouth that this case was far too dangerous to allow Jenny to get mixed up in. I would have to find a way of distancing myself from her while I looked into it. I would have to tell her straight that she should not involve herself. The trouble was, I was pretty certain she wouldn't take a blind bit of notice of me. At the same time, it was vital that I found Magdalena in order to protect Jenny. I didn't doubt for one moment that the Dingleman would carry out his threat.

We were given a table near the stage and the tickets included a bottle of Johnnie Walker provided by the Dingleman; we didn't even have to pour it ourselves or pay for the soda water. We were a couple of swells. I had only been to the Astoria two times before, once to see a clown and once when the orphanage choir sang here at Christmas. I didn't know much about Johnny Chattanooga, although I had seen the posters. Jenny told me his real name was Charlie Milliner and his younger brother, Harry, was the one playing the 'gobble-pipe'. They played some lively tunes. 'Is You Is or Is You Ain't My Baby', 'There's a Silver Moon on the Golden Gate', 'Kiss Me Goodnight, Sergeant Major' . . . We danced for some of the slow numbers.

Then the band took a break and Jenny said she had to go to the om-tiddly-om-pom. When she returned I asked her, 'What's a gobble-pipe?'

'Saxophone.'

'Oh, I see. So what's . . . an accordion?'

'Groanbox. The drummer is a skin-tickler, trombone is a tram and the string bass is a doghouse.'

'How do you know all this?'

'An American soldier told me during the war. Guess what type of jazz they are playing?'

'What types are there?'

'Sweet, hot, corn, salon, lollypop, schmaltz, dillinger, gut-bucket, clam-bake, barrel-house.'

'I wouldn't have a clue.'

'You have to guess.'

'Lollypop.'

'Clam-bake.'

A chap in full evening dress, including a cummerbund, passed close to our table. He was accompanied by a lady. A white fox stole was draped over her shoulder and the eyes of the fox gleamed in the spotlight and seemed to stare at us.

'I expect they are a couple of people from your first class, Jack.'

'I expect they might be. Do you dislike them for that?'

'No, why do you think that?'

'I thought your voice sounded a touch harsh. People occasionally do dislike such people. Sometimes when I have been called to assist at an incidence of drunkenness in third class, I have been called names.'

'What do they call you?'

'The actual words are not important—'

'If you'd rather not say.'

'I'm not ashamed to say. If a man calls me a name and it is not true, it does not hurt me. I was called a butler once. I think I knew what the chap meant. Some sort of lackey, I suppose.'

'What did you do to him for calling you a butler?'

'I did not do anything to him for calling me that. He was making a nuisance of himself and I asked him to temper his exuberance.'

'Temper his exuberance!'

'Is there something wrong with saying that?'

'No, it's just that a normal person would have told him to shut his pie hole or something.'

'I suppose you would say I am not a normal person.'

Jenny reached across the table and touched my hand. 'Of course you are not a normal person. That's why I like you.'

I must admit I was quite affected by those words of Jenny's. I expect everyone quite likes it when someone says such a thing.

'The look on your face!'

'Why?' I said. 'Is there something wrong?'

'No, it's . . . it's you. Anyone would think a girl had never told you she liked you before.'

'They haven't. Why would a girl say such a thing?'

Jenny rolled her eyes and then, perhaps feeling she had made me uncomfortable, changed the subject. 'I saw that horrid doctor again. I told him I wanted to take Aunt Agatha home and he said that was out of the question. So I said, "What right do you have to hold her here?" and he wrote it down for me.' She took a piece of paper out of her handbag and unfolded it. 'He said he was empowered under the Mental Deficiency Act of 1913 as administered by the Board of Control for Lunacy and Mental Deficiency to detain indefinitely and at his pleasure all idiots, feeble-minded persons and moral imbeciles. To wit Miss Wilberforce had been categorised as a feeble-minded person, meaning one whose weakness does not amount to imbecility, yet which requires care, supervision or control, for her protection or for the protection of others.' She looked up. 'Then he said he had to catch his bus and advised me to stop questioning his authority. He said the line between feeble-minded person and moral defective was a thin one and he could easily adjust his diagnosis, particularly if I continued to make a nuisance of myself, and then I wouldn't be allowed to visit her at all. Can you believe that?'

It must have been the Johnnie Walker because I got rather tight during the course of the evening. The conversation was so gay and Jenny was such fun. I made the mistake of revealing to her details of the case that it would perhaps have been wiser to keep under wraps. I told her what the Dingleman said about the letter from the nuns of 1915. Not surprisingly, she was beside herself with excitement to learn that her aunt might have witnessed the theft of this astonishing item. She started making plans for how we would work together on the case. I tried to dampen her enthusiasm, but it wasn't easy. It really would have been wiser not to say anything.

'Well,' said Jenny with an air that suggested the matter was settled, 'we will have to find Magdalena and that letter. If Aunt Agatha really did see a letter being stolen rather than . . . a murder . . . well, whoever put her in hospital must want the existence of this letter kept secret. We must find it and demand they release her.'

'I'm not sure if that's wise—'

'Wise?'

'For you, I mean.'

'Don't be silly.'

'It could be dangerous.'

'I can't just leave my aunt sleeping like that.'

'I'm sure she's being well looked after.'

'And I'm sure they are trying to make her forget what she saw. No, we must—'

'I really think it's too dangerous for—'

'Are you scared, Jack?'

'Not for myself but, you see, there is something I didn't tell you. The day after you came to my office I received a visit from some rather unsavoury chaps who suggested I would be better off leaving this case alone.'

'I see, so you are scared.'

'Not at all.'

'Who were they?'

'One of them was Lord Apsley, who used to be at the orphanage. The other two said they were . . . from Room 42.'

'Where's that?'

'I don't know.'

'Well, I'm from number 37 Moreton Crescent and I mean to get to the bottom of this. We must find Magdalena. What places does she frequent?'

'I'm not sure if she *frequents* anywhere, it depends on . . . who she's with.'

'Isn't there somewhere you can ask?'

'Before the war she used to visit the Star and Garter. There was a chap there, I never met him, a Lithuanian called Andruis. He looked like Desperate Dan, they said.'

'Then we must go there and ask.'

'To be honest, if Magdalena doesn't want to be found, it will be very difficult. She's very good at not being found.'

'In that case, we must find the nuns.'

I laughed.

'If they sent the King a letter they can't be very far away . . . don't you want to win the Heinroth Prize and find your mum?'

'Yes, I do, but I don't see how that will help your aunt.'

'We could go and ask the nuns what was in the letter . . . then we could go and see the King.'

'No, Jenny, I know this is all rather exciting, but—'

'Oh, Jack!' She flashed me a look of such intensity that it almost made me jump.

I made a dismissive gesture with my hands. 'Well, if you can find the nuns you are a better girl than all the other Railway Goslings combined.'

'You said the chap who wrote the missing 1931 Gosling annual found them.'

'Cadbury Holt? Yes, so they say.'

'Tell me about him.'

'Cadbury was the oldest, nine years older than me, so he seemed like a grown man. He was good at everything. He could run faster, and was stronger. Unlike the rest of us he wasn't scared of fierce dogs. He was the best boxer and won cups competing with boys at other schools. He was good at maths and scripture and English. He was good at woodwork. He could make dovetail joints that held without the need for glue. He could tie sailor's knots. Even the potatoes he grew in the garden behind the kitchen seemed better than ours.'

'Oh dear, he sounds like a goody two-shoes.'

'No, no, really he wasn't. He wasn't afraid to get into trouble. He was charming, and quite . . . dashing. After he left in 1918 he came back a month later sporting a pencil-thin moustache on his top lip, like the film star Jupien Duvalier. It was as if he had always had it, even though I knew he didn't. You remember you asked about the Chinese temple boxing? It's not really a secret. Cadbury taught it to me and the other boys. He had learned the art from a scripture master who spent nineteen years as a Protestant missionary to China. It's quite amazing what you can do if you know the pressure points. It's saved me from many a beating and possibly worse over the years.'

'Hmm, I'm still not convinced he wasn't a goody two-shoes. Tell me something really bad.'

'He could be wicked, I can assure you. He even smoked cig-arettes. Cheadle used to run away quite a lot and we would be sent out looking for him. One day Cadbury and me were together looking for Cheadle and we met the priest's daughter sitting on a wall by the canal. She blew a raspberry at us. And Cadbury gave her three cigarettes if she would . . .'

'Yes?'

'Well, if she would . . .'

'What?'

'If she would say the words "Bloody Christ".'

'Did she?'

'Yes! And smoked the cigarettes.'

'OK, that's better. Where will we find him now?'

'In a lion's stomach I suppose.'

'What happened to all his files and papers?'

'Mr Jarley at Lost Property has the archive . . .'

'There you are, you see, you can ask Mr Jarley for Cadbury Holt's papers. There's bound to be a clue in them. What about his friends?'

'There's only one really, Cheadle Heath. You remember I told you, he . . . he's not a Gosling any more, he blotted our copybook.'

'Yes, I remember, but you didn't say what he did . . .'

'I would prefer not to.'

'Was it so terribly shocking?'

'Yes, frankly it was. He . . . he went to live with a woman.'

'A woman!'

'In sin.'

I could see Jenny making an effort to contain a sly smile. 'Oh, Jack! When you told me in the Lyons tea shop that he'd blotted everybody's copybook, I assumed he must have murdered a priest or something. But this is much worse.'

That really was perhaps the most shocking thing I'd ever heard and there was half a second's silence. Then Jenny giggled and I found myself laughing too. It really must have been the liquor. I'd never laughed at what Cheadle did before.

'Where does he live?'

'He used to live above the Chinese laundry in the Shambles. I haven't seen him since 1938.'

We went to the Star and Garter to find Andruis. The saloon bar was half empty. The landlady had fat jowls and a big bosom piled high with beads; she stood looking bored behind the hand pumps. Three men were standing next to the cribbage table, smoking and looking shifty. This pub did not have a good reputation. I ordered a bottle of pale ale for myself and a glass of lemonade for Jenny. We stood and observed the men while we drank. They were thin and nervous, with sallow complexions, the sort acquired by men whose main job is to sell stolen goods in pubs. They seemed at home here. I told Jenny to wait and carried my drink over and interrupted their conversation. I asked them if they knew a man called Andruis.

They exchanged glances and their eyes contained the glint of expectation, as if the evening had finally started to get interesting. One of them spoke. He differed from the others in being a good nine inches shorter, and skinnier. His ears were slightly too big for his head and he had bright sparkly eyes. Strangest of all, his head seemed placed too low into his collar, giving his face the slightly startled look that I have noticed characterises the weasel.

'What does he look like?' said the weasel.

'I'm afraid I really couldn't say. I've not had the pleasure of his acquaintance.'

The response to this was very caddish. They all swapped glances but in a way that involved looking down their noses as if to say 'La-di-da'.

'I realise that might strike you—'

The door to the gents' lavatories swung open and the squeaking hinge drew their attention. A man who looked like Desperate Dan emerged. He was tall and wide at the shoulders, his nose was comically snub and he had a lantern jaw. He was built like a stevedore, but gave the impression that an honest day's work was not something he greatly cared for.

When he reached us, the weasel said, 'This chap is looking for someone called Andruis.'

'Andruis,' Desperate Dan repeated. 'What does he look like?'

'I was told he was quite . . . a tall chap, like you. I was hoping you might be able to help me find an old friend, Magdalena. She used to come here quite a lot, before the war. My name's Jack.' I held out my hand to shake. He ignored it.

'What war?' he said.

I think this was meant as a joke and certainly his companions treated it as such. If you ask me, it was a very poor joke, especially in view of the many terrible things that took place during the war and which were still very fresh in the minds of every decent person.

'Who told you he was here?' said Desperate Dan.

I paused to consider. His tone was unfriendly and I decided this was futile and it would be best to leave. 'A chap.'

'A chap?'

'Yes. A chap told me.'

'Does he have a name?'

'I . . . I'm afraid I don't know his name.'

One of the others chimed in. 'Sounds a bit fishy to me. Chap told him but he doesn't know the chap.'

Andruis glanced at his friends. Their faces wore the stiff vacancy that tough chaps like to hide behind, but there was also the beginning of a smile brewing on their countenances. You could tell they thought some sport was about to begin.

'I just wanted to get a message to her, but if it's a trouble to you—'

'Perhaps she's gone to Barking,' said the weasel in a manner that suggested he was uttering a private joke.

Andruis stepped forward and pointedly stood too close to me. 'Since you are here, why don't you have a drink with us?'

'That's very kind of you but I have company.'

The men sniggered. Conversation in the pub had stopped and people were looking towards us. The landlady stopped halfway through pulling a pint, and stared.

'It wouldn't be polite to leave and welsh on your round, would it?'

The others agreed.

'Nothing worse than a man who sneaks out just as it's his round. Worst type of chap that is,' said one of them.

Jenny, who had been observing keenly from across the bar, came over and stood by my side.

'Are you ready to leave, Jenny?' I asked. 'Well, it's been nice meeting you.'

'Charming,' said Andruis. 'Would you like to leave a visiting card?' He positioned himself between us and the path to the door.

'Would you step aside please?'

He looked at me with a cruel smile. 'No, I don't think I care to.'

'I would prefer to avoid unpleasantness.'

He made a comic face.

'Andruis!' The landlady's voice rang out. He looked across. She didn't say anything but gave him a look that said clearly that she didn't want any broken furniture.

'Who's causing trouble?' he asked.

I turned to Jenny. 'Please would you be so good as to go outside and wait for me at the end of the street?'

'I'm not leaving you.'

'Please, Jenny, I require you to.'

'I'm not going outside until you do.'

I moved my face closer to hers and whispered, 'There might be blood and it would shame me for you to see it.'

Her eyes watered. 'Jack, if they hurt you—'

'I don't mean my blood!'

I turned to Andruis. 'Would you step aside, please, sir?' I touched his arm to encourage him. He grinned again and screwed back his fist. This was quite a surprise. Given the manner in which he conducted himself, I expected him to be a better fighter than to signal his intentions so clearly. He wouldn't have lasted five minutes fighting like that at the orphanage. When the punch came I stepped inside it easily enough and then gave him a sharp crack to the ribs above the heart. It looked quite casual but I well knew the power in that blow, the punch to the ribs that breaks the heart of the prize-fighter and makes him kiss the canvas like a sweetheart. The pain shivered through Andruis and made him gasp. He slumped to his knees, made an effort like a drunken man to get up and then fell backwards, flat on his back. There was a crash as he did, like a tree falling. His men looked down at him in disbelief. He lay still, staring wide-eyed but unconscious at the ceiling. A rattling noise came from his throat. This was not a safe position to leave him in. I knelt down and pulled his arm over and brought him on to his side, so that his tongue did not block his air passage. I looked up at the weasel. 'Would you be kind enough to give me your coat?'

'What for?'

'To put under his head.'

'I don't want blood on it.'

'There is no blood.'

'But there will be if you finish him off.'

'I'm not going to finish him off, I want to make him comfortable, he seems to have taken quite poorly.'

'Give him the bloody coat,' said one of the others. The weasel took off his coat and handed it to me in a bundle. I put it under Andruis's head, then stood up. 'I'm sure he will be all right in a little while. You might like to chafe his wrists to hasten his recovery, or some smelling salts would help too.'

Jenny handed me my hat, which had fallen off in the fight. I placed it on my head and addressed the weasel. 'You, sir, would you tell me what you meant by that remark about Barking?'

'I didn't mean anything by it.'

Another of them chimed in. 'Magdalena's sugar daddy is Joshua Barker, the chap who owns Barker & Stroud's.'

I thanked him and we left.

Outside, we stood on the pavement and looked at each other. For once Jenny seemed lost for words. She looked at me with a strange mixture of expressions. Fear and excitement, and that soft look of shock one wears after treating a matter too lightly and being corrected by events.

We stood in silence for a full minute and I reflected on how derelict of my duty it was for me to lead Jenny into danger like this.

'Bravo, Jack,' she said softly.

I shook my head. 'This is no place for bravos, Jenny. This has to stop now.'

'What does?'

'You know very well. You cannot become embroiled in this case.'

'I can if I want.'

'Well then I shall have to forbid you.'

'I will follow you then. It's my aunt, remember?'

'You won't have anything to follow. I have decided not to take this case.'

'You can't do that.'

'Can't I? I think you will find I have full discretion—'

'Not take the case? We'll see about that.'

'And I must tell you that you are on no account to get involved.'

Jenny stared at me, poised with pent-up anger, like an arrow about to be released. 'Not get involved? Hmmph!' She marched off into the night shouting as she went, 'Not Pygmalion likely!'

After she left, there was silence: the traffic seemed to have gone to bed. I looked down at my fist, still balled from punching Andruis. I slowly relaxed the fingers. During the war, when the army medics performing the physical examination read on your form that your occupation was GWR fireman, they waved you through.

It wasn't true, of course, that I was not going to work on the case. In fact, I did precisely as Jenny had suggested. First thing Monday morning I did three things. I put in a requisition for Cadbury Holt's case files. Then I placed a telephone call to Barker & Stroud's. The lady who answered told me Mr Barker was away on business in London and she was not sure when he would be back. She took my name. Lastly, I telephoned the Chinese laundry leaving a message for Cheadle. Half an hour later he returned the call. It was a bad line, his voice crackling in and out like a radio station drifting on the wireless. I pressed the Bakelite harder into my ear. At first, I did not realise it was Cheadle.

'Jack? Jack? Is that you?'

'This is Jack Wenlock.'

'I tried ten minutes ago and couldn't get through. I was worried you might have already been cashiered.'

'Cashiered?'

'Just over three weeks till new year's eve, now. The end of the Great Western.'

'Who is this, please?'

'Don't you recognise me? You used to. It's Cheadle.'

My grip on the telephone receiver relaxed. 'Oh, Cheadle, yes.'

We arranged to meet at the turntable in half an hour. I replaced the receiver and hurried downstairs to fetch my bicycle from the tool room in the yard. I cycled out to Wildernesse where the turntable lay on the south side of the engine shed. Some people wonder about the need for a turntable. Can't steam engines operate in reverse, they ask. The answer is, yes, of course, they can, but the driver gets tired of looking over his shoulder for seven or eight hours. The biggest misconception among the general public, particularly among ladies, is that the turntable moves by clockwork. In truth it is either steam operated, in which case the driver attaches a pipe from the engine to provide the steam, or, as in the case of the one at Weeping Cross, it is manually operated, which means the driver and his fireman push it round. They put their backs into it to get it going, but after that it is fairly easy.

The wind whistling across the siding was biting and sharp. I stood on the footbridge and looked south. There was a wail. The rails below began to sing, the air to quiver. A train approached. You could feel the rumble in the ground, as if beyond the horizon a herd of buffalo was stampeding in our direction. The old stone bridge began to hum, and my stomach quivered in expectation of the moment the thunder struck. Seen at a distance there was a curious disparity between the sedate progress and the fury of the smoke chuffing out of the chimney. It disappeared when the train got closer. Suddenly all was violence. She was snorting furiously now, coughing fire and gobbets of smoke into the grey morning. Oh my! Her arrival slammed into the bridge like a giant hammer, throwing an earthquake into my lap. She slipped under the bridge like a whale blowing spume – a delicious fog that filled my nostrils and heart with the intoxicating scent of nursery smells: brimstone and smoke, coal and scorched steam, hot oil and cold ash. Sparks and smoke and screams everywhere. Then carriage roofs, studded and veined, grey, clattered past with the thundering clickety-clack of a giant's printing press. Instinctively, like all small boys taken by their grandmothers to watch the trains, I turned and rushed to the other side, to watch her go.

Cheadle approached quietly, almost sheepishly. I sensed his presence more than heard him. We shook hands. He smiled, a thin smile in a thin face, the sort of smile that did not reach the eyes and suggested life had been hard for him in the ten years since he blotted our copybooks.

He turned and began to walk and I fell in lock-step although I had no idea where he was heading.

'I expect you think I'm a pretty poor sort of chap,' he said.

'I didn't rightly know what to think, Cheadle. None of us did.'

'It's not like how they describe it, in books and at the flicks. It's downright Devilish a lot of the time, being with a woman.'

'Did you really live in sin?'

'Yes, I'm afraid I did. It was pretty ghastly. More like rotting than living.'

'Rotting?'

'I can't think of a better word for it. Some might call it life. I was able to find work for a while as an insurance investigator. We rented a small room, and it was passable, but it was all rather . . . sordid. I missed the railways too. Then our landlady found out that we were not married and so we had to leave. They say you can't outrun your past, Jack, and they are right. It's like your shadow. Or the Mark of Cain.'

'But Cain murdered his brother.'

'Some people think what we did was worse.'

'But what did you do? Why? Was she terribly pretty?'

'She wasn't really pretty at all, Jack. I expect that will surprise you. I was rather surprised myself to discover how it all worked. The things they taught us about taking a cold tub first thing in the morning, and doing physical jerks, and praying for strength, none of that made a blind bit of difference. There are things, you see, that happen . . . as I said, it was all rather Devilish and to tell you truly, well, I wasn't terribly good at it. There, I've said it.'

I nodded with what I hoped was a face of understanding, but the truth be told, I didn't know what he meant. What wasn't he terribly good at?

'She began to mock me. I'm rather afraid I raised my hand to her.'

'Oh, Cheadle!'

'I know. It shames me to say this. But have you . . . I mean I doubt rather that you have . . . have you ever had relations with a girl? No, I can see that you haven't. You're lucky. Take my word for it. It's Devilish. You probably can't imagine anything worse than a man who raises his hand to a lady but a lot of them do it. I never imagined I could ever do such a thing.'

Cheadle suggested we might like to take a glass of ale and I got the impression that he would like it more than me. He was quite choosy about the pub, though, and we passed the Railway, the Union and the White Horse before he settled for the King George. After we passed the third I formed the impression that he was avoiding pubs which were known to be popular with railway men. The George was still empty although they had built a nice fire in the grate and we took our pints of bitter and sat at a round table near the fire.

For a while we did not speak but preferred to let our frozen limbs warm up in the heat.

'Will they be keeping you on then?' he said.

'I haven't heard anything, and to tell the truth, I don't know who to ask. Or even whether I should.'

'If it was me, I'd say nothing. They'll probably forget about you.'

'Yes, I'm sure that's right,' I said, although I did not believe it.

'Haven't heard from you for a long time, then this. You wanted to wish me happy Christmas, did you?'

I looked up from my pint and our eyes met. I felt a pang of guilt. There was no avoiding the issue. 'I rather hoped you could tell me about Cadbury.'

He looked as if this piece of news confirmed his own presentiment.

'Got the bug, have you? Everyone does eventually.'

'Bug, Cheadle?'

'The nuns. It comes to every Gosling.'

'I was just curious, that's all.'

'Is it all?'

'Aren't you curious?'

'There's enough trouble in my life without that.'

'You were closer to Cadbury than anyone. Is it true what they say? That he found them?'

He didn't answer immediately. It was as if he were reluctant to broach the subject but knew in his heart that he was going to.

'I saw him. Just once. Ten years ago now, just after I moved to Hereford. A boy came to my digs and told me there was a man outside who wished to speak with me who wouldn't give his name. We went outside but there was no one there and then the boy led me to the railway viaduct where a man was waiting under the arches. It was dark, as you can imagine, and I was a bit unnerved. He stood in the shadows and refused to come into the light where I could see his face. I challenged him directly on the matter and he said, "I cannot let you see my face, Cheadle. Be content that it is me, the brother that loves you." Those were his exact words. I remember them precisely.'

'You've no doubt it was him?'

'I knew it was him, in a way I cannot explain to you. I knew that he was greatly changed from the man I had known. Almost as if he had died and been reborn, but that is just a figure of speech. I do not mean it except as a way to try and explain the difference I discerned. He felt much older, too, for some reason his presence recalled a phrase to mind from one of the hymns we used to sing, the Ancient of Days. His voice was the voice of a man at the end of his life. He told me that his life was in constant danger, that he lived in the shadows of this world, scarcely ever remaining in one place for more than one night and that he was taking a great risk in coming to see me. I asked him if this danger had to do with his quest for the nuns and he agreed that it did. He told me he had after years of searching discovered the answer to the riddle, he had seen the nuns. "So they are still alive, then?" I said. He said they were very much alive although not in a fashion commonly understood by that expression.'

'What way then?'

'I really couldn't tell you. Cadbury told me it would be dangerous if he were to reveal to me what he had discovered. I'm telling you this, Jack, to warn you. Sometimes it is better not to know things. They call it forbidden fruit, don't they? That's what happened in the Garden of Eden, isn't it? They ate the apple from the tree of knowledge and everything went wrong after that. I did the same. I found out what it would have been better for me not to have known. And so did Cadbury. It seems to me that you of all of us have a good life. You strike me as a happy man. And happiness is something that once lost is never entirely repossessed.'

'How can a Gosling live happily not knowing the answer to the great mystery of the nuns?'

'With a steadfast determination not to know that which being known will do him no good. If you can know in advance that certain knowledge will bring only suffering and sully your soul's tranquillity for ever, what good can there be in pursuing it? Just for the satisfaction of a curiosity that will lead to your doom? An itch that you cannot resist to scratch?'

'Can the truth really be so very terrible?'

'Can it be so very wonderful? You do not possess the truth, but what is missing from your life?'

'Did he tell you nothing about the mystery?'

'He told me some things. He said no man would find them, until he learned to look in a fresh way. He said he had found

93

them but it had taken many years and it required him to forget all that he thought he knew. Finding them was a task beyond the wit of most men, he said, but he did and he lived among them for a while. But harder than finding them was finding the way back.'

'Is it so very far away?'

'I do not think he meant it like that. It could be in the next street, but a man having uncovered the truth of their fate would never again find peace in his soul.'

'It seems to me he said a lot without actually saying anything that a man could grasp with his two hands.'

'I did not doubt the truthfulness of what he told me. But some of it struck me as a bit . . . well, to be frank I didn't understand much of it. He said they had committed a crime, they stole something . . . something very ancient.'

'The holy sisters?'

'Yes. It was a map, they stole it from a library. I don't know where. He said the map showed the location of the River Pishon. Do you know what that is, Jack?'

'It's the fourth river of Eden.'

'That's right. He didn't say any more. The week after we met, he sent me a chit of paper. He didn't even sign his name to it, it was just a paragraph of hastily scribbled words. It said, if I truly wanted to understand, I should go to London Zoo. There was a fellow there, Mr Clerihew in the ape house – he spent some time in Africa and saw the nuns with his own eyes.'

'Mr Clerihew at the zoo?'

'Yes, those were his words.'

'And did you go?'

'I'm rather afraid I didn't. I never seemed to find the time, and to be honest, the errand struck me as rather foolish.' He laughed without mirth and pushed his glass away as if to indicate our time together had come to an end. We both stood up to leave.

For a few seconds we stood in the doorway of the pub, preparing to part in different directions. 'We must do this again some time,' he said.

'Yes, I would like to.'

A cold wind blew a piece of newspaper along the pavement and wrapped it round Cheadle's legs. He made an ineffective attempt to kick it away. We said goodbye and then he grabbed me by the arm. 'Jack, if you ever find yourself a girl, will you promise me something?'

'I'll do my best. What is it?'

'If . . . if you love her, Jack, take my advice, don't talk to her about trains all the time.'

THE BOY'S OWN
RAILWAY GOSLING ANNUAL

Vol.VII   1931   Price: 1/-

Replies to our readers' letters

CEDRIC OF DUNSTABLE—Your fishmonger is right: the driver (but not the fireman) of a mainline steam locomotive on the Great Western Region is permitted under certain circumstances to perform the marriage ceremony.

LUCY J. OF MOTHERWELL— Ignore your brother and heed the wiser counsel of your cook. Pemmican is a form of concentrated foodstuff made from drying meat such as elk, moose and buffalo, and fortifying it with lard and other fats. Its purpose is solely intended for expeditions into perilous wildernesses. For your proposed journey to Devon we suggest fish paste sandwiches, sausage rolls, jellies and perhaps an apple.

THE CONTINUING ADVENTURES OF RAILWAY GOSLING
CADBURY HOLT – ON THE TRAIL OF THE MISSING NUNS!

At the Feast of One-eyed Jheg

After the feast was over and the dancing which went on into the early hours was spent, One-eyed Jheg turned to me and expounded upon the quest that had brought me thither. He assured me that the stories were untrue. It was not his brothers the noble Jhabra that had sold the English holy sisters into slavery, but those jackals and curse-ridden fiends from the deep south, the Alhaj'abhra. With each sentence One-eyed Jheg spat into the fire, which hissed like a snake. He said, 'The Jhabra are Lords of the Sun, they do not enslave and sell the darlings of Allah into perpetual night.' He, One-eyed Jheg, was there that day and had seen truly with both eyes for this was in the days before the claw of the desert lion took his right eye. With two young sharp eyes he witnessed the raid on the fort when the holy sisters came in search of their lost brethren. They were armed, he said, with Bergmann M15 machine guns, Luger side arms and a flame thrower. He pulled up the sleeve to reveal the withered burn tissue where the cruel fire had consumed his arm. 'My friend,' said One-eyed Jheg, 'I tried to reason with them but they were possessed by the holy fire and refused to listen. They sacked our beautiful library and stole the Great Map that showed the source of the River Pishon.' One-eyed Jheg threw down a creased black-and-white photo. It depicted a U-boat belonging to the Imperial German navy at anchor in a bay fringed with palm trees. *U-33* it said on the conning tower.

'This is how they arrived,' he said. 'In the dhow that swims like a fish. And in this the devil's dhow, they took away the Great Map.'

'The River Pishon?' I said in disbelief.

'Indeed!'

'*And a river went out of Eden to water the garden,*' I said, incanting the words that I had heard so many times as a boy, '*and from thence it was parted, and became into four heads. The name of the first is Pishon: that is it which compasseth the whole land of Havilah, where there is gold . . .*'

'Oh yes,' said One-eyed Jheg. 'The River Pishon. The last undiscovered of the four rivers of Eden.'

Chapter 8

I RETURNED TO my office to find a message from Mr Dombey at the bookshop, Master Humphrey's Clock. Mr Dombey said he had been contacted by a lady claiming to have a 1931 Railway Gosling annual for sale and who was due to visit his shop at four o'clock. It seemed too good to be true, but there was no way I could miss the opportunity and set out shortly after three. I arrived in plenty of time and decided to take a cup of tea in the café across the Square. A young lady with a Veronica Lake hairstyle stood just inside the door. She turned as I entered, took one look at me and said, 'I knew it!'

'Jenny! How funny to meet you!'

'Oh yes!' she said in a voice that sounded a bit harsh. 'So funny I forgot to laugh.'

'Is there something wrong? You seem a bit flustered.'

'Of course not, it's a trifle warm in here, it makes me go red. What brings you here?'

'I was going to pay a visit to the cobblers.'

'Oh, were you, indeed? You won't get rid of me that easily.'

'Get rid of you? In what way?'

'You know exactly what I mean. Don't you come the innocent with me.'

'But, Jenny—'

Her eyes flashed and I took a step backwards and brushed

against the arm of a lady who had been raising a cup of tea to her mouth. 'I'm so sorry,' I said.

'You should be more careful,' she said in a sour voice.

'Yes, it was clumsy of me, I'm terribly sorry.'

'Well, it's too late saying that now, isn't it?'

'Is your arm broken?' said Jenny turning sharply. The lady looked at her arm and then thought better of herself.

'No, of course not!'

'It sounds like it, the fuss you are making. All he did was brush your arm.'

'He jumped back very sharply. Look at the mess he's made on the tablecloth.'

'That's what the tablecloth is for, isn't it? To mop up spills.'

'I'm just saying . . .'

'Say it to me then, I'm the one who made him jump back.'

I took Jenny gently by the arm. 'Shall we go outside, it's a trifle stuffy in here.'

Outside on the square, Jenny pushed herself close to me and told me in no uncertain terms: 'I don't believe you are going to the cobblers. You are probably investigating the missing nuns and don't want me tagging along.'

'I really am just going to the cobblers.'

'Which one? I'll walk with you.'

'As it happens, I think I might pop into the bookshop for a browse, I'm a bit early.'

'Early? Do you have an appointment with your shoe mender?' She sighed. 'Jack, I know you are going to see the chap here about a lady with a 1931 Gosling annual.'

'But—'

'I'm the lady. I knew you were only pretending when you said

99

you weren't going to take the case. Let's go in and ask about the thingybob plates.'

No bell tinkled when we walked in, but the floor squeaked so loudly it was hardly necessary. The shop felt like the inside of a ship made of books. Timber beams rose from the floor, through piles of books, towards a ceiling of yellow plaster that bowed like a lumpy mattress. Wooden shelves rose up on every side forming avenues in a labyrinth of musty books. Every space had been filled, and papers and files of documents were wedged between the book tops and the shelves above. An old man sat hunched over a desk, with snow white hair reaching down to his shoulders. He wrote into a ledger with a fountain pen. It was clear he was aware of our presence, but he took his time, mumbling softly to himself as he wrote. He finished writing with a flourish and stabbed a full stop. Then he looked up. His face was entirely covered with surgical gauze, fixed in place with adhesive tape attached to his ears. There was a thin crack, like the opening to a pillar box, where his mouth should be, two holes in the covering for his nostrils, and two perfect ellipses for his eyes, which twinkled sadly within the darkness. He wore a pair of half-moon glasses balanced on the bandaged bridge of his nose.

'Yes?'

'We're looking for a Railway Gosling annual,' said Jenny.

'I have them all.'

'The 1931 edition?'

'Ah!' He tutted. 'Except that one.'

'We've tried everywhere,' she said.

'Everyone has tried everywhere.'

'The booksellers in London told us to come here.'

He tutted again. 'They really have no business saying that.'

'They told us it was printed here,' I said.

'Did they indeed? I spy a great desperation in your face. Do you drink tea?'

'Yes, I am very fond of tea.'

'I couldn't trust a man who was not. Wait!' He ambled to the front of the shop and let the door off the latch. He turned the sign saying CLOSED to face the street and then passed to a tiny kitchen at the back. We heard the sound of a kettle being filled. We waited. Once the tea was brewed he returned holding a tray with a pot, three cups and a plate of digestive biscuits. He placed the tray down unevenly upon the papers, causing the biscuits to slide off the plate.

'Guess how long I have worked in this shop?'

'Quite a long time I shouldn't wonder,' I said.

'Have you ever devoted much study to the phantasma we call Time?'

'Only in relation to the smooth operation of the railways.'

'Yes, yes, I can see I was not wrong about you. The railways of course are responsible for the unification of time on our island. Before the railways, each town had its own time, worked out from the mayor's sundial, and each town was different. Leeds was six minutes behind London, Bristol ten. Is it not so?'

'So I understand.'

'For a while railway station clocks had two minute hands, to register the different times, but that measure was but a halfway house. It was the electric telegraph that defined the modern age of unified time. As Charles Dickens said, it was as if the sun itself had surrendered to the Great Western Railway. The station clock is a marvellous instrument, but it represents a regrettable refusal to accept the most obvious truth about Time, namely that it is malleable. You wonder, perhaps, how long I have worked in this shop, but really you should wonder how long have I not worked here, and the answer I should give would be this: there is no time that I have not worked here. I was born upstairs in the room overlooking the square, I was cradled upstairs in the back room overlooking the foundry. I was schooled in the garret and receive my clothes through the post from a man who has never met me but adjusts the size according to the passage of the seasons. Would it surprise you to learn that I have only once left this shop? And that was in 1938 when I made a journey to London, during the course of which I lost my suitcase.'

'I think I would be more than a little surprised to hear of that,' I said.

'I have never met anyone who wasn't. Even when my dear sweet mother died, I did not leave the shop; and neither did she.' He paused and considered, then said, 'I need hardly tell you, of course, that no copies of the 1931 annual exist.'

'But were they printed here?' said Jenny.

'Yes, they were printed upstairs under conditions of total secrecy, I wasn't even allowed to peek. When the printing was finished it was taken away in an ambulance marked "St Ignis Fatuus Hospital". Along with the galley proofs and the original manuscript. The printing press was smashed up with hammers. The ambulance returned, but the manuscript did not.'

'What about the thingybob plates?' said Jenny.

'No thingybob plates were made.'

'Why did they do this?' I said. The man turned his palms to the sky and shrugged.

'Who were they?' said Jenny.

'The people from Room 42.'

'That doesn't tell me much,' said Jenny.

'It's not intended to.'

'But where is the room?'

'I am unable to say.'

'You mean to say the whole print run was taken away?' said Jenny.

'Oh yes.'

'How many books did they print?' I said.

'Just one.'

'That couldn't have taken very long to print.'

'It didn't. Did I say it took a long time? No, I said no such thing.'

'Why did they do this?'

He stirred the tea and then poured. It was so dark it was almost the colour of ox blood.

'You ask why but I think you already know why. Because the 1931 edition was written by the only Railway Gosling to go off in search of the nuns and succeed in finding them. Oh yes, do you think I could not tell what your business was? You are the chap from the railway station to whom I sent the note. It was a simple courtesy to inform you of this development, but the same courtesy requires me to confess that you are almost certainly wasting your time. I have no faith that the lady who telephoned me was bona fide. I get such calls from time to time. Perhaps it amuses them. Yes, I knew you straightaway. I have seen so many men come here seeking the solution to this the greatest of mysteries. Each one is like you, dressed in a long raincoat that seems woven from the same material they make shadows from; his hat pulled low and beneath the brim, along the rim of which raindrops cling, there is a darkness and gaunt and forlorn shade in which the eyes peer with a bright and demented intensity. Yes, I have seen that look many times in the visage of those who seek the missing Gosling annual. To each I have rendered whatever small assistance it was in my power to give, and each has made the promise and never kept it. So, why should you be any different?'

'What is the promise?' I asked.

'That they will come back and tell me of their adventures.'

'We'll come back, won't we, Jack?' said Jenny.

'Yes, you say that now, but everyone abandons me in the end. For a time I used to receive visits from that Cadbury Holt. He was quite a chap. He used to tell me stories about the Railway Goslings and his time at the orphanage.' He tilted his head back slightly as if trying to recall, and then laughed. 'He told me how he and another boy had been out looking for a boy who had run away. Instead of him, they found the vicar's daughter down by the canal and –' he chuckled softly – 'they offered her three cigarettes to show them her drawers. And she did! Wait! I will fetch the book on Frau Troffea.' He stood up and walked down one of the aisles to a bookcase at the back. He searched for a book and retrieved it with a small cough of triumph. As he did, Jenny stared pointedly at me, but I refused to look her way. I could tell without looking that she was grinning and no doubt found the story Mr Dombey had just told very droll.

He returned and laid the book carefully on the desk. It was a leather-bound quarto, with gold edges on the pages and green mildew in the text. He searched carefully with a familiarity that suggested he had done this often. 'Cast your mind back to 1518 if you will. Strasbourg. Ah yes, here, see!' He laid his fingers as if in a caress on a woodcut of medieval peasants dancing in the street. 'They dance! See! They called it the Dancing Plague or the Dance of St Vitus. In 1278 a bridge across the River Meuse collapsed under the weight of the dancers. In 1374 an outbreak began in Aix-la-Chapelle and spread to Cologne, Flanders, Franconia, Hainaut, Metz, Strasbourg, Tongeren and Utrecht. This is Frau Troffea. In July 1518 she began to dance. She could not stop, she danced all day and all night, all week. Soon she was joined by others, until by the end of the month there were more than four hundred. The priests fulminated against the depravity from the pulpit, physicians went among them, but nothing could stop it. They danced until their poor hearts gave way and they fell down dead in the dust. And see here, the Chronicle of Kleinkawel written in Strasbourg in 1625:

> Amidst our people here is come
> The madness of the dance.
> In every town there now are some
> Who fall upon a trance.
> It drives them ever night and day,
> They scarcely stop for breath,
> Till some have dropped along the way
> And some are met by death.

'And they do not simply dance, they squeal and howl, as if in torment, they lash out and leap into the air.'

'How does this relate to the nuns?' said Jenny.

'I was just coming to that.' He turned a page. 'Look! The Dancing Plague of Strasbourg is closely associated with an even more famous event, one that you will be familiar with from your schooling, namely the disappearance of more than a hundred children from the small German town of Hamelin in 1284, led by a mysterious piper in clothing that was . . . pied. Or piebald. Derived from the word for magpie. You see? Black and white, like a nun. Is that a coincidence? I think not. You must examine the legend of the Pied Piper. Three children were left behind. One because he was deaf and could not hear the instructions; one who was blind and could not follow; and one who was lame and could not keep up. There are always some left behind. You must seek the nun who missed the boat. Or perhaps I should say "missed the train".'

'Did one miss the train?' said Jenny.

'Yes. Sister Beatrice.' He turned to a page that held two newspaper cuttings. He handed the first to me. 'The nuns were from the Lacrismi Christi convent in Povington. Sister Beatrice was left behind.'

The clipping showed a photo of a nun with thick spectacles dominating her face, under the headline 'Lucky escape for Sister Beatrice'. The story told how Sister Beatrice had responded to a call for astigmatic nuns to take part in a special top secret War Office mission. However, it transpired that she had been the victim of a clerk's typing error and the call had, in fact, been for stigmatic nuns and so Sister Beatrice was rejected. She said she had been very disappointed at the time, and had always regarded her astigmatism as a burden, but now she gave thanks in her prayers every night for her deliverance and never ceased to marvel at the ways of the Lord.

'El Greco was astigmatic, too,' said Mr Dombey. 'Although I have discovered no connection between these two facts.' His voice became distant as he pondered that mystery. 'And here, see!' He pointed to the second cutting, which had a picture of a circus strongman flexing his biceps, wearing nothing but a paper fig leaf over his private parts. The headline read 'Daughter of Russian Bear among missing nuns'. 'You see? This is the famous Greco-Roman wrestler Yevgeny Preobrazhensky, from Estonia. They called him the Russian Bear. Before the First World War he used to wrestle five men a night and one bear. His daughter Ludo was a novice at the priory. They say she was the biggest nun the world has ever known.'

We thanked Mr Dombey for his help and left. Outside the shop we stood and faced each other on the pavement.

'I think we have a clue,' said Jenny.

'But, Jenny—'

'It was my aunt and if you think you are going off looking for the nuns without me, you've got another thing coming. If you don't want my help, I'll just carry on on my own. I expect I'll solve it before you.'

'Well, you're jolly likely to get bashed over the head if you carry on like that.'

'That will be your fault, then, won't it?'

'I don't see how, I won't be the one bashing you.'

'Who will then?'

'Anybody could.'

'It's up to you to keep an eye on me.'

I put my hat on. Jenny adjusted it and said, 'Do you always put it on skew-whiff, or just when I'm around?'

'I put it on the way I always do.'

'In that case you have been walking around all your life with your hat on skew-whiff. Aren't you glad you met me?'

'Well, yes, I suppose I am.'

Jenny rolled her eyes. 'I see we are going to have to do some work with you. Oh just say yes, for Pete's sake. Don't you see you've got no choice? I'm just going to follow you otherwise.'

'But mustn't you go to work?'

'I've left the Anaglypta Mill. I found Aunt Agatha's Premium Bonds. There was £97. I'm going to find another job.'

I stood staring intently at her. She balled her fist in an amusing show of threatening to box me.

'Don't make me do it,' she said.

'All right then.' I relented. 'Have it your way.'

She held out her hand and I saw no other option but to shake it.

'Where are you taking me now?' she said.

'I really don't know. Where would you like to go?'

'Somewhere nice.'

I thought for a moment. 'Have you seen the Severn Junction signal box?'

'Oh, Jack, I'm sure you take all your girls to the signal box. Take me somewhere . . . somewhere . . . I know, let's go to Barker & Stroud's and ask to speak to Magdalena's sugar daddy.'

'I've already telephoned. They told me he's away for the time being.'

'Did you know about him and Magdalena?'

'I must say I didn't. Although it should have been obvious, really.'

Jenny interlocked her arm in mine and we wandered through town. Whether by chance or intention we arrived at the Lyons tea shop where we went on that first day. We went in and ordered coffee. This was not something either of us would normally do, but Jenny insisted that our new partnership needed to be sealed with some sort of celebration.

'Mr Barker always had a soft spot for her, you see. That's why he chose her as the model for the Lindt Chocolate mural on the wall of his shop. He had a friend who worked in Harley Street, a special doctor who came to see her.'

'Was she ill?'

'She had a very rare condition that made her senses become distorted, like Alice in Wonderland. Sometimes she would feel herself very tall, so her head was almost touching the ceiling; and other times she would feel tiny, no bigger than a mouse. Or sometimes she said she could smell a noise, or hear a colour.'

'That sounds rather fun.'

'She said it was frightening. She also complained about an intruder, a girl dressed like her, knocking on the glass and demanding to be let in. But we always searched the grounds when that happened and never found anything. Even one time when it snowed, we didn't even find a footprint.'

'Did the doctor cure her?'

'No, there is no cure. It's connected with migraines, which was this chap's specialism. He wanted to write about it and call it Alice in Wonderland Syndrome. I think he probably liked her, too. Everybody did. It was quite a black day in the home when she was beaten.'

'What did they beat her for?'

'For saying she wouldn't go into service. All the girls were trained for this employment. She once told me about all the rules they were taught. You wouldn't believe it. When meeting a member of the family in a corridor, you should turn your face to the wall. You must never speak unless with a specific necessary request or errand. You must on no account smile at an amusing story told by a member of the family in your presence, or even in any way indicate that you had heard it.'

'I don't think I would have liked to learn all that either.'

'No, she didn't. Then one day we had a visit from Lady Susan Seymour who talked to us about her travels and showed some lantern slides of Moon Beam, the Potawatomi Indian princess. She asked Magdalena what she wanted to be when she grew up and received the answer, Suffragette. That's what she was beaten for. Magdalena knew quite a lot about Suffragettes because once a lady died and left to the orphanage her collection of the *Illustrated London News*.'

'When you telephoned, they didn't say when Mr Barker will be back? In that case, we must go and find Sister Beatrice first. Where is Povington?'

'Near Chirk, about an hour north of here on the train. But I understand the priory has been closed for many years.'

'We could still go. Sister Beatrice might still be there.'

'How would we find her? All we know about her is she is astigmatic.'

'We could ask the local optician. I know,' she said suddenly, 'we will return her lost Bible.'

'Where will we get her Bible?'

'Couldn't you get one from Lost Property?' said Jenny.

Chapter 9

I F YOU WANTED to create an inventory of every item on this earth, and write all these items down in a ledger, you might think the task would be too much for one man and he would need to bequeath it to his son. But you would be wrong. Such a ledger already exists in the form of the Weeping Cross Railway Lost Property Book. False teeth, coffins, funerary urns, books, manikins, skulls, dead bats, live bats, cows, pigs, goats, monkeys, snakes, spiders, wooden legs, eye-patches, dead octopi, prams, musical instruments, old masters, gramophones, parasols, Japanese fans, stone giants, elephants' tusks, elephant-foot umbrella stands, stags' heads, small boys . . . everything that man is capable of losing has been lost and handed in. The Book is an inventory of the human race. Mr Jarley in the Lost Property Office was low in spirits because of a heavy cold but my request for a small travelling Bible, a rosary, a group photo of nuns and a pair of spectacles of a sort worn by astigmatics filled him with delight. The same delight, I suspect, exhibited by the hotel concierge who, after years of being asked to supply theatre tickets to see *The Mousetrap*, is one day asked to procure a ticket on the Trans-Siberian Railway all the way to Vladivostok.

Mr Jarley said he had drawers full of group photos of nuns. Did I want it in a frame, a locket, loose, sewn into a tea cosy or in an album? What sort of album? One containing other group photos of nuns with scenes from nunnery life? Or as the record of the life of the particular nun, beginning perhaps with a faded and creased photo of a blissful man in a backyard somewhere, holding a newborn baby as his wife looks on adoringly. And then progressing through the Christening, first steps taken, the birthdays and Christmases, a snap of her crying in the bath tub on the kitchen table, the first school photo and awkward onset of youth and with it the troubled countenance, the evidence of a heart torn by conflicting currents; and then, perhaps, the chap in battledress, painfully young, scarcely started shaving, staring out from the ellipse with a forced smile filled with uncertainty? The one who never returned and thus precipitated the decision to enter the convent? I said, if you've got one like that it would be ideal. To which he replied that he had many like that. What about a name? I told him Beatrice was the name but I was fully capable of writing it on the flyleaf myself. Mr Jarley answered that if I permitted him to swap photographs between albums he could provide me with one that perfectly answered my needs in all respects. Of course, he added, once you have finished with it, you will have to return the item. It will remain property of the Railway all the while it is in your possession, and he needed to have it back in case the lady in question should ever turn up and ask for it. What material did I want the rosary to be fashioned from? Wood, ivory, ebony, carved bone? And the Bible, which translation? King James, Tyndale's, Taverner's, Webster's? In leather, cloth or wood? He had them all. And as for spectacles of a sort worn by astigmatics, he was able to offer a variety of frame materials from simple wire to tortoiseshell and narwhal horn, and corrective lenses in a range of dioptric powers. I wondered aloud, as was my custom at such times, whatever would we do without him. He replied, sadly, that we should soon all find out the answer to that time-worn question because he had just that morning received a letter regretfully informing him that his services would not be required after Christmas.

The small travelling Bible, rosary, group photo of nuns and a pair of spectacles of a sort worn by astigmatics were all duly delivered to my office before the end of the day. The consignment also included the Cadbury Holt case file I had requisitioned. Or rather that particular file marked G–H. This included his notes on the numerous German counts he had disarmed of their swordsticks, the notorious case of Henbane Henrietta, and the Hail Mary Celeste. I had arranged to meet Jenny the next day at the ticket barrier, and the prospect of a jaunt to Povington, although I did not hold out any hope that it would prove fruitful, put a spring in my step as I left the office that evening.

As I entered the street, a car engine started up. A seal grey Morris 1000 moved away from the kerb and slid up alongside me. The driver reached across and wound the window down. Our eyes met in a look of mutual recognition. It was the chap who appeared in my office the day after Jenny came, the elder one.

'Jack!' He pulled the handle and shoved the door ajar. 'Have you got a minute? We need to chat.'

'I am rather busy.'

'It won't take long.'

'Where do you want to take me?'

'Nowhere, just around the block.'

I climbed in and closed the door.

113

We drove to the top of Dandelion Hill and parked looking out over the town below. Fog and smoke and fumes filled the valley, fed by the chimneys of the biscuit works, the textile mill and the Anaglypta Mill. Two chimneys pumping out beige smoke, and one pouring out fumes that were dark brown and made the eyes water. The smoke curdled the sky. Gasometers added a sallow, gassy smell. Up here the air was slightly better. This was good for the men with bad lungs, but not such good news for the knocker-up boy employed by the railway company to cycle round Weeping Cross knocking on the doors of the drivers and firemen in the middle of the night.

Mr Old spoke. 'We're all good chaps, Jack. You must believe that. Good chaps. But sometimes being a good chap can involve . . . methods that some people don't understand.'

'I don't understand.'

'There's no reason why you should, you have to trust us.'

'Why?'

'Because we love England. Because you love England.'

'Is it true Jenny's aunt saw a letter being stolen? A letter from the missing nuns of 1915, addressed to His Majesty the King?'

'What will you do if I tell you?'

'As a man I will do my duty.'

'Your duty is to mind your own business.'

'In my opinion the worst form of cad is the one who steals a postal order from a child's birthday card. I have to say a chap who steals a letter from the King runs a close second. If I find this letter I would have no hesitation returning it to the King.'

'But would you read it?'

'No, of course not.'

'Even though it contains the solution to the greatest mystery

114

in railway history? What man, what Gosling could forbear? It doesn't matter what assurances you gave, we wouldn't believe you. You would read it and then we would have to hang you.'

'What sort of Gosling would I be if I shirked my duty?'

'You have a greater duty.' He turned to me with an imploring look in his eye. 'You have to try and understand the situation the country was in in 1915. Unrestricted submarine warfare – such a thing had never been known before. Our merchant ships were going to the bottom of the ocean in appalling numbers. We were being exsanguinated, Jack, like a stag with its throat cut, hung up to drain. There was less than a week's food left in the whole country. Do you know what that means? We would have had to contemplate the unthinkable. Can you guess what that was? What the stark choice facing us was? Can you?'

'I'm afraid I have no idea. Build airships and drop bombs on them?'

'Oh no, too late for that. Surrender. That was the only option. To the Hun!'

'No!'

'You see! One of our chaps in Berlin got hold of the German War Plans. It made shocking reading. They weren't just going to vanquish us. That wasn't good enough. They wanted to complete the job left unfinished by their Hun ancestors and smite us utterly. The cities would be ploughed into fields and sown with salt; the men would be turned into human dray-horses, pulling the ploughs . . . pulling ploughs, Jack! And as for the women, don't ask!' He paused and looked at me as if to gauge the effect his words were having. 'In Belgium they tied

115

the priests to their own bell-clappers. Did you know that?' He shook his head in disbelief. 'The bells ran red with gore and clerical pulp.'

'Did you know a lot of our chaps played football with them on Christmas Day in 1914? In No-man's-land.'

'Yes, yes, but those men were traitors. Never forget that. They allowed themselves to fall for the wiles of their enemy. No honourable soldier does that. It is tantamount to treachery. They should have been shot.'

'I met a chap once who played football with them that Christmas. He swapped buttons with one. Said they were chaps same as you and me. He struck me as a good man.'

'And therein lay his undoing. Chaps like him can't imagine what we are dealing with, all their lives they live in England's bosom and encounter straight-dealing and goodness. They are as easily deceived as babies. They don't understand: the German soldier is a perfumed dandy in lace socks, but his heart is blacker than pitch. War is a foul business, Jack. You can't afford to play by the Queensberry Rules. You say you met a chap who played football with them. I met a chap too. He had a different story to tell. He lost his brother. You know what they did to him? I quake to tell you. The German war machine needed glycerine, and for that they needed fat. They had a secret factory in the Black Forest. Totally hush-hush, but you can't keep something like that secret. They used our chaps. Prisoners of war. Boiled up and rendered down. Threw them on the conveyor belt with pitch forks. Pitch forks!'

'But how can you pitch fork a man? It's not possible.'

'Two men holding the same pitch fork could do it. But you are missing the point, it doesn't matter how they did it.'

'What is the point then?'

'The point is, no one could countenance surrendering, appealing to the mercy of such inhuman brutes, but we would have had no choice. You know why? Because there is a fate even worse than surrender.' He paused and spoke again in a softer register. 'Do you know what happens in a city under siege? People swap cats, did you know that?'

'No, I didn't. Why do they swap cats?'

'So that they don't have to eat their own. That's how it is. How it has been since the dawn of time in all cities under siege. Dogs, cats, rats . . . they all go. Then they eat the zoo if there is one. This is what desperate people do, and hunger, Jack . . . hunger of a type you have never experienced and almost certainly cannot imagine, drives men and women to the very limit and beyond. Some people give up, they prefer to die. But those who don't, they become beasts utterly without conscience. They boil up leather and bones, make soup from sawdust, they eat joiner's glue, toothpaste, cough mixture, wallpaper paste, cold cream . . . anything. A fur coat buys you a pound of flour, a woman can be had for a tin of spam. A boy will murder his granny and boil her up rather than face the pangs of hunger. Amputated limbs are stolen from the hospital. Corpses are dug up from the cemetery. When hunger stalks, everything stops – no police, no water, no fire brigade, civilisation disappears overnight. You know what the Bible says? They knew what happened in sieges. *And I will cause them to eat the flesh of their sons and the flesh of their daughters, and they shall eat every one the flesh of his friend in the siege.*'

'I would rather die than surrender to the Hun.'

'That would be your right. But do you have the right to

117

condemn a nation to the terror of the siege? What would you do to avoid it all? What would you sacrifice, Jack? To save the country you love? Would you sacrifice a town? Twenty thousand men died on the first day of the Somme. That's all the men in Weeping Cross. It carried on for another one hundred and forty-one days. What's a handful of nuns compared to that? You wince, you twitch your nose in disdain, like a rabbit, but what would you do? Have you ever stopped to wonder? No. I'm sure you haven't. That's the trouble with fastidious people like you, you have it easy. You stand on the sidelines and hold court. You condemn. It's easy to condemn. Much harder to act in a way that is right but still invites condemnation.' He sat up and turned the ignition key. 'I'll take you home.' As the engine shuddered into life he added, 'If you want someone to blame, blame the Americans. Where were they when we needed them?'

That evening after tea, I received a visitor at my digs. One of the chaps came into the kitchen to say there was a man standing on the doorstep asking for me. This was very rare. It turned out to be the Dingleman. I invited him up to my room on the second floor. We climbed up bare wooden stairs, for which I apologised. I explained that the stair carpet had fallen prey to a soaking last spring when the pipes broke on the fifth landing. I felt a slight embarrassment for the bare and humble features of my life. My room had a small sash window commanding a view of the recreation ground, although it was dark now. There was a single bed, a chair, a wireless on a table, a wardrobe and a gas fire. A clothes horse was positioned in front of the table and this was draped with socks. The fire was not lit and clothes took a long time to dry. Ron sat on the bed and

I fetched a bottle of brown ale from the cupboard under the stairs, and we shared this.

'I just wanted you to understand,' said the Dingleman, 'in case you didn't, how serious I am.'

'I think I do.'

'I always hoped Magdalena would marry me, but she won't. But that's not the point. Now that you've got a girl, you may feel about her the same way. If you do, that gives us a problem.'

'Ron, I sense you are repeating your threat.'

'I am.'

'I must tell you . . . you probably don't think I'm much of an opponent, not someone to be feared, but—'

'No, no, Jack. I do. When you make a living in the ring, you learn to get the measure of a man. I'm never wrong. That's why I've come here tonight. I know what you are capable of, even though I'm not sure you do. We're in a fix.' His expression became morose. 'My boy is very poorly.'

'I must say, it was famous of you for taking him in like you did. I think a lot of people would be very surprised to learn about it.'

'Well, that's one surprise they won't enjoy. I don't want you blabbing.'

'I won't. I sincerely hope he gets better for Christmas.'

'Even if he does, they say he will be in that iron lung all his life.'

'I've heard there will be a vaccine by 1960.'

'I've heard that too. But not for people who already have it. Do you remember what it was like to be in a firebox?'

'Yes, of course.'

'How did you feel?'

119

'To be honest I didn't like it at all. I was frightened. Most boys are. But they have to go, don't they? Because only little boys are small enough.'

'I wonder if that's how he feels.'

We finished our beer and he left without saying any more, but leaving me in no doubt that he was earnest about his threat to Jenny.

THE BOY'S OWN
RAILWAY GOSLING ANNUAL

Vol. VII   1931   Price: 1/-

Replies to our readers' letters

G. I. LAWRENCE, BASILDON—It all depends on how far the flea jumps. The practice you describe first appeared during the siege of Theodosia in the 14th century when the besieging Mongol army catapulted plague-infested corpses over the city walls. Whether the bubonic plague could traverse the entire length of the train by flea jump alone in the space of a typical mainline journey of some six hours is very much open to doubt. Records show not a single instance of this occurring on any British train. There have been cases where drivers have been suddenly overcome by food poisoning. None of these have resulted in derailments of the type you describe, nor of conflagration sweeping away an entire village community.

THE CONTINUING ADVENTURES OF RAILWAY GOSLING CADBURY HOLT – ON THE TRAIL OF THE MISSING NUNS!

I First Make the Acquaintance of Mr Gape

'Pishon!' he cried, with breath so sodden with gin it made a bird drop dead from a tree on the river bank. 'Pishon! You mad fool, there is no such river and even if there were what would be the point of spending all that trouble getting there? We have cemeteries just as good here in Port Bismarck!'

Mr Gape lay slumped on the floor of the pilot-house, his back wedged against the port hatch. The *Nellie* was a squat, thirty-footer, flat-bottomed boat with an iron hull and a deck that had once been wood but which now was so rotten it glowed like forest mushrooms. The pilot-house was built from timbers so damp you could bore your own finger right through. A tattered awning covered the last six feet of the stern. The boat exuded a reek of decay commingled with the putrescent aroma of rotting vegetables. The engine and boiler were amidships with a tall funnel that could occasionally be coached into coughing some puffs of black smoke into the sky. The only part of the *Nellie* that inspired confidence was the brass plaque on the pilot-house gable inscribed with the words '*Isaac J. Abdela of the Abdela & Mitchell shipyards at Brimscombe, Gloucestershire. 1895. May the Lord have Mercy on All Who Sail in This Vessel.*'

'You crazy, crazy fool,' Gape said again and added emphasis to his diagnosis by saluting with a hand that clasped the neck of a gin bottle.

I answered him as calmly as I was able. 'I have it on good authority that the river exists and that you are one of the few white men to have knowledge of its whereabouts.'

Gape stared at me the way a man might examine a five-legged horse. 'You do not strike me as the sort of chap who desires to end his days in a cannibal's cooking pot.'

'The fate of my mortal remains concerns me not, so long as my soul is not in the pot with them.'

'Pishon, eh? You want to go to the River Pishon. The fabled lost river of Eden. Just like that! Just load up with stores, fill the boiler and off we go. Just like that!'

'I don't see any reason why not.'

'That just goes to show what a crazy fool you are, and an ignorant crazy fool to boot.'

'Please do not be tedious. I shall, of course, pay for your services.'

'Pishon! First we'd have to sail up the Sulabunga here for three weeks until she became nothing more than a trickle. Then we'd have to hire some porters to help drag the *Nellie* over a small volcano and put her down in the Lunga-Lunga, a river better known to you as the Pishon.'

'That sounds like an excellent plan.'

Mr Gape belched most disgustingly. 'Well, it might be if it didn't require us to steam through the territory of the Segembwezi. They are a proud people who do not take kindly to strangers passing through the territory, at least not ones who fail to pay the tribute.'

'Then we shall pay the tribute.'

'That's a good plan, except that the Segembwezi make the tribute rather high.'

'How high?'

Mr Gape threw back his head and laughed. I waited patiently. Ordinarily I should have boxed his ears and thrown his loathsome bottle into the river, but all my information told me he was the only man insane enough to undertake a journey beyond the first set of rapids.

'The children of the Segembwezi chase after you,' said Mr Gape. 'They cry, "Niama. Niama!" Did you know that? At first you fancy they are asking for beads or a gift, but no, it means "Meat. Meat!"'

'You are not succeeding in frightening me, if that is your purpose.'

'They like to cut off your face and boil it up in your own stomach along with a bit of rice and goat.'

'I'm quite fond of a bit of goat myself.'

'Are you indeed! And what of the delicacy they prize the most, the part they reserve for honoured guests and visiting kings?'

123

'If you mean brains, I have eaten sheep brains and not suffered.'

'I do not mean brains! I mean that part of a man which it is most unfortunate for a man to lose, for in doing so he loses that which makes him a man.'

I could contain my disgust no longer. I rushed forward and seized the wretch by the rag he called a shirt and shook him. 'You are a disgrace! A disgrace to the England that bore you . . . to the noble country that first gave you suck, that fed and clothed and schooled you, and gave you her tender green ways to wander in.'

He started to fall sideways, forcing me to prop him up.

'Good old Blighty!' he said and grinned vilely. 'How jolly lucky I am.'

'Have you no sense of shame? What sort of example is this to show to the Savages? You have a responsibility, Mr Gape, nay, a duty . . .' My words petered out as it became apparent Mr Gape had become insensate.

Chapter 10

SHREWSBURY, CHESTER, BIRKENHEAD & LIVERPOOL

Week Days—contd.

Weeping Cross	1.15p.m.
Shrewsbury	1.40p.m.
Leaton	1.48p.m.
Oldwoods Halt	1.51p.m.
Baschurch	1.58p.m.
Stanwardine Halt	2.01p.m.
Haughton Halt	2.07p.m.
Rednal and West Felton	2.13p.m.
Whittington Low Level	2.19p.m.
Gobowen	2.26p.m.
Weston Rhyn	2.30p.m.
Chirk	2.34p.m.

Jenny was already waiting for me at the ticket barrier as the clock struck one. A phone call to the stationmaster at Chirk had reassured me that there were two opticians in the town, but only one – Lowell & Chambers – had been in business since the turn of the century. Jenny and I had some debate about this as we climbed the stone steps to the platform. My intention had been to approach the town's optician with the items from Lost

Property and ask if he might know where to find Sister Beatrice. But Jenny felt he might see through our ruse and we would stand a much better chance of gaining the information we sought if we simply approached someone in the street.

Our train arrived in Weeping Cross twenty minutes late as a result of an accident involving a goods train derailed in a tunnel during the night. By all accounts it had not been a serious accident but all the same one does not like to hear of such things. It is like hearing news of a bereavement in the family. An accident in the darkness of a tunnel is all the more alarming. Few passengers reflect on the courage it takes to drive a train into a tunnel. A man who walks down into his cellar holding a light becomes frozen with fear if his light fails. He dares hardly move, and feels his way gingerly back to the surface. But a train driver entering a tunnel can see nothing. If you have been caught in a room when a gale blows the smoke back down the chimney you will know what it is like in a tunnel. Smoke, ash, sparks and hot cinders blow back into your face and eyes. As a passenger you assume the footplate team are keeping their eyes peeled for danger. In truth, they are most likely both on their hands and knees in the cab, faces covered in wet cloths.

There is one advantage to the accident taking place in a tunnel: you won't see it. Out in the open, if a driver sees a train ahead into which he shall shortly collide, there is little he can do. He will of course apply the brakes, and turn off the regulator, but it takes miles to stop a 500-ton train travelling at full pelt. Once having done that he can do no more except save his own skin by leaping clear of the cab. But should he? This is a vexed issue. No point can be served by his remaining, but in jumping he is saving his skin by availing himself of knowledge unavailable to the passengers. In practice most drivers and their firemen, when all else is lost, do jump from the cab, although they very often do not survive the jump, and those that do, perhaps, spend the rest of their lives regretting their decision. For they relive the experience every night in their dreams, having witnessed an event that no man should ever have to behold: two trains in collision. And pity the poor chap at whom the finger of blame will eventually point. Good men who lead lives of diligence, toil and sober hard work. Who dedicate their long days to the service of the railway company and the passengers, and who never acquire a black mark against their names but are ordained by the cruelty of fate to make an error. The sort of simple human error, the very performance of which marks us out as men and not infallible immortals, the sort that in any other walk of life would hardly warrant a mention, becomes a moment on the railways that destroys a man's life. Men such as Magdalena's father, who in a moment of befuddlement put the troop train on the wrong line and forgot about it.

Many of the safety features that we take for granted today came about as a result of crashes. People would be greatly surprised to learn the most important safety feature, implemented after a crash on the Great Western near Reading in 1841, was to put a roof on the carriages.

Magdalena's father achieved a certain renown for his error for a few years, but some men achieve a notoriety that outlasts them. Men such as John Benge, whose name is remembered by posterity for his part in derailing the train on which Charles Dickens was travelling in 1865. Benge was the foreman of the track gang given the job of replacing some timber on a bridge and chose to do so in the small window of time between two trains. This was accepted practice, but he made an important mistake: in order to find a suitable period in which to carry out the repair work, he consulted the railway timetable. But the timetable made no mention of the boat train on which Charles Dickens was travelling, because boat trains, like excursions and troop trains, are not listed in its pages. A boat train is dispatched to meet a boat, and boats, depending as they do on the vagaries of tide and the weather, arrive at all sorts of times. When the train in which Dickens was travelling reached the bridge, it wasn't there. The train plunged into the river. Charles Dickens was not killed but never fully recovered. John Benge is regarded with particular disdain by literary scholars since it is because of him that we will now never know who killed Edwin Drood.

During the journey we discussed the disappearance of the nuns.

'Wasn't there some sort of official inquiry?' said Jenny. 'They must have found something out.'

'The findings were not made public but the version that was given to me was about something called ergotism. This is a sort of madness brought on by eating grain that has a fungus growing on it. It happened a lot in olden times. The explanation was the nuns must have eaten contaminated Host – made from mouldy rye – and been consumed by madness and all wandered off the train and then they all fell down a mine.'

'Did they look down a mine?'

'There were no mines to look down. Although there was Box Tunnel. But that was the first place they searched. The police and the army. It was the seventeenth of May 1915. The train left Swindon at 7.25 in the morning, and reached Bristol Temple Meads at 8.25.'

'What did the guard say?'

'He disappeared too. There were twenty-three nuns and the guard, all of whom vanished. There were police road blocks and checkpoints throughout the south of England and a watch was kept on all ports and aerodromes, but nothing was ever seen of them.'

I took out the case file of Cadbury Holt, and spread the items relating to this case on the seat. There were newspaper clippings and letters from foreign countries. *The Times* front page for 18 May 1915 ran the headline 'Holy Sisters vanish into thin air, German foul play suspected'. Cadbury had also included a report of a Zeppelin bombing raid on Southend-on-Sea. There was an envelope of photographs showing police and Boy Scouts searching along the railway track; photos of police and soldiers conducting road blocks and checkpoints; soldiers at unidentified ports checking identity papers. One picture stood out: a photo of an unfortunate man surrounded by an angry crowd. Cadbury had scribbled on the back that he was an innocent Ukrainian suspected of being German on account of his accent. The country was awash with rumour that German spies were coming ashore from U-boats disguised as nuns.

Cadbury's file contained a number of subdivisions, and in the back was a letter from the Commissar with Responsibility for White Slavery attached to the International Red Cross in Geneva. The text of the letter described a report received from the British consul in Kuching, British North Borneo, about a seafaring vagrant called Hershey Lindt who claimed to have seen one of the nuns in the belly of a tramp steamer aboard which he had been Shanghaied in 1927. It was clear that the consular official gave little credence to the story but reported it

129

for form's sake. Mr Lindt had been an expatriate American who specialised in the export of elephant-foot umbrella stands in Port Bismarck on the coast of West Africa, fifty miles north of the mouth of the Congo. One night after having drunk too much rum in a particularly seedy dockside bar frequented by cutthroats, pirates and wretches running from the noose, he found himself abducted aboard a tramp steamer in the charge of the notorious Captain Squideye. They were bound for a tiny island off Sumatra called Skull Island where it was said there lived a monster who could only be appeased by being fed from time to time the flesh of a white woman. Mr Lindt claimed to have glimpsed one of the nuns chained up in the belly of the ship and maintained that the stoker told him in hushed tones appropriate for such skullduggery that this nun was the next intended sacrificial victim. Captain Squideye, when questioned some years later, denied all knowledge of this whilst at the same time contradicting himself by claiming that they were making a feature film. Mr Lindt eventually jumped ship in Sarawak, northern Borneo.

Outside the station at Chirk there was only one thoroughfare to investigate. We decided to adopt Jenny's plan and ask the first person we met. It turned out to be a district nurse who had just finished loading her bicycle's basket with parcels from the collecting office. Her reaction was unexpected. She stood astride her bicycle and stared at the items I had procured from Mr Jarley, the Bible, rosary and spectacles. Then she said, 'Would it surprise you to know that Sister Beatrice was not astigmatic?' There was a moment's silence, and then she continued, with barely disguised disdain, 'Yes, I thought as much. Who is it this time? Are you from the press? You don't look it, you look more like an insurance investigator. We're quite tired of your sort, you know. You never stop to think about the pain you cause, do you?'

'Madam,' I said.

She pointedly turned her handlebars aside and prepared to ride off. 'Well, you'll get nothing out of me. Nor anyone else round here, I should imagine. Sorry if you've had a wasted journey. I must congratulate you on the audacity of your pantomime. I've never seen that one before. Lost Property indeed.' She cycled off, leaving us both rooted to the spot, lost for words as we watched her cycle away uncertainly, wavering from side to side.

It began to spit with rain, and without speaking we ambled up the road, following her, towards a bridge over the canal. As we did a motor car past us rather swiftly and careened from side to side as if the driver and passenger were both wrestling with the wheel. The car was a Bentley and halted on the bridge. The passenger-side door flew open. A lady in a fur coat jumped out and appeared to be in some distress. She slammed the door but her coat became caught in the door frame and prevented the mechanism locking. The driver opened his door and climbed out with what seemed to be an exaggeratedly slovenly attitude, designed to infuriate the lady.

'You stay there, George Spencer,' she cried and then, extricating herself from the door frame, ran across the bridge and climbed on to the parapet.

I shouted, 'Hey, I say!'

The chap sauntered round the car towards her, not seeming to be greatly concerned.

'Please, madam!' shouted Jenny.

'Do not concern yourselves,' the chap said with an insolent

grin on his face, 'it's only about three feet deep this time of year. The greatest danger is to her coat.' He turned to her. 'You could at least take it off first, darling. You know how much it cost.'

'You . . . bugger!' she cried, and then turned and jumped. Half a second later there was a splash.

'You really do like to be the centre of attention, don't you?' said the chap as he wandered across to the parapet and looked over. The lady began to scream. I rushed over, jumped on to the wall and then scrambled down the bank to the canal. It may well have been no more than three foot in depth, but she was certainly giving every appearance of drowning. I took off my coat and jacket but there was no time to disrobe further. I jumped in.

'Would you like me to send for a boat?' the insolent fool shouted down. Although the water was shallow, the lady was thrashing around in a most violent fashion and I was obliged in the interests of her safety to give her a punch on the jaw in order to knock her senseless. The chap on the bridge shouted, 'Bravo!' The lady went limp in my arms and I scooped her up and carried her up the bank and noticed that the district nurse had joined us. She rolled out a blanket on the ground and I placed the lady down. 'She's not drowning,' I said, 'just a bit stunned.'

'She's not the only one,' said the chap. 'Well, I'll be damned if I'll let her ruin the upholstery. I only just got the old girl. Connolly hide.'

Jenny and the district nurse knelt down beside the lady and chafed her wrists and slapped her face gently. I took out my Gosling hip flask and poured a tot of brandy into the cap. I held

132

it to her lips and she opened her eyes and sipped with rather more gusto than was perhaps seemly. The chap laughed in a sardonic sort of way and said, 'Attaboy!' and then added, 'I would be a bit careful if I were you: give her a drink every time she jumps in the river and she'll be doing it morning, noon and night.' I turned towards the chap. It was clear that he was a gentleman, in dress at least. His suit was of tweed and cut in the style favoured by men given to filling their leisure hours with fishing and shooting.

Jenny looked up. 'She could catch her death.'

'Yes, that's normally what happens to people who go swimming in the open in winter. Bloody fool.'

'I must ask you, sir, not to use profanity in the hearing of a lady who has just been rescued from drowning.'

He looked puzzled for a second and then said, 'Oh, I shouldn't worry about that. Elvey likes a bit of sailor talk. Just ask her groom.'

'Even so, sir, the lady has had a most unpleasant experience—'

'It's her own bloody fault, isn't it?'

'That's twice now, sir. I won't ask you again.'

'Oh really, what are you going to do about it?'

'I have a good mind to give you a blue eye.'

'Oh you do, do you? I'll have you arrested for that.'

The lady, who had regained her senses, said, 'Coward!'

'In that case,' I said, 'I will give you two blue eyes.'

The man looked at me. He was a bit younger than me, late twenties perhaps, but I could see he was yellow. He swallowed. The lady snorted. He turned and went back to his car, saying to her, 'I'll let them know at the house where you are.'

He climbed in. 'I wouldn't worry yourselves too much about this. She plays tricks like this all the time.' He drove off.

We were later to learn that this was the Countess Elvira Evegne de Castille-Sanchez, daughter of the Castille-Sanchez petroleum family. We read about the affair in the newspapers. It appeared that the argument which led to the countess jumping into the water had ensued after she told the chap that she was carrying his child, whereupon he first accused it of belonging to someone else and then broke off the engagement. You probably remember the exchange at the trial which caused such a fuss it was in all the papers. He asserted there were quite a few other men who could lay claim to the honour of being the father. To which the countess responded by saying she could be quite sure of the paternity on account of simple family resemblance, namely that just like his father the baby took great pleasure from kicking her in the heart.

Within ten minutes a more sedate-looking car, driven by a chauffeur, arrived and the countess took her leave of us, seemingly having fully recovered her sparkle. The nurse, who had introduced herself as Mrs Stevens, invited us to her cottage where she was kind enough to give me a hospital dressing gown and array my wet clothes on a clothes horse placed in front of the fire. She made us some hot cocoa and apologised for her rudeness earlier, although I did not see why she should.

'There really is no need to apologise,' I said.

'Did you mean it when you said she was not astigmatic?' said Jenny.

Mrs Stevens ran a hand down my clothing drying in front of the fire, and moved the clothes horse closer to the hearth.

'No,' she said. 'I just wanted to take the wind out of your sails.

134

I didn't believe your story, you see. We get all sorts coming here to ask about the missing nuns, some of them can be rather . . . ghoulish, and frankly it can get a bit tiresome. There is a great deal of affection around here for the holy sisters. They still talk about Sister Ludo.'

'That was the daughter of the Russian strongman,' I said.

'Yes. Ludmilla Preobrazhenskaya, but they all called her Sister Ludo. No one who was there will forget the day she lifted a calf above her head at the St Swithin's Day Fair. She once caught two chaps stealing lead from the pantry roof; got them both in a bear hug then tied them up. One of them managed to wriggle free enough to reach the priory telephone receiver and call the police for help.' We chuckled and Mrs Stevens smiled as if secretly pleased at the effect of her words. 'Are you really from the railway company?'

'Yes,' I said. 'Although perhaps not exactly acting in an official capacity.'

'Were you hoping to visit the priory? If so, you're in luck. Usually the gunners are firing every day in December right up until Christmas Eve, but this year they stopped at the end of November. It's a nice walk across the fields.'

'I don't quite follow,' I said. 'Are you talking about the Army?'

'Who else?'

'But what has that got to do with the priory?'

Mrs Stevens looked a touch confused. 'The priory is on the firing range, of course.'

'Is it?' said Jenny. 'We had no idea . . . do you mean a real firing range?'

'The Army took over the whole hamlet of Lower Povington by compulsory purchase in 1915.'

She took one look at the expressions of bewilderment on our faces and said, 'I'll just be a tick.' She stood up and walked across to a sideboard and pulled open the drawer. She rummaged through the contents and took out a folded-up letter and handed it to me. It was from the War Office, dated 2 June 1915.

TRAINING AREA, LOWER POVINGTON

DEAR RESIDENT

In order to give our troops the fullest opportunity to perfect their training in the use of modern weapons of war, the Army must have an area of land particularly suited to their special needs and in which they can use live shells. For this reason you will realise the chosen area must be cleared of all civilians.

The most careful search has been made to find an area suitable for the Army's purpose and which, at the same time, will involve the smallest number of persons and property. The area decided on, after the most careful study and consultation between all the Government Authorities concerned, is the hamlet of Lower Povington, comprising approximately five square miles centred on the chapel of Povington Priory.

For more precise information, see the map pinned to the chapel door.

It is regretted that, in the National Interest, it is necessary to move you from your homes, and everything possible will be done to help you, both by payment of compensation, and by finding other accommodation for you if you are unable to do so yourself.

The date on which the military will take over this area is the 9th June next, one week from now. All civilians must be out of the area by that date, and there will be no possibility of return.

The Government appreciate that this is no small sacrifice which

you are asked to make, but they are sure that you will give this help
towards winning the war with a good heart.

For the sake of clarity, no attempt will be undertaken to restore the
burned-out priory.

C. H. MILLER

Major-General I/c Administration,

Central Command

Jenny moved next to me on the sofa and put her head on my shoulder. We read the letter together. When we had finished, I handed it back.

'We had no idea. What does it mean about not restoring the burned-out priory?'

'There was a terrible fire, in May 1915. They were all killed.'

'How awful!' I said.

'Do you mean,' said Jenny, 'twenty-three nuns took the train and disappeared, and the ones who didn't go on the excursion were . . . were . . .'

Mrs Stevens made a pained expression. 'Yes, the ones who stayed home were burned in the fire. All twelve of them.'

'And then the Army took over the land?'

'Yes,' she said in a whisper.

'Don't you find . . . isn't that rather fishy?' said Jenny.

'We don't talk about it,' she answered simply but in a voice that seemed to contain a collective sense of shame, as if to say she knew jolly well these things should have been spoken of, but no one had possessed the temerity to, and with the passage of time it had become harder to look into the dark past. 'We prefer not to.'

'Was Sister Beatrice burnt too?' said Jenny.

'Some people think she is the one who set the fire. At least, that's what the police said. She wanted to go on the excursion, you see. It was something to do with the War Office and she applied and . . . was rejected.'

'We read about it in a newspaper cutting,' said Jenny.

'So where is she now?' I asked.

'I really couldn't tell you. The police never caught her. Some people round here say they've seen her over the years, but I doubt it.'

'But she might be alive?' said Jenny.

'She might, but I couldn't even begin to tell you where to look for her.'

'Do you believe she set the fire?' said Jenny.

'No, I'm sure she didn't. I'm sure it was just an accident. As I said, we prefer not to talk about it.'

'I'm awfully sorry,' I said. 'I'm sure you are all heartily sick of this matter.'

'Yes, we are.'

'You must do a lot of cycling as a district nurse,' I said. 'I rather fancy that was a Super-eeze from the Birmingham Small Arms Company I saw you riding, with a three-speed hub, am I right?'

Jenny shot me rather a fierce glance and said to Mrs Stevens, 'Is there anything left of the priory?'

'The roof has gone, and much of the great hall. Robbers have helped themselves to the lead and anything of value. There are trees growing out of it all now.'

On the step of her cottage Mrs Stevens pointed us in the direction of a path which took a short cut to the priory across some fields. After about a quarter of a mile we came to a stile and notices warning us that we were entering an Army live fire range and forbidding us to proceed any further. But there was no fence, and so we carried on. After a while, the shattered fragments of building could be discerned amid the trees ahead, and rising above them a church spire. Beyond that we could see the broken roof of the priory, with a tree growing through the rafters. It continued to drizzle, lending the whole scene a forlorn aspect, although one should imagine it could be quite pleasant in summer with numerous drowsy bees humming and birds twittering. Mrs Stevens told us the area was full of animals, rabbits and foxes and deer, who were not deterred by the occasional explosion and were happy to occupy the land vacated by man. But today there was not even a bird. The path arrived at what would once have been the main street of the village. Grass and weeds had broken up the surface of the road and it appeared like a green lane. There were the ruins of shops and cottages on either side. The post office had a red posting box set in the wall with most of its bright red paint gone, revealing the metal beneath. The windows were broken and the door hung from one hinge. Within we could see a counter; some paper was scattered on the ground, and the smell of damp and mould came from the piles of broken timbers tangled up with plants. Next door was what had once been the shop. An enamel sign still advertised that they sold Vimto and hot chocolate. We looked around, talking in whispers for some reason. It was not that we feared being apprehended by the soldiers, of whom we saw nothing, but the general sense of being in the company of ghosts. At the end of the main street, adjacent to a brook, was the chapel and graveyard, accessed by a rusty iron gate. The yard was a mass of brambles, but one or two graves had the dried remains of flowers placed on them. Not recently but certainly within the past year. There was a yew tree patiently presiding, no doubt having seen many things, good and bad, in its life. In its shadow we found the twelve gravestones of the holy sisters who had died in the fire. Twelve headstones all bearing the same date of 29 May 1915. We stood and stared solemnly, as if come to pay our respects.

'Do you believe it was an accident?' said Jenny. 'Twenty-three of them disappear from a train. And then the ones who didn't go, who might be able to reveal what happened, were all killed in a fire. Then the Army took over the town and cleared everybody out.'

'I really don't know what to believe. Maybe Sister Beatrice started the fire.'

'I don't believe that. If you ask me, she's the scapegoat. That's just a story so people don't search for the real explanation for the fire.'

'So why did she go missing?'

'She guessed what the game was, I suppose. First the fire, then the police looking for her. She must have known they wouldn't believe she had nothing to do with it.'

'But the police, Jenny, would they really accuse Sister Beatrice of deliberately setting the fire if they didn't—'

'No, it's too fishy, the Army taking over the land like that. Do you believe it was just a coincidence?'

'I have to say it would be very easy to believe it was not a coincidence, but to think that would require one to imagine the people who run our country capable of an act so wicked, so heinous that, well, really!'

'Perhaps they are.'

'Do you really think so? To deliberately fake an accident, burn twelve nuns to death, in order to, I suppose, stop them talking?'

'We know the ones who disappeared from the train were on some sort of secret mission for the War Office. That suggests the War Office knows what happened to them. Or at least has a very good idea.'

'Jenny, we are not Germans. We are English. All around the globe, right now as we speak, the people of our colonies and dominions give thanks to us for taking them out of the dark night of tyranny and savagery. They love us because through our mercies they too can be English.'

'You sound like the chap on the Pathé news.'

'Jenny!'

'If they are so grateful, why do we need so many soldiers to keep them in order?'

'What has that to do with the nuns?'

'Nothing, everything. I don't know. It doesn't make sense. You say they are grateful and yet we have armies in their countries, why do we need them?'

'To protect them from the jealousy of nations who are not so well favoured as to fall under the reign of His Majesty. They love the King.'

'What happens to the ones who don't love the King?'

'I don't know what you mean. Why would anyone not love the King?'

'You read about it in the papers. Rebellions. Sometimes they don't seem to love the King at all and they are put down by the Army.'

'Quite right too, you can't allow that sort of thing to spread.'

'But when the Army put down a rebellion what they mean

is they shoot them, they fire at them, at women and children . . .'

'No, Jenny, I'm sure they don't do that.'

'You mean when they fire into a crowd to put down a rebellion they don't shoot women and children?'

Jenny stopped and stared at me intently, possessed by a passion that I had not seen before. She looked at me as if hoping I had the answers, but I didn't. 'Jenny, a rebellion in Africa is a different matter, isn't it?'

'I don't know. You say you can't believe our people would kill the nuns, but is it really possible to believe it was a coincidence?'

'I would rather believe that than believe our chaps . . . I mean, think it through: you would need to order soldiers to do it . . . kill them in their sleep or something.'

She shrugged helplessly.

'If . . . if I thought our chaps were capable of that . . . were capable of ordering chaps to do that . . . all my life I have believed in the goodness of—'

'I know, Jack. So have I, but look at the ground.'

Stupidly, I did, even though I had already seen the gravestones.

'We should dig them up,' said Jenny.

I gasped. 'Jenny!'

'That way we'd know. Don't you want to know?'

'How would it settle the issue?'

'Because we would see if they had died . . . differently. If they had been shot, or beaten with an iron bar or something . . .'

'What if they were smothered?'

'Then I suppose we wouldn't be able to tell. But surely they would shoot them, smothering is just too ghastly.'

'It's all ghastly. I'm sorry but I cannot bring myself to perform such a . . . dreadful act.'

Jenny nodded.

'I mean, I just can't believe they would . . . it would be so . . . I can't believe anyone would . . .' But I was unable to finish my sentence. I recalled the words of Mr Old as he described the horrors of a city under siege. *What's a handful of nuns compared to that?* And then I saw a vision of the men on the first day of the Somme, walking into the machine-gun fire because they had been ordered not to run. News of the terrible losses had produced an appropriate shudder of horror throughout the land, but it didn't make them stop. Whoever was running the show carried on like a fireman shovelling men into the flames for another four years. *What's a handful of nuns compared to that?*

There was silence for a while, then Jenny said with a sigh of resignation, 'What are we going to do?'

It was a good question. I wondered whether another chap might simply have fetched a spade and started digging. Is that what Jenny expected of me? It began to drizzle more strongly and we took shelter in the porch of the church. We sat on a bench against the wall and ate our picnic. Jenny had packed raspberry jam sandwiches and a flask of tea and, despite the mournful surroundings, it did taste splendid and our spirits revived a little.

For a while we did not speak. We ate our sandwiches and listened to the patter of raindrops on the porch roof. When the sandwiches were finished, Jenny poured the tea. She had brought a china cup to complement the cup provided with the flask and which served as screw-on top. The tea was still hot; we nestled together and held our cups so that our knuckles touched. Jenny spoke: 'This morning I telephoned the hospital again. They told me Aunt Agatha was still sleeping. That's ten days now, Jack. That can't be right, can it?'

'I'm afraid I really don't know. It does sound peculiar.'

'Can someone die from too much sleep?'

'I . . . I'm sure they know what they are doing.'

'Are you? What if they want her to die?'

'Jenny, that is silly.'

'Is it? Why?'

I puzzled the question. 'I'm sure if they wanted to kill someone they could find a simpler way of doing it.'

That seemed to pacify Jenny for a while. I said: 'You know, after you . . . the day after our disagreement outside the Star and Garter I went to see Cheadle.'

'The one who blotted all your copybooks.'

'Yes.'

'Was he still living in sin?'

'No, I think that all ended a long time ago. He strikes me as very lonely now. He told me Cadbury visited him once. This would have been around 1937 or '38 I believe. Cadbury said the nuns were still alive. He told Cheadle that if he wanted to understand he should go and speak to a chap called Mr Clerihew, who works in the ape house at London Zoo. Apparently he grew up in Africa and said he'd seen the nuns with his own eyes.'

'In Africa?'

'I'm not sure if he meant he had seen them in Africa, just that this chap was originally from there.'

'Did Cheadle go?'

'No, he didn't.'

'Then there is nothing else for it, Jack, tomorrow we must go to the zoo.'

'Yes, we could ask one of the monkeys what it all means.'

'That is what we should do. We could go to Selfridges and look at the Biros, too.'

'And the television receivers.'

'Yes, yes.'

'I'm rather afraid we would have to travel in third.'

'Jack!'

'Yes, I know but really—'

'No, I mean, I was only joking.'

'Were you? I thought you wanted to go to London.'

'Oh, I do. But . . . you . . . I was teasing, I never imagined you would—'

'It really isn't too difficult to arrange, I'm just worried you might find it rather dull.'

'Would you really take me to London?'

'Of course.'

'When? Tomorrow?'

'If you like.'

'To the zoo?'

'Yes. Although I have to say I would be deceiving you if I thought . . . well, I'm sure this Clerihew chap left a long time ago, it's completely hare-brained.'

'Oh completely. It's the most hare-brained thing I've ever heard.'

'You see?'

'Oh, I see, oh I really see. It's just so wonderfully hare-brained. A whole herd of hares. Do they have herds?'

'I'm sure they must.'

'Fibber. I can tell from the way you spoke that they don't. What do they have, Jack? Flocks? Do they have flocks of hares?'

'I seem to remember reading somewhere that a group of hares is called a husk.'

'A husk? Oh, that is perfect. The idea is a husk of hare brains. You read that in one of your Gosling annuals, didn't you?'

'Yes, the 1935.'

'All the same, it might not be quite that silly. Would Cadbury Holt go to all that trouble of finding his lost friend Cheadle to tell him something that was no use whatsoever?'

'That's precisely it, I really don't think he would. Cadbury Holt wasn't a foolish chap. If he really did find the nuns and return to tell Cheadle, I don't believe he would have misled him or played a practical joke on him.'

'Then we must go.'

'Yes.'

'Although I'm not completely convinced he wouldn't have been joking, he does seem to have had quite a sense of fun. I mean –' Jenny changed the tone of her voice to a saucy whisper – 'did you really ask the vicar's daughter to show you her drawers?'

'I was wondering how long it would be before you brought that up.'

Jenny giggled. 'Oh, Jack, don't be a sour-puss. I think it's really funny. In fact, I'm thrilled.' She paused and said, 'Please don't think I'm wicked, but do you . . . was that brandy I saw you give that lady?'

'Yes, I carry a small flask for medicinal purposes.'

'Medicinal purposes?'

'Yes, for ladies who faint and suchlike.'

'I feel faint.'

'Are you serious?'

'Very faint. I thought it might be nice to add a tot to our tea. Aunt Agatha used to do that before bed.'

I took out the hip flask and did as I was bid. 'You realise, of course, that I could be dismissed on the spot for this.'

Jenny giggled and touched her cup to mine. 'Here's mud in your eye.'

We sat there lost in a reverie and I found myself wishing we could stay there for ever and never have to leave.

'That chap was beastly, wasn't he? Would you really have given him a blue eye?'

'I think I might have, he certainly asked for it.'

'I wish you had. I expect you see a lot of his sort in your first class.'

'It is quite unusual to encounter one as ill-mannered as that.'

Jenny made a hmmph sound.

'You mustn't think I only serve the gentlemen. I help everybody. In fact . . .' I stopped.

'Yes?'

'I suppose you will find me a total bore now if I tell you the most serious of all the crimes I investigate is the theft of a young boy's postal order, or young girl's, of course. There! See! I knew you would mock me.'

'Jack! Please! I'm not mocking, I'm grinning because you are so . . . so . . . oh, I don't know. Please go on, please tell me about the postal orders. Why are they so important?'

I paused again, partly because I did not entirely believe that she was not making fun, but then I realised it didn't matter. She grabbed the lapel of my coat and shook in frustration.

'Well,' I said. 'I suppose the point is, a lot of people will assume because of the modest sums that are generally involved with the theft of a postal order the matter is of no great moment. But nothing could be further from the truth. Whether the amount stolen be five shillings or fifty guineas or . . . or . . . five thousand guineas it is all one. No, I would go further and say the gravity of the offence is all the greater with the postal order than, say, the theft of a pearl necklace from the travelling bag of a lady of the aristocracy. Such ladies are used to the ways of thieves. To steal a lady's necklace, though a mean thing to do, does not destroy the lady's faith in the goodness of mankind. But consider a seven-year-old girl waiting for her birthday. Already two weeks before she starts to stare at the postman as he walks down the street. She knows it is impossible that he will have anything for her, he seldom ever does, the postman delivers only to the grown-ups and she is only too aware of this. Receiving parcels and letters strikes her as being so wonderfully exciting but she never gets any. Except on her birthday. Then she is queen for the day. So she starts to watch every day with an agony in her heart, an agony that only increases in strength the nearer the day approaches. Imagine it! Not only does she know that soon she will get some letters addressed personally to her, but one of them will be from her aunty in Scarborough who will send her five shillings to spend on anything she pleases. Five shillings for a girl who has never had more than a halfpenny on occasion to buy sweets. Her mother will take her to Barker and Stroud's, to the toy department, and for a brief afternoon she will be in Heaven. Just think of how her expectation builds over the days leading up to her birthday – like a kettle on the stove, her poor heart will be whistling by the day before. And when the day comes, she stands at the window, nose pressed to the glass, watching for the postman. And there he is! He comes sauntering jauntily down the street, he approaches, he's whistling, the bag seems more than usually heavy today, now he's one house away. He walks up the drive and posts the letters for next door, it seems to take ages but really it can't take any longer than usually. He's done, he's back on the pavement, no more than ten steps away now, nine, eight, seven . . . and then something strange happens, something terrible, unheard of, dreadful beyond this little girl's comprehension. He walks past.' I stopped, to catch my breath. 'Don't you see? A cad who steals a child's postal order is not just stealing money, he's stealing a child's belief in the goodness of the world.'

Jenny stared into my face, her eyes wide with astonishment. 'Oh, Jack,' she said. 'I'd never seen it like that before.' She pulled herself towards me on the bench and held her face nestling next to mine. I laid my cheek on the top of her head. Her hair tickled and filled my nostrils with a sweet clean wet scent, like a lawn after a shower. Since she did not pull back in protest, I allowed myself to press my head against hers more firmly. And she in turn pressed herself closer to me. Jenny sighed and spoke into the folds of my coat.

'I wish someone had stolen my postal order.'

Chapter 11

W E ARRIVED BACK in Weeping Cross shortly after six. I walked Jenny to her bus stop and said goodbye. Then I returned to my office to check the post. The door was ajar and a faint scent of coal tar soap greeted me as I opened it. It called up a host of other smells: boiling cabbage, laundry steam, Kiwi shoe polish, floor wax, paraffin, smelly feet, a sort of faint musk that collects behind the ears of boys who do not wash very carefully, Kipper's wet fur and doggy odour, chalk dust and the heavy cologne of the masters, candles, ink, disinfectant, TCP antiseptic, chlorine bleach, and many others. It was the smell of the Railway Servants' Orphanage. Sitting in my chair was Magdalena.

'Hello, Jack.'

I stared into her face. When Mr Barker came to the orphanage to choose a girl to put in the Lindt advertisement, there really was no doubt about who he would pick. Magdalena was beautiful with a sadness in her eyes that could put a spell on you. When she stared into your eyes she made you feel very uncomfortable or very much abashed and in love. We were all charmed by Magdalena, no one had any choice in the matter. And though there was a lot of jealousy when she left every morning to pose for the artist, no one could really begrudge her the special treat when the painting was finished. It was wonderful. A Swiss milk maid wearing a pink dirndl and holding a bucket of creamy milk. Behind her was an alpine background of intensely blue sky, vivid green meadows and a dazzling snow-capped peak. The Swiss maid had wild tousled hair the colour of treacle, bright eyes and cheeks with exaggerated apple-red spots, like a tin soldier.

'Magdalena!' I stuck out my hand. She shook it solemnly. She was mocking my stiffness, I knew that. But I did not mind. Magdalena's teasing sprang from a heart that cared.

'You look like you've seen a ghost,' she said.

'To tell you truly, Magdalena, you also look rather like a ghost. Have you been poorly?'

'I've been better, that's for sure. You seem to be keeping well. I hear you've got a girl. That's not like you, Jack. She must be very nice.'

'I'm afraid Ron Dingleman has got the wrong end of the stick, there.'

'Just tell me to mind my own business, it's fine.'

'She came to see me on business, her aunt was a passenger that got into a fix; we went to the Lyons tea shop.'

'As I said, it's none of my business.'

'She's a very nice girl, Magdalena. You'd like her. I would like to introduce you, I'm sure—'

Magdalena laughed in a soft and bitter sort of way. 'That's probably not a good idea.'

'I'm sure you would like each other immensely.'

'No, I'm pretty sure we wouldn't.' She reached into her bag with fingers that trembled slightly and fished out a cigarette. I lit a match for her and she drew until the cigarette was alight.

'Your hands are shaking.'

'I had a migraine earlier.'

'I thought they stopped.'

'They did. Now they are back. I'm in a bit of a pickle.'

'I'm sorry to hear that.'

'I stole a letter.'

'Yes, the Dingleman told me.'

'I expect he told you all about it, then.'

'He said it was addressed to the King.'

'He told you to find me, didn't he?'

'No, of course not.'

She smiled as if to say she didn't believe me, but it didn't matter. 'Will you buy me a bottle of brown ale?'

'I'd be happy to.'

'Your telephone rang just now, I answered it. I hope you don't mind.'

'I don't mind in the least. Did you take a message?'

'Yes. I wrote it down, see.' She pointed at a slip of paper next to the phone. 'It was the man from that bookshop on the square. He said he was going away and wanted you to help him with his suitcase.'

I picked up the slip of paper and read. I slipped it into my pocket. 'I will go and see him first thing tomorrow morning.'

'Tonight. He said it had to be tonight.'

'To help him with a suitcase?'

'He said it was a matter of life and death.'

Outside, a thick smog had fallen on the town, and the sound of St Bede's chiming seven was muffled and faint. It was so bad even the cinema had closed. They said those sitting further back couldn't see the screen. If you held a yardstick out, you couldn't see the end of it. The buses passed at walking pace, with a chap

152

holding a burning rag walking in front. The lights glimmering reminded me of the lights of a ship that passes in the night. It was like being blind, and yet the blind were the only ones who knew their way in it.

Magdalena didn't want to go to the Central across the road, so we walked down the street with no pub in mind. She said she couldn't see her feet, and it was true.

She took my hand and held it as we walked.

'It's just so we don't lose each other,' she said.

'Yes, that's a good idea.'

'It could easily happen in fog like this.'

'Yes, it could. You are quite right.'

She squeezed my hand and pressed herself next to my side.

'Do you think it's true what they say,' she said. 'Mothers losing their prams in this and never finding them again.'

'They could certainly lose them for a while, but I can't see why they wouldn't find them when the fog lifted.'

'Yes, that's true. I'm glad. I would hate to think of the baby in the pram and no one coming to feed him ever again.'

'I heard about a chap who wheeled his aunt in her bath chair to Boots to exchange her novel. He left her outside and when he came out she was gone. He didn't have the first idea where to start looking. It was so thick you had to feel your way forward on your hands and knees. He found a police box and telephoned the police station and they sent two men to help, but it was no good. They had to go home and come back when it had cleared the next day. Turned out the aunt had been there all along, but the fog was so thick inside Boots the poor chap got confused and left by the wrong entrance – the one on Priory Gate instead of Monk's Row.'

153

'Hmm, smell that!'

'It's from the traffic policeman, he's burning rags I think, soaked in petroleum.'

'I do so like that smell.'

We walked slowly, shuffling our feet rather than picking them up in the usual fashion; it was safer that way, otherwise you could step off the kerb without realising it and twist an ankle. The normal noises of the city were muffled, as if we had cotton wool in our ears. I also had the feeling that there was somebody following us. I didn't really see how they could and I tried to push the thought away. It was probably the eerie quality of the night working on my imagination. In the distance, as we walked, we heard the crack of small explosions, which I knew to be the detonators they lay on the track to warn the driver of the presence of signals he would otherwise not see. Drivers hate fog. You can't even see the top of the signal. The fireman has to climb down from the cab, walk up the track to the signal, climb up the ladder and feel the position of the signal with his hand.

'Let's go in here,' said Magdalena. 'I don't like walking in this any more. It's . . . it's green. Don't you think the fog is green?' She pushed her face close before mine to make sure I understood her drift and I could see she was unnerved too.

'Yes,' I said, doing my best to sound cheerful. 'It definitely has a . . . a sort of dirty green tinge.'

The pub was the Seven Stars, and seemed as good as any and we ducked in gratefully. It was like entering a smoke-filled room. There was little colour and the drinkers were grey shapes. But the warm yellow lights and the bright fire in the hearth made it feel inviting and cosy rather than oppressive. There was an air of conviviality and camaraderie that one suspected had been partly fostered by the unusual circumstances of the evening, the way neighbours who do not normally exchange greetings will stop and talk on the occasion of a particularly deep snow fall. I bought two bottles of ale and we stood in the corner near the fire and wished each other good health.

'What have you done with the letter?' I said.

'I can't tell you that. I'm going away.'

'Where to? Perhaps I could come and see you? I could bring Jenny—'

'It's best that you don't know.'

'You're trembling.'

'She's back, you know.'

'Who?'

'That girl from the orphanage, remember, the one who was banging on the glass, pleading to be let in?'

'You've seen her?'

'Yes, still wearing my clothes.'

'I must say we never really believed you at the time. Even when we went out to search the grounds, we never found anything.'

'You were looking in the wrong place. She was in the mirror.'

I blinked as I registered the puzzling explanation. Magdalena gave a thin laugh.

'That's a very strange thing to say. In the mirror?'

'Yes, and sometimes there was no one in the mirror at all.'

'That's even stranger.'

'That's what the doctor from Harley Street said. Alice in Wonderland Syndrome. He was quite excited about it. I was his first.'

'It was kind of Mr Barker to arrange that.'

'Yes, I always was his favourite, wasn't I?'

I peered at Magdalena and realised how tired she looked. 'Mr Barker, was he . . . were you—'

'I think they will kill me.'

'No, Magdalena, why would they? Surely not. You don't kill someone for stealing a letter.'

'For reading it.'

'Can't you seal it up and tell them you didn't read it?'

'The seal is broken. And it wouldn't matter anyway, they wouldn't believe me.'

'I'm sure there is a way out of this. I suggest you approach His Majesty the King and appeal to his honour. Tell him, yes, you are a thief but you would never dream of stealing anything belonging to the King.'

'But I did.'

'Yes, but not intentionally. If you had known whose letter it was I'm sure you wouldn't have taken it. If you explain that to him, I'm sure—'

'No, Jack.'

'Yes, just say you wish to apologise and return the letter. I expect he would be very grateful. The King is a good man. I'm sure he would be very kind to you.'

'The King is an idiot.'

It was as if she had kicked me in the shin. 'Magdalena!' I looked over her shoulder and around to see if anyone had heard. Magdalena was not well.

'He couldn't save me even if he wanted to. He does what he's told, like everyone else.'

'I find that hard to credit. A King does what he likes.'

'Only in fairytales. In real life he's like a stationmaster. He wears a smart uniform but only so long as he turns up at the station every day and waves at the passengers.'

'I'm sure the King—'

'He won't help, he can't.'

'But—'

'Do you remember in 1917 when the King announced he was changing the name of the royal family?'

'Yes, of course.'

'Why did he do that? One moment they were the House of Saxe-Coburg and Gotha and the next they said they were called Windsor.'

'I don't know.'

'He's in it up to his neck. Jack, don't get involved.'

'But you know I have to. A letter stolen on the railway.'

'It's not worth dying for.'

'Won't you tell me what is in it?'

'It's from the missing nuns of 1915. They've written to the King. There are powerful people in this land, they were responsible for what happened in 1915. They are still around, still in power.'

'Are they . . . are they Room 42?'

'Yes.'

'But who are these people?'

'It doesn't matter.'

'Of course it jolly well matters! I want to know. You can't just have a room and no building. How on earth would the postman find them? It's completely ridiculous.'

'I don't think the room is in a particular building . . . or maybe it is. I don't know. I know a chap . . . a sugar daddy. He looks after me sometimes. He knows someone who knows someone. They decide what happens.'

'Is this sugar daddy Mr Barker?' I felt rather impertinent saying it and expected a rebuff, but she just smiled, and nodded. She didn't expand. There was a moment's silence until I realised there was nothing more to say. What did it matter who it was? I said, 'What do you mean, they decide what happens?'

'The important things that happen, matters of state I think you'd call it.'

'But that's what the government is for, isn't it?'

'Not really. Mr Barker says the government are just there to make it look respectable.'

'Are they responsible for what happened to the nuns?'

'Yes.'

'But—'

'Jack, none of this matters. The point is, if the contents of this letter are published, the people from Room 42 will be lynched.'

'It sounds to me like they jolly well deserve to hang.'

'I'm sure they do.'

'Where will you go?'

'That doctor from Harley Street, he's abroad now. He conducts research into neurological disorders at a famous hospital in . . . a city. Apparently he's making quite a name for himself. He's written to me a number of times offering to pay my fare and living expenses if I go out there and take part in his research. He wants to write a book about me. I've decided to go.'

'The thing is, if you don't give the letter to the Dingleman, he will do something bad to Jenny.'

'No, he won't. He's just trying to scare you.'

'He has succeeded in scaring me. I don't think he makes idle threats.'

'He's not like that any more. He's not violent. In the old days, when he took over that other chap's territory, yes, he was. But not now.'

I remembered the bloodstained false teeth and knew that she was wrong. 'But if you give him the letter he will make sure everybody is safe. He knows how to handle these matters.'

'You don't negotiate with Room 42. They always double-cross you. Mr Barker told me not to trust them. He said I should get out of the country.'

A gust of cold air told me the door had opened. Magdalena was staring over my shoulder. Her eyes widened. She put her glass on a window ledge then clasped my face in her hands and peered urgently into my eyes. She brought her face up close to mine; I could feel her hot breath. 'I have to go. Promise me you'll forget all about it. Promise me, Jack.'

'But, Magdalena—'

'Promise me, please . . .'

She stopped pleading and kissed me before walking hurriedly towards the back of the pub and the rear door.

I turned and saw the Dingleman's man with the Plasticine nose. He spotted me and walked over. 'Mr Dingleman sends his regards.'

'That's kind of him, but I must ask you to contact me some other time.'

'Must you now? How very nice.'

'I'm not sure you understand.'

'I understand, Jack. Mr Dingleman is anxious for news of Magdalena.'

'I'm working on it.'

'That's good.'

'These things take time.'

'Of course they do. I saw you earlier with a girl. Luckily for you the fog was too thick to—'

'It was Jenny.'

'I see. Just gone to spend a penny, has she?'

'I really don't think—'

'Whoever it was seemed to leave quite hurriedly. Make a pass, did you?'

My fist balled. 'Look here, you . . .'

He smiled, a cold smile. 'You don't want to start any trouble in here.'

'It's jolly lucky for you that I don't.'

'Yes, I know. You were a fireman on the Great Western and so you have a punch to the ribs that breaks the heart of the prizefighter and makes him kiss the canvas like a sweetheart. Isn't that how it goes?'

'Yes, and it's true.'

'Have you ever been on the receiving end of one?'

'No, I haven't.'

'Now's your chance. I used to be a prizefighter. But the prizes were not big. We can step outside if you like.'

I looked at him in disbelief.

He flicked my lapel rather insolently with the back of his hand and said, 'I'll be going now, but not far. Next time we meet, I'll expect you to have better news for me, that's if you want to keep your teeth in your head. Good night.'

I stared at him as he left. Most people who know would say I am far from being a coward, and I don't consider myself one.

But the chap's words evoked an icy slither in my insides. My hand in my pocket felt the slip of paper with the telephone message. I walked out into the night to visit Mr Dombey.

A small courtyard separated the garage from the back kitchen at the bookshop. The walls rose like the faces of a cliff. By craning my neck I could see high above a lozenge of mauve drizzle-filled sky. The interior of the garage was gloomy. Inside, an ambulance gleamed like a fish in a dim pond. It was the colour of butterscotch with big shiny bells attached to the front either side of the radiator. It took up almost all the space in the small garage. Mr Dombey's face was still obscured by gauze.

'You see,' he said, 'the vehicle in which the manuscript of the 1931 Gosling annual arrived. Soon I will leave by the same means, but first I need you to help me with my suitcase.'

'Are you going to drive it?' I said.

'I am still looking for a driver.'

'Where will you go?'

'All I can tell you is my time has come. You have no doubt noticed how I have aged in the few days since we met.'

'I am rather surprised to hear you ask such a thing since your face both now and when we first met has been entirely covered by bandage.'

'But I have shrunk. My suit, don't you see?' He held an arm out, the cuff reached as far as the knuckles of his fingers. 'I am like a boy in a man's suit, is it not so?'

'I wouldn't go so far as to say that, some men prefer a looser fit.'

'You do not need to spare my feelings. I have shrunk and will

161

continue to do so. And my hair, too. Does it not now seem disproportionately large for my face?'

'I am unable to see your face.'

'Would you like to?'

'Well . . .'

'I would not recommend it. It is disfigured by carbuncles. They are spreading. It is impossible for me to serve customers with such a frightening face. Soon I will leave this shop for good. I shan't be sorry.'

'Have you seen a doctor?'

'I have seen many, but there is no remedy. I was warned many years ago that one day this would happen.'

'Where is your suitcase?'

'I have no idea. Why do you think I sent for you?'

'I thought you wanted me to help you with it.'

'That is true.'

'Is it particularly heavy?'

'No, it is very light compared to the suitcases that the travelling public generally prefer. Where do they get all the things to put inside?'

'Then perhaps it is placed somewhere too high for you, on top of a wardrobe.'

'How can you possibly know such a thing?'

'Because I am wondering why you need my help.'

'I want you to find it, otherwise I will be unable to travel.'

'So you have lost it?'

'Oh yes. Assuredly. I last saw it on the Paddington to Taunton express, the one that left at half past seven in the evening on the twenty-third of January 1938. I got out at Reading and clean forgot my suitcase.'

162

'That was ten years ago.'

'Almost to the day. Naturally I applied to the Lost Property department. They said they couldn't find it, but that can't be true. It has to be there somewhere. There is no other place it could be. You will find it for me. A small pigskin case, not much bigger than a briefcase. It is unremarkable but for one thing. The leather bears a small motif: a ship's anchor much like a sailor might have inked on his bicep; and the name of a ship, the *Laura Bell*. It shouldn't be hard to find, but you must be quick.'

'I would be very happy to inquire, but I would not wish to encourage your hopes of a speedy—'

'No, no, you must find it quickly. Don't you understand? Don't you see? Without it I cannot travel. I have not long left now.' He peered into my eyes, as if urging me to share his vision. 'Don't you see? I have heard it . . . twice now in the night watches, while sitting alone in my shop, I have heard it.'

'What? What did you hear in the night?'

'The beating, and I felt the breeze waft, from nowhere it came, there was no door ajar nor window open, but still it came. I saw it lifting the papers on my desk. And I shuddered.'

'But what was it?'

'It was the beating of . . . angel wings.'

THE BOY'S OWN
RAILWAY GOSLING ANNUAL

Vol. VII   1931   Price: 1/-

Replies to our readers' letters

P. T. MILLS, HULL—You are thinking of Christian Friedrich
Schönbein from Switzerland who discovered the remarkable qualities
to which you allude when his apron exploded in 1846. He was
working in his kitchen and happened to spill nitric acid on his
kitchen table. He used his apron to mop up the mess, unaware naturally of the remarkable effect of combining concentrated nitric acid
and cotton. When he hung his apron up to dry it exploded and this
became the beginning of the gun cotton munitions industry. We are
given to understand that the best gun cotton can be obtained from
Waltham Abbey Royal Gunpowder Mills, although we emphasise they
have a strict policy of not selling their wares to small boys.

THE CONTINUING ADVENTURES OF RAILWAY GOSLING
CADBURY HOLT – ON THE TRAIL OF THE MISSING NUNS!

My Headstone Ordered from Mozambique

Our gunwales were weighed down with the rolls of cloth, boxes of
beads and rolls of wire that would be our means of purchasing the
supplies we would need. In addition we had one double-barrelled
breech-loading rifle, one elephant gun, two American Winchesters
and various side arms. Although Mr Gape devoted a great deal of

attention to the purchase of these weapons he affected not to greatly care whether we took them along or not. Bullets were useless these days, he told me, since the savages had long ago learned the way to tackle the white man's 'thunder-spouts' was to remain invisible and not present a target. He gave it for his opinion that we would, as a matter of course, be attacked with poison arrows from archers hidden in the foliage along the river banks. The steam whistle attached to the funnel was a far better means of frightening them off.

'I never met one yet who wasn't afraid of the whistle,' he said and tamped the tobacco down into his pipe bowl with a thoughtful air. As he did this he kept the wheel holding our course with his knee. I offered to take the wheel while he prepared his pipe, but this offer elicited a look of withering contempt.

'Would you offer to sleep with a man's woman while he filled his pipe?' he asked.

The question was so absurd and impertinent that it left me tongue-tied.

'I rather expect you wouldn't. In this part of Africa, though there may be circumstances in which it would be deemed appropriate to sleep with a man's wife, you touch his boat at your peril. Even making eyes at it will result in your skull being emptied of those dear sweet warm brains that mean so much to you, and the space used for storing manioc.'

'Mr Gape, I can see you are going to be champion company on this journey because your capacities as a fabulist are really first rate.'

'Do you doubt me, sir? Then perhaps you would be kind enough to examine the sugar bowl aft and see if there is not something disturbingly familiar about its smooth white curves.'

'Oh no, Mr Gape, I entertain no doubts about a man's head being turned into a sugar bowl. I was rather doubting your infamous remark

165

to the effect that a man might sleep with another chap's wife round here. They don't strike me as being the understanding types.'

'What bliss it is to be a child and have a child's understanding of the world. Of course you cannot simply sleep with a wife uninvited but if you are a guest in one of the villages then your host as a matter of courtesy will offer you one of his wives to sleep with. It would be deemed insulting to refuse, even if she is not comely. Insulting and dangerous. I tell you this as a warning since it strikes me as precisely the sort of wrong-headed, bumbling mistake someone like you would make.'

'Tell me about the poison arrows.'

'There are numerous poisons: the sap of the Gaboda Tree, the gall bladder of the green-toed frog, the thorax of the black widow ant . . . the savages are spoilt for choice. All the poisons are deadly and death occurs within hours or at most days. The only difference is in the agony of the death. If they like you, the suffering can be mercifully short.'

'How short?'

'Two, maybe three hours.'

'That doesn't strike me as short.'

'That's because you have never had to listen to the dying moans of someone with black widow ant poisoning. According to the Arab slavers whose libraries in Khartoum hold many mysteries, there is only one pain that can compare and that is the pain of crucifixion, although a particular form of crucifixion: not the one where they put the nails through your hands, but the variety where they hammer them through the ulnar nerve in the wrists. You are familiar with the ulnar nerve, it is the one that gives you such discomfort when you strike your funny bone.'

'Is there no medicine that can save a man's life?'

'No, the only remedy is to steam down the centre channel away from either river bank. Because of the deadliness of the poison they have never bothered to perfect the art of archery like our English bowmen. Their arrows are toys and do not travel far out into the stream.'

'Is it always possible to avoid the river banks?'

'Usually, but not always.'

'I don't think I'd like to have a nail driven through my ulnar nerve.'

'There is certainly nothing funny about it.'

With that utterance Mr Gape went silent for a while and seemed to be troubled by a thought. His eyes narrowed as he stared forward and the little boat butted its way upstream with a frisky joy that reminded me of a puppy. The rising sun had soon burned off the mist and the air began to acquire a fierce enervating heat that the cool of the river did little to efface. The very trees began to sigh, and the cries of the monkeys from the treetops became muted. Unprompted, my heart began to sing, and then even more strangely so did I. Or rather I began to hum, 'Yes, we have no bananas.' I decided to assay a touch of levity to coax Mr Gape out of his reverie.

'You know, Mr Gape, in view of the decidedly bleak view you take of my chances of survival on this trip, it really was rather short-sighted of you to order just one headstone from that chap from Bojumi. You could have got a much better price if you had ordered two.'

He looked at me, still slightly absent, and then said, 'Oh no, I did. I ordered yours as well. Mozambican limestone.'

Chapter 12

THE NEXT MORNING, Jenny and I caught the 7.25 from Shrewsbury which was due to arrive in Paddington at twenty past eleven. In the cold light of dawn, the idea of going to the zoo struck me as rather silly, but at the same time rather marvellous too. As we climbed aboard the carriage, the thought occurred to me that I had only ever rarely done things in my life that were silly. In fact, I couldn't think of any.

We sat by the window, facing each other. Two chaps joined us. The first walked in after peering at us for a few seconds through the glass from the corridor. He sat down without removing his coat and proceeded to fidget with his feet in a manner that I found annoying. Just before we left the station another gentleman entered, this time without scrutinising his fellow travellers, and took the seat opposite the man with the nervous feet. He wished us all a good morning, placed his mackintosh on the rack above our heads, then opened a small case, took out some papers and began to read. Rain began to patter against the window.

'What happens to the animals when it rains, Jack?' said Jenny. 'Are they allowed indoors?'

'I'm afraid I couldn't say. I suppose it must depend on the animal.'

The man reading the papers from his briefcase looked up. 'They should give the animals a coat like mine,' he said.

Jenny and I exchanged glances. 'Why do you say that?' I asked.

He took out a flask from his case and retrieved his coat from the rack. 'Watch this,' he said. He poured some hot tea from the flask into the top which served as a cup and then carefully poured a few drops on to the sleeve of his coat. The tea spilled off the surface like water from a duck's back. 'What do you think of that, then?'

'That's quite something,' I said.

'Is it a special type of tea?' said the other man.

'Oh no,' the chap replied, 'it's the material of the coat. It's entirely new—'

'What's it called?' said Jenny.

'The material? It's called polyethylene terephthalate.' The man with the annoying foot reached into the hip pocket of his coat and took out some small cheaply printed pamphlets that bore the title 'Temperance is next to Godliness'. He reached across and held them out to us, fanned like a hand of playing cards. 'There are other ways to stay dry, if you take my meaning.' He smiled and urged us with the intensity of his stare. We each took a pamphlet and thanked him.

'That is a very witty comparison,' said the man with the coat. 'But perhaps wasted on me. Even at Christmas I wouldn't suffer a drop to pass my lips.'

'Indeed. Why put a thief in your mouth to steal your wits?'

At Wellington he expressed regret that he had to leave, claiming it was his stop, but I got the impression he was just moving to a different compartment in order to disseminate more of his pamphlets.

'What a flat tyre,' said Jenny, 'making people feel guilty about a drop of the giggle water.'

'One drop can lead to perdition,' said the man with the coat.

'I've never heard it called that before. Most people say barrelled or something.'

'Perdition is a place, not a state of inebriation.' He reached out his hand to shake. 'My name's Beeching, Doctor.'

'Wenlock.'

'Pleased to meet you, Mr Wenlock.' He didn't ask Jenny's name.

'What was the name of your marvellous coat again?' I asked.

'Polyethylene terephthalate.'

'Poly-what?' said Jenny.

'Polyethylene terephthalate.'

'It's a bit of a mouthful,' said Jenny. 'Maybe you should shorten it.'

'What to?'

'Oh, I don't know. Terry-lene, or something.'

'That doesn't have the ring to it that polyethylene terephthalate does. This product will revolutionise the clothing industry. For thousands of years man has been a slave to the elements, his every enterprise contingent upon the good graces of the gods of Rain and Shine. But no more! Thanks to my coat, man will become an all-weather animal, more versatile than the duck, moving with equal ease in summer and winter, impervious to the onslaughts of the weather.'

'Bad news for the weather forecasters,' said Jenny.

'Indeed,' said the man. 'But you can't halt progress. The invention of the pneumatic car tyre was a bad day for the manufacturers of horseshoes, but that is no reason to reject the motor car.'

'Trains are much nicer than motor cars, though, aren't they?' said Jenny.

'I'm afraid you are completely wrong about that,' said Doctor Beeching.

'Oh am I?' said Jenny, with a tone in her voice that made me think the chap needed to watch his step. 'And what makes you say that?'

'Is it not obvious? A motor car can travel anywhere its owner wills, whereas a train is confined to the prison of its track. It's like comparing an eagle to a weathercock.'

'You can get lots more people in a train,' she persisted.

'Is that supposed to be an advantage? People should stay at their workplaces. Life is a serious business, not a works' outing.'

'People like trains.'

'What does that prove? Only those who wallow in ignorance can admire trains. All it takes to stop a train is a tiny gradient, one or two inches, and the wheels spin and the fireman has to put sand on the rails to help the wheels adhere. Is that the modern way of transport, to apply the methods of the pharaohs? A motor car could climb to the top of Everest. Think of the colossal waste of manpower needed to build a railway line without gradients. When you build a road you shape the road to fit the contours of the land, but with a railway line it is the other way round, you shape the world to fit the line. The line must be level and so if the land is not high enough, you build it up with embankments, or construct bridges and viaducts. If the land is too high you slice through it and create a cutting. If it is still too high, you bore a tunnel through it at a loss of ten chaps through death for every mile. At other times the rails are raised on stilts, or cut into the edge

171

of escarpments, or somehow tacked to the sheer face of a seaside cliff.'

'But this is precisely why the railways are so wonderful!' I cried out, startling the chap. 'The Great Western Railway line between Paddington and Bristol Temple Meads is a marvel – the platform at Swindon is the same height as St Paul's Cathedral. They call it Brunel's billiard table.'

'Swindon!' Doctor Beeching threw up his hands in horror. 'And how, pray, did Swindon come to be born? The great railway engineer Daniel Gooch threw his ham sandwich out of the window with the words, "Wherever this sandwich falls, there will I build my town." Thus Swindon was born.'

'Are you an admirer of the pharaohs, Doctor Beeching?'

'As chemists they were unspectacular, but as builders, as engineers, probably the finest that the world has ever known.'

'Well, I am sorry to gainsay you but the achievements of our railway builders knock those of the pyramid builders into a cocked hat.'

'Poppycock! Says who?'

'Mr Gibson C. Chesterton in his seven-volume historical masterpiece, *Railways of Albion*. It's the most authoritative book on the subject in existence. According to his estimate – which I may say has been approved by the steering committee of the Royal Society of Calculators – more earth was moved in the construction of the railway line from London to Birmingham than is contained in the entire Great Pyramid of Cheops.'

'Oh really!'

'The Great Pyramid of Cheops contains 5,733,000,000 cubic feet of stone. When they built the London to Birmingham railway they moved four times that much. It took more than

100,000 men twenty years to build the Great Pyramid, but the London to Birmingham railway was built by 20,000 men in five years. Compared to our great railway engineers, the achievements of the pyramid builders are very modest. In fact, if you sought a fitting comparison to the great railway-building epoch of the nineteenth century you would, according to Mr Chesterton, do better to look back to the construction of the medieval cathedrals.'

'I'm sorry but to compare the construction of railway lines with those sacred wonders the great cathedrals is . . . well, in order to do it a man would have to talk directly through his hat! The cathedrals of Lincoln, Salisbury, or Rheims, Cologne, Notre Dame in Paris . . . really! These are the sublime representations of God's goodness petrified in stone for all time. The railways, on the other hand, insofar as it is even possible to associate them with the Divine, are merely the . . . the hair that clogs up His sink plug.'

'No!'

'Yes, and all to what end? To provide an easy means whereby the feckless can skulk off from work and travel to the seaside? How is the nation served if half the people whose role is to manufacture our goods are sitting on Brighton beach eating cockles? And that social evil pales in comparison to what took place during the construction of the railways – the whole country filled with marauding, violent, drunken oafs.'

'They were heroes!'

'To you perhaps, but not I suspect to any man who had a daughter and lived in a town through which this army of diggers and drunkards passed. Every time they got paid there would be a three-day pitched battle requiring the magistrate to call out the dragoons to quell their madness. Do you defend that too?'

'I certainly don't, and I don't deny that such unpleasant scenes took place from time to time, but I would say that the gravity of this has been greatly exaggerated by historians who have not taken the trouble to inquire into the true facts.'

'Oh, is that so!'

'Yes, Doctor Beeching, I rather think it is. Most of the tales of drunken brawling are lurid exaggerations. The reality is of a sober and hard-working body of men who endured privations beyond what we today can even imagine, living in camps that moved with the track, engaging in the most arduous back-breaking and dangerous work. Scarce a mile moved without at least one of their number killed, blown up by dynamite, or crushed by falling rock, or cruelly maimed in such a way that a man would never be able to work again. They were cheated by all they had financial dealings with, their names constantly blackened by all; wherever they went, men's fists were raised against them. These brave and fearless men, and the courageous women who accompanied them, were, despite the false reputation laid at their door, for the most part temperate, sober and God-fearing. And in the sweat of their brow and salt of their faces they carved out engineering miracles that were the foundation of this country's greatness, of which you spoke earlier. The great empire we were born of, the greatest the world has ever known, would not have been possible without the railways. But there is more to it than that. The railways are the very soul of our land now: there is hardly a village or hamlet that does not lie on or close to a line. Railway stations are every bit as important and dear to our hearts as the village church. All life is there. There can scarcely be anything sweeter or more rhapsodic than the quiet of a summer's afternoon on an English railway station, waiting for the train to arrive, aware that it may be quite some time yet, but not caring because in standing amid the quiet and contemplating the world in such a lovely spot, against a background hum of happily chirruping insects, the distant lowing of cattle, the sleepy walk of a station cat . . . why I know not how to express it save to say that during the war, when far from home in the Sudan, it was the remembrance of these things that supported me in the dark hours. And what about the station names? Appledore, Chacewater, Swanbourne, Waterfoot and Temple Combe, Lossiemouth, Ambergate, Kiplingcotes and Kissthorns . . . is this not poetry?'

'Yes, if the index at the back of an atlas counts as such.'

'Doctor Beeching, where is your heart?'

'My heart is a pump, not a toy box.'

'I really can't allow the calumny that the navigators were bad people. I would like if I may to read you a short passage from Mr Chesterton's history. It's a small thing, really, nothing to make a fanfare about, but I have been so deeply struck by the words that I carry them with me.' I took down my hat from the rack and removed from within the inner band a piece of paper which I unfolded. 'This is what I believe is known as an oral history. It is the testimony of one Sarah Devereux, the wife of one of the navigators who built our railways. It was written down in 1858, by a woman working for one of the many Temperance Societies that took up the cause of the navigators. Like many people she initially took them to be an army of villains fit only for a terminus in Hell, but she found her views profoundly altered when she encountered first hand these people in the flesh. These are the words of Sarah, as dictated to the lady:

'*One Saturday night he took out his money and said us would tramp to Yorkshire. For he'd worked there before and it was all rock, and beautiful for tunnels. I didn't know where Yorkshire was, I had never been more than twenty miles from Bristol before. We were gone four years, and I wasn't but just seventeen year old, and I didn't want to go. And 'twas then us began to quarrel so. He took his kit and I had my pillow strapped to my back, and off us set. Us walked thirty mile a day, it never stopped raining, and I hadn't a dry thread on me night and day, for us slept in such miserable holes of places, I was afeard my clothes would be stole if I took them off. They was a rough lot there; then us seen and things I wish I'd never heard of.*'

I finished reading and looked directly at Doctor Beeching. 'Just imagine it, Dr Beeching, seventeen years old, owning nothing but a pillow, walking from Bristol to York . . . four years they were away . . .'

'Four years is not such a long time. I spent longer than that studying at Imperial College.'

'Yes, and I don't doubt you had very comfortable lodgings. Have you ever been in a position where you were scared to take your clothes off for fear they might be stolen and they were the only ones you had? It really should make us humble, if you ask me. Instead of blackening their remembrance we should honour them for their heroic achievement, one that has few equals in the history of the world, and from which we benefit without thinking every day of our lives.'

Doctor Beeching gathered up his belongings as we were approaching Wolverhampton High Level. 'It's a very pretty speech you made and you would look good making it on a soapbox, but I am a rationalist. I can assure you, the railways will come to be seen as a colossal mistake and future generations will assuredly rid our land of their disfiguring presence. The future of transport, and I speak here with the authority of a scientific man, is the motor bus.' He moved to the door and took hold of the handle.

'If you don't like trains, then why are you travelling on one?' asked Jenny.

He seemed annoyed by the question. 'Because my car wouldn't start this morning.' He slid the compartment door aside and said, 'Good day.'

'Au reservoir,' said Jenny.

'What a disagreeable chap,' I added.

Paddington was a scene of chaos. Rivers of people flowed by up and down the platform; porters struggled against the flow carrying baggage. All bent upon two rituals that define our lives, arriving and departing. We stood rooted on the platform, like a tree stump in a river as the people flowed past. Jenny looked up and around and then said, 'Oh, Jack, listen!' It was a platform announcement made over the system of electronic loudspeakers. I turned to gaze at her face; it was shining and I felt an upsurge in my breast of something I suspected might be pride.

'Yes, yes, it really does sound as if the man is inside your head, doesn't it? But he's not, he's over there!' I pointed to the control room hanging in a mezzanine structure above the concourse, in front of the Great Western Hotel. We walked down the platform and as we passed the first-class compartments Jenny stopped and pressed her nose against the glass. 'Ours was much more cosy,' she said.

We caught the bus outside the station and got off at Regent's

Park and walked. The rain had stopped and it brightened a little. We were not so impressed by the famous Mappin Terraces. Mountains made from concrete that really look nothing like mountains and surely wouldn't fool an animal. The most popular animal in the terraces was Susie, a polar bear brought to the zoo after being lassoed in Greenland by a party of Cambridge students. She had a sweet tooth and would catch sticky buns thrown to her in her mouth.

In the ape house we found a gorilla sitting on his own looking rather forlorn in a small cage. He sat and stared out through the bars, and seemed to peer beyond the faces of the school children who had lined up to taunt him. He seemed bored and if the taunting children had ever upset him in the past it seemed they had lost the power to do so. We watched for a while and both became possessed of the same feeling of dejection. After a while, the school children filed out, leaving an old lady wearing a headscarf. A zoo employee passed through and we asked him if he knew Clerihew, the keeper. He gave us a funny look and walked on. The woman turned to us and said, 'I come most days, he doesn't remember me any more, he's getting old.'

'Who?' I said.

'Clerihew.'

'You know him?' said Jenny.

'Of course.'

'We're looking for him, you see.'

'What do you mean?' said the lady. 'You've found him, haven't you? This is Clerihew.' The woman nodded at the gorilla. Jenny and I exchanged glances of surprise. 'I remember him arriving in 1932. Queue halfway across the park, back then. The little mite was difficult to see then because he was so small. Just a baby. He had a little suitcase.'

'What was in it?' said Jenny.

'Hot-water bottle, teddy bear and a pair of pyjamas in good quality Egyptian cotton.'

'Did he wear his pyjamas?' asked Jenny.

'He did for a while. If you came early you could still catch him in them. But he grew so quick, it didn't take long before he was out of them. The suitcase was on display in the museum for a while but it had to be withdrawn.' The woman leaned in closer and said, 'It was made of human skin.'

Jenny squeaked in surprise.

'Some woman turned up and claimed it was her late husband. There was a mark in the leather. She said he used to have a tattoo just like it.' The woman nodded, wished us a good day and moved off, saying, 'Come here often enough and you get to meet all sorts.'

We wandered to the zoo's small museum. There was a display about Clerihew. There were photographs of the crowds queuing round the block to buy tickets, and one of the baby gorilla wearing a nappy, looking as vulnerable and anxious as a human baby. There was also a picture of the African potentate, King Jhorumpha, officially handing the gorilla to the chairman of the British Rotary Club in Port Bismarck. King Jhorumpha was wearing what appeared to be a Mickey Mouse tie and grinning broadly. The caption explained that he had given the gorilla as a present to the King of England, whose postage-stamp collection he greatly admired. Jenny read the accompanying article from *The Times* that had been framed and affixed to the wall. Subset within it was a smaller story about a woman who had become hysterical whilst visiting the new star attraction at London Zoo and had to be taken to the infirmary. The lady, Mrs I. Gape, had convinced herself that Clerihew's suitcase was made from the skin of her missing husband, who was also called Clerihew. The suitcase had been withdrawn from display and later sold to an American collector of curios called Hershey Lindt. This name had cropped up before, in Cadbury's case file. I remembered there had been a report from the consul in British North Borneo relating the testimony of a seafaring vagabond called Hershey Lindt who claimed to have seen one of the nuns in a tramp steamer. Was it the same Hershey Lindt? To an English ear the name was unusual, but maybe in Switzerland Lindt was as common as Jones.

It would have been nice to take our tea and sandwiches on a bench in the park, but it had turned into quite a raw December day and really was too cold. Fortunately the zoo had made available a room in which it was deemed acceptable to eat sandwiches that one had brought along oneself and we went there. It was quite a drab place, with no windows, just a skylight and trestle tables in rows, like a works canteen, but it was warm and dry. To tell the truth, I was enjoying Jenny's company so much I really didn't mind about the room. We decided that after lunch we would take the bus to see Buckingham Palace, and then before catching the train back from Paddington we would visit Selfridges and look at the television receivers.

'So, Clerihew is the gorilla,' said Jenny.

'Yes, it rather looks like it.'

'Do you still think Cadbury wouldn't play a practical joke on Cheadle?'

'It is certainly very droll, but I think there is method in his madness. The gorilla must have some significance. I need to think about it.'

'I telephoned the hospital again last night,' said Jenny. 'They said Aunt Agatha was still asleep but that she was feeling much better.'

'I see.'

'How can they know she is feeling better if she is asleep?'

'I really couldn't say.'

'She can't feel anything if she is asleep.' She reached into her handbag and took out a packet of cigarettes. She offered me one and we both smoked in silence for a while. Jenny said, 'I had a dream about Sister Beatrice. It was horrible.'

'Jenny, you mustn't.'

'They killed her and then pretended she had gone missing, when really she was already dead. Then they blamed her for setting the fire.'

'I'm sure your dream was inspired by the ghoulishness of that place. Sister Beatrice is probably alive and well somewhere. We will have to find her.'

'How will we do that?'

'I really don't have much idea.'

We sat in silence for a little while, lost in our own thoughts but probably the same oppressive forebodings. Jenny said in a brighter tone: 'Is the case of the missing nuns the most baffling you have ever encountered?'

'Pretty much, I'd say, although I have one on my desk at the moment which is pretty mysterious.'

'That sounds intriguing. Are you allowed to tell? Or are you one of those wicked chaps who get pleasure from teasing a poor girl?'

I pondered for a second whether it would be proper to tell about the case of Driver Groates and Fireman Stalham. There had been a small write-up in the newspapers so I decided there was no reason to be coy.

'I will tell you,' I said, 'but you must promise not to reproach me if the whole thing gives you a headache. It has certainly given me one.'

'I promise. Guide's honour.'

I explained the details of the case. 'Even more peculiar, the light in the ceiling had a bloody handprint on it.'

'Whose hand?' said Jenny.

'The blood, of course, belonged to the dead driver, but the handprint was that of Fireman Stalham. There were also smears of blood on the outside of the door. Fireman Stalham was in such distress that they took him to hospital and he walked out in his dressing gown sometime between 3am and 4am. He has not been seen since.'

'Driver Groates was dead with a bashed-in skull,' said Jenny, repeating the details as if wanting to be sure she had got it right. 'There was glass inside the compartment, but no sign of the thing Fireman Stalham claimed had been thrown in and which hit his driver. Fireman Stalham has done a bunk and no one knows where he is. There was a bloody handprint on the light bulb in the compartment roof.'

'That's it. So what happened?'

'I give up.'

'I don't blame you, but if you ever manage to work that one out, I will speak to Mr Jarley at Lost Property and ask him to let me know the first time someone hands in a Biro.'

After the zoo, we took the bus to see Buckingham Palace and

182

the Houses of Parliament. Then we walked up to Oxford Street to Selfridges, where we made straight for the radio and gramophone department. The television set they had was an RGD and was already receiving a broadcast as we entered the department. On the screen was a chap explaining about the latest development in London called a supermarket. It was an American idea that represented an entirely new way of shopping in which you do most of the work yourself. He said, soon we should all be supermarketers. The salesman, noting our interest, walked over and explained some of the features. It was a 29-valve television sound and vision receiver of the cathode-ray type. Picture size of 10 inches by 8. This was the same size as a blown-up photograph and meant more than one person could watch it in comfort. No more family arguments about who got to watch the television. It was available on hire purchase for an initial down-payment of £5 and 16 shillings, and twelve monthly payments of £4 15s and 9d. That didn't include the aerial installation, of course. All the same, it struck me as quite reasonable, and really a television set could be had for an outlay not much more than the cost of a motor car. As we watched, the pictures of the supermarket reminded me, for some reason, of Magdalena visiting me last night, and the fear that had been in her eyes. Magdalena was no coward, and I could not get out of my mind the frightened way she had darted from the pub when the Dingleman's chap arrived. I thought, too, of the gaiety with which Jenny had suggested the idea of digging up the graves of the nuns, as if we were in a sensational novel. But of course we weren't. I began to reflect on the danger into which I had been selfishly leading Jenny. I knew if I were honest with myself that the reason I had allowed her to take part in the investigation of her case was most irregular. It was because I liked being with her.

We wandered back towards Paddington station through Hyde Park and I determined the time had come to put an end to things before someone got hurt. I decided I would tell her when we reached the point where we would have to leave the Park. But when we got there it occurred to me that we had been walking for some time in silence and that this was not the awkward silence that sometimes exists between two people but a completely different one that felt very nice and I reflected that I hadn't ever enjoyed a silence in that way before. So I postponed my remarks until we reached the station. When we did I still found I lacked the courage and waited until we were on the platform.

'Jenny,' I said, 'I think it's probably best if I investigate this case alone.'

'Not on your nelly.'

'Yes, I knew you would say something like that but it really is too dangerous.'

'I'm not scared.'

'No, I don't imagine you are, all the same—'

'Didn't I tell you I would do it anyway, no matter what you said?'

'Yes, indeed you did, but, well, you see I ran into Magdalena yesterday, and—'

'Oh.'

'She's scared for her life. She won't say why, but this letter – she seems to think they will kill anyone who reads it.'

'That's nice.'

'Is it?'

'I mean, it's nice that you saw Magdalena.'

'Yes, I suppose so. All the same . . .' My words trailed off as the whistle of the approaching train attracted our attention. We said no more until the drama of arrival was past. Pish, posh, shhhh, ker-shhhhhhhhhh. So many steam sounds. I don't think there lives the man who is entirely unmoved by the theatrical bravura of a steam engine arriving or departing.

Once we were seated in our compartment, Jenny pressed her face to the window.

'You see, she was quite windy and that's not like her at all.'

'You don't say.'

'She said she was going away . . . to hide. There's no chance of her giving us this letter, so I think the only thing we can do now is find the nuns.'

'Really.' Jenny's tone was quite flat and lacking in warmth.

'Yes. We must find them and ask them what was in the letter and then appeal to the King. But the whole thing is fraught with danger and I really couldn't—'

'Do you know, whenever you say "Magdalena", your voice changes pitch slightly?'

'Does it?'

'It's like a catch in your voice.'

'I didn't know that.'

'The way some men speak differently when they talk of their dead mother.'

'How interesting!'

'Were you sweet on Magdalena, Jack?'

'I hardly ever see Magdalena—'

'That's not what I asked – I asked if you were sweet on her.'

'Everyone was sweet on Magdalena.'

185

'That's not what I asked either, I don't give two hoots about everyone.'

'Jenny.'

'You see? When you say my name there is no catch in your voice. So, were you sweet on her? I imagine you must have been if everyone else was.'

'No, you don't understand. We grew up together, like brother and sister, so I didn't think about her like that. I mean, she was awfully pretty and . . . Magdalena was like a bird that has fallen out of its nest. She was odd in a very nice way. We were all shocked when Tumby died—'

'Who's that?'

'He was one of the Goslings.'

'Last time you said you didn't want to talk about him.'

'No, I said I didn't want to talk about Cheadle. I don't think I mentioned Tumby.'

'So what did he die of, then? Measles?' There was an edge to Jenny's voice that I hadn't heard before. I frowned and stared at her. She flicked her eyes away from the window, to me, and then back as if there was something very interesting going on outside, but there wasn't.

'He was caught stealing from Kipper our collecting dog and Lord Apsley was forced to thrash him before the whole school.'

'And he died?'

'Yes. During the thrashing, Magdalena cried out in pain as if she were the one being beaten. In a way she was. Because of her Alice in Wonderland Syndrome, she would get migraines that made her senses swap over so she could hear colours, and see sounds. She told us she felt each stroke of the cane. She begged them to stop and said Tumby didn't steal the money.

They asked how she knew, and she said Kipper told her. They had to drag her outside for some air.'

'Drag?'

'Help.'

'So why say "drag"?'

'I don't know. I didn't mean anything by it. Once outside in the yard she screamed again and said, "He's dead!" Then Lord Apsley stopped and said, "Don't be silly, he's just sleeping." And he carried Tumby off to the infirmary.'

'They beat a little boy to death?'

'He had a weak heart.'

'They always say that.'

'Who does?'

'People.'

'Magdalena and Tumby were very close.'

'The dog told her it wasn't Tumby?'

'Yes.'

'She sounds stupid.'

'I don't think she was.'

'Bully for you. I'm sure you thought she was just lalapaloosa.'

'I don't know what that means.'

'Super-colossally fantabulous.'

I was aware of a growing sense of vexation within me. I didn't know what had happened but the sun had slid behind a cloud. 'Would you like some tea?'

Jenny banged her head against the window glass. 'Oh yes, everything will be just spoony if we have a cup of tea.'

'Spoony?'

'Snazzy Jack, super-solidly Fifth Avenue, groovy and totally cheezle-goddam-peezle.'

'You really have some funny expressions. Where did you get them from?'

'An American soldier.' Jenny's voice became different when she said that. Softer but with a weary sad bitterness. 'He was our lodger for a while. I moved in with my auntie and he put his snore rack in my room.'

'A GI?'

She saluted sarcastically. 'Yes, sir! From Chocolate Town, USA.'

'I didn't know there was such a place.'

'Hershey, Jack, Hershey Pennsylvania, where they make the chocolate.'

'The town is called Hershey?'

'They named it after the chocolate.'

'Well, that's—' I stopped.

'It's what?'

'I didn't know.'

'Well, you do now.'

'Were you . . . was he . . .'

'He was funny.'

'He stayed in your room?'

'Where else?'

'So there was the three of you, then. I mean, your auntie would have always been there with you.'

'Not always.'

'Not?'

'Sometimes she went out, and then there was just the two of us.'

'But . . . was that wise?'

'Oh, I wonder. Let me see now, was it wise?'

'I mean two of you—'

'That's right, a boy, a girl, both of whom could count to two.'

'But that's not . . . how old was he?'

'As old as his tongue and a little older than his teeth.'

'Same age as you then.'

Jenny glanced away from the window again. I was aware of having made a joking remark, but I hadn't intended it so. I wasn't laughing.

'Two years younger actually. He was nineteen. So yes, we were both very wise.'

'I think you are misunderstanding me, all I meant was . . . was whether it was proper—'

'It's a bit late to act the fire extinguisher, and anyway you can hardly talk, can you?'

'What do you mean?'

'A bit of a cheek, I call it. You gushing on and on about Marvellous Magdalena and then getting all shirty because we had a lodger. We were doing our bit to win the war.'

'Who's being shirty?'

'The King of Timbuktu.'

'Timbuktu doesn't have a king. Just a vizier.'

'Fancy that. Did you read it in your Gosling annual?'

'Cheadle told me.'

'Fuck Cheadle.'

'Jenny, how dare you be so . . . waspish!'

'Cheadle ruined you all, Jack.'

'I don't see how.'

'I know that.'

'Just because he blotted our copybooks—'

'He fell in love, for God's sake. With a woman, instead of a train. He probably wasn't the first.'

'But he—'

'A man can love a woman as much as a train, Jack, he can! He can. More!'

'More?'

'Oh, don't you see? More, so so much more. There is something, something so much more.'

The whistle wailed and I sensed the train beginning to slow down. Blotches of wetness appeared on the window as snowflakes fell and melted on the warm glass. Jenny continued to stare intently at the grey nothingness. We remained in silence as the train proceeded at dead slow. Eventually I spoke.

'What was his name?'

'Cooper.' Jenny's eyes glistened.

'You know, when you said that, your voice changed slightly.'

She nodded, almost pressing her face into the glass. 'Yes, I know. But not as much as when I say yours.' She sighed. 'Anyway, you don't need to worry. He bought the farm on Omaha.'

'In Omaha.'

'On Omaha. It's a beach. You should go there some time. You could build a sandcastle with a little tunnel for your trains.'

Chapter 13

THE TRAIN WE caught home was the 6.10 from platform 2, the one that travels via Bicester. It arrived in
Weeping Cross quite late, about twenty past ten.
There was a restaurant carriage as far as Wolverhampton but
Jenny wasn't hungry. By the time we reached Weeping Cross the
snow had begun to stick. Jenny did not want me to see her to
her bus. I walked towards the town centre; my heart was in
turmoil but I only dimly understood why. This day that had
started so marvellously had ended . . . I could not recall ever
feeling such overwhelming consternation in my heart. What had
I done to make Jenny go like that? I had to see Cheadle, he
would know. Perhaps of all the Goslings only he could tell me
this. It was late, getting on for eleven, but I could not sleep until
I had seen him. Outside the Astoria a man sidled up from the
shadows and I could see without needing to turn and look that
he meant to ask me for money or a cigarette or something.
Whatever today's hard-luck story was. Well, he could go and
sing for his supper. He touched my arm softly, and said, 'Sir.' I
jerked my arm away.

'Sir.'

'Go away, man, you'll get nothing from me.'

'Please, sir.'

'Go away, I tell you!'

He gripped my arm and I flung my arm up and outward, almost striking him across the face. He fell back and stumbled. I stood rooted to the spot, watching him slope away. What had become of me?

As I entered the Shambles, a car slid past. It was a Rover sports saloon with a silver Viking's head on the bonnet and black paintwork with a thin red pinstripe down the coachwork. It pulled up and parked across the road from the Chinese laundry. I sensed that the occupants were watching me. I walked up to the front door of the laundry and knocked. The lights were off and I had to knock for quite some time before someone answered. It was a small Chinese boy, about ten or eleven, who opened the door. A week ago I would never have dreamed of such impertinence. To bang on the door of a strange house and rouse a sleeping family like this. The boy was holding an oil lamp and seemed not greatly surprised to see me. He turned and walked down the passage as if it were understood that I would follow and that it was equally clear who I had come to see. There were stairs at the end of the passage and he began to climb. I followed. On the first landing a Chinese man stood in a doorway watching. He looked at me and said, 'You not Lord Apsley.'

We climbed five storeys to the roof. Cheadle was in the garret, lying in a bed so high off the floor that he had a soap box to act as a step. His bed was, in fact, a mattress on crates containing soap powder and ammonia. He was staring at the ceiling, and spoke without turning to look at me.

Fear no more the heat o' the sun,
Nor the furious winter's rages;

Thou thy worldly task hast done,
Home art gone, and ta'en thy wages;
Golden lads and girls all must,
As firebox cleaners, come to dust.

I smiled patiently.

He turned his head to see me. 'Hello, Jack.'

'Are you well, Cheadle?'

'Just a bit tired.' He coughed. Doors banged downstairs. 'This house is Tudor, did you know that?'

'No, I didn't.'

'I expect, over the years, a lot of people have died in this room, staring up at the sky through this window. We come and we go, it all seems so . . . important, so urgent, our little lives filled with little cares and pains. Lots of those. But when you look back, it's quite affecting to see how small and without meaning those cares were. If only I had known it sooner, I might not have taken things to heart so. Is it snowing?'

'A few flurries, not sure if it's going to stick. It's chilly though, the wind is from the north-east.'

'Would you like a cup of tea? I can send the boy. It's Chinese tea, tastes like water you boil peas in, but it's pleasant enough.' He turned to look at me properly. There was a candle on the bedside table. He picked it up and held it closer to my face. Then he gasped. 'Oh dear, I'm so sorry. Oh, you poor man. There was me waffling, oh, you poor man.'

'Cheadle, I—'

'It's come, hasn't it? I see it in your face. A terrible darkness where before there was such gaiety. Those cruel fiends.'

'Cheadle, I—'

'To throw you out just before Christmas.'

'No, you misunderstand.'

'You've received the letter ending your employment?'

'No, I haven't. Not yet.'

'But then what on earth has happened to make you look like this?'

'I've met a girl.'

His face, which had been grey and taut with suffering, became transformed. It was as if his face had been a Halloween turnip and someone had lit the candle inside. He turned quickly to me.

'Oh, Jack, that is good news!'

'I never expected to.'

'You never do, that's the glory of it. Oh, Jack, you cannot know how much joy this news brings me.' He drew himself up in bed on his pillows, as if finally this were news worth living for. 'You must grab! Grab it! Seize your happiness as it passes you in the street, and not let go. You will spend the rest of your days in regret if you do not. Quick! On the mantelpiece, glasses. Fetch them!'

I duly did as I was told.

'Your Gosling's brandy, you have it?'

'Yes, but—'

'No buts!'

'It's for medicinal purposes.'

'Physician, heal thyself!'

I took out the flask and filled the glasses. We wished each other good health and drank.

'Seize your happiness, seize it, I say.'

'I think it may be too late for that.'

'No! Tell me her name.'

'Jenny.'

He closed his eyes and nodded happily as if the name could not have been more perfect. 'Jenny,' he repeated. 'Do you love her?'

'It's a bit soon for that, Cheadle, I hardly know her.'

'It's never too soon, that's not how it works. You come here late at night wearing a face like Lord Byron and tell me you are not in love? Pish!'

'But—'

'If you heard her cry from the street now and you rushed out to find some ruffian trying to steal her handbag, what would you do?'

'I would smash his teeth in, Cheadle.'

'Good! What else? What if he hit her?'

'Oh, Cheadle, I don't dare think what I should do, I think I should grab the fiend round the throat and throttle the life out of him.'

'Good! You see? I knew it! I could tell.'

'Knew what?'

'You are in love.'

'How can you tell?'

'Oh, I can tell.'

'Then I am doomed. I thought she liked me but now I think she hates me.'

'Good!'

'Good?'

'Oh yes, that's a very good sign.'

'But I don't understand.'

'Of course you don't, that's another good sign. This all fills me with the most wonderful felicity.'

'We had a picnic, it was all going so well. Then I did something wrong and I can't for the life of me think . . . I don't know what I did wrong.'

'Oh no, you never do!'

'Never?'

'At first everything you do is right, but then that all changes and everything you do is wrong. Everything! Even when you are trying your hardest, it's not good enough. That's when you know her heart is yours.'

'This all sounds topsy-turvy to me.'

'Of course, did you think being in love was the same as firing a train?' His eyes glittered with mirth.

'Well, I'm glad to see my troubles supply you with entertainment. That's very good, that is. Chap finds himself in a fix and . . . I felt a bit giddy coming here this evening, and . . . and I struck a man in anger for no reason. I'm not myself.'

'Oh, Jack, do not mind my enjoying your fix, as you call it. If only you . . . if only you knew how lucky you are and how keenly I envy you.'

'I can't believe you are telling me this, not long ago you said—'

'Does it matter what I said?'

'I don't know what to do.'

'Oh that's easy. Apologise. You must apologise.'

'What for?'

'Anything you like! It's not important. Do it now, do it tonight!'

'Surely I have to know what I am apologising for?'

'What on earth for? That's not necessary at all. Say for being a horrible beast. She's hardly going to contradict you.'

'And if I do that, will she forgive me?'

'Of course not!'

'But that is intolerable.'

Cheadle paused to catch his breath. When he spoke again it was in a lower, quieter register. 'I've seen more of this world than you, Jack, and I have to say I don't care greatly for much of it. It's a pretty poor sort of place for the common folk, and as far as I have been able to make out, it always has been.'

'Is it really so awful?'

'I rather think that it is. There is so much pain and most folk sort of laugh it off and say mustn't grumble, but really they have every right to grumble. But the reason they put up with it are those rare times when things are special. At those times you forget, you see. You forget the dreary days of toil and grim determination. It all goes out of the window. You must forget about your worries and fears, you must take your sweetheart somewhere, somewhere nice, the seaside perhaps. Has she been to the seaside? Or Ireland? I'll warrant she hasn't been there. Take her, you can go from Fishguard to Rosslare. It's a new vessel, too, the SS *St Patrick*, built by Alexander Stephen & Sons, Glasgow, and divided into thirteen watertight compartments. All sorts of modern features – lifeboats fitted under davits, buoyant seats distributed throughout and a wireless installation equipped with direction-finding apparatus. She'll be tickled pink.' He grabbed my arm and squeezed. 'Jack! When you came to see me, I said you must think I am a pretty poor sort of chap. I who blotted our copybooks and paid the price. I was penitent, but I didn't mean it. I was just pretending, it was a lie. I said it so as not to hurt you. I don't regret a bit of what I did. You find yourself at a crossroads. You have to make a choice. I won't tell you what the choice is, you must work it out for yourself. You are lucky in a way that they are nationalising the railways because it makes it easier.'

'I don't see how.'

'Really, they won't want you in their new railway.'

'That's not certain. People will still be wicked on the trains. They may still need me.'

Cheadle's face was hidden in the dancing shadows of the candle, but I could sense the intensity of his gaze. And though I contested his words, they made me feel like a fool or one who walks his whole life in blindness. I asked, 'Why did that Chinaman downstairs mention Lord Apsley?'

'He was here earlier.'

'Lord Apsley? What on earth for?'

'He comes to see me from time to time.' He let go of my arm and sank back into the pillows. 'Go now, and find your girl. As for the other thing, I will send the boy round tomorrow with the book.'

'What book?'

Cheadle looked slightly surprised. 'Oh, Jack, the book, for your trip to Ireland. That's what you came for, isn't it?' He pulled me closer and whispered, 'It will tell you what to do . . . about the Devilishness.'

I looked at Cheadle in astonishment. He returned my stare and hissed, 'It's got pictures you can follow – racy ones!' He winked and said, 'You lucky perisher!'

Out in the street, the frost had deepened and made my cheeks smart. The crunch of my footsteps in the fresh snow was the only sound in the world, apart from the engine of a car starting up. The Rover parked opposite was still there. It pulled out and did a U-turn, pulling up alongside me. The rear window wound slowly down. Lord Apsley sat in the rear, and invited me in. I walked into the street to enter by the door on the driver's side. The interior smelled of old leather and barley sugar sweets. The red leather seat had an armrest down the middle and the carpet was thickly piled scarlet. After I got in, the car moved off, driven by a chauffeur in a dove grey suit and peaked hat who observed me through the rear-view mirror.

'Bit late to be visiting the laundry, isn't it?'

'I dropped some collars off. I'd been walking, you see. Didn't realise it had got so late.'

'Something on your mind, Jack? A man who takes a walk late at night has generally got a bee in his bonnet, in my experience.'

The car pulled out of the Shambles and crossed the square. The engine purred and made hardly a sound. The world outside seemed almost as bright as day because of the snow but devoid of all sound, the silence accentuated by the flakes of snow that danced before us as we drove. In the darkness I could not see Lord Apsley but felt his presence. His cologne was dark and sickly, containing the scent of roses left too long in a vase. I remembered the words of Cheadle and found myself uttering sentiments the like of which had never crossed my tongue before.

'Lord Apsley, I have always . . . I have always regarded you as a good egg. Moreover, I have always regarded the Great Western Railway as the finest organisation of men to be found anywhere in the world, perhaps with the exception of the British Army. And I have never doubted for one second of my life that my country is the best in the world and that the people are the best chaps in the world.'

'Hear, hear! I hope nothing has happened to make you reconsider those thoughts.'

'You read a letter to me the other day that you said was from my mother.'

'Jack, I shouldn't have done that. It was thoughtless.'

'All the same, it came as a great surprise to me to discover that you had such a letter.'

'Yes, it would. I can see that.'

'You should give it to me, shouldn't you?'

'And what good would it do you?'

'She was my mother.'

'You already have a mother. The Great Western Railway. Has she not been good to you?'

I drew myself up and said, 'I must tell you frankly, Lord Apsley, that I regard it as . . . as a pretty poor show that you have held on all these years to a letter addressed to me from my mother.'

His tone became sharp. 'Don't get uppity, Jack, remember your place. You are bright but you are still only a boy from the orphanage. You shouldn't concern yourself with matters of state; they are above and beyond your grasp.'

'I agree that there are many things I don't understand but a mother . . . every man can grasp that.'

'Can they indeed? How would you know? Let me tell you about mothers. People talk a load of ballyhoo about mothers. Unlike you, I had one, but I can't say it ever did me a lot of good. You shouldn't listen to other chaps. Some of them even cry for their mother on the battlefield when dying, did you know that?'

'No, I had no idea.'

'Rotten cowards they are, bringing dishonour on their regiment in their finest hour. I once had a man shot for mewling under fire. Believe me, mothers are no good. You know what I wanted to be when I was a boy? An actor. Can you believe that? Vaudeville. A painted man in tights. I cringe to think of it now. But I had a loving father who mercifully beat that dream out of me. It took a long time to completely extinguish it. Many thrashings. At first, I blubbed. But I learned to bear my correction with fortitude. My softhearted mother tried to intervene, to prevent the beatings that were making me whole. I shudder to think what may have become of me if she had had her way. It's a good chance I would have turned into one of those . . . those . . . sodomitical dandies rouged up and powdered, who meet at night over in Wildernesse. It could so easily have happened, and if it had been left to my mother it probably would have. Do you think she did me any favours with her cowardly pleading? No, Jack, take my word for it, you are better off without a mother. You don't realise how lucky you are.' He broke off as the chauffeur pulled up outside the gentleman's club, Marmaduke's. 'Sturridge, take Mr Wenlock home.' The chauffeur gave a tiny nod of acknowledgement.

'Sturridge will take you home,' he said, returning his gaze to me.

'There's really no need, I'm just as happy to walk.'

'In this weather? Out of the question.'

Sturridge opened the rear door and held out an arm to help Lord Apsley. Before climbing out he put his hand on my forearm and drew me towards him. 'That filly who came to see you. Have you seen her again?'

'No, Lord Apsley. After you told me she does not love England, I broke off all communication with her.'

'Good man! And Magdalena, have you seen her?'

'No, Lord Apsley.'

He peered into my eyes as if wishing to gauge the truthfulness of what I had said. 'You said you loved England. If you do, if you truly love her, you must have faith in what I say.'

'I'll try.'

He tightened his grip on my forearm and leaned across as if what he needed to say could not be overheard by the chauffeur. 'We have great plans, great plans for you, Jack.'

'But won't I lose my job in January?'

He frowned slightly and said, 'Perhaps initially, yes. You must trust us. If you find Magdalena, let us know. If the contents of that letter are revealed, there will be no answering for it. There will be no Goslings ever again. Probably no trains at all. We need to find Magdalena. We have to hang her. Do you see?' He released my arm. 'Keep it under your hat, there's a good chap. And love your true mother, the one from whose loins you sprang: England. Now is the hour of her need. Do not desert her like your flesh and blood one abandoned you.'

We watched him enter the club. Mr Sturridge drove off without a word and then once in the stream of traffic said, 'May I ask where you live, sir?'

'Devil's Curtsy, but really you can drop me at the bus stop.'

'I'm sure it's quite all right, sir.'

In the passing light of a streetlamp I saw something resting on the seat next to me, left behind by Lord Apsley. It was a Chinese newspaper.

'I think Lord Apsley has forgotten his newspaper.'

'Don't mind that, sir, that's mine. It's for my boy . . . my son. He'll be seven this February.'

'Surely he doesn't read Chinese?'

'Oh no, but he likes to pretend he does.'

'Young boys have a wonderful imagination. I met one the other day who wants to drive a rocket in outer space.'

'I wish mine did. My boy wants to be an engine driver. He dreams of it every night. I tell him it's a lot more pleasant firing a steam engine while snug asleep in bed. In truth, it is a hard, back-breaking job, and filthy dirty. But what do boys understand of dirt? They like getting dirty.'

'It's certainly a hard life from what I hear.'

'I hear the same. Freezing cold and scalding hot at the same time. But he met a driver once, you see. Filled his head with all sorts of fine pictures. He told the boy how the smartest people in the land walk up the platform at the journey's end to shake the hand of the driver and his fireman.'

'It's true, I've seen it.'

'He told him a man can bear a lot of hardship in return for such a handshake. He told him about driving at night, when you pass through all the sleeping towns, when all is calm and only the snoozing dogs cock half an ear in their sleep to mark your passing, he told him that in all the bedrooms in the houses where young boys sleep, they are dreaming of one day being an engine driver.'

'I'm sure it's true.'

'Yes, if you are the driver of a mainline express. But hardly any man rises so high, do they? I say to him, "Would you like to be the man who empties the ash tray under the train?" You see, sir, everyone sees the driver and his fireman and queue to shake their hands, but no one gives a thought to the ashmen, covered in soot like chimney sweeps. I don't know whether you have seen it, sir, but the ash and clinker has to be removed with shovels with handles fourteen feet long. The ashmen have skin on their palms like leather, so thick they can pick up hot coals with their bare hands and smile as they do it. They wear rubber boots because leather ones would catch fire, and wear overalls that are never washed, for how could they be washed? When they reach the end of their life the overalls are burned in the firebox. Every boy who joins the railway dreams of firing the Scotch Express, but for every one who drives there are twenty to clean and scrub. It's not like you get any choice in the matter.'

'And I fancy, Mr Sturridge, he doesn't take a blind bit of notice.'

'No, indeed. All he can think of is those gentlemen shaking his hand and pressing a sixpence on him.'

Mr Sturridge ignored my request to be dropped at the bus stop and insisted on taking me home. When I gave him the address on Devil's Curtsy it seemed from his face that he was familiar with it and regretted having been so expansive to me on the subject of the railways. A lot of railwaymen live up here, he said, and I agreed.

'Mr Sturridge,' I said, 'I hope this does not strike you as intrusive, but would I be right in thinking that this man who filled your son's head with wonderful pictures of life on the railway was your good self?'

He smiled. 'Indeed, it was. I lost my position on the railway. I'm not able to see him as often as I'd like now. He lives with his grandmother. So when I do see him, I give him the newspaper.

I tell him I'm driving the train to China these days. Hence the long absences.'

I shook his hand and pressed a Gosling's Friend badge into his palm.

'Next time you see him, please give him this and wish him luck in achieving his dream.'

THE BOY'S OWN
RAILWAY GOSLING ANNUAL

Vol.VII	1931	Price: 1/-

Replies to our readers' letters

S. G. P., INVERNESS—We know of no correspondence course that might instruct you and if we did, in view of what you said about your sister, we would certainly not tell you.

M. SCHOFIELD, MARGATE—It all depends on whether you wish to be hanged or shot.

A. BARLOW, CHESTERFIELD—There are no instances of two goods trains carrying dynamite colliding head on.

THE CONTINUING ADVENTURES OF RAILWAY GOSLING
CADBURY HOLT – ON THE TRAIL OF THE MISSING NUNS!

More Wimples than Heads

For seven days in a row, we kept to the centre of the stream. Even at night, Gape preferred to take our chances drifting with the current, rather than risk tying up to the river bank. In all that time, he refused to speak to or look at me, instead grasping the wheel with both hands as if it were a lifebuoy and he a drowning man. He was so scared, for a while he didn't even drink. For my part I could do nothing but pray, and stare with wonder at the river, which changed colour during the course of the day like a salamander. At dawn it glowed lemon, later it turned green and then cocoa, before finally catching fire at dusk with flames of rose madder. By the eighth day, Gape was satisfied we had passed through the territory of the Segembwezi. He became more relaxed, returned to his gin and finally spoke to me.

'The land of the Segembwezi was where we lost Sister Gertrude,' he said without turning to look at me, still staring fixedly at the far horizon. 'All they found of her was her head.'

'Good Lord! Her head?'

'It was hanging from a tree. In contrast to her custom while alive, she was smoking a pipe – a calabash containing a sweet aromatic tobacco that gave off the scent of cherry. We still had some porters with us, hired in Port Bismarck. The news that one of the holy sisters had been decapitated did not seem to bother them much, but the sight of the pipe filled them with terror. They all recognised it, you see. It had been a distinguishing feature of the German consul in Port Bismarck who had been reported missing six months previously. The German consul had been much feared in the district. He used to sit on his veranda taking pot shots with his rifle at anyone with a dark skin who happened to pass by the house. He once found a leaf on his lawn after the maid had swept it and had her given fifty lashes of the chicotte, which is a whip made of rhinoceros hide. They say that more than fifty lashes will kill a man but even half that is enough to break him in a way that Time can never mend.' Suddenly, as if his trance had been broken, he turned to me and stared with an intensity that was unsettling. 'I was given fifteen lashes once in the gaol at Port Bismarck. I was in a delirium for a month afterwards.'

Behind us the sun had slipped below the canopy of trees and the jungle came alive. A monkey screeched, and a chorus of those insects the natives call karishka-karishka began the dusk chorus, making the noise that gave rise to their name. Men say the sound is caused

207

by the demented rhythmic scraping of the insect mandible over its exoskeletal eyelid.

'Tell me, Mr Gape, there is one aspect of your marvellous tale that strikes me as odd. You claim that you journeyed with the holy sisters up the Sulabunga in the German U-boat. But when I came to find you I was obliged to undertake a day's march from Port Bismarck on account of the famous staircase of cascades that no boat can pass. So how, then, did the U-boat negotiate them to reach the navigable part of the river?'

'Porters. How else?'

'You mean to tell me they carried the U-boat?'

'Pushed mostly, on rollers. Not so very difficult with a team of good men. But of course our team didn't come anywhere near to deserving that epithet. They were hired from the prison and since the enterprise was considered suicidal no one in his right mind would have volunteered. Since that time I have spent many years in the sorts of seamen's dives along the western seaboard where the customary greeting to a stranger is to cut his throat. But I never saw a more hopeless bunch of wretches than that team of porters. Monkeys would have been better.'

'Is it not greatly surprising that such a crew did not simply murder the nuns in their beds and run off into the jungle?'

'They would have done, but for one thing. Sister Clodagh turned out to be a wily old bird. When they brought her Sister Gertrude's head, she did not throw the pipe away, as we expected. Instead she cleaned it out and attached it to her rosary. She said she wished to present it to the German authorities, but no one believed her. You should have seen the gleam in her eyes when she counted her beads that night. It made my skin crawl. Mojumbha told me the verdict of the porters: the spirit of the Great Mother was sick. But perhaps there was a method in her madness too. The next morning when we rose an unusual silence filled the camp. There was not the customary melee of preparation, no breakfast had been cooked. It was a mutiny: the porters refused to continue unless they were paid in full now and revised terms agreed for the remainder of the journey. The other sisters were remonstrating but the men refused to budge. But then a collective gasp went up. Sister Clodagh appeared from her tent smoking the German consul's pipe. The men looked on with horror and instantly went to work. There was no more talk of mutiny after that.'

Chapter 14

I WAS FAR too agitated to consider sleeping. I kept hearing the words of Cheadle echo through my mind, that I should find Jenny this very evening and apologise. I borrowed a bicycle from the shed. I wasn't sure exactly whose bike it was – most of the chaps in my digs had one, and they all looked the same in the dark. I just hoped whoever it belonged to would not be a driver or his fireman due to clock on in the middle of the night. There was no more grievous sin than a footplate team arriving tardily and making the train late. It was unforgivable. This was why they sent a boy round to knock them up in the small hours. I pushed the possibility from my mind, gripped the handlebars with a grim determination and rode downhill in the direction of the gas works. I knew from the index card she had filled in at the milk bar that Jenny lived in Moreton Crescent. When I arrived, the house was in darkness and my attempts to rouse the occupants succeeded initially in waking only the dogs of the neighbourhood. Soon there were five or six of them bellowing in chorus. It was as if they were overjoyed to be given this opportunity, that barking angrily in the middle of the night was the thing they liked doing best of all, even more than going for walks or fetching sticks. After a while, a sash window in Jenny's house was thrown up with an angry squeak and a man leaned out to demand to know what the devil I thought I was doing. He threatened to come down and give me a knuckle sandwich, and I told him I would be quite content for him to do that just so long as he first informed Jenny that I was here. He ducked back in and a minute later reappeared to say she was not at home. Then he closed the window and extinguished the light.

My eyes smarted. This was madness, the second time that evening that I had disturbed the sleep of respectable people in a manner that would have filled me with contempt a week ago. The contempt would have been for what I had always regarded as a weakness of character. I had encountered it many times in my working life, the lack of self-respect and discipline that was characteristic of the behaviour of ruffians. Many such men acted in ways that were quite desperate and I had always wondered how it was that they could permit themselves to lose control like that – didn't they know how despicable they appeared? And now tonight I was struck with a piercing revelation of understanding. Of course they jolly well knew how despicable it appeared! They weren't blind. But such considerations were utterly beside the point to them, such was the nature of the passion which gripped them. I returned home and lay wide awake for hours, staring at the ceiling and listening to the far-off moans and cries of the trains that passed through Wildernesse. It is, of course, a frequently observed irony attendant upon such restless nights that sleep finally comes when it is time to rise. Some time after six I dropped off and so, for the first time ever, I was late for work that morning.

I arrived shortly after ten to find a man with his back to me rifling through the papers on my desk. I turned the light on. He froze. 'A common thief in the night, eh?' I said. 'We'll see about that. Raise your hands very slowly and then turn round so I can see you.' The intruder complied. It was a woman.

'Please, sir, I am not a thief.' She was thin and bony, wearing a drab khaki coat and a headscarf. She looked to be between sixty and seventy.

'Well, you are behaving rather like one.'

'Please don't shoot.'

'How could I do that? I don't have a gun.'

'But you told me to put my hands up.'

'More fool you then.'

'That's not fair.'

'Perhaps you would have liked it better if I had walloped you over the head with a Great Western Railway fireman's shovel. I have one, you know.'

'You wouldn't hit a lady.'

'Is that what you think? Well, it just so happens I punched a countess on the jaw not two days ago.'

'You are a fiend then.'

'Perhaps you would like to sit down and be so good as to tell me what you are doing here.' I removed my coat and draped it over the hatstand. 'You can take your coat off too, if you like.'

'I'll keep it on if it's all the same to you. I feel the cold something terrible these days.'

She sat down. I went to the hearth, picked up the poker and stabbed at the embers, then placed some more lumps on from the scuttle. I returned to my desk and sat down. 'What are you doing in my office?'

'I've come to say my piece.'

'You were looking for something on my desk.'

'I was just tidying things up. My name is Iphigenia Gape. You have been making inquiries about my late husband, Mr Clerihew Gape.'

'I can assure you I have done no such thing.'

'In that case I have arrived just in time to stop you making those inquiries. I expect you will be wanting to offer me a cup of tea.'

I left Mrs Gape with the admonition not to pry into my belongings and went to make the tea. When I returned she sat with the air of one striving hard to look innocent.

'I eloped with Mr Gape when I was seventeen in 1910. He was a vagabond, common thief, inveterate card sharp and all-round confidence trickster who would turn his hand to anything provided it was against the law. You will wonder what a young girl could possibly see in such a degenerate man and I will answer you this: if you knew him, you would not need to ask. For Mr Gape was dashing. Devilishly handsome, although he would have been even more so if he could have contrived to forswear alcohol until at least after sunset. My father was an elocution tutor who had fallen on hard times. For a while he made a good living teaching members of the mercantile classes how to improve their speech in order to pass for their betters. A pleasing diction is the key to the doors of opportunity, he used to tell me; well, as with most things in life, he was wrong about that. He fell from grace when a lie was circulated about him and, no longer able to find the work the Lord had prepared him for, we became fishing-net repairers.

'We lived with seven other families in a tenement in Hull that bore a great resemblance to the shoe in which the old woman in the fairy tales lived, although our life was no fairy tale. In short, Mr Wenlock, we were poor and even at the young age of seventeen I could see there was very little prospect of my achieving anything in life much more exalted than the lowly position of my parents, unless fortune would smile. This was in Hull. I met Mr Gape one day when he came to collect a net, and one might say Fortune had at least winked because he was just then doing an honest day's work and this was the only time that I ever knew him to do such a thing. As soon as I set eyes on him I was utterly consumed with passion for him. Even if I had known about the full extent of his rascality, it would have made no difference. I would gladly have followed him through the Gates of Perdition. We started to meet in secret and in the course of these trysts I fell from Grace in a manner that was hardly without precedent in this world. This left us in a sorry situation. Mr Gape had no money and no prospects and nothing to offer me except a heart the size of a whale. That was more than enough for me and I gladly accepted his offer of a seat beside him on the coach travelling pell-mell to Damnation.' Mrs Gape reached over, lifted the lid of the tea pot, and gave the leaves a stir. Then she poured the tea, and after a making a noise in her throat to indicate satisfaction, returned to her story.

'My father, of course, saw things in a different light. He beat me black and blue, making me deaf in the left ear and knocking out my front tooth. The night after the beating I eloped with Mr Gape to Grimsby. It would be many years before I saw my father again, and that was when he was in his coffin. We were married the following day after first bribing the priest: it took a whole bottle of whisky and two slices of Dundee cake to convince him I was twenty-one. That same afternoon Mr Gape acquired some funds by pawning various items of silverware that looked very similar so those which had lain on the altar of the church. Our wedding night was spent in a dockside drinking establishment popular with Swedes, Latvians, Lascars and rats, where my new husband played cards for the boat of Captain Brig who had been looking for some time for a means to retire from the arms of his erstwhile mistress, namely the North Sea. The boat was called the *Laura Bell*; named, I believe, after a notorious nineteenth-century strumpet. The game went on long into the night during which Mr Gape staked more stolen silver, numerous other items in his possession and a final crowning bid that I found out later was none other than my maidenhead. Well, Captain Brig and Mr Gape were both excellent cheats but my new husband finally prevailed. Before the week was out, Mr Gape had negotiated a stipend from the coastguard to enter his boat into employ as a lightship, anchored to the north east of Lindisfarne Island. Mr Gape reasoned that being paid a modest sum to do nothing but sit at anchor and shine was as near as one could hope to get to the good life. And so we lived together on his lightship and most agreeable it was too. The money for shining was rather modest, and so Mr Gape supplemented this stipend by acting as a seaborne warehouse for illicit traders in guns, whisky and on occasion white slaves. This proved to be a very successful addition to the household economy and I had to admit that for all his lowly beginnings Mr Gape was a man of enterprise. But alas he got greedy and in pursuit of an especially large reward decided to collect a shipment of whisky from the Isle of Moira himself, and this necessitated him abandoning our anchorage and sailing north. We might have got away with it but Mr Gape forgot to turn off the light. We were apprehended by a royal naval corvette and my new husband was sentenced to ten years in Wormwood Scrubs with hard labour. I returned to Grimsby where I was taken in by the Salvation Army and given a tambourine which I banged in return for my keep. I visited Mr Gape as often as I was able and found him in disconsolate mood. Then the war broke out and Mr Gape's fortunes changed.' Mrs Gape stood up and walked to the door. She looked out into the corridor and, after assuring herself that there was no one in a position to overhear our conversation, returned to her seat and continued.

'In 1915 he received a letter from His Majesty the King advising him that His Majesty had been gracious enough to grant him a pardon. I was overjoyed at this news, even more so than my husband, who had a very strong inclination to smell a rat or at least suspect the presence of one even in a rose garden. Nothing in this world, he said to me, comes without strings attached, royal pardons notwithstanding. Fie! I said, this is the King of which you speak, not some lowly cut-throat from one of your dockside gambling dens. Oh no, he replied, men do not get to be kings by accident. Men who fill that office have the guile of a fox and the morals of a highwayman. How else do you survive in such a hotly contested position? Kings, he said, are descended from men who knew how to strike a hard bargain and you will find it is the same here. And indeed it was. The King had a little errand for my husband to perform in return for his royal pardon. It entailed his participation in something called Project Babel. From what I could gather, this was an enterprise every bit as hubristic as the Biblical project which inspired the name.' Mrs Gape paused and said, 'Why are you meddling in my affairs, Mr Wenlock?'

'I wasn't aware that I was.'

'Then perhaps you are meddling in my affairs without realising it. You went to see the gorilla yesterday.'

'How do you know? It sounds like you are meddling in my affairs.'

'Until yesterday afternoon I was unaware that you existed. Then I received a telephone call from a man called Mr Old who told me that you had been to see Clerihew and you would probably seek me out. He said on no account was I to talk to you.'

'Would I be right in surmising that you are the lady who fainted in 1932 when she saw the gorilla's suitcase?'

'Yes, indeed. Of course, I was mocked as a madwoman, but I was as sane then as I am today. There was no doubt about it: the mark on the little gorilla's suitcase was the tattoo of *Laura Bell*, complete with anchor, that my husband had on his right forearm.'

'That is quite a fantastical claim.'

'But none the less true for that.'

'Surely it was nothing more than a misunderstanding? That your husband had a *Laura Bell* tattoo and the suitcase had the same motif embossed in the leather does not necessarily imply that they are one and the same, that the suitcase was made from a piece of your husband.'

'How else do you explain it?'

'Perhaps the suitcase belonged to someone who served on the *Laura Bell* and enjoyed such a period of happiness there that he had the name embossed on his suitcase.'

'Mr Wenlock, you have a charmingly rose-tinted image of

the conditions aboard that ship and of the sort of human ship-wrecks that served on her. You would no more find one in possession of a suitcase than a top hat. Moreover, my late husband would turn in his grave right now if he thought it possible that anyone who served under his command could have taken away such fond memories of his servitude that he would have the name of the vessel tattooed on his suitcase.'

'Nonetheless, it is quite common for sailors to tattoo the name of a ship on their arms. All sailors do it, even when serving under tyrannical masters. That being the case, there may be any number of men walking round with the words *Laura Bell* inked on their bicep. Indeed, "Laura Bell" strikes me as a common sort of name and there must be quite a number of ships so christened. If you will allow me that, then I put it to you that even if the case was made from the skin of a man, which I doubt, it would not necessarily be the skin of your late husband. It could be the skin of any number of crew members from any number of ships called the *Laura Bell*.'

'It had his mole, too. Three inches to the left. And a scar where I stabbed him one night with the bill of a swordfish. Explain that.'

'I would explain that by saying it was a figment of your imagination induced by the shock of seeing that tattoo on the gorilla's suitcase. What happened at the zoo?'

'When I came round from my fainting fit, I was taken to a military hospital where I received a visit from two very shady gentlemen who were quite rough with me and told me that if I didn't shut my trap I would lose my pension.'

'If you were seventeen in 1910, you couldn't have been more than forty when you had your fainting fit in 1932.'

'This was no ordinary war widow's pension; it was a special dispensation granted by His Majesty the King in recognition of services rendered to him by the Gape family.'

'This afternoon when Mr Old called, you were told not to talk to me and yet you came?'

'I'll say to you the same that I said to Mr Old when he telephoned. "Talk to him?" I said. "I'll take my rolling pin to him if he thinks he can interfere with my Special Dispensation."'

'I think no such thing.'

'It'll take more than words to convince me of that; men often achieve ends they never intended. My rolling pin is in my handbag in case you doubt my earnest.'

'I have every confidence that were I to look into your bag I should find a rolling pin just as you say. All the same, I would never dream of depriving a lady of her pension. What was Project Babel?'

'Mr Wenlock, you strike me as being a man in his thirties and so perhaps you will not remember the mortal peril that faced our island in 1915. The Germans had embarked on a policy of unconditional and unrestricted submarine warfare. Their dreadful U-boats had brought our island so close to starvation it was said we were only a fortnight from having to surrender to the Hun. The larder of dear old England was bare. The cruellest blows to our merchant fleet were in the North Atlantic to the north and west of Ireland. Against this background, a party of nuns from the Lacrismi Christi convent in Povington wrote to the War Office with a proposal which became Project Babel. Perhaps you will tell me what your business in this affair is. And please do not play the innocent. Just from talking to you it is abundantly clear that you are meddling in my affairs.'

I glanced at the clock above the door as the whirr that preceded the chime drew my attention. It was 11.00. I wondered what I should say. I did not see what could be achieved by misleading Mrs Gape. 'I am investigating a crime that took place on the Great Western Railway. At the moment I have no clear idea in what relationship it stands to the affairs of your late husband.'

'What sort of crime?'

'A robbery. Why are you worried about your pension?'

Mrs Gape pressed her lips together as if deliberating. 'After his hurried release from prison, I heard no more from my husband apart from a postcard. Later that summer I received a letter from the War Office informing me that he had been lost at sea during a secret mission and that they were awarding me a pension on the understanding that I didn't speak about it to anyone. This pension has kept the wolf of hunger from my door ever since. I had no reason to doubt their word, but then in 1935 I received a letter from the British consul in Port Bismarck in West Africa, regretting to inform me that my husband had been murdered. The French authorities had apprehended a deserter from the Foreign Legion, a criminal well known to them, called Le Chou, who appeared to be using the identity of Clerihew Gape. He was wearing his clothes and carrying Mr Gape's passport. Under questioning Le Chou denied having murdered Mr Gape but claimed to have won the clothes from him in a card game. I knew then, of course, that my husband must be dead since no one could beat him at cards. My understanding is, he was later returned to his barracks where the military police, not satisfied with Le Chou's story, used a hand-wound telephone generator to administer electrical shocks to his tongue. He duly amended his account and said he traded Gauloises cigarettes for the clothes with a chief of the Segembwezi in 1931. Either way, I decided it best to say nothing since I had been in receipt of a pension based on the presumption that he had died at sea in 1915 and if it were determined that he had died in Africa in 1931 they might ask for the money back, which I hardly need tell you, I was in no position to provide. What sort of robbery?'

'An important letter has been stolen. What was the nature of Project Babel?'

Mrs Gape pulled her coat collar together around her throat and stood up. 'You don't know what Project Babel was?'

'I know it had something to do with the nuns who went missing.'

'Well, as long as you don't know any more than that, I think my pension will be safe for a while.'

'It seems odd that they would release your husband from prison . . . were his qualities so rare that they could not find someone suitable on the outside?'

'Mr Gape wondered the very same thing and came to the conclusion that the quality that distinguished him in their eyes was his worthlessness. A man whose death they would no more mourn than the death of a fly.'

'All the same, there must have been many men who fell into that category.'

'But how many of them owned a lightship?'

'Was that necessary to their plan?'

Mrs Gape paused as if to consider, then said, 'The project the holy sisters wrote to the War Office about involved anchoring a lightship in the sea lanes of the North Atlantic, in the place where our merchant seamen were going to their deaths. They offered to crew the ship and pray for the dying, to offer succour to those poor wretches they managed to fish from the sea.' A sly grin spread across her face as she registered my reaction. 'Of course, I suspect the War Office had something else in mind when they accepted this proposal.'

'And yet somehow they disappeared from a train.'

She gathered her coat around her, pressed her handbag against her chest and stood up. 'Is that what you think?'

'Do you doubt it?'

She smiled and then walked to the door and said at the threshold, 'It is my duty to tell you to be careful. Mr Old told me that if you continued to make a nuisance of yourself they would hang you.'

'Won't you stay a while longer?'

'I've spent all the time here that I need to. Good day to you.'

'No, no, stay a while . . . I must—'

But she had gone.

I listened to her footsteps echo down the corridor, followed by the soft hum of the lift. Two things were apparent. Two days ago Mr Dombey at the bookshop had authorised me to find a suitcase that he had lost on a train twelve years ago, a case that bore the name of a ship, the *Laura Bell*. Now Mrs Gape came to see me claiming her late husband had been the captain of the *Laura Bell*, and she was of the opinion that he had been turned into a suitcase. She based this claim on the similarity she discerned between the name on the case and the design of her husband's tattoo. I had already submitted the requisition form on behalf of Mr Dombey at Lost Property.

But what did it mean? What could it mean? I picked up a pen from the inkstand and began to jot down some notes. Jenny's aunt had witnessed the theft of a letter which allegedly came from the lost nuns of 1915. Their mysterious disappearance was part of a top secret War Office project called Project Babel. The nuns left behind died suddenly in a fire and their convent was taken over by the Army. It was reasonable to conjecture the fire had been deliberately set with the intention of shutting up the remaining sisters who might otherwise start asking awkward questions. According to Mrs Gape, her husband, Clerihew Gape, had been released from jail by royal pardon in order that he could captain the *Laura Bell* in Project Babel. Mrs Gape never saw him again and was told by the War Office that her husband had died at sea. She was given a pension on the strength of this, but later received word that he had died in Africa in 1931. When Clerihew a baby gorilla arrived at London Zoo in 1932 she, like many others, queued up to see him. She became convinced that his suitcase was made from the skin of her husband. This was denied but the suitcase was taken off display and eventually acquired by an American collector called Hershey Lindt. This was also the name of an elephant-foot-umbrella-stand merchant Shanghaied aboard a tramp steamer in 1927 who told the British consul in Singapore that he had seen a nun held captive in the basement of the ship. And it was an exporter of elephant-foot umbrella stands who received the gorilla as gift to the British nation on behalf of the Port Bismarck Rotary Club in 1931. Who was Hershey Lindt? He seemed to be everywhere. I took out Gibson's *Atlas of Colonial Railways* from the second drawer of my desk and opened to the page on Africa. Port Bismarck was situated at the mouth of the Sulabunga River, near the border of the Congo Free State and the French Congo. I decided I would send a telegram to the Port Bismarck Rotary Club asking for information about Mr Lindt.

THE BOY'S OWN
RAILWAY GOSLING ANNUAL

Vol. VII   1931   Price: 1/-

Replies to our readers' letters

B. G. BENSON, WIGAN—Stick to blow football and if your urge to shoot postmen is not to be assuaged with the advent of maturity you may wish to consider joining the French Foreign Legion.

MASTER GRAINVILLE, YEOVIL—Your first step would be to practise handling non-venomous snakes such as the grass snake. But try not to practise on the same one. Life is already difficult enough for a snake.

THE CONTINUING ADVENTURES OF RAILWAY GOSLING
CADBURY HOLT – ON THE TRAIL OF THE MISSING NUNS!

The Mountains of the Green Dawn

The next morning, his eyes two dark saucers of pain from the drinking, Gape continued his tale of the previous evening. I sensed he had begun to recognise that the end was approaching.

'A beach in Algeria, empty, save for some wild ponies. It was fringed with orange groves. Paradise.' His hands trembled on the tiller. Somewhere in the forest canopy a wild animal screeched. 'In the distance we saw a town. Sister Philippa, Sister Bryony and four others decided to walk there to barter for provisions. While they were away we discovered a young girl in the orange groves, a shepherdess with her flock. Sister Clodagh spoke to her in French. Her name was Bashirah, but since this was considered a heathen Mohammedan name the holy sisters baptised her in the sea and gave her the name Prudence. She left, seemingly quite pleased with her new name, and returned that evening with the news that the party of nuns had been captured by the Alhaj'abhra. She gave us to understand they had been taken to the slave market at El Gaberdine. This was half a day's march away and after some discussion the girl hinted that her uncle Farooq might be willing to make his motor bus available in return for some English pounds. The U-boat's safe contained gold Swiss francs, and after examining them the girl agreed that they were suitable. The next morning she arrived with the bus, driven by her uncle Farooq. He regretted that he wouldn't be able to accompany the party because he had an agreement with the other bus drivers not to poach passengers from El Gaberdine. And so off they went on their own. Sister Ludo at the wheel and the entire armoury of the U-boat pointing out of the windows of the bus, making it look like a hedgehog.' Mr Gape paused and turned to look at me. I was staring at him as entranced as a child at a magic show. He shook his head as if even today it defied his belief. 'I stayed behind to guard the U-boat, so I can only give a second-hand report about what happened. By the time they reached El Gaberdine the day's trading was over and the six holy sisters had been sold to a merchant in Khartoum. They were already heading south-east in one of the big Alhaj'abhra caravans. This news put the holy sisters into such a rage that they sacked the great eleventh-century library that Farooq had recommended for sightseeing. There they stole the famous map showing the location of the River Pishon.' Gape squinted ahead, his attention drawn to some change in the prospect that I could not discern. He turned to me suddenly.

'What do the instruments say?'

'What instruments?'

'The damn compass, you fool!'

'I really must ask you to—'

'You can ask me to go to Hell for all I care, but kindly answer the question!'

The compass needle was spinning continuously in one direction like the hand of a drunken clock.

'It's . . . it's . . .'

'It's spinning, isn't it?'

'Yes. Yes, it is! What does it mean?'

'It means we have fallen off the map. Yonder, see beyond the tree line, those are the Mountains of the Green Dawn.'

I stared at the distant mountains with wonder. 'Where does Eden start?'

'Beyond the mountains. It is a hard terrible journey through the Pass of Gabriel and down into the place the ancients called locus amoenus, the pleasant place.'

'It must be truly marvellous.'

'Yes, if you consider a leper colony marvellous.'

'Leprosy in Eden?'

'And much else besides.'

'Your blasphemous tongue will see you damned, Mr Gape. I wonder that you can be so sure that you found the blessed realm.'

'You can wonder all you like.'

'Did you have any cast-iron proofs to attest to the truth of your discovery?'

'Not cast iron, gopher wood.'

'You jest!'

'No, Mr Holt, I do not. They built a school house from wood

provided by the natives, the trees in the valley being deemed unsuitable. It was an unusual wood, resinous and aromatic with a sweet talcum-powder scent. We had never seen its like before and asked the natives what it was called. Gopher wood, they said. They told us a legend their people tell, from long ago, about a man who appeared one day and bought a large amount from them in order to build a boat. This he then stocked with animals, two examples of each. That's good enough for me, Mr Holt.'

'But even so—'

'Enough quibbling! We are at journey's end and it is time to pack your bags.'

'You surely do not mean to cast me out here in this wilderness?'

'I do indeed. I have fulfilled my half of the bargain, or as much of it as I care to. The holy sisters you seek lie there beyond the Mountains of the Green Dawn.' He reached out his hand. 'Goodbye, Mr Holt, you are an amiable fool, but a fool nonetheless. I wish you luck. You will need it.'

Chapter 15

TOWARDS EVENING THE temperature plunged and it became bitterly cold. I stood for a long time up on Devil's Curtsy, numb with the wind flapping at my coat. Below me the lights of the town twinkled more sharply than ever in the clear cold air. For the first time in my life I wondered what should become of me. Working for the Great Western Railway I had never needed to concern myself with such thoughts; it seemed no more likely that the railway would disappear than the sea would freeze. But the newspaper rolled up in my inside pocket told me that the North Sea had indeed frozen. They said the wind had come all the way from Russia, and warned you not to walk on frozen sea. It struck me as odd that the Russians were our enemies now. Most chaps I knew who had met Russian soldiers in Berlin spoke very highly of them. I couldn't understand why they would turn on us like this. Was Jenny right to think the nuns who stayed behind had been murdered in their beds in order to shut them up? What did they know? If this were true, if our own chaps could commit such a wicked act, then the Russians would have had good reason to turn against us. They would be right to erect their iron curtain to keep us out. I walked over to the seat and sat down and held my head in my hands. The wind was swirling down below in the valley, making a keening sound. It swirled in my heart too. I thought of Jenny. Who was she to me? Just a lady who walked into my office ten days ago. Plenty of ladies had sat in that chair over the years, but never had there been one who entered my life as well as the room, the way Jenny did. When I left work and returned home I easily dismissed them from my mind, put them aside the way one puts one's gloves on the hall table and gives them not another thought until after breakfast the following morning. And yet Jenny had somehow remained in my thoughts the whole time. And now unwittingly I had offended her.

I heard myself gasp at the thought and I understood why. I had gasped upon contemplating the return to the life I had led before she came, the life that had struck me up until then – insofar as I gave the matter any thought – as highly acceptable. Now it seemed as empty as a burned-out house. And I no longer wanted to return to it, no more than a family forced from their home by fire would want to go and live in the burned-out shell. Was this the Devilishness of which Cheadle spoke? But what exactly had I done to make her talk to me in that waspish manner? Cheadle understood these things but he was as baffling as she was. First he told me to beware, to shun the company of ladies, and the next time we met he told me it is wonderful news, and the most wonderful of all, the best sign, was that I had upset her. This he told me is a marvellous development, and further- more, if I were so fortunate as to win her heart, she would be upset with me all the time and I would never know why. In which case, why would I want to win her heart? The 11.23 Taunton to Manchester Piccadilly cried out as it entered Wildernesse, and the answer to the question was clear enough. To win her heart and live a life in which everything I did was wrong would still be glorious compared to the life that had sufficed me up until now but which now filled me with aversion.

I pulled my coat closer to keep out the bitter cold and trudged through the snow that was lying thickly on the ground now. The flakes were like cold butterflies flying in my face. At the top of the hill I opened the little wooden gate and stepped into the street. At the end, where Dandelion Hill joined the road, a woman stood under the streetlamp. I knew straightaway it was Jenny, just from the attitude with which she held herself, a mixture of defiance and nervousness. My heartbeat became insistent. I pulled myself erect and strode as purposefully as I could. What should I say? She turned to look at me. She began to move towards me. A policeman passed on his bicycle, the lamp flickering with a feeble glow under the power of his dynamo. 'Evening!' he said in passing and I echoed the single word in reply.

'Jack,' said Jenny.

'Jenny, how nice—'

'Oh, Jack, I'm so sorry, I was such a cow. Please don't send me away.'

'But, Jenny—'

'Please don't, even though I deserve it. I wouldn't blame you, if I were you, I wouldn't have anything more to do—'

'Jenny—'

'You don't have to say anything—'

I stepped forward into the penumbra of the lamp, and took hold of Jenny's shoulders gently. 'But, Jenny, I have no intention of doing that. I was about to . . . I was about to ask you if you would mind very much if I took you to Ireland.'

She stood and gazed at me as if my face was covered in writing that was too small for her to read.

After a long silence she said, 'Ireland.'

'Yes, in . . . in . . .'

'In Ireland.'

'That's the one. I thought, that is, I assume you have never been. Have you ever been?'

'Jack! Of course I have never been. How on earth would I have been to Ireland? Oh, you are not joking, are you? I don't think I could ever forgive you if you were.'

'Well, that depends on whether you agree. I was rather afraid you would think it impertinent, in which case I would say—'

'Jack.'

'No, I'm not joking. Wouldn't it be . . . rather . . .'

'Yes, it would, it would. We'll have to take a boat.'

'Yes, it leaves from Fishguard every day at nine sharp.'

'How sharp?'

'I expect as sharp as they come. The SS *St Patrick* entered service on the Fishguard Rosslare line only in July this year so she's still very new.'

'When will we go?'

'Next week. I thought we could travel down to Fishguard on Monday and catch the boat on Tuesday.'

'We'd have to stay in Fishguard then?'

'Yes, I can make arrangements with the Railway Hotel there.'

'We could travel as Mr and Mrs Wenlock.'

'But that would be—'

'Or Mr and Mrs Zanzibar O'Hanlon. Or we could be Dexter G. Scoopermooker the Third, and his wife Mary-Lou.'

'Jenny, do you really want to travel under an assumed name?'

'Wouldn't it be fun?'

'Yes, I suppose . . .'

'Unless you already have a wife, I've never really asked, so . . .'

'Jenny, you know very well I have no such thing. You are wicked.'

'I'm only teasing. Oh, Jack, it sounds wonderful. I've never been on a boat. Are they rather fun?'

'I'll say! The cabins have a new system of thermo-regulating louvre ventilation which allows each one to be heated or cooled separately according to the wishes of the passenger.'

'That sounds wonderful. Has it got a big engine?'

'Two independent sets of Parsons' combined steam turbines, each set driving its respective shaft through single-reduction gearing. Steam is provided by four oil-fired Scotch boilers . . . Jenny, am I boring you?'

'No, no, please go on, please, tell me about the boilers. Tell me everything. Will we be able to go on deck?'

'I'll say! There are three promenade decks, with the topmost being on a level with the navigating bridge. The first- and third-class dining saloons are located on the promenade deck and have large picture windows so we can draw the full benefit from the view and sunshine. The first-class saloon is decorated in mahogany and seats sixty-eight passengers at small tables, while teas are served in alcoves on either side. The galley is fitted with the latest electric grill and refrigerating chambers . . .' My words fizzled out as I became aware of a look of bewilderment taking hold of Jenny's face. 'Jenny, tell me I'm not boring you—'

'I thought I heard . . . listen.'

We listened. From the darkness of the park a feeble voice called out. 'Please help me.'

'Who is that?' I cried.

'Please help me, please, sir.'

'Who are you?'

'Please.'

'You stay here under the lamplight, I will go and see who it is.' I walked back to the little wooden gate and through into the park and downhill in the direction from where I thought the sound had come from. 'Hello?' I called. There was silence. I trod gingerly, I could hardly see a thing. 'Hello?' There was a rustle. A dark figure stood up in some bushes and began to run away from me, downhill. 'Hey!' I cried. Up above me from Devil's Curtsy there came the sound of a woman's squeal. Not long drawn out, but short, like a yelp. As if someone had been surprised and a hand placed over her mouth to stifle her complaints. A car door slammed. Tyres screeched. I turned and ran back, but by the time I reached the street, the car and Jenny had gone.

Chapter 16

I T WAS CHRISTMAS Eve. Twelve days had passed since they took Jenny away. Most of the time I had sat silently in my office, staring at the phone. The police had been very kind. They had done all that could be expected: mounted a search of the area, and knocked on doors, house-to-house. They had asked after Jenny down at the Anaglypta Mill. But the one piece of information that might have helped them, I withheld. I did not mention the Dingleman. I assumed he had abducted her because I had failed to deliver the letter to him, in which case he would surely contact me. But he didn't. And when I asked after him at his usual haunts it seemed he had gone to ground. No one knew where he was. I sat and stared at the phone, reasoning that he was no fool and since nothing could be gained by hurting Jenny, this episode would serve as the prelude to giving me another ultimatum. I sat in my chair, like a boxer stunned to his knees by a well-placed hook, who, impelled to beat the count, rises too early; who looks in bewilderment at the baying mob in the ring seats and wonders who and where he is.

I returned to my office after lunch to find a letter in a buff envelope bearing the initials of the Great Western Railway. I took a quick glance at the contents to confirm what I had suspected: it was a letter of dismissal. The letter told me my employment would be terminated on the fourteenth of January.

At the beginning of the year, as 1947 passed into 1948, God's Wonderful Railway, and the other three great railway companies, would cease to exist. In their place would be the new railway company called British Railways, whose symbol would be a lion riding a unicycle, something previously only seen at the circus. On the stroke of midnight, all the trains in the land would toot their whistles. I returned and sat at my desk, shivering. The fire was dead and the coal scuttle had been emptied in a manner that suggested the economies that were required of the new railway company were already in effect.

I fetched my hat and sought a well-thumbed piece of paper inside.

One Saturday night he took out his money and said us would tramp to Yorkshire. For he'd worked there before and it was all rock, and beautiful for tunnels. I didn't know where Yorkshire was, I had never been more than twenty miles from Bristol before. We were gone four years, and I wasn't but just seventeen year old . . .

The railways were built by these people. Who had the right to end the great railway companies? Who? All my life, I had never asked for anything except the permission to serve the railway. They tell you never to leave a baby unattended in its pram out in the back yard. Because a magpie would peck out the baby's eyes. The magpie is cruel. But men are worse. My eyes smarted and tears brimmed up. I groaned like a cow in an abattoir. I pressed my eyelids tightly shut. But the tears were squeezed out and slid down my cheeks. I felt the cold trickle, and heard the soft thud as the drops fell to my desk.

I placed my hand over my eyes and wept. *Damn it. Damn them*

236

and bloody, bloody bugger them. I picked up the client's chair, raised it above my head and dashed it to pieces on the ground. With the pieces I lit a fire in the grate. I built a pyre over some crumpled newspaper and then lit the paper. In less than a minute I had a fine blaze and the room began to warm. I turned out the light and sat for an hour at my desk, listening to the crackle from the grate and the distant moaning of the engines at the station below. Periodic wails, sighs, gasps, clanks and the sweetest sound of all: chuffing.

I went for a walk. In the High Street I stopped outside Barker & Stroud's and stared at the Christmas display in the show window. It was a crib, rather a grand one: a wooden shed made by a skilled joiner, two realistic manikins of Mary and Joseph in a scene littered with toy sheep and donkeys. A Salvation Army band approached along the pavement, playing silver tubas and trombones; the insistent rhythmic thrashing of the tambourines reminded me of a steam engine climbing a gradient. As they passed someone put a gentle arm on my forearm. Serge cloth, a blue so dark it was almost black, edged with red trim. It was the tambourine player. I looked into her face and realised it was Mrs Gape.

'Are you all right, Mr Wenlock? You look most unwell.'

'Hello, Mrs Gape.' I forced a smile and we stared into each other's eyes. I saw a kindred spirit. 'Mrs Gape, I must ask you, when you were in my office, you hinted . . . or rather expressed doubt that the nuns did indeed disappear from the train.'

'What do I know?'

'It seems to me you know an awful lot.'

'Now is not the time. Perhaps in the new year I will come to your office and we can—'

'I'm afraid you may not find me there if you do. You are aware of the government's plan for the railways.'

'Yes, but . . . you do not mean to tell me they have given you your marching orders?'

'I am afraid so.'

Her face became suffused with sympathy. 'Oh, I am so sorry to hear that.'

'Please don't concern yourself.'

The rest of the Salvation Army band had reached the corner of the street. Mrs Gape cast swift glances, anxious not to lose them. 'You may recall during my visit to your office I mentioned a postcard from Mr Gape. It was sent from Bristol, on the day Southend was bombed by a Zeppelin. That was the tenth of May 1915. They set sail that day. And yet the nuns were reported missing from the train on the seventeenth of May. How can that be? It is my belief that the disappearance and nationwide search was a fiction, designed to disguise what had really become of the nuns, something . . . terrible. And before you ask, I don't know what that is.'

I walked along the canal towpath. It was dark and dank; the waters glistened like treacle, the lamps from the streets above glimmering in the depths. I walked, enjoying the crunch of gravel under the soles of my shoes. Every hundred yards or so the path ducked under a bridge. Above, men cycled to or from work, dark shapes with weak flickering dynamo lights on their bicycles. Under the bridges, water dripped in the murk. I could tell from the pungent smell of yeast and hops on the night air that we were passing the Trencherman's Brewery and beyond that the smell of sulphurous fumes from the gas works mingled with the stale oil of the canal. I wanted a drink with a fervour that is normally foreign to my nature. After the gas works the smell gave way to the sewage works, and this indicated we were in Wildernesse. I climbed the dark bank at the next bridge and clambered over the wall, landing with a crunch on to the side of the road. I followed it to the wasteland and headed towards the lights at the main road up ahead, the yellow light that came from a pub window. I thought of those tales of Cornish people who used to set up false lights on the coast to lure ships to their doom so that they could plunder them. I was struck by just how cruel a trick that was. It really is quite infamous when you consider it, far worse than sticking a man up on the highway. I walked across the remains of the bicycle works. It had been making munitions during the war and been bombed. Amid the piles of rubble and shattered brick there could still be seen glinting twisted machinery. People said it was not wise to walk across this ground at night, it had become the home of people who were up to no good, but tonight I didn't care. Because, for perhaps the first time in my life, I was up to no good.

I had spent a lifetime confronting men who were 'up to no good'. Violent men who fought with bloody faces, men who stole from others, who drank themselves silly and caused a nuisance to other sober and respectable passengers. For the first time tonight, I understood why they did it. I understood the plain truth that had eluded me all the years. They did it not because they were bad people who found entertainment in being reprobates, but because there was nothing else left to do. They were desperate. The sober and respectable people preferred to read of this desperation in a newspaper kept at arm's length, which they could fold up and leave behind on the seat when they left

239

the train. I had been appointed to preserve their right to read undisturbed. They were no better, just luckier. They had never known desperation. Tonight, I had nowhere left to go. I considered the words of Mrs Gape. If it were true, as she surmised, that the nuns had not really disappeared from the train, but secretly embarked on the *Laura Bell*, and that the search had been an elaborate pantomime to cover up their disappearance, what difference did it make? They were just as lost. Even if they really had fetched up in Africa and Mr Gape had been turned into a suitcase, it made no difference to the plight I found myself in, the only one that mattered, the disappearance of Jenny. If the Dingleman had taken her because I had failed to deliver the letter, what could I do? Magdalena had the letter and made it quite clear she would not surrender it. Perhaps if I could find her and tell her about Jenny . . . but she said she was going away and no one knew better how to disappear and not be found than Magdalena. As for Jenny's plan of finding the nuns and appealing to the King, even if I could find them, what good would it do? Did not Magdalena say the King was in it up to his neck? Which meant such an appeal would presumably incur his displeasure. There was nowhere left to turn, except the place that desperate men find comfort in for a while.

I walked into the Kingfisher. It was just after 8pm and it was full with men from the biscuit works and those coming off shift at the Anaglypta Mill. So full, in fact, that I had to be careful opening the door. I pushed through to the bar and ordered a pint of bitter and a whisky chaser which I knocked back in one and asked the barman to refill. He did so without looking at me but with a slight pause that indicated he had noticed the eager way in which I had drunk it. I expect a chap working in a bar gets to see every type of drinker there is and has a pigeonhole for them all. What type was I tonight? I did not know, but I'm sure he did.

I'm not used to getting tight, but tonight I got drunk, and quickly. I had three more whiskies, a gin and orange, another two pints and a bottle of brown ale. I began to feel rather pleased with myself. I began to see things more clearly. I did not believe the Dingleman would harm Jenny straightaway. He would use her as a bargaining chip. He would have to contact me, and when he did, I would rescue her and that would be an end of it. Indeed I began to wonder why I had made such a fuss. I would sort the situation out first thing tomorrow morning. It would probably take most of the day to find her, but I saw no reason why we shouldn't have tea at Lyons that night, and, who knows, perhaps next day we could go shopping for a Biro.

I began to laugh at myself. What a silly fool I had been! I thought of that first day when we went to the Lyons tea shop; it seemed like it happened a thousand years ago although it was just over three weeks since she had said 'Abyssinia' at the tram stop. The remembrance was like a blow to the heart. All we did was take tea and an egg, a slice of bread, but I could not recall ever having had a happier meal. It was . . . it all seemed so . . . golden. This was precisely the Devilishness of which Cheadle had spoken. He said when you look back even the most hum-drum moment will appear magical and he was entirely right. And here was I crying for no reason. I had done something that I never in my wildest dreams imagined that I would. I had found a girl. And I found that I liked it. Most remarkable of all, a wonder that I could not believe, she appeared to like me. I should be celebrating, not drowning my sorrows. I ordered two more straight gins.

A young lady to my right caught my eye and smiled. I nodded back and I dare say she mistook my smile for a sign of friendship, for indeed I was smiling broadly now. She moved over and chinked her glass against my pint without asking and said,

'You seem to be having a merry time.'

'Yes, yes, I rather suppose I am.'

'Well, isn't that nice! You rather suppose that you are.'

I wasn't sure how to respond to that comment; I didn't sound all that friendly. She was quite a strange-looking fish. Her face was caked in make-up, not particularly well applied, and her lipstick, which was the colour of a pillar box, extended so far beyond the rim of her mouth that she almost looked like a clown. Her hair was a very bright shade of blonde and worn in what I believe is called a permanent wave, and yet it didn't seem to fit her face. I believed it might even be a wig. Perhaps she was an actress.

'To be honest,' I said, 'I'm celebrating.'

'Oh, is it your birthday?'

'No, it's better than that, I challenge you to guess.'

'Guessing special occasions is thirsty work,' she said, waggling her empty glass. I became aware that her companions standing at the corner of the bar were watching us quite intently and seemingly making comments to each other. They were grinning too, and I have to say there was something not entirely normal about them but I wasn't sure what it was. I bought her a gin and tonic and laughed when she asked if I was celebrating winning the football pools.

'No, unfortunately that is not the case.'

242

'What do you do for a living then? If you tell me that I will guess what you are celebrating.'

'Oh, that's easy, I work for the railway.'

'You like soldiers, though?'

'I don't dislike them, why do you say that?'

'I just thought you would, being in here and that.'

'Why, is this pub popular with soldiers?'

She laughed for some reason. 'You're a funny one, aren't you? I don't believe you work for the railway. I think you work in the music hall.'

'No, I can reassure you on that point. As a matter of fact, I'm a Railway Gosling.'

'What's that?'

'Well, I suppose you would say it is a form of detective.'

She didn't look too pleased at this news, which surprised me. Normally people react very warmly when I tell them I am a Railway Gosling.

'A bobby?' she hissed.

'No, not exactly, as I said, I work for the railways.'

'You trying to get me into trouble?'

'No, of course not, why should I?'

'If I were you I would keep your mouth shut about it in here. Some folk might not take too kindly to finding a . . . whatever it was you said, among them.'

'My name's Jack.' I held out a hand to shake, but she did not take it.

'And mine's Arthur,' she said. 'Hold on, I need to go to the you-know-what.'

I watched her move and was surprised to see her push other men aside in quite a forceful way and these men retreated from her looking rather fearful. I noted too that her companions were still watching me intently, in fact, quite a lot of people were, and I have to say I found the attention not to my liking. And then I saw among them a man who looked just like Lord Apsley, but he was wearing a wig, too, and theatrical rouge. Behind him I caught a glimpse of a man who looked like Desperate Dan. The thought that it might be that Lithuanian chap, Andruis, whom I had humiliated in the Star and Garter, unnerved me and made me feel suddenly alone, and far from home. I stumbled towards the door and spotted the girl, at the far end of the room now, do the most confounded thing. She walked into the gent's lavatories. I pushed the swing door and plunged into the cold, refreshing air.

Outside on the pavement a man accosted me. It appeared he had been waiting out in the cold.

'Mr Wenlock, sir?'

'Yes . . . do I know you?'

'We have not been introduced, but you did strike me across the face last week outside the railway station. I have a message for you and would be very grateful if you did not strike me again.'

I stared into his face and remembered how I had rudely cuffed him outside the station after the trip to London. A fortnight ago, but it seemed much longer. 'I'm sorry I struck you the last time we met. I wasn't well.'

'It does not matter. I intended to warn you, sir. And now the event concerning which I meant to warn you has come about. I have a message from Mr Old and Mr Young. They require you to deliver to them by new year's eve the letter that Magdalena stole.'

'But I don't have the letter.'

'I wouldn't know about that, sir. They said if you didn't give them the letter they would be forced to hurt Jennifer.'

'Jenny? Are you saying they have Jenny? I thought the Dingleman—'

'I have no understanding of the contents of the message, I was just asked to deliver it.'

'Not the Dingleman?'

'As I say—'

'Yes, yes. They said they will hurt her?' The thought of them hurting Jenny made me lose my balance. I stumbled and the chap supported me. He pressed a scrap of paper into my hand. 'They said you can telephone them on this number when you are ready to hand over the letter. I must go now, sir. A merry Christmas to you.' He wandered off into the night.

I walked back across the wasteland. How did this news alter things? Once, in the Sudan, I saw a dog with rabies chase its own tail, with a terrifying fury. Round and round until it eventually collapsed from exhaustion. In the same way did my thoughts race round and round getting nowhere. I clasped the scrap of paper and determined I would telephone the number. I quickened my pace. I could hear the distant pub door swing open and a group of men leave. They took the same route as me and the sound of their drunken laughter got nearer. I didn't particularly like it and thought that I should make haste, but unfortunately I was overcome by an urgent desire to relieve myself, which had to be obeyed. The voices stopped and I assumed that they had turned off and were no longer following me, so I returned to the path. There was a clank as something hit me on the back of the head. I think it was a shovel. I fell over and the world started spinning. I found myself flailing, trying to get up, but there was a group of chaps gathered round me punching and kicking me. They were laughing too and jeering at me with words that I did not catch. I tasted blood in my mouth. The beating subsided and I lay on my back looking up at their silhouettes against the night sky. Arthur was one of them and other chaps I did not recognise.

'I think he needs to go for a swim,' said Arthur and this resulted in general agreement.

'Best place for a bobby,' said one of them and the others agreed. They lifted me up and I fancied I saw the face of Desperate Dan among my attackers. They carried me towards the sewage treatment pool. It was round, with a piece that moved slowly round like the hand of a clock. There was a fence too and it took them a while to manhandle me to the top. Once they did they heaved me over and let me fall, laughing at the splash. More insults were thrown at me and then they left, all breaking into a run. I could hear their voices get fainter, voices of laughter and hatred.

There was no denying I was in a pickle now. I managed to swim to the side. The steel walls were too smooth to get any purchase. There was no rail nor hook protruding. I felt like a spider unable to climb out of a sink. The sewage farm was bounded on the south side by the railway viaduct. The arches rose high above my tank like a cliff face, a cliff so close I could almost touch it. How I longed to be on the viaduct looking down. I pushed myself round the tank with my palms into a section illuminated by the glow from the railway lights high above me. I found a vertical crevice in the wall, where the metal had been joined. It was too narrow for my fingers to enter, but if I could wedge something into it, I would have a makeshift handle. That was when I thought of my Formica. I took it out of my pocket, and inserted it. By raising it slightly like a railway signal and gently applying my weight, I was able to keep my body stable, my head above the water.

Time passed, a distant clock chimed 9.30. It was still early but there was little chance of anyone passing this way tonight. I began to shiver and when the clock chimed the hour I noticed that the water level had risen and was approaching the level of my handhold. I would see the 10.05 Hereford train, but would I see the one an hour later? Should I pray? I seldom did and it occurred to me God would consider it impertinent of me to appeal to him now when I had ignored him in the past. But then I had worked for His wonderful railway, surely that counted for something? I decided it might be worth a try but then I wondered what I should say; it seemed rather silly to ask for a ladder. I contemplated, aware that my shivering was beginning to get more violent. There was no sound apart from the tinkling of the water against the side of the tank and my breathing. Not even a dog disturbed the night. Had the whole world gone to bed? No. There was a sudden wail, and then two more. It was the night train to Hereford. And then I heard a sound that filled my heart with joy – that unmistakable double cough in the chuffs. It was 4070 *Godstow Castle*. If this should be the last train I saw, I could not imagine a better engine to pull it. As if understanding my need, the train proceeded over the viaduct slowly, so slow I could make out the shadowy shapes of the driver and fireman on the footplate, dark figures against the copper glow from the firebox. Ah! Chaps, if only you would look out now and see!

And then something happened that, had I prayed to God

earlier, I should certainly have regarded evidence of His answer. The last carriage before the guard's van glided past and slid into the penumbra of the lone trackside lamp and the light revealed to me an extraordinary sight. A chap was leaning precariously out of the carriage window, leaning so far that he would have fallen out were it not for the fact that another chap inside the compartment was holding his legs. The compartment from which he emerged was dark, in contrast to the brightly lit one next door, and into which he appeared to be peering. He was playing the peeping Tom! But what on earth could be happening in the adjacent compartment to make him risk his life like this? As he passed, he looked down and saw me, perhaps the last thing on earth he expected to see – a man in the sewage tank. It all took place in a second or two, but in those short seconds, which seemed longer than normal seconds, our eyes met.

I cried out to him. 'Can you help me, sir? You will be at the station in a minute or so. If you could report my predicament . . . otherwise I think I shall drown.'

The train passed and the astonished man was engulfed by darkness. The thought occurred to me that he had better climb back into the compartment pretty sharpish or he would hit the bridge and so would pass my last prospect of rescue. I began to shiver uncontrollably; perhaps it was the cold water that now the effect of the alcohol subsided I noticed with a sharp and keen pain. The water was like ice and it seemed quite possible that I would freeze before I drowned. I had attended to many incidents over the years in which vagabonds had been found frozen near the tracks in winter. It was a common form of death. I had no way of knowing if the man had heard my plea but even if he had he would no doubt have dismissed it as the raving of

248

a madman or a drunken man. And are they not the same? But my dark presentiments were wrong. Ten minutes later the sound of men could be heard approaching. I cried out and before long they were staring over the parapet surveying the scene below with a policeman's light. I was saved. And what is more I had solved the mystery of Fireman Stalham and Driver Groates. The driver must have been leaning out in a similar fashion and hit a bridge.

THE BOY'S OWN
RAILWAY GOSLING ANNUAL

Vol. VII	1931	Price: 1/-

Replies to our readers' letters

ABIGAIL, CREWE—You could indeed fashion a tourniquet from such material. However, if your brother really did behave in the manner you describe we suspect you would benefit more from the services of an undertaker.

G. R. ROGERS, CANTERBURY—Absolutely not! For one thing the blowpipe dart you envisage would almost certainly not penetrate the postman's tunic.

RAJIV, BANGALORE—Good quality chain or a stout rope will do the job. However, you would struggle to convince a jury that you tied the lady to the track in the heat of the moment.

THE CONTINUING ADVENTURES OF RAILWAY GOSLING
CADBURY HOLT – ON THE TRAIL OF THE MISSING NUNS!

The Well-spoken Cannibal

The two warriors threw me on to my knees before the Chief. He grinned.

'Railway Man, I have decided to beat you no more. Are you pleased?'

The vines wound around my wrist bit deep into my flesh, making me wince. I answered the Chief. 'Whether you beat me or not, it is all one to me.'

'Railway Man, you are a spoiler of sports. For three months I thrash you daily. Now I tell you that I intend to beat you no more and you are not even curious. Railway Man, play the game!'

'Chief Jhorumpha. If it pleases you to beat me, you will. If the sport loses its savour, you will stop.'

'My medicine doctor will tend to your wounds. You will be given good food and clean water, straw to sleep on. I will make you whole again. Shall I tell you why? Because I propose to remove your skin after your death, and from your hide I will make myself a hat and coat so that I too may pass for a white gentleman and travel in this first class which you have told me about. Do you approve of my plan?'

I was determined to deny the Chief the pleasure of seeing me quail.

'Your plan to turn me into a hat and coat is not a bad one. However, you seem to underestimate the measures necessary for you to pass yourself off as an Englishman. Moreover, it is my duty to warn you that my person, humble though it is, carries with it the protection of His Majesty the King of England.'

'Oh yes, King George. I hear he collects postage stamps and sticks them in a book. What is the purpose of this strange behaviour?'

'I warn you, Chief Jhorumpha, you dice with death when you impugn the honour of the King of England.'

'Why don't you invite him to my country so that we can wrestle?' The Chief laughed, and all the other warriors laughed along, even though not one of them spoke English. 'No, Railway Man, your stamp collecting King will not save you. You are not the first to come in search of the holy nuns. The sons of England are cry-babies. I have had many Englishmen in my cooking pot and they all cried.'

251

'This behaviour you describe is characteristic of an Italian, not an Englishman.'

'Are you sure?'

'No son of England would cry upon being put into a heathen cooking pot.'

'I am curious to test this hypothesis.'

'What? And ruin your new coat?'

'Yes, what a quandary I find myself in, the choice of the man you call Hobson, I believe. Perhaps I should be less ambitious and turn your hide instead into a travelling suitcase.'

Chapter 17

M
Y RESCUERS TOOK me to a hospital where the
doctors gave me an anti-tetanus injection that
made me very poorly. They called it an adverse
reaction and for a week I drifted in and out of consciousness, beset
by the most frightful dreams. And then on new year's eve, the last
day of God's Wonderful Railway, I opened my eyes at eight in the
morning to find a chap sitting on a chair next to my bed. He was
holding a cloth cap tightly in both hands and staring intently at
me. I was in a dormitory, coloured a drab shade of green, light-
ened with beige. The floor comprised square tiles in shades of
chocolate and fawn. Wintery sunlight filtered in softly from two
large windows at one end. At the other end was the door through
which now a nurse pushed a trolley from which she dispensed hot
drinks: tea, Milo, Ovaltine. Men lay awake, staring at the ceiling
or reading newspapers. There was a hum from somewhere. The
nurse, on seeing me awake, left the trolley and hurried out.

'Good morning,' I said to the man at my bedside.

'Are you feeling better, sir?'

'I'm really not sure if I could say, but I take that as a good
sign.'

'Yes, I fancy you would know if you weren't feeling so well.
My name is George Binks. I'm the chap you waved to from . . .
from . . .'

'I think it was a sewage treatment pool.'

'That's what they told me. Rotten place to find yourself. They said some toughs had thrown you in.'

'And hit me on the head with a shovel. I'm lucky to be alive, thanks to you. I owe you a great debt of gratitude.'

'It's not necessary to thank me, sir, I did what any Christian man would do. I've come here to ask a favour of you.'

'Of course, just name it.'

'Have you spoken to anyone about it all yet?'

'You are the first man I have spoken to since that night.'

'I wouldn't normally intrude like this, but you see, I recently became a father—'

'My congratulations.'

'Thank you. I'm a fireman for the Great Western Railway. I'm not sure if you have had many dealings with the railway. A lot of people have fanciful ideas about the driver and fireman. They imagine we are quite rich fellows but nothing could be further from the truth. It isn't easy making ends meet and now we have a new mouth to feed, well, I would be in an awful fix if I were to lose my employment.'

'But why should you do that? You saved my life.'

He looked down at the cap in his hands, and twisted it some more. 'This isn't easy for me to say, but there is no . . . well, let me put it this way. When you called to me from the water, what did you see?'

'I saw you leaning with half your body out of the window, with another chap holding on to your legs. And I have a suspicion you were trying to look into the compartment next to you. I also believe you had put out the light in your own compartment by unscrewing the bulb.'

'You are a sharp one.'

'Not that sharp, I don't know what you were doing. Were you playing a joke on a friend in the next compartment?'

'Not quite, sir.'

'My name is Jack Wenlock.'

'Not quite, Mr Wenlock. It pains me to say this, but I was spying on a chap in there with his sweetheart.'

'You were a peeping Tom?'

'I'm far from being the only one to do it. My driver and I were travelling home on the cushions . . . it's quite common.'

'Well, I don't know what to say.'

'If you could tell them you waved to me but not tell them what I was doing . . . I should be very grateful. I don't want to lose my job.'

'Mr Binks, your secret is safe with me. I can assure you, I would not dream of reporting the man who saved my life. All the same, I think it is my duty to warn you that if you persist in this activity it could lead to your ruin. I happen to know a driver by the name of Groates was killed doing precisely the same as you not two months ago. He hit a bridge, you see. And his fireman Mr Stalham has gone missing – hidden his face from the world for shame, I should imagine.'

Mr Binks shook his head. 'Oh no, sir, Fireman Stalham is not missing if you know where to look. He's working as a chauffeur for Lord Apsley.'

'I happen to know Lord Apsley's chauffeur is called Sturridge.'

'Whatever name he chooses to go by, it's the same chap. He's not hiding from the world for shame, as you put it, but to stay out of prison.'

'Well, then I will reassure him on that score. Although his employers will take a dim view of his activity as a peeping Tom it is hardly a crime worthy to send a man to prison for. What happened was a terrible accident.'

'That all depends on what he saw through the window of that train carriage, doesn't it?'

'And what did he see?'

'No, perhaps I've said too much.'

'What did he see? What could he see, that—'

'He saw two chaps.'

'Two chaps?'

'Behaving in a way . . . a way . . . they could be arrested for it.'

I sank back into my pillow and emitted a gentle puff of air and said softly, 'Two chaps. On the Great Western Railway . . .'

'Not just any chaps. One of them was rather important.'

'Who?'

'Lord Apsley. And he was with that other chap who hangs around with that sort. Cheadle Heath.'

'Cheadle Heath? No!'

'Do you know him?'

'Yes. But he's . . . he's not—'

'Everyone knows it.'

'But why would Fireman Stalham having witnessed such a thing go and work for Lord Apsley?'

'I expect for the same reason any man who had a family to feed would go and work for a man of means. The question, perhaps, should be why Lord Apsley would employ him knowing what he knows.'

'Well, why would he?'

'Because that way he can make sure Stalham shuts his trap.'
He stood up and said, 'Well, I've said my piece.'

After he left, the doctor arrived. I told him I was leaving that very minute and, although he deemed that unwise, he did not make a great effort to stand in my way. My clothes were returned and it seemed the hospital had been kind enough to have them dry-cleaned. The sight of them reminded me of that evening a week ago and of the chit of paper bearing the telephone number I should call. I fished it out of the trouser pocket only to discover that it, too, had been dry-cleaned and the number was no longer legible.

On my way out I ran into Ron Dingleman. He was walking along the corridor, wearing a dressing gown and pyjamas. He had a bandage round his forehead. We stopped and faced each other in the corridor as if meeting for the first time in many years.

'Where you off to all in a hurry?'

'I'm going to see Cheadle.'

'I fancy I should wish you a happy new year.'

'I would prefer it if you didn't, to be honest, Ron.'

He looked pained and nodded. 'Yes, there's not much happiness about that I can see.'

There was something about that phrase and the voice in which he uttered it that took me aback. This seemed to be a shadow of the Dingleman who faced me. All the vitality and cocksure insolence had gone; he was like a deflated balloon.

'What happened to your head?'

'Got hit by a hammer.'

'Oh Lord! How dreadful. Did someone attack you?'

'You could say that.' He seemed oddly uncertain. 'Did your girl enjoy the show?'

'Oh, Ron, they've taken her. To Room 42.'

He nodded as if this news didn't greatly surprise him. 'They said they would spare Magdalena if I gave them the letter. But she knew better than me, she knew better than to trust their word.'

'But where is Room 42?'

'I don't think it is anywhere in particular. Magdalena said they shoot people there.'

I looked at the bandage around his head. 'This chap who attacked you . . . I suppose you must have made a lot of enemies over the years.'

'Yes, but most of them are in the ground.'

'Do you know the man who did it?'

'Oh yes, known him all my life. You are looking at him.'

'Are you telling me you hit yourself with the hammer?'

'I am.'

'But what on earth for?'

'I've had enough of the place.'

'The hospital?'

'The world.'

I narrowed my eyes with puzzlement. Ron Dingleman really was the last person I would ever have expected to talk this way.

'That's not much of a reason.'

'My boy died.'

I paused in shock and cried, 'No!'

He gave a grimace in answer. He patted my arm as he moved past and said in parting, 'When you see Cheadle, tell him I know who stole the money from Kipper. I've always known.'

*   *   *

Cheadle stared up at me from his bed, sunk into his pillow like a stone thrown from a building landing in snow. He seemed to have shrunk, and receded from the world.

'You remember Tumby Woodside,' he said. 'The day Lord Apsley thrashed him to death.'

'Don't play games with me, Cheadle. You know very well I sat in the same assembly hall as you and watched.'

'Yes, I know. But there is so much you don't know.'

'What has Tumby got to do with this?'

'He was thrashed for stealing the money from Kipper's collecting box. But it wasn't him. It was me.'

I took a step back and almost lost my footing. If he had punched me on the nose the effect could not have been stronger. 'No, Cheadle.'

'Yes, Jack. I did it. And I watched Apsley beat Tumby knowing that he was innocent.'

'You stole from a dog?'

'Yes, I stole from a dog. That's another blot on my copybook.'

'I can't believe it.'

'It's not hard. I was fifteen and had never tasted chocolate. Then they painted that Lindt advertisement on the wall by the station, do you remember?'

'Of course.'

'Switzerland. You can't imagine what longing that picture unleashed in my heart. The Matterhorn so white, that spotless blue of the sky, the green grass and Magdalena as the milk maid . . . Where was this place? I thought it was called Lindt, a country near to Heaven. If you tasted the chocolate it would transport you there. That's what I thought. Every day I stared at it, Lindt. A funny word, but one that has come to dominate our lives, really, hasn't it?'

'I don't see how.'

'No, Jack, you don't. I never met anyone who was quite so good at not seeing the wood for the trees.' He reached across and grasped my hand. 'It's good to see you though.'

'I can't believe you watched him being thrashed like that,' I said.

'What would you have done?'

'I would never have stolen from Kipper.'

'I gave him some too.'

'Kipper?'

'He liked it. There was none left on his mouth afterwards.'

'Jolly lucky for you. If Lord Apsley had seen it—'

'It wouldn't have made any difference. He knew I had done it. Don't ask me how, he was always watching me. He used it against me, you see. I had to do what he wanted.'

'Beastliness!'

'Yes, Jack, beastliness.'

'When?'

'All my life. I can't stop, even though I want to. I rather fancy it is the same power that the torturer has over the man he torments on the rack. It's a form of bewitchment. It never goes. I don't want ever to see him again, but still I do. I don't expect you to understand and, to be frank, I don't greatly give much of a damn whether you do or not. It's all wretched.'

'Why didn't you . . . tell on him?'

'Think about it. Tumby was thrashed for stealing. The evidence was the chocolate around his mouth and the Lindt wrapper in his pocket. Where did they come from?'

'A kind gentleman in the street gave them to him.'

'I gave them to him.'

'But—'

'I gave them to him. Do you know what that means?'

'You . . . he . . . why didn't he say?'

For answer Cheadle simply stared at me, eyes glittering with a lifetime's accumulated pain.

'He took the beating rather than betray his friend.'

This time he spoke, but in a whisper so soft it wouldn't have disturbed a mouse. 'Yes.' Tears welled up at the corners of his eyes. 'I warned you. I told you to take your happiness and be grateful for it, not to inquire into things that would not make you happy, but you chose to ignore me and here you are.'

'But Lord Apsley . . .'

'He's not the man everyone thinks he is. He's rotten, Jack, rotten right through. A coward and a—'

'I know he's rotten, Cheadle. It's all rotten. But surely he's not a coward. He's a hero . . . isn't he?'

'What? The hero of Elandslaagte? No, Jack, he's not. Did you never wonder what it was, the shame deeper than beastliness? It's blubbing. At Elandslaagte he cried for his mum on the field of battle. The men refused to serve under him; he had previously had a man shot for blubbing, you see. That's why they sent him home and gave him the Gosling project.'

'I went to Povington Priory. I saw the graves. The nuns who stayed behind, I suspect they were killed. By our chaps.'

'Yes, I daresay they were.'

'Nuns, Cheadle.'

'Oh, fuck the nuns!'

'How dare you!'

'Fuck the nuns, Jack, fuck them all. Who cares about the nuns?'

'I thought we all did.'

'I don't.'

'Don't you care about England?'

'Not particularly. Did she ever care for me?'

Cheadle lay still for a while. The distant tower of St Bede's chimed nine. Machines hummed downstairs, there were shouts. The smell of chemical cleaning agents stored in the room seemed to grow stronger.

'Cheadle, where is Cadbury? I believe you know.'

'I don't know where he is now. I hope he's still abroad, for his own good. Did you read his case file?'

'Yes.'

'There's a chap who keeps popping up in the story, Hershey Lindt.'

'Yes, he's everywhere. An exporter of elephant-foot umbrella stands, from Port Bismarck, big-game hunter, seafarer. I've sent him a telegram.'

'Didn't the name strike you? The Lindt advertisement. Chocolate?'

'Hershey, Pennsylvania. Chocolate Town, USA. Are you saying Hershey Lindt was Cadbury? That's rather a silly game to play, isn't it?'

'Is it? Quite droll, I would have thought.' A rare smile cracked the mask of his face. He sighed the world-weary exhalation of a man whose sinews still function but whose heart has given up.

'So, was it all a lie then, about you living in sin with that woman?'

'Oh no, it was a blessed truth! Her name was Florence. She

was a shop girl, in a haberdasher's. I had an office in Cheltenham Spa station at the time—'

'Which one?'

'Malvern Road. I caught her standing on a footbridge about to do some desperate mischief to herself. She pretended at first she was just watching the trains, but it's odd how you can tell, isn't it? Some instinct warns you. I persuaded her to go with me to a café for a cup of tea. She told me she had lost her position as a result of a misunderstanding and did not know how she would support herself. Her husband had been a merchant seaman during the war and died when his ship went down in the channel. I wouldn't say she was pretty, Jack, I rather think life had taken its toll on her, but occasionally I managed to make her laugh and when she did . . . well, she made me laugh too. I insisted on taking her home to her digs and made her promise to meet me again in two days' time, to reassure me that she was feeling better. Then I did something rather extraordinary. I went to see her employer and persuaded him to take her back. Well, you should have seen her face when we met two days later. She gave me a bobbin. I expect you will laugh. What would a chap like me need with a bobbin? She laughed too, she said it was all she had. I've still got it.' He stopped and pressed his lips together, and his brow creased. 'I've still got it.' He went quiet for a while, before continuing.

'She didn't last long back in her job. Someone had been telling tales about her. When she was dismissed again, we went to Ilfracombe together, posing as man and wife. I arranged it with one of our railway landladies, it was foolish I suppose, but once in a while everyone deserves the chance to be foolish. We had such a lovely time, walking along the prom holding hands and eating ice cream. In the evening we ate fish and chips and sat on a bench and admired the illuminations. We knew it couldn't last, even though neither of us could have said exactly why. So we gulped our pleasure and did not give a fig for tomorrow. I've discovered this is the only true philosophy. You stumble on happiness but rarely, like you stumble on half a crown in the road. When that happens the only sensible policy is spend it and have the pleasure of it. Put no store in tomorrow. When we returned, I was dismissed. Someone had been telling tales on me, too. So we moved to Hereford, where we hoped we would not be known, but misfortune dogged us all the way. We had no money, life became very difficult. That's when we began to quarrel. I still shudder to recall those fights. The words we exchanged. That's when I raised my hand to her. I rue the day, Jack. Then she left. That's it really.' He gave a thin smile. 'But Ilfracombe ... that was ... remember those summer trips to Barmouth?'

'Yes, I remember.'

'Weren't they grand?'

'They were, Cheadle.' He gave me a sharp stare and suddenly looked relieved. He hadn't been wrong. Those days at Barmouth as children had been grand.

'But who could have been telling tales on you?'

'Who do you think?'

'Not Apsley?'

'Who else? Who else in the world would care enough? He wanted me back. He needed me.'

'What a rotten, rotten bloody scoundrel!'

'He's the unhappiest man I ever met. You know what he wanted, don't you?'

'I think I would rather you didn't tell me.'

'It's not what you imagine. He wanted me to hold him and say, "There, there . . ."'

'There, there?'

'Does it surprise you?'

'Of course it does. Lord Apsley, the hero of Elandslaagte. He would have had you shot for saying something like that.'

'That's how it works, isn't it? The mind.'

'I don't pretend to know how the mind works. The stuff I've heard, about these analyst chaps . . . sounds like mumbo jumbo to me.'

'I expect most of it is. But some things you see for yourself in life. We hate in others the faults we deny in ourselves. Those analyst chaps have a word for it, but I can't remember what it is. It hardly matters.'

'Why then, after all that, did you go back to him?'

'Because I am a coward. Always was.'

'No.'

'If I didn't go back, he was going to tell the Dingleman about Tumby. Dingleman always swore he would kill the real culprit if he ever found out who it was. He made a promise to Magdalena. As I said, I'm a coward.'

'But the Dingleman knew about Tumby. He knew it was you who stole the money.'

'No?'

'I saw him before I came here. He told me to tell you. I think he's always known.'

He nodded slowly, as if this crowning irony was no more than he deserved. 'As I said, Jack, I'm a coward. I used to envy Cadbury so much. He wasn't scared of anything.'

'You were what you were. You didn't choose it, no more than Cadbury chose to be fearless.'

'Yes, you are right. We don't choose to be the way we are. But there are times in life when we can choose. You now, Jack. Think on what I have told you. We had a lovely time at Ilfracombe. We stayed a week, but my only regret is we didn't stay a month.'

'Cheadle, how can I find Room 42?'

'Not easily, Jack. In the old days it was easy. They used to wear plumed hats and big fat jewels to help you. They turned up on your wedding day and debauched your bride. If they didn't like you they took you to the Tower. They left you in no doubt. But they are smarter now, more subtle. They don't advertise. They are sly and conceal the vulgarity of their power behind a facade of stupefying dullness.'

'But the . . . the wickedness of it.'

'No, they are not even wicked. They don't have the passion for it.'

'If they are so powerful, what are they afraid of?'

'You, Jack. And me. People. They are afraid of the common folk.'

THE BOY'S OWN
RAILWAY GOSLING ANNUAL

Vol.VII	1931	Price: 1/-

Replies to our readers' letters

S. MARIGOLD, TAUNTON—There are no recorded instances of a cow flying through the air after having been hit by an express train.

FRUSTRATED, ST IVES—Wouldn't it be better to follow the example set by our Lord and forgive him? He is only eight.

THE CONTINUING ADVENTURES OF RAILWAY GOSLING CADBURY HOLT – ON THE TRAIL OF THE MISSING NUNS!

Through the Land of the Giants

There were five porters ahead of me and five behind and each was laden with a basket on his head, except the one immediately behind me who held a spear pointed at my kidneys. The baskets contained gifts, and goods to exchange for the supplies that we would need. I carried the box containing the Chief's tribute. It gave off an odour of carrion and by noon of the first day had turned black with flies.

There was no attempt made to catch game along the track. Instead we ate dried unleavened breads and strips of cured meat that they assured me through a series of preposterous mime displays was monkey; but yet I declined because of a presentiment deep within my bowels that it may have been the forbidden flesh of that particular breed of ape that the natives call 'monkey who wears a hat'. I discovered later that there was a reason for not stopping to hunt. The bearers were most anxious to complete the journey as soon as possible as they were all mortally afraid of Mama !Mkuu. Most of the time the forest canopy closed above our heads, cutting off the light and making our world as gloomy as a coal mine. But occasionally we would enter an area less densely entangled and lo! The mountains would loom above us, impossibly high, pale green in hue and snow-capped.

Behind us the forest retreated until we could turn and look out upon a carpet of green stretching for hundreds of miles and from which no individual tree could any longer be distinguished. The River Pishon glinted like pewter in the green, and as the afternoon faded and the sun began to wane, this colour brightened to liquid silver. It began to grow chilly. As we climbed, the wall of the mountain grew sheer and a stone staircase began to traverse its face, moving horizontally. The sky blushed and ravished our hearts with a rose garden in the clouds, just as we arrived at a door in the edge of our world and which the very sun begged us to desist from entering. From a distance I had assumed it to be a rock outcrop but, as we approached, the brooding dark resolved itself into twin effigies of giant faces set in the towers overseeing an entrance into the mountain. The faces had the ancient haunting quality of those one finds in the postcards travellers send from Easter Island, or in the Sumerian friezes at the British Museum. The lips were carved into a snarl betokening their haughty contempt for us feeble leprechaun invaders; but mostly was my heart abashed by the cold obsidian of their eyes. They seemed to contain within their dark pools the cruel certainty of those lost giants that we were unworthy vermin and our tiny hearts would be crushed by the unbearable secrets and wonders contained in the world to which we insisted on travelling against all sensible advice; crushed as the Soley-Soley moth beneath the elephant's foot. We passed the gate; our hearts quailed and the very core of our being was sickened with presentiments too heavy for mortal flesh to bear. We passed into a tunnel that had been bored through the face of the mountain. The tunnel was dark, sporadically illuminated by the flickering light of torches set in the wall. The air was thick with the reek of burning pitch. The light of the torches writhed like drunken plague victims in the dance of death, and the wall sparkled, returning the reflex of the flames from mirrors that I knew with rising terror were human eyes lodged in a thousand faces belonging to a thousand heads, spitted on pikes set in the walls, and which lined the way like a procession of sightseers at the Devil's Coronation. This was the work, they said, of Mama !Mkuu.

Chapter 18

As I walked through town Cheadle's words echoed in my mind like footsteps in a long corridor. They are afraid of the common folk. I now knew what I had to do. I would need to return to the station to fetch the implement that would be the undoing of the people from Room 42: my Great Western fireman's shovel. There were not many folk about, it was still early, but those that I saw seemed already possessed of the anticipation that builds on new year's eve. The ringing of bells heralded the arrival of a fire engine. It raced past me. I looked up and saw smoke above the rooftops, coming from the direction of the town square. People began to move in that general direction. Even before I reached the square I could feel the warmth. Mr Dombey's shop was ablaze, fiercely so. Orange and yellow flames roared from the window, like rivers of fire disappearing upwards into the night. I stood behind the lines of people gathered to watch, held back by the heat. The firemen stood far back too, aiming their hoses at the flames but unable to enter. Inside, a black timber crashed down, throwing off showers of sparks. A wooden framed building filled with dust-dry books, there was no way to stop it. A man in front of me explained to the new arrivals: the owner was dead, they took him out in an ambulance earlier, before the blaze fully took hold. Overcome by the smoke. It seemed a fitting end for the shop that had printed the missing Gosling annual, on this the last night in existence of the Great Western Railway. I was sick at heart and weary. When I retrieved the shovel from my office I found also a telegram slipped under the door. It was from Hershey Lindt.

HAVE NEWS THAT MAY SAVE YOUR LIFE STOP ARRIVING
BRISTOL 31 DEC SHIP KOWLOON STAR STOP CABOT WHARF
BERTH 5 STOP MEET AT SEAMAN'S MISSION 10.25PM STOP
WILL WAIT 30 MIN NO MORE STOP

I glanced at the clock. It was just after ten. There was a train to Bristol this evening at six which would arrive at 10.05. The train to Chirk took an hour and twenty. The walk to Povington Priory about a quarter of an hour. This should give me more than enough time to get there and back in time for the evening train to Bristol. It would depend on how long I spent at the priory. But how long does a man need to dig up a grave?

It was foggy as I alighted from the train at Chirk, a cold clammy veil that contained pinpricks of water which the wind puffed into my face, like those greenfly sprays that lie on the potting-shed table. There were probably a thousand other men carrying a shovel that afternoon on the eve of new year, but I felt as if the whole world could see into my heart and discern my terrible purpose. The walk from Chirk railway station to the priory seemed much longer this time. There was no soul about, and no owl hooted to mock me. I stood at the grave's edge, stared down and slammed the shovel into the earth. *To the layman, a shovel is a shovel, but not to the fireman who wields it. The GWR shovel*

is considered to be the best, even by the men from the other companies . . .
The blade sliced into the earth. I put my foot on it and pressed my weight down. I levered the handle and forced the clay apart. The shovel fell again. I dug. Before long the metal hit wood. Ten minutes later and sufficient soil had been removed. I stepped down and knelt on the coffin. The wood was wet and spongy, rotten. It did not put up much resistance. I pulled pieces away to make a hole; it was no more difficult to break apart than the crust of a meat pie. A smell rose up, similar to the smell from a sack of potatoes that has lain at the back of a garden shed, in which the potatoes have been consumed by a white rot. I clicked on my torch light and trained the beam down into the hole. It gleamed on bone. Yellow. The thin eggshell of a nasal cavity. Darkness either side. Below that the gleaming grin of teeth. And before the teeth, five grey twigs pressed against another five twigs; these were her fingers pressed together in prayer. Her wrists were enclosed by metal bracelets that were joined by a chain. Shackles. They glimmered in the light of my torch. The metal was darkened with a bloom that was familiar to a man who had worked on the footplate of a steam engine. The metal had been scorched. They are afraid of the common folk, Cheadle had said. And what of me? Had I become a Jacobin?

A voice broke the silence with an insolence that I recognised. 'Are you having a nice dig?'

I turned. It was the boy, Mr Young, who appeared in my office the day after Jenny came, and whom I had threatened to hit with the shovel I was now holding.

'This is a revolver, in case you were wondering.' He wiggled his hand and the barrel of his pistol sparkled. 'I seldom get a chance to use it, so bear that in mind.'

'Is that your way of saying you would like to use it?'

'Oh yes.'

'Have you ever shot a man? I can tell that you haven't.'

'Well, there's always a first time, and I doubt I will have many opportunities as good as this. You are trespassing on Army land, probably a spy I shouldn't wonder. There would be very little paperwork. Maybe none.'

'You've chosen a good spot for it.'

'Yes, it's quite a popular place for getting rid of nosy parkers.'

'What do you want me to do?'

'Turn round and walk towards the gate. I will be right behind, hoping you give me a good reason to shoot.'

I did as I was told. At the gate he directed me right and past the great hall on to the main thoroughfare. I walked slowly up the road, wondering if there was any point in running. We passed the ruined post office and came to what had once been a village hall. A seal grey Morris 1000 was parked outside. There was music from within. I paused at the threshold and the boy gave me an encouraging prod in the back with his revolver. I pushed the door open and walked in. The room was mostly bare. Some paper decorations hung from the light fittings, paper chains in a gaudy rainbow. A trestle table was laid along one wall. It was covered in a festive paper tablecloth and the remains of a small buffet; there were sandwiches and cake and jelly, and some white paper plates. A gramophone record was playing, a voice crooning 'A Nightingale Sang in Berkeley Square'. Chairs were stacked against the opposite wall and five of them were gathered in front of the buffet table, around an upturned tea chest that acted as a table. Somehow it accentuated the emptiness of the hall. Mr Old sat on a chair, smoking a cigarette. 'This is a pleasant surprise,' he said.

'I found him doing some gardening,' said Young.

'Come to wish us a happy new year, no doubt,' said Old. His voice was slurring, infused with a bitter tone that often comes to unhappy men after the initial joy of a drink has faded. 'Digging, eh? Are you rehearsing for a part in *Hamlet*? Alas, poor Yorick . . . is that who you are, Jack? Hamlet? Are you well? You don't appear to be yourself.'

'I'm not sure if I am myself. To tell the truth, I am no longer sure I know what myself is.'

'So you are Hamlet. Or have you come to bandy modernist philosophy?'

'There's nothing modern about it. I think it's pretty old-fashioned. A man dedicates his life to the service of those he was told were his betters and he discovers one day that the people he had served were rotten scoundrels—'

'Oh dear, who told him?'

'You are a lot of scoundrels. Where is Lord Apsley?'

Mr Old chuckled quietly to himself. 'You missed him. Is he a scoundrel too?'

'He is. Moreover, I have reason to suspect that His Majesty the King might also be a scoundrel.'

Mr Old gave a sour laugh.

'You should be careful what you say. Mr Young might shoot you for treason. I'm sure he'd like to.'

I turned to face Mr Young and raised the shovel.

He smiled but there was fear, too, in his eyes. He said, 'Drop the shovel.'

I tightened my grip on the handle. I raised the shovel as if winding up for a swing. It was a bluff and it fell flat. He stepped smartly backward, out of range, and levelled the pistol at my chest.

Mr Old said, 'I'd drop the shovel, if I were you. He'd like nothing more than to kill a man. He thinks it will compensate for all the things wrong with his character. That one simple act of murder. He's like a savage who eats a lion's heart thinking it will give him the lion's courage. I try telling him it won't make any difference, but he won't listen. He's young.' He picked up a whisky tumbler and swirled the contents before taking a gulp in a sharp and world-hating act.

'It's up to you, Wenlock,' said Young.

I lowered the shovel but did not drop it.

'Suppose you tell us what you are doing here, digging things . . .' said Old. He reached for his glass on the table and finding it empty, stopped and looked puzzled. 'And calling the King names.'

'What have you done with Jenny?'

'I'm afraid you're a bit late. You've missed her, she was here but she had to . . . leave.'

'Leave to where?'

'Somewhere she will be taken care of,' said Old. 'She got a bit upset when Mr Young told her that her aunt had died. Understandable, I suppose. There is no easy way to break such news.' He was quite morosely drunk now and giving vent to a lifetime's pent-up bitterness.

'Isn't that right, Mr Young?' There was no answer. 'Lord Apsley took her away. He'll be back in a while. You can have a drink. Give the man a drink.'

Young looked affronted and said, 'Why should I?'

'Of course,' said Old, 'in this sort of set-up the man with the gun almost never has to make the drinks. And I don't see how I can oblige, I can't stand up from my chair.'

'I don't want a drink. I desire you to tell me where they have taken Jenny.'

Mr Old looked at me through a mist of confusion and blinked it away. 'You know, I'm not sure if I can remember.'

'Room 42,' said Young. 'That's where she is. Trouble is, no one knows where that is. Maybe it's here.'

'It used to be a hotel room,' said Old. 'All decent hotels have a Room 42. You could rely on it. It was where a chap would go when he'd let the side down, to blow his brains out.'

'Your girl got quite flighty when we told her about her aunt,' said Young. 'Caused quite a scene.'

'Yes, Mr Young had to lay the law down, didn't you, eh? He's good at laying the law down with people who can't hit back.'

'Shut up!' said Young.

'But what am I saying? She did hit back, didn't she? Gave you quite a wallop. Although not compared to the one you gave her.'

I faced Mr Young with eyes narrowing. 'Did you . . . raise your hand to Jenny?'

He looked at me and, even though he was pointing a gun at me, he swallowed with fear. 'No,' he said.

Old gave a bitter and mirthless laugh designed to contradict that utterance.

'Where has Apsley taken her?'

'To get some steak,' said Old. 'To put on her blue eye. We only have sausage rolls.'

'It was her own fault,' said Young. 'Silly cow.'

Inside me, a cold fury was building.

'Own fault,' Old repeated.

'Shut your trap,' Young said. 'I've had as much as I can take from you.'

'Damn fool was supposed to take care of her.'

'I said shut it.' He turned to me. 'Your girl is fine, she just slipped, that's all.'

Old mumbled into this whisky glass. 'Slipped.'

Young flinched. 'In fact, she was jolly lucky she was with me, and not him. He's a fine one with the ladies.'

Old laughed, the way a man does sometimes when words hit home.

'Yes, why don't you ask him what happened to Sister Beatrice?' He raised his voice, addressing Old. 'Tell him what you did to her.'

Old made a sigh of contempt.

'She's here, you know. You can see her if you like. But you'll have to dig. He buried her deep . . . isn't that right?'

I cast a glance at Mr Old.

'Mr Old gave her a lift in his car, didn't you? Always the gentleman.' He returned his attention to me. 'By the way, if you were looking for her, you were digging in the wrong spot.'

'My supposition was that you people did something terrible to her so that it could appear she had gone missing. And you could blame her for the fire.'

'Bravo,' said Young.

'I didn't want to believe such a thing.'

'Too bad, as the Americans say.'

I turned to Old. 'If you don't mind me saying, Mr Old, I think you are . . . well, I don't quite know how to find the words. I've never met . . . never believed an Englishman could behave in such an unconscionable manner.'

Young sniggered. Old intoned softly,

> *The river of death has brimmed his banks,*
> *And England's far, and Honour a name,*
> *But the voice of a schoolboy rallies the ranks,*
> *Play up! play up! and play the game!*

He gave another sour laugh. 'That's what old Apsley sings when he's in his cups, isn't it?' He looked up from his glass and it seemed as if the alcoholic fug that had clouded his brains and slurred his words cleared for a second or so. 'Believe me, sonny Jim, you don't win a war by playing the game. You win by being the first to gouge the other chap's eye out with your thumb.'

Our attention was distracted by the sound of a car pulling up. Doors opened and were slammed. We looked to the door. Three people came in. Sturridge, the chauffeur, Lord Apsley, and Jenny, her hands bound with packing string, in front of her like a posy. She turned to me, and cried out, 'Jack!' The area around her right eye shone a livid blue, but worse than this were the dark rivulets of kohl down her cheeks that indicated she had been crying. She darted towards me. Mr Young, keeping the gun trained on me, took a step to one side and shoved her violently with the open palm of his hand. She tripped and fell heavily on her face, unable to use her hands to cushion the blow. A droplet of blood fell from her nostril on to the cold floor. 'You swine!' I said to Young and swung the shovel. It was the same fluid movement of a fly-fishing man casting his hook. The blade that had seen so many breakfasts sizzle and fry in the firebox smashed into his ear and crushed it as if it had been a fried egg. He cried, 'Oh!' and in the same moment he fired the pistol. I should have been dead, but having stepped towards Jenny, and his not having corrected his aim, I was hit not in the chest but in the left bicep, where the bullet passed straight through. At the same time he fell to the ground, reeling from the shock of the GWR shovel hitting his ear. I looked down. My left arm hung loose, my shirt sleeve became hot and wet with blood. It hurt like blazes. Young had lost hold of the gun and was still bewildered in a world of pain and confusion. Driven by instinct he fumbled like a blind man for the gun on the floor. I kicked it away, but too forcefully. It came to rest at Lord Apsley's feet. He did not bend down but, keeping his eyes on me, reached into his coat and drew out his own gun. It was a Webley Mark II .38. The official service pistol of an officer in the British Army. 'More than happy to shoot you, Jack, if that is your wish,' he said.

I turned my gaze to him.

'Drop the shovel, there's a good chap.' Our eyes met. 'Sturridge, pick up the gun.' The chauffeur obliged.

'Now, Wenlock,' said Apsley, 'put down the shovel. Do it now. I would no more hesitate to shoot you than I would a wog.'

Sturridge pressed the gun barrel into the temple of Apsley, and said, 'Nor would I you, you old queen.'

Lord Apsley did not move, hardly reacted; but the tiniest change in the way he set his jaw indicated that, along with everyone else in the room, he knew the tables had been turned. Sturridge continued to press the barrel of the gun against the lord's temple whilst gently reaching round and taking the Webley service pistol. He held it out to me without looking at me. I walked over and took it. Lord Apsley asked if he might sit down.

279

His tone was calm, cold, and contained within it the sense of repressed fury, a fury I saw once long ago at the orphanage when he beat Tumby in a manner out of all proportion to his minor crime. A chair was provided and he lowered himself gratefully, exhausted. Mr Old wore a grin on his face, an exaggerated one, partly from the last stages of drunkenness, but partly of amusement as if this were the best joke yet. On the floor, Young made an attempt to rise, but the gasp of pain that accompanied the attempt showed that the shovel had exacted a heavy toll on him. He wasn't seriously injured but for a while, at least, it didn't look like he would be going anywhere. Blood trickled from his ear.

Jenny, Sturridge and I walked out into the cold afternoon. Sturridge shot the tyres out on the Morris 1000 and we left in Lord Apsley's Rover.

We made good time driving back to Weeping Cross. Sturridge was a good driver. There was little traffic and he drove fast without in any way being risky. The mood in the car was a cocktail of conflicting emotions, perhaps dominated by a repressed exultancy and disbelief at what had transpired. There can't have been another group of travellers on new year's eve with quite such a strange tale to tell.

'I really can't thank you enough for that Gosling's Friend badge,' said Sturridge as he kept a keen eye on the road ahead. 'My boy found it in his stocking on Christmas morning. His little face really was a picture.'

As we drove through the darkened countryside, Jenny helped me remove my coat and jacket and attended to the bullet wound. She tore a strip of silk from the lining of her coat and fastened a bandage as best she could.

'I wonder what will become of me now,' said Sturridge.

'Mr Sturridge, you must become Fireman Stalham once again.'

'Chance would be a fine thing.'

'I see no reason why you shouldn't. You really have done very little wrong, other than to be the victim of an unfortunate accident. My employment officially extends until the middle of the month, and I shall submit my report. I will say poor Driver Groates was trying to retrieve his hat which had blown out when he collided with the bridge. I shall recommend you be reinstated. Provided you stick to the story, there is no one to gainsay it.'

'Except Lord Apsley.'

'What would he gain by revealing the truth?'

'He might want to be awkward. He won't forget what happened back there. We've stolen his car, have we not?'

'Since you are the chauffeur, I'm not sure if it counts as stealing, but it hardly matters. I recommend you remove yourself to a safe place and telephone Lord Apsley. You must tell him that you know all about his cowardice in the face of the enemy, how he cried for his mother on the battlefield.'

'I could not condemn a man for crying, Mr Wenlock. There is a lot in this world that can make a man cry.'

'I couldn't either, but this man once had a soldier shot for crying, and yet cried himself. It is no shame in my book, but it is in his and we must take advantage of that. I expect those chaps at his club, Marmaduke's, esteem him quite highly?'

'Oh indeed. Old soldier, they all look up to him.'

'Then I imagine he would be loath for them to learn the truth about him. I expect, too, in the conduct of your duties as a chauffeur, you have witnessed him in numerous other indiscretions?'

'It would make your toes curl what I've seen.'

'There you go then. You merely have to make a deal – your silence for his. I can't see what he would have to gain by disagreeing. After all, the very reason he took you into employ as his chauffeur was to shut you up.'

The clocks of the town were striking a quarter past five as he dropped us at the station. We shook hands and made our parting. Since we still had time to spare, Jenny and I went to my office. It was cold and dark but strangely comforting. Once inside, Jenny spun round then jumped into my arms. I held her with my good arm, for a while, as the other hung limp by my side. I pressed my cold cheek on to the silky top of her hair. A distant rumble approached, the floor hummed, the room filled with the smell of sulphur before fading again. The 5.17 to Hereford, just like on the first day she came to my office. Jenny pulled back and looked up into my face. Her eyes glittered in the darkness.

'You never gave me a Gosling's Friend badge, you rotter.'

'I would have, but I thought . . .'

'What?'

'I was worried you might consider it beneath you.'

'Shows you how much you know me then, doesn't it?'

'Yes, yes, I expect it does.'

There was a slight pause and Jenny said, 'That was your cue to say you would like to get to know me better.'

'Oh yes, yes, I would.'

'It works better if I don't have to prompt you.'

'Yes, I know. But I'm really not very good at—'

'I know.'

Half her face was darker than the room; the right-hand edge held a pale yellow gleam from outside. There was an intensity to the light that suggested the snow was sticking on the awning above the platform. We listened to the shrill cry of a whistle, shouts, doors slamming. I moved a strand of hair from the corner of her mouth and touched her bruised eye. She flinched.

'What beasts these people are,' I said.

'They killed the man in the bookshop. Mr Dombey. They started the fire. I heard them talking about it.'

'Why would they do such a thing?'

'They think he might be Cadbury.'

'No,' I whispered. I squeezed my eyes closed at the horror of this casual murder of an innocent man. 'No.' I picked up the telegram from the table. 'Cadbury is Hershey Lindt. I'm sure of it. He's arriving tonight at Bristol.'

We caught the York to Bristol Temple Meads. It would be the last journey the train would make as part of the Great Western Railway. Tomorrow the train would make the same journey at the same time, but it would be different. I did not know in precisely what way, but it would be different, and not as good. The thing that made it different, the thing that would be gone after midnight, is not something you can see. Not something you can touch or hold. You cannot even rightly say what it is. It's like when you walk into a church and you lower your voice. You feel something you cannot describe. For hundreds of years simple folk would have gathered there and looked up in hope or fear. Over the generations the something accumulates. It gets into the old wood and stone, the way perfume left in a drawer leaves a scent that lingers long after the perfume bottle has gone. You cannot hold it in your hand, or put it in a bottle, you cannot point to it or describe how to capture it. You cannot name it. But the strongest things can be things like this. All over the land people meet and part, they undertake journeys that they hope will change their lives, they return from journeys a different person to the one that left. This is the perfume of a railway station. In a church it is the smell of mildew and candlewax, or wood polish and soft disinfectant on tiled floors, dusty cassocks and mouldy air from high in the roof where it is always chilly, or oil lamps and brass polish. In a railway station it is smoke and steam, sulphur and ash; or wet raincoats and wet dogs, carbolic and coal tar soap, Kiwi dark tan shoe polish, lady's perfume from Boots, hot Bovril and tea from flasks; tears. It is the accumulation of joy that builds in the heart when people are reunited with those they love, or the sadness when they part at the ticket barrier. The paraphernalia of the station platform, the trolleys and porters, the bags, the trunks, the hanging signs and enamel Player's signs, the gleaming track and distant signals, all these are props on the stage of our lives. They quicken the heart as we scan the horizon for the first signs, the little puffs and far-off wail. The railway journey is a small piece of wonder in our sombre lives. It is always undertaken with a secret thrill at the possibility of what may happen. It is a thing called Hope.

Our world as we steamed through the night was a dim compartment lit by yellow lights that were reflected in the dark glass and seemed to accompany us outside too, a second room containing the both of us, travelling alongside our train. As we journeyed, I mentally composed the report I would write on behalf of Fireman Stalham; and I pondered the telephone call he should make to Lord Apsley. As events were to transpire, Fireman Stalham was later reinstated to his former employ without needing to make the telephone call. Cheadle broke off relations with Lord Apsley, and some time towards the end of January, Apsley travelled to a cold and deserted seaside town where he went to the desk of a drab hotel and asked for Room 42. He had no suitcase and said he wished to retire early without taking dinner. He ordered instead a glass of whisky. About an hour after it was delivered they heard a shot.

We spent most of the journey lost in our own thoughts. From time to time, wayside halts or crossing gates would rush up like ghosts and disappear again just as fast. For a brief moment there would be half a glimpse; the five white bars of the gate, and a disc the colour of blood; a man and boy and dog, standing by the gates; a car waiting perhaps, but not many cars tonight; as midnight approached, fewer people were travelling. Our train was nearly empty. We sat in a dark cell, like two people posing for a photograph. Sometimes, we saw the lights of hamlets where folk would be preparing for the arrival of the new year. There was an otherworldly quality to the prospect, as if we were viewing the passage of their lives from a remote height and had been granted a privileged view that revealed their urgency, the way our lives pass by sometimes, flash by like a train in the night, and it reminded me of the words that Cheadle had uttered with so much passion when he told me about Florence. We all assumed the episode with his lover was a source of perennial regret to him, but in truth it was the one thing in his life he did not regret. The single episode of joy that would nourish his heart like honey as he looked back on his life from his death bed. Cheadle did not give a damn for his blotted copybook, and what after all was that but a means to blind us, to conceal from us the truth? It shocked me that a man could be made so blind, have the course of his whole life determined by such a childish admonition as a blotted copybook. I knew with a pain in my heart that I had been the most blind of all. For had I not so arranged my life, this wonderful precious gift that my mother . . . yes, I had so often dreamed of her making that lonely journey on the 27 bus to the orphanage, but had I ever really understood the pain it must have caused her to give me up? A mother who gives up her son so that he will have a chance in life? For that act contains within it the recognition that the circumstances of her life were so broken and without hope that they could never be fixed, and she gives up all hope for herself and invests it in the boy, believing that those to whom she entrusts his future will honour that covenant. But they cheated her. Cheadle was right. We had all been taught to scorn him, but he had been the wise one.

Another wayside halt swept into view, a man alone at the crossing gate staring with wistful confusion at the thunder of the passing train, snowflakes swirling sadly about his face. I turned to Jenny and asked her to marry me. I was going to explain to her the urgency, how we must hurry because tonight held such a special status in the annals of days, because on the stroke of midnight the authority vested in the captain of a ship and the driver of a Great Western Express to join man and woman in the bond of matrimony would be rescinded. But I said it not, because Jenny said yes, yes, yes, before the words of my explanation could even form. And then she kissed me and pressed her face against mine, and I realised that it no longer mattered if we were married tonight or five minutes after midnight, because I no longer gave a hoot.

THE BOY'S OWN
RAILWAY GOSLING ANNUAL

Vol. VII   1931   Price: 1/-

Replies to our readers' letters

MISS DAISY C., PINNER—No English schoolboy has ever been hit on the head by a falling meteorite. You will have to find other methods of dealing with your brother.

HARRY BIGGINS ESQ., INVERNESS—It is true that the eye in certain specialised ophthalmic procedures can be removed from its socket and reinserted, all the while still attached to the optic nerve. While outside the socket, however, it does not 'see' anything. Even if it did, no surgeon would be so frivolous as to perform the trick you describe.

QUENTIN PEASWORTHY, WINCHESTER—The effect on your cook, though dramatic, would not be as you envisage. Steamrollers operate more like the iron your housekeeper uses on your shirts. Only in cartoons do they flatten everything in their path.

THE CONTINUING ADVENTURES OF RAILWAY GOSLING
CADBURY HOLT – ON THE TRAIL OF THE MISSING NUNS!

A Prospect of Havilah

But this was no simple tunnel through a mountain, it was a staircase to another world, an ancient land older than time itself, begotten in the deep earth's womb. There was no sun and no source for the light that we could see, it was everywhere and nowhere, as if the world itself glowed like the embers of a fire. There was vegetation, not the soft and smiling trees we had left on the surface but dark and stunted cauliflowers larger than a man at which buzzed winged lobsters that snapped at us with their dark pincers as we passed. We stood on a ledge and looked out upon the land. Black, still waters glistened and the leader of our party gave me to understand through a simple pantomime of a man writhing in a deathly agony that I was not to drink the water. But fool that I was, so parched was my throat, that I could not forbear to drink some droplets from the calyx of a flower and within an hour was afflicted with a terrible delirium. I was unable to walk and the porters carried me trussed on a pole in the way I had seen them do with their favourite hunted food, chimpanzee. For a week I raved, as we slowly traversed that blasted world, and what dread visions and phantasms appeared to me during that mania! I saw the towers and broken spires of a shattered city standing beside a sea that gleamed like the eye of the leviathan in the deep. Sleep withheld her gentle grace from me and I beheld the days as wide-eyed and fearful as men in gaols who await the kiss of Caiaphas at dawn.

At times I imagined myself being attacked by giant birds, but instead of claws raking the top of my head, it was the feet of angels that scuffed me. Angels? I know not what other word to use although I stretch the term beyond breaking. They had the blue white skin of a man who has festered twenty years in a dungeon such that he no longer even remembers the sun and would go blind did he ever behold it. And yes they had the arms and trunk too, although clothed in a filthy rags like the dress of a demon doll on the day of her wedding; a dress that was filthy and torn and

289

shimmering with parasites. The cloth was patched and sewn with the stitching a man might achieve if both his hands were broken and his eyes put out. On their backs were wings of grey mite-eaten feathers. They were called chrorguhs, mongrel beasts spawned by some diabolic miscegenation between the race of man and the race of eagles.

I beheld slime-covered marble palaces, and dim city streets from whose buildings trembling tentacles reached out. Strange streetlamps lined our route and, as my madness deepened, I saw they were not streetlamps but crosses from which hung the rotting skeletons of crucified goats. Spread along the arms of the cross, as upon the telegraph wires that line our blessed railway lines, were crows, grown too fat to fly. Above us rose the ramparts of the Dark Tower protected by great wooden gates, each the size of a ship.

And then on the eighth day, my fever broke. I felt a scented breeze on my face and we emerged into the daylight, on to a rocky terrace high on the mountainside. Eagles circled below us and beyond lay the vast green realm of Havilah. We rejoiced as men once dead whom Providence has restored to life. In the valley below we could see a settlement of small huts within a stockade on the river. We stopped and gazed in wonder, drinking in gulps from the sweet cool air and squinting into the piercing blue light. Above us the mountain towered into snowy crags like broken teeth biting the sky.

'*Nyumba kubwa ya mama!*' the men pointed and cried. 'Big Mama's house!'

I gasped in wonder, and gasped again and again, adding a soft harmonic to the shrill keening of the wind. Then I wept. '*Nyumba kubwa ya mama!*' the men cried again. 'Big Mama's house! Big Mama's house!'

I was so entranced that I stumbled and dropped the box Chief Jhorumpha had given me containing the tribute for Mama !Mkuu. It fell open on the floor and spilled its contents. A hundred human eyes rolled out and bounced down the steps that led to the valley.

Chapter 19

THE SNOW LAY as a smooth blanket upon the road, occasionally marked by the lines of car tyres. The train had been delayed by thirteen minutes and so we took a taxi in the yard outside the booking hall. The driver drove carefully and slowly over the icy cobbles and the minutes ticked away. It was 10.29 when we pulled up outside the seaman's mission adjacent to berth 5. The air was mauve and sparking with ice crystals. The hull of the *Star of Kowloon* rose up from the dockside as sheer as a white cliff. Railway tracks criss-crossed the oil-dark ground, derricks loomed like shadows in the gloom; a cat's cradle of hawsers between ship and berth. Two gangways led up to little dark openings in the ship's side. The air was thick with the reek of tar, brine and smoke. The seaman's mission was a low hut set amid cranes and piled-up crates. It bore a simple cross at one end and welcomed, so the small sign said, members of all Christian faiths, regardless of denomination. There was an old, 1920s era ambulance, the colour of butterscotch, parked before it and a man sat in a bath chair in front of the wheel arch. He was smothered in tartan blankets, and his face entirely obscured by white gauze that matched the colour of the snow. A nurse stood with her hand cast gently on his shoulder.

This man was Hershey Lindt, and yet I also knew him as Mr Dombey, whose shop had recently burned down. Many years ago in the orphanage I had known him as Cadbury Holt. The nurse was Magdalena. We walked across. The ship gave a long deep moan on the horn and the snowflakes flurried upwards as if similarly agitated. I knew without a word passing, perhaps from the sound of the horn, that Cadbury was not arriving on the *Star of Kowloon*, as his telegram had implied, but leaving on it.

'Jack,' said Cadbury simply, but with a tenderness in his voice that almost betokened longing. I looked into the ellipses that were cut into the gauze on his face. He seemed to have shrunk even more, making his hair seem more luxuriant, the way it does on the shrunken heads taken by the savages of Borneo. The blankets enveloped his small frame and it was as if he were shrinking before our gaze. I peered into the depths of his eyes, as if looking into a well, and wondered how I could have missed the imp that his eyes contained and that was such a clear sign of my lost brother. Is it possible that the twinkle in someone's eye can be recognisable? Distinctive as a voice? I thought it was. I saw the same bright gleam that I did the day all those years ago when we got into trouble with the vicar's daughter. The reason I had not spotted it in the shop was that I had never expected to find it there.

Magdalena pressed down on the handles of the bath chair and turned to wheel Cadbury inside, out of the cold. Jenny rushed to open the door and once inside we sat at a table near a steamed-up window through which the ship was a vague silhouette. The room was empty apart from three dark-skinned merchant seamen at one table talking in a language I did not recognise. A tea urn shone brighter than a Salvation Army captain's tuba and a lady stood drowsily behind the counter lost in a reverie. Jenny fetched four teas which Magdalena fortified with a bottle of brandy.

'I knew you the moment you walked into the bookshop,' said Cadbury.

'You had the advantage of me there.'

'Yes.'

'Hello, Jack,' said Magdalena.

'Magdalena is coming with me,' said Cadbury. 'I do not think I could manage the voyage alone.'

I looked at Magdalena, remembering her saying she was going to stay with the brain specialist. She explained, 'As far as Port Bismarck, that's where we will part. I am going on to Cape Town.' She reached across the table and placed her hand on Jenny's. 'I'm so glad Jack has met you.'

Jenny nodded and managed a faint smile.

'You must look after him.'

'Yes,' said Jenny, 'I will.'

We drank our tea and Magdalena poured more brandy into our cups. We raised them and chinked them in a toast.

'Your health,' said Cadbury. We reciprocated and he said to Jenny, 'I'm so pleased Jack has found such a nice girl. That's more than I ever did.'

Jenny's face brightened. 'And I'm so pleased he had such a wonderful brother. He's told me quite a bit about you.'

Cadbury made a dismissive gesture with his hands.

'Did he really pay a poor girl three cigarettes to show him her drawers?' Magdalena giggled, and Cadbury laughed.

'He got into awful hot water for it. He took a beating from the masters.'

'You didn't tell me that,' said Jenny.

'To be honest, I'd forgotten all about it. And, really! I think this is hardly the time—'

Magdalena gave me a gentle push. 'Oh, Jack, we all think it's funny.'

I looked at the grins on all their faces and suddenly I laughed too. It did seem rather funny, although for some reason it had never really struck me like that before.

'You never told, though, did you?' said Cadbury. 'You never told them I was with you.'

'So only you got the beating?' said Jenny. 'That seems a bit unfair.'

'To tell you the truth,' I replied, 'it was fair enough. I know I told you it was Cadbury's idea, but actually it was mine.'

Jenny looked at me with a strange gaze as though there was nothing in the world she approved of more than this revelation.

Cadbury raised his glass again. 'Here's to Jack, for not telling.' They toasted me. Then Cadbury said, 'Have you retrieved the suitcase?'

'I have put in a requisition, it's no simple task.'

'On the contrary, what could be simpler? A suitcase lost at Reading in January 1938, embossed with the words *Laura Bell*? Mark my words, it should not be difficult to find. I have absolute faith in Mr Jarley in Lost Property.'

'If it was so easy to find, why have you not managed it yourself?'

Cadbury looked surprised. 'Because I have not tried! Don't you see? It was necessary for me to hide the case, and what better method?'

'You mean,' said Jenny, 'you deliberately abandoned the case, knowing it would be stored in Lost Property?'

'Yes! If I had chosen a conventional hiding place, why, they would surely have found it. But who would have thought of looking in Lost Property? Even if they had, what chance of finding it? Only one man in the world could find it. Mr Jarley. Mark my words, it will be there still, somewhere, and he will retrieve it for you.'

'Is it really made from the skin of Clerihew Gape?'

'Yes, I'm afraid it is. That man was the bane of my life but I wouldn't have wished that fate upon him. I obtained the suitcase originally in order to give him a decent burial but things didn't turn out the way I planned.'

The ship's horn sounded, three times. Cadbury glanced at a clock on the wall behind the counter. It was ten to eleven.

'We sail at a quarter past,' said Cadbury.

'I understand much, but not all,' I said. 'The nuns from Povington Priory wrote to the War Office with a proposal to crew a lightship anchored in the North Atlantic, to pray for the drowning sailors. The proposal was adopted and a ne'er-do-well called Clerihew Gape was released from prison to captain the ship. According to his widow, they set sail on the tenth of May, the day Southend was bombed. But the nuns were reported as having vanished from the train a week later. So I suspect this was a ruse to cover up the true fate of the nuns. But what was it? Subsequently they appeared to have turned up in Africa, after travelling in a German U-boat. How did they get there?'

Cadbury nodded and his eyes sparkled behind his mask, as if he was pleased with my progress.

'What made you seek Mr Gape in the first place?' I asked.

'It was a German count,' said Cadbury. 'I caught him travelling with a forged ticket somewhere between Banbury and

Leamington Spa in 1927. He sat there cool as you like, every bit the English gentleman in a burgundy frock coat over grey check trousers, a lilac-and-cream-striped woollen waistcoat. His cologne was lavender. His English was entirely without fault or even the slightest hint of the land that gave him birth. He even had a copy of the show catalogue for Gulliver's Gentleman's Emporium resting on his knee. But the ticket for Taunton had a slight glitch in the uppercase T that we had been warned about. He knew straightaway the game was up and made a run for it. Jumped from the train and ran down the embankment and hid in a barn where his presence was betrayed by some hens that loved England. There was nowhere for him to go so he drew his swordstick, which considering my reputation was very much the stupidest thing he could do. Seconds later, I had him on the ground –' Cadbury picked up a fork from the table and held it out as if re-enacting the scene – 'the point of his own sword pressed into his Adam's apple . . .'

He put the fork down and continued: 'He bought his life with the most outrageous story I had ever heard. It was about the missing nuns. He told me about Port Bismarck, a stinking, rat-strewn, fly-infested town of brothels and warehouses at the mouth of the Sulabunga, near the border of Angola and the French Congo. He told me about an Englishman who lived there, passing his days in the seedy drinking dens and bars at the harbour's mouth, with a tale so crazy that not a single soul believed him. He told me this man, Mr Clerihew Gape, had first arrived there in 1915, travelling in a U-boat along with a party of English nuns. Of course, my initial reaction was to dismiss the wild tale, but there was something in the calm and unper-turbed manner in which he told it that gave me pause. That blackguardly count was unafraid to die and his tale, though insane, had the ring of truth. In short, I could not rest until I knew. I set out to find Mr Gape. I spared the count's life, delivered him into the hands of the police, and spent the next few years scouring the ports of north and west Africa searching for Mr Gape. On my first trip to Port Bismarck he was not to be found, although he was well known. I spent years searching, for a while even enlisting in the ranks of the Foreign Legion. Eventually I found him in a drunken stupor in the wheelhouse of his boat, the *Nellie*. This was 1929. Gape confirmed the story. He told me how he had arrived there in a German U-boat with the twenty-three nuns, how six of them had been sold into slavery at the market of El Gaberdine. And how the angry sisters mounted a rescue raid and stole the Great Map from the Library of El Gaberdine. The map, as you know, showed the whereabouts of the lost river of Eden, the Pishon. He accompanied the holy sisters as they sailed the U-boat up the Sulabunga in search of this. To negotiate the cascades they hired porters from the town gaol. After that they sailed for a month inland until the river became too shallow and there they dragged the U-boat on rollers fashioned from jungle trees over the mountain and set her down in the Lunga-Lunga. Gape went with them as far as the Mountains of the Green Dawn, after which they let him go. He returned to Port Bismarck.' Cadbury indicated to Magdalena that his cup was empty and she refilled them all. 'At first, he was very reluctant to repeat the trip but my offer of gold was enough to persuade him. He agreed to take me as far as the Mountains of the Green Dawn, but would go no further on account of this –' Cadbury touched the gauze on his face. 'Leprosy. A most unexpected feature of Eden. I do not know exactly what became of him. I can only assume that after he left me he fell into the hands of Chief Jhorumpha, who had him turned into a suitcase. Later when Chief Jhorumpha presented the baby gorilla to the Port Bismarck Rotary Club, as a gift to the people of England, the suitcase went along. I have to say,' Cadbury added with perceptible exasperation, 'Chief Jhorumpha was the most damnably facetious chap I ever met.'

'So did you find the nuns?' said Jenny.

'Yes. I spent four years living among them. Or rather four years elapsed in the outside world. In Havilah time passes differently, or, to be more precise, it doesn't seem to pass at all. The only gauge by which you can measure its passing is through the advance of the leprosy carbuncles that all eventually fall victim to.'

'What happened to the guard on the train the nuns had supposedly been travelling on?' I asked.

'My understanding is he was a stooge working for Room 42.'

'And the nuns sold into slavery?' said Jenny.

Cadbury whistled softly and fluttered his fingers as if to indicate the flight of migrating birds. 'From Khartoum, they appeared to have been sold on to all corners of the earth. The other Goslings went in search and met untimely ends.' He turned to me and said with more intensity, 'Now it is time for another Gosling, the last one, to go and bring them back. I knew one day you would find me. I laid the trail to me as well as I could. But of course not too well – it was devised as a test to see if you were worthy.'

'You told me you were born in the shop, and had never left even when your mother died.'

'I was acting a part.'

'Even so, that was rather a tall tale to tell, wasn't it?'

Behind the gauze, Cadbury's eyes glittered with mischief. 'Extremely tall.'

I was about to remonstrate but then it occurred to me that, knowing now that it had been Cadbury all along, it did seem rather funny.

'I'm sorry I had to mislead you,' he said. 'I needed to be sure.'

I laughed. 'I should have guessed it was you. Who else would come up with a cock-and-bull story like that?'

'But I don't understand,' said Jenny. 'How is it that a party of nuns travelling on a train from Swindon to Bristol Temple Meads in 1915 could vanish into thin air and turn up on a beach in Algeria, aboard a German U-boat?'

'Ah that was the most dastardly part of the plan.'

THE BOY'S OWN
RAILWAY GOSLING ANNUAL

| Vol. VII | 1931 | Price: 1/- |

Replies to our readers' letters

T. ATKINS, YORK—Judging from the quality of your handwriting, you have no chance whatsoever. Consider a manual trade.

F. G. PRENDERGAST, CROMER—There are many reports of decapitated heads winking at the crowd gathered for their execution but we suspect the best explanation is the same nervous spasm that causes the headless chicken to run. As for speaking after the guillotine blade has fallen, these reports are far less reliable.

ANONYMOUS, BERWICK-UPON-TWEED—Keep pure, and pray for strength.

THE CONTINUING ADVENTURES OF RAILWAY GOSLING CADBURY HOLT – ON THE TRAIL OF THE MISSING NUNS!

In the Court of Mama !Mkuu

Slowly I dragged my eyes up to behold the human scarecrow sitting behind the desk. She was dressed in black rags that might once have been a nun's habit, but which time had turned into a spider's web of dark threads in which scraps of the original cloth were caught like giant flies. Underneath this outer garb she wore a girdle woven from bones. Each of her bosoms, which otherwise swung free of the black cloth, was encased in the skull of an anteater. Her hair was wild and tangled, descending to the desk in an overflowing cascade, like jungle creepers at the margin of a river.

Her face lay in shadows. Somewhere off to my right a bright silver horn shone above a spinning shellac disk and the voice of Enrico Caruso, sounding as if he sang from a manhole beneath the street, filled the Eden night with the tinny refrain of Europe. I stood before the desk straining in the gloom to see the face of Mama !Mkuu, but her head, supported by the thin blue-white fingers of her right hand, was lowered as if she were reading the Bible, though I could tell that it had been many years since she had done that.

A torch on the wall threw quivering pools of light upon the desk. The top was fashioned from a single great slab of dressed stone, and this was laid upon the ribcage of a beast so large it seemed not even a rhinoceros could have supplied it. The gleaming ribs curved like the spars from a ship of bone. Out of the belly of which fantastical beast did it derive? Surely it could only have come from those cold-hearted saurians that bellow in our darkest dreams and roamed this earth before the wickedness of Man so tested the patience of our Merciful Father that he was forced to destroy us all. A candle was seated in a silver holder. I watched transfixed as a fat globule of wax over-brimmed and fell precipitously down the candle side the way a human sacrifice falls when thrown from a cliff's edge. My gaze was drawn with fascination to the infernal candelabra itself; it was covered with the most intricate designs of intertwining serpents and young ladies disrobing and entwining with the beasts in lascivious traffic. Next to the candle was a Bible of a size that would take two men to carry it to the table. It was opened to a page in Genesis and I saw with dismay that the page had been covered in scrawls and rude stick figure drawings of men and women in the same acts of defilement emblazoned on the candlestick. A quill made from an ostrich feather lay resting on the page, with inky blobs obliterating the verse. I could feel two eyes watching me keenly, the way perhaps a snake observes the mouse into whose eyes he will spit his venom.

I opened my parched mouth and whispered the words, 'Mama !Mkuu.'

Slowly, gingerly, she raised her head. The candle painted her more golden than a Flemish Madonna. I saw with shock that her face, too, was ravaged by the cruel blisters and carbuncles of leprosy; her nose was enlarged and cratered like a potato; this lent the look in her eyes a quality that pierced the heart. It was the same aching puzzlement you saw in the eyes of a gorilla who has spent a lifetime captive in a zoo. The look with which he regards you through the bars contains a deep heartache for the green African trees of his half-remembered youth. And since he has known nothing but kindness from the human who daily tends and feeds him it never occurs to him that humans would be the ones responsible for his life sentence in prison. Instead he assumes some other among the animals – the wolf perhaps – must be responsible and that his keeper is a captive too. Thus, when evening comes and the keeper catches a bus home to his family, the gorilla thinks he has been locked up for the night in some dungeon similar to his own. And each morning when the keeper reappears and shares his food with the gorilla, the poor beast's heart is wrung for pain at the gesture for well he sees the keeper does not eat the food himself, but gives it all to his friend while he himself grows thin. Thus does the gorilla love and pity the keeper. And the pale aching melancholy in his eyes was the same I saw that night in the eyes of Mama !Mkuu. Was this the dark secret Mama !Mkuu had discovered here at the umbilicus of the world? That we were the gorilla in the prison house we call earth? And was the pain in the agonised waters of her

303

eyes the recognition that Christ was the keeper who betrayed us? Or was it merely a trick of light, the reflection of a candle in eyes seared with rheum and weary of staring out from a face that disease had laid waste and hardened into bark?

In the gloom our eyes met, and she said, so softly that I struggled to hear the words,

'Did you bring any gramophone records?'

Chapter 20

THE LADY FROM behind the counter came across and told us they would be closing in ten minutes. It was eleven. She asked us if we would like any more tea and gave our cups a meaningful stare that indicated she knew we were drinking brandy. We said no and wished her a happy new year. She began to close shop.

'You mustn't have too much,' said Cadbury. 'You have an ambulance to drive.' He registered my look of surprise. 'I think it best, don't you?' He took out a ring of keys and slid them across the table. 'This is the ignition key. The smaller key will open the *Laura Bell* suitcase when you find it. I expect you have guessed its contents.'

'Yes,' I said. 'I assume it to contain the missing Railway Gosling annual.'

'The manuscript, no more. I fibbed to you when I said a copy had been printed. It was never printed. The case also contains the accounts sent to me by the other Goslings who went in search of the nuns sold at the slave auction. One day you will publish it. One day, when it is safe to reveal its contents. Until then, the responsibility falls on you, the last of the Goslings, to keep it safe and, of course, to keep yourself safe from harm.' He placed his palms down on the wheels of his chair and pushed himself closer to the table. 'The plan the holy sisters came up with was completely hare-brained, of course. There was no reason why they would need to be actually in the North Atlantic in order to pray for those who were unfortunate enough to be sunk in it. The Lord is not known to be deaf and can hear a prayer from Povington just as well as one from the ocean. But those devils in Room 42 adopted the proposal because they had something far more base in mind than the creation of a floating chapel.' Cadbury paused for a second as if even now he could not quite believe the truth he carried in his heart. 'You must prepare yourself, Jack, for what I am about to say.'

'Cadbury, I do not think I have much faith left to shake.'

'Yes, good, good. You see . . .' He paused, as if wondering how best to tell the dark secret. 'Dear old England was standing on the edge of a cliff. Days away from surrender. There was only one hope. To drag the Americans into the war. The American public was violently opposed, but public opinion is a fickle thing and could easily change. And what could be more calculated to bring about that change than the greatest atrocity story of all time? What if the beastly Germans torpedoed a ship carrying twenty-three nuns engaged on a mission of the Lord? Twenty or so holy sisters bound for the cold and deathly North Atlantic shipping lanes where they would pray for the souls of the dying and dead? Perhaps there was not a man among them who would have devised the idea himself. I don't imagine there was a man in Room 42 capable of inventing such a scheme. But when the letter from the nuns arrived, perhaps the idea suggested itself. They probably thought they had no alternative. Maybe they didn't. It was decided to leak the exact position of the ship to the Hun. But there was a problem. The Germans were too honourable to sink a ship full

306

of nuns, so they had to be sold a lie. Hence the secrecy sur-
rounding the affair. They were told the ship contained the
British war cabinet escaping to Ireland, en route to America.
Well, you can imagine how that revelation was received in
Berlin. The idea that the cowardly rascals in Westminster in
order to save their own miserable hides would counterfeit a
lightship . . . The Germans sent their U-boats out to sink it
without a note of compunction.'

'Magdalena said it was the reason the King had to change his
name in 1917, but why?' I said.

'He changed his name for the same reason a common burglar
adopts an assumed name and whistles a tune of feigned
innocence.'

'I don't understand,' I said.

'You see, I have told you how the information was received
in Berlin, but how did it get to Berlin?' Cadbury paused with
the air of a conjuror about to embark on his greatest trick. 'How
do you think the Germans found out?' Cadbury repeated. 'King
George telephoned his cousin the Kaiser and told him.'

There was a small pop of air as we all exhaled in surprise.

'A treasonous act, I think we can agree.'

'It was all so long ago,' said Jenny. 'Would it really matter now
if the truth came out?'

'Ah, that is the point,' said Cadbury. 'Perhaps if it were not
for this tide of Communism sweeping the world, things might
be viewed differently. But consider, what might happen in this
brave new world if the truth about the King became known?
All those working men and women who fought in the war, who
lost their brothers and sisters, mothers and fathers to the
Germans . . . and what for? To build a fairer society. Who knows

307

how they might feel? Is it inconceivable that a popular uprising might sweep away the old order entirely? Would you bet against it? That is what they fear.'

'So how did the nuns end up in Africa?' said Jenny.

'Simple,' said Cadbury. 'The nuns commandeered the U-boat. The German U-boat intercepted the *Laura Bell* and fired off a torpedo. It hit her amidships and the *Laura Bell* began to sink. The U-boat rose to the surface prepared to provide aid to the survivors and lo! What did they see? To their horror, instead of the British war cabinet, the sea was filled with nuns. The German mariners rescued them. And that is where the tale takes the most remarkable twist. The holy sisters commandeered the U-boat. It was Sister Ludo who did most of the fighting. Sister Clodagh stole the captain's pistol and with it they took over the ship. The German sailors were locked below and the armoury raided. The sisters armed themselves and forced the captain at gunpoint to show them how to sail the U-boat. He perhaps was undecided but his mind was made up by the appearance at that point of a Royal Naval frigate on the horizon. The nuns, thinking rescue was at hand, signalled their presence by semaphore. The frigate fired upon them and they were forced to dive. An hour later they surfaced and radioed the frigate advising the captain of his mistake. But the frigate fired again. They turned tail and the frigate chased them south. At first, they assumed it was simply a terrible mistake: that the English captain was unaware that the U-boat contained the British nuns. But after the third encounter it became quite clear that the English captain knew precisely who they were and was under orders to sink them. They fled. It was the German skipper who worked it out. The Royal Navy continued the chase and the nuns sailed south and off into the realm of mystery and myth.' Cadbury paused, and emptied the last of the brandy into the cups. We raised them once more in toast and wished each other bon voyage. The ship's horn sounded insistently, and the clock showed ten past. From far off we could hear the sound of singing. 'They put the German sailors ashore on a quiet stretch of coast in Portugal. They were later shot as traitors by the German authorities. The Kaiser was as anxious as anyone to keep a lid on the affair.'

At a sign from Cadbury, Magdalena stood up and placed her hands on the bath chair. 'So now you know it all,' said Cadbury. 'My advice to you both is to assume new identities, and be very cautious. Jack, you are the last of the Goslings, and the duty falls to you to preserve the truth, to publish the missing annual. The duty also falls on your shoulders to find the other nuns, the ones who were sold at the slave market. Shanghai, Chicago, Peru . . . the South Seas, the trails lead everywhere. You must find them, Jack. But in order to do any of this you must make sure you stay alive. In order to do that I suggest you make use of the contents of this.'

Magdalena opened her handbag and took out a letter. She placed it on the table.

'The letter,' I said.

'The letter,' repeated Magdalena.

We stared at it. Lilac envelope edged with crimson and blue chevrons. Three stamps: bananas, a pineapple and a king's head in profile. I placed my hand on it.

'We must go,' said Cadbury. 'You must keep the letter hidden in a safe place and let it be known it will be published in the eventuality of your untimely death. Then you will be safe.'

'Have a good life, Jack,' said Magdalena. She kissed me lightly on the cheek, and then kissed Jenny. The horn of the *Star of Kowloon* sounded once more, and Magdalena wheeled Cadbury away.

Epilogue

THE *STAR OF Kowloon* and the old ambulance left the port at around the same time. The ship was bound for a small settlement on the western seaboard of Africa, and the ambulance drove north through streets that were beginning to fill with revellers moving to the final public house in which they would spend the moment when the year turned. We had no destination in mind, we merely sought a stretch of railway line in the quiet of the country with a level crossing where we could bring a Great Western Railway train to a temporary halt. No particular one, any train would do. It turned out to be the 11.40 Bristol Temple Meads to Liverpool. The driver and his fireman were not particularly surprised to discover a signal against them a few miles north of Yate. What happened next greatly surprised them. A man and a woman appeared at the side of the engine and said they urgently needed to be married – in the next five minutes; and the ceremony absolutely had to be performed by the driver of a mainline GWR express. This privilege of office would, they explained, expire in five minutes. The fireman helped them aboard and the driver removed from the breast pocket of his jacket a small leather Book of Common Prayer that he had carried all his life in anticipation of such a moment but had never once had to use. He performed a short ceremony. As the young couple said the words, 'I do', the fireman pulled on the whistle and in answer there came an eerie echo across the land. It was midnight and all the trains in the country were sounding their whistles to salute or lament the passing of the four great railway companies and the creation of the new British Railways.

The train in which the marriage ceremony was performed was number 4070 *Godstow Castle*, the one with a sloping throatplate in the firebox and the characteristic double cough in the chuffs. Perhaps for a man with a stone heart, the reappearance of that old friend on their wedding night – the same engine whose sweet double chuffs had serenaded them on their first encounter – might be dismissed as a coincidence, and not as evidence of the directing hand of the Great Stationmaster. But none of those present on the footplate that night, nor indeed on any footplate on any night during the time of the Great Western Railway, could ever be said to have such a thing as a heart of stone.

Appendix 1

Letter found in the estate of Jack Wenlock

The Sisters of Lacrismi Christi
Leprosy Sanctuary
Havilah
Eden
Africa

Wednesday 3 September 1947

To His Majesty King George VI of England
Buckingham Palace
London

Your Majesty,
I write to you from a land beyond the Mountains of the Green Dawn, and beyond all imagining.

I have every reason to suppose the contents of this letter will astonish you and I recommend Your Majesty finds a suitable chair before reading further. Some weeks ago a chest of drawers was found floating in the Sulabunga River and the natives, perceiving it to be a white man's machine, had it conveyed to us here in Havilah. We found the top drawer to be lined with an edition of the Cape Town Times dating from April 1947. The front-page

*story described Your Majesty's Royal Tour of South Africa. Well, imagine
our shock to discover England has a new King! The last news we had of
dear old Blighty was in 1929, when your brother was on the throne. Your
Majesty, if you are a kind man – something which the noble countenance in
your photograph gives me hope to believe – would it please you to give leave
for we lost souls here in Havilah to return to England?*

Our dearest wish is that we might die in the arms of the land that bore us.

*I include with this letter a manuscript setting out a full and detailed
account of our wanderings since we disappeared from the pages of history
in 1915.*

*If Your Majesty is kind enough to reply, he might like to know that no
postman will venture up the Sulabunga for fear of being eaten. However, a
note addressed to Chief Jhorumpha and left with the secretary of the Port
Bismarck Rotary Club will stand a good chance of reaching us, eventually.
I hope Your Majesty will not regard it as impertinent if I add that a packet
of Peek Frean's Garibaldi biscuits included with his message would make
some old ladies very happy.*

I remain in hope, your humble and obedient servant,
Mama !Mkuu

Appendix II

THE ORDER FOR THE BURIAL OF THE DEAD

Fifteen years later, in 1963, Her Majesty's Stationery Office published a document entitled *The Reshaping of British Railways* by Dr. R. Beeching. More popularly known as the Beeching Report, it recommended for closure 5,000 miles of railway line and the following 2,363 stations:

Abbey Town
Acrow Halt
Acton Central
Addingham
Adlestrop
Ainsdale
Airmyn
Aldeburgh
Aldermaston
Aldridge
Alford Town (Lincs)
Alfreton and South Normanton
Alresford (Hants)
Alrewas
Altofts and Whitwood
Alton Towers
Ambergate
Andover Town
Apperley Bridge
Appleby (Westmorland)

Appledore (Kent)
Ardsley
Ardwick
Armathwaite
Armley Canal Road
Armley Moor
Arram
Arthington
Ascott-under-Wychwood
Ashbury
Ashburys for Belle Vue
Ashby-de-la-Zouch
Ashby Magna
Ashcott
Ashdon Halt
Ashey (Isle of Wight)
Ashington
Ashley Heath Halt
Ashley Hill
Ashperton

Ashton Charlestown
Ashton Gate
Ashwater
Ashwell
Askham
Aspley Guise
Athelney
Avoncliff Halt
Avonmouth Dock
Awsworth
Aynho for Deddington

Bacup
Baguley
Bagworth and Ellistown
Bailey Gate
Ballingham
Balshaw Lane and Euxton
Bamford
Bank Hall
Banks
Baptist End Halt
Barcombe Mills
Bardney
Bardon Mill
Bardsey
Barlow
Barnard Castle
Barnoldswick
Barnstaple Town
Barnwell
Barrow Haven
Barrow-on-Soar and Quorn
Bartlow
Barton-on-Humber
Basford North
Bason Bridge
Bassenthwaite Lake
Bath Green Park
Bathampton
Bathford Halt

Battersby
Baynards
Bebside
Beccles
Bedlington
Bedworth
Bedwyn
Beechburn
Beeston Castle and Tarporley
Belmont (Middx)
Belper
Ben Rhydding
Bentham
Bere Alston
Bere Ferrers
Berkeley
Berkeley Road
Berry Brow
Berwick (Sussex)
Besses-o'-th'-Barn
Betchworth
Bexhill West
Bickershaw and Abram
Bideford
Binegar
Birch Vale
Birkdale
Birkenhead Woodside
Bishop Auckland
Bishop's Lydeard
Bishop's Nympton and Molland
Bishopstone
Bitton
Blaby
Black Dog Halt
Blackdyke Halt
Blackhall Colliery
Black Horse Road
Blackpool North
Blackrod
Blackwell

Blacon
Blaisdon Halt
Blandford Forum
Blaydon
Bleadon and Uphill Halt
Bleasby
Blencow
Bletchington
Blockley
Bloxwich
Blue Anchor
Blundellsands and Crosby
Blyth
Bodmin General
Bodmin North
Bollington
Bolton Abbey
Bolton-le-Sands
Bolton Percy
Bootle (Cumberland)
Bootle Oriel Road
Borrowash
Botanic Gardens
Botley
Boughton Halt
Bow (Devon)
Bow Brickhill
Bowker Vale
Box
Box Mill Lane
Brackley Central
Bradford Peverell and Stratton Halt
Brading (Isle of Wight)
Bradwell (Bucks)
Braintree and Bocking
Braithwaite
Bramber
Bramley and Wonersh
Brampton (Suffolk)
Brancepeth
Brandon Colliery

Bransford Road
Braughing
Braunton
Braystones
Breamore
Bredon
Brent (Devon)
Brent Knoll
Brentor
Bricket Wood
Bridestowe
Bridport
Brigham
Brightlingsea
Brimscombe
Broadbottom
Broad Clyst
Broad Green
Broadstone
Brockholes
Bromfield
Bromham and Rowde Halt
Brompton (Yorks)
Bromyard
Brondesbury
Brondesbury Park
Brookland Halt
Broomielaw
Brownhills
Bruton
Bryn
Buckingham
Bude
Budleigh Salterton
Bugle
Bulwell Market
Buntingford
Bures
Burgh-by-Sands
Burgh-le-Marsh
Burlescombe

Burley-in-Wharfedale
Burslem
Burton Agnes
Burton Joyce
Bury Bolton Street
Buxted
Buxton

Cadishead
Callington
Calne
Calstock
Calverley and Rodley
Camelford
Cannock
Carbis Bay
Carcroft and Adwick-le-Street
Carlton and Netherfield
Carnaby
Carville
Castle Ashby and Earls Barton
Castleford Cutsyke
Castlethorpe
Castleton (Yorks)
Cattal
Catterick Bridge
Cattistock Halt
Causeland Halt
Cavendish
Chacewater
Chalford
Challow
Chandlers Ford
Chapel-en-le-Frith Central
Chapel-en-le Frith South
Chapelton
Chappel and Wakes Colne
Chard Junction
Charfield
Charlbury
Chatteris

Cheadle (Cheshire)
Cheadle Heath
Cheddleton
Cheltenham Spa Malvern Road
Chester-le-Street
Chester Northgate
Chesterton Lane Halt
Chetnole Halt
Chilcompton
Chilsworthy
Chilvers Coton
Chilworth and Albury
Chipping Campden
Chittening Platform
Chorlton-cum-Hardy
Christian Malford Halt
Churchdown
Church's Hill Halt
Churchtown
Churston
Cirencester Town
Clapham (Yorks)
Clare
Clatford
Clay Cross
Claydon (Bucks)
Clayton Bridge
Clayton West
Cleckheaton
Clevedon
Clifton Bridge
Clifton Down
Clough Fold
Cloughton
Coaley
Coalville Town
Cobridge
Cockermouth for Buttermere
Codnor Park and Ironville
Cole
Collingham

Collingham Bridge
Colnbrook
Colnbrook Estate Halt
Colyford
Colyton
Combe Halt
Combpyne
Commondale
Coningsby
Cononley
Consall
Cooksbridge
Coombe Junction Halt
Copplestone
Coppull
Corbridge
Corby
Corkickle
Corsham
Corton
Cotherstone
Coundon Road
County School
Cowes (Isle of Wight)
Cox Green
Cranleigh
Creech St Michael Halt
Creekmoor Halt
Cressing
Cressington and Grassendale
Crigglestone
Croft
Croft Spa
Cromford
Crook
Crossens
Cross Hands Halt
Crouch Hill
Crowcombe
Crowhurst
Croxley Green

Crumpsall
Cudworth
Culcheth
Culgaith
Culkerton Halt
Cullompton
Cutnall Green Halt

Daggons Road
Daimler Halt
Danby
Darby End Halt
Darfield
Darlaston
Darley Dale
Darlington North Road
Darsham
Dartmouth
Dauntsey
Davenport
Deepdene
Defford
Delabole
Denby Dale
Denstone
Dent
Denton
Derby Friargate
Derby Nottingham Road
Desborough and Rothwell
Desford
Devizes
Devonport King's Road
Dewsbury Central
Didsbury
Diggle
Dinting
Dinton
Disley
Doleham Halt
Donnington

Dorchester West
Dore and Totley
Dorking Town
Doublebois
Dove Holes
Downton
Draycott and Breaston
Drax
Drigg
Dronfield
Droylesden
Dudley
Duffield
Dulverton
Dunball Halt
Dunmere Halt
Dunsbear Halt
Dunsland Cross
Dunstable North
Dunstable Town
Dunster
Durston

Earlestown
Earswick
Easington
East Anstey
East Budleigh
East Langton
East Leake
Eastrington
Eccles
Eccleston Park
Eckington
Edale
Edenbridge
Edge Hill
Edington Burtle
Egloskerry
Egremont
Egton

Ellerby
Ellesmere
Ellesmere Port
Elmesthorpe for Barwell
Elmton and Creswell
Elswick
Embsay
Emerson Park Halt
Entwistle
Etherley
Ettingshall Road and Bilston
Evercreech Junction
Evercreech New
Evershot
Ewood Bridge and Edenfield
Exeter St. Thomas
Exminster
Exmouth
Exton

Fairfield for Droylsden
Fakenham East
Fawley (Herefords.)
Fazakerley
Featherstone
Felixstowe Beach
Fencehouses
Fenny Compton
Fenny Stratford
Fernhill Heath
Ferryhill
Filleigh
Finchley Road and Frognal
Finstock Halt
Firshy
Fishponds
Fiskerton
Fitzwilliam
Five Mile House
Fladbury
Flax Bourton

Fleetwood
Foleshill
Ford (Devon)
Fordingbridge
Forest Row
Formby
Four Crosses
Fourstones
Fowey
Foxfield
Frankton Halt
Frant
Fremington
Freshfield
Freshford
Fritwell and Somerton
Frizinghall
Frodsham
Fullerton
Furness Vale
Fyling Hall

Gainford
Gargrave
Garsdale
Garstang and Catterall
Garston
Garswood
Gateacre
Giggleswick
Gilsland
Glaisdale
Glastonbury and Street
Glemsford
Glossop Central
Glynde
Gnosall
Goathland
Godley Junction
Godstone
Golant Halt

Golcar
Gomshall and Shere
Gorleston Links Halt
Gorleston-on-Sea
Gorton and Openshaw
Gospel Oak
Goxhill
Grampound Road
Grange Court
Grange Road
Grateley
Great Ayton
Great Bridge North
Great Bridge South
Great Linford
Greatstone-on-Sea Halt
Greenhead
Green Road
Gresley
Gretton
Grimstone and Frampton
Grindleford
Grogley Halt
Groombridge
Grosmont
Guisborough
Guiseley
Gunnislake
Gwinear Road

Hadham
Haigh
Hailsham
Halberton Halt
Halesworth
Hall Road
Halton (Lancs)
Halwill
Ham Green Halt
Hammerton
Hammerwich

Hampstead Heath
Ham Street and Orlestone
Handborough
Hanley
Haresfield
Harpenden East
Harringay Stadium
Hartfield
Hartley
Hatherleigh
Hathersage
Havenhouse
Havenstreet (Isle of Wight)
Haverhill
Hawkesbury Lane
Hawsker
Hayburn Wyke
Hayfield
Hayle
Hazel Grove
Heads Nook
Heathfield (Sussex)
Heaton Park
Heckmondwike
Hednesford
Hedon
Heeley
Heighington (Durham)
Hele and Bradninch
Hellifield
Hellingly
Helmshore
Helpston
Helsby
Hemingbrough
Hemsworth
Henbury
Hendford Halt
Henfield
Hensall
Henstridge

Henwick
Hesketh Bank
Hesketh Park
Hest Bank
Heswall Hills
Heswall Hills
Heyford Halt
Highbridge for Burnham-on-Sea
Higher Poynton
High Lane
Hightown
Hillside
Hindley South
Histon
Hole
Holme Hale
Holme Lacy
Holmsley
Holsworthy
Holt
Holt Junction
Honley
Hoole
Hope
Hopton-on-Sea
Horam
Horden
Horfield
Hornsea Bridge
Hornsea Town
Horsebridge
Horton-in-Ribblesdale
Horwich
Hucknall Byron
Humberstone Road
Hunwick
Hurstbourne
Hutton Gate
Huyton
Hyde Central
Hyde North

Hykeham
Hylton

Idmiston Halt
Ilfracombe
Ilkeston Junction and Cossall
Ilkeston North
Ilkley
Ince and Elton
Instow
Irthlingborough
Isfield
Itchen Abbas

Kegworth
Kempston Hardwick
Kenilworth
Kensal Rise
Kentish Town West
Keswick
Ketton and Collyweston
Keyingham
Kibworth
Kidlington
Kidsgrove Liverpool Road
Kildale
Kildwick and Crosshills
Kimberley East
Kingskerswell
Kingsley and Froghall
King's Cliffe
King's Nympton
King's Sutton
Kintbury
Kiplingcotes
Kirby Muxloe
Kirkandrews
Kirkbride
Kirkby
Kirkby-in-Ashfield East
Kirkby-in-Furness

Kirkby Stephen West
Kirkstall
Knaresborough
Knightwick
Knottingley

Lacock Halt
Lake Side (Windermere)
Lancaster Green Ayre
Langford and Ulting
Langley Mill and Eastwood
Langport West
Langwathby
Langwith
Latchley
Launceston
Launton
Lavington
Layton (Lancs)
Lazonby and Kirkoswald
Lealholm
Leamington Spa Avenue
Leamington Spa Milverton
Leek
Leicester Central
Leigh (Lancs)
Leigh (Staffs)
Leigh Court
Leigh Halt (Kent)
Leiston
Lelant Halt
Levisham
Leyton Midland Road
Leytonstone High Road
Lichfield Trent Valley High Level
Lidlington
Lightcliffe
Lilbourne
Limpley Stoke Halt
Linby
Lincoln St Marks

Linton
Littleham
Little Salkeld
Little Sutton
Littleton and Badsey
Liverpool Central
Liverpool Road Halt (Staffs)
Liversedge
Llanymynech
Llynclys
Lockwood
Londesborough
Long Eaton
Longhope
Long Marston
Long Marton
Long Melford
Long Preston
Long Stanton
Longton Bridge
Longtown
Longwood
Looe
Lostock Junction
Lostwithiel
Loughborough Central
Louth
Lowdham
Lower Ince
Lowestoft North
Low Moor
Lowthorpe
Lowton St Mary's
Lubenham
Luckett
Luffenham
Luton Bute Street
Luton Hoo for New Mill End
Lutterworth
Luxulyan
Lydd-on-Sea Halt

Lydd Town
Lydford
Lydney Town
Lyme Regis
Lympstone
Lyng Halt

Mablethorpe
Maddaford Moor Halt
Maiden Newton
Maldon East and Heybridge
Malvern Wells
Mangotsfield
Manningford Halt
Manningham
Mansfield Town
Mansfield Woodhouse
Manton
Marazion
Mardock
Marfleet
Marishes Road
Market Weighton
Marsden
Marsh Gibbon and Powndon
Marsh Lane and Strand Road
Marston Magna
Martock
Masbury Halt
Matlock Bath
Mayfield (Sussex)
Medstead and Four Marks
Meeth Halt
Meir
Melksham
Melmerby
Melton Constable
Melton Mowbray Town
Menheniot
Menston
Mersey Road and Aigburth

Mickleton
Middleton (Lancs)
Middleton-in-Teesdale
Middleton Junction
Middlewood Lower
Midford
Midgham
Midsomer Norton South
Midville
Milborne Port Halt
Milcote Halt
Miles Platting
Millbrook (Beds)
Miller's Dale for Tideswell
Mill Hill (Isle of Wight)
Mill Hill (Lancs)
Millhouses and Ecclesall
Millom
Milnthorpe
Milverton (Somerset)
Minehead
Minety and Ashton Keynes
Mitcheldean Road
Moira
Montacute
Monton Green
Montpelier
Moor Row
Morchard Road
Morcott
Morebath Halt
Morebath Junction Halt
Morecambe Euston Road
Mortehoe and Woolacombe
Mossley (Lancs)
Mottisfont
Moulton (Yorks)
Mountfield Halt
Mow Cop and Scholar Green
Mumby Road
Mundesley-on-Sea

Nanstallon Halt
Nantwich
Narborough
Neston North
Nethertown
Newark Castle
New Basford
Newbiggin
New Bolingbroke
Newcastle (Staffs)
Newchapel and Goldenhill
Newchurch Halt
New Holland Pier
New Holland Town
Newland Halt
Newlay
New Longton and Hutton
New Mills Newtown
Newnham
New Passage Halt
Newport Pagnell
Newport (Isle of Wight)
Newport (Salop)
New Romney
Newsham
Newstead
Newton
Newton Heath
Newton Kyme
Newton-le-Willows
Newton Poppleford
Newton St Cyres
Normacot
Northampton Bridge Street
North Elmham
Northenden
North Filton Platform
Northorpe North Road
North Seaton
North Tawton
North Thoresby

North Wylam
Norton Bridge
Norton Halt
Nottingham Victoria
Nunthorpe
Nutfield

Oakamoor
Oakham
Oakington
Oakle Street
Oakley (Hants)
Oaksey Halt
Old Dalby
Old Hill High Street Halt
Oldland Common
Ormesby (Yorks)
Orrell
Ossett
Otley
Otterham
Ottery St Mary
Ottringham
Oulton Broad South
Oundle
Overton

Padbury
Padstow
Pallion
Pampisford
Pans Lane Halt
Pant (Salop)
Park (Manchester)
Parkhouse Halt
Park Leaze Halt
Park Street and Frogmore
Partington
Partridge Green
Paston and Knapton
Patney and Chirton

Patricroft
Patrington
Peak Forest for Peak Dale
Pear Tree and Normanton
Pebworth Halt
Pegswood
Pelsall
Pemberton
Penda's Way
Pendleton
Penns
Penruddock
Penshaw
Penshurst
Penwortham Cop Lane
Petrockstow
Pewsey
Pickering
Piercebridge
Pill
Pilning Low Level
Pinhoe
Pitts Hill
Pleasington
Plumpton (Sussex)
Pocklington
Point Pleasant
Polsloe Bridge Halt
Pontefract Monkhill
Pontefract Tanshelf
Pool-in-Wharfedale
Poppleton
Port Isaac Road
Portishead
Porton
Portsmouth Arms
Powerstock
Poyle for Stanwell Moor Halt
Poyle Estate Halt
Prees
Prescot

Preston Road (Lancs)
Prestwich
Pudsey Greenside
Pudsey Lowtown
Purton
Puxton and Worle
Pye Bridge
Pylle Halt

Quintrel Downs

Radcliffe Central (Lancs)
Radford
Radstock North
Radway Green and Barthomley
Rainford Junction
Rainhill
Ramsbottom
Ravenglass
Ravenscar
Rawcliffe
Rawtenstall
Reddish South
Redland
Repton and Willington
Ribblehead
Richmond (Yorks)
Ridgmont
Riding Mill
Ringstead and Addington
Ringwood
Ripon
Roade
Robin Hood's Bay
Roby
Rocester
Roche
Rockingham
Rodmarton Platform
Rolleston Junction
Romaldkirk

Ropley
Rose Hill Marple
Rossett
Ross-on-Wye
Rotherfield and Mark Cross
Rowfant
Rowsley
Royston and Notton
Royton
Rudgwick
Rugby Central
Rugeley Town
Rushwick Halt
Ruswarp
Ryburgh
Ryde St John's Road (Isle of Wight)
Rye
Rye Hill and Burstwick

Saddleworth
Saffron Walden
St Albans Abbey
St Andrew's Road
St Bees
St Budeaux Victoria Road
St Columb Road
St Helens Shaw Street
St Ives (Cornwall)
St Ives (Hunts)
St James Park Halt
St Kew Highway
St Keyne Halt
St Michaels
St Peters
Saltaire
Saltmarshe
Sampford Courtenay
Sampford Peverell Halt
Sandown (Isle of Wight)
Sandplace Halt
Savernake for Marlborough

Saxmundham
Scale Hall
Scholes
Scorrier
Scorton
Scotswood
Seaforth and Litherland
Sea Mills
Seascale
Seaton (Devon)
Seaton (Rutland)
Seaton Delaval
Seaton Junction
Seend
Seghill
Sellafield
Semington Halt
Semley
Settle
Severn Beach
Severn Bridge
Shalford
Shanklin (Isle of Wight)
Shap
Shapwick
Sharpness
Sheepbridge
Shepley
Shepton Mallet Charlton Road
Sherburn-in-Elmet
Shildon
Shillingstone
Shipton for Burford
Shirebrook West
Shirehampton
Shoscombe and Single Hill Halt
Shrivenham
Sidley
Sidmouth
Sidmouth Junction
Sigglesthorne

Sileby
Silecroft
Silloth
Silverdale (Staffs)
Silverton
Skegness
Skelmanthorpe
Slaithwaite
Sleights
Slinfold
Snaith
Somersham
South Acton
Southam Road and Harbury
Southcoates
Southease and Rodmell Halt
South Elmsall
South Molton
Southrey
South Tottenham
Southwater
Sparkford
Speeton
Spofforth
Spondon
Spon Lane
Stacksteads
Staines West
Stainton Dale
Stalbridge
Stamford Bridge
Stamford Town
Standon
Stanley (Yorks.)
Stanley Bridge Halt
Stanlow and Thornton
Stanton Gate
Stapleford and Sandiacre
Staple Hill
Starbeck
Starcross for Exmouth

Staverton Halt
Steeton and Silsden
Stepney
Steventon
Stewartby
Steyning
Stickney
Stixwould
Stockbridge
Stockport Tiviot Dale
Stocksmoor
Stogumber
Stoke (Suffolk)
Stoke Edith
Stoke Works
Stonegate
Stonehouse Bristol Road
Stoulton
Stow Bedon
Stratton Park Halt
Streetly
Strines
Stubbins
Sturmer
Sturminster Newton
Suckley
Sudbury (Suffolk)
Summerseat
Sutton Junction
Sutton-on-Hull
Sutton-on-Sea
Sutton Park
Swanbourne
Swavesey
Swimbridge
Swinderby
Swine
Syston

Tackley Halt
Tadcaster

Tanhouse Lane
Tattenhall Road
Tavistock North
Tebay
Templecombe
Tetbury
Thatto Heath
Theddingworth
Thorner
Thorney and Kingsbury Halt
Thornford Bridge Halt
Thornton Abbey
Thornton-in-Craven
Thorp Arch
Thorpe (Northants)
Thorpe Culvert
Thorpeness Halt
Thrapston Bridge Street
Three Oaks and Guestling Halt
Threlkeld
Thurgarton
Tinker's Green Halt
Tipton St John's
Tisbury
Tiverton
Tiverton Junction
Todd Lane Junction
Toller
Tollerton
Topsham
Torrington
Tower Hill (Devon)
Trench Crossing
Trent
Trentham
Tresmeer
Trouble House Halt
Troutbeck
Trowell
Tumby Woodside
Tunbridge Wells West

Tunstall
Tyldesley

Uckfield
Uffington (Berks)
Ulceby
Ulleskelf
Umberleigh
Upholland
Upper Holloway
Upton (Cheshire)
Usworth

Venn Cross
Ventnor (Isle of Wight)
Verney Junction
Verwood
Vulcan Halt

Wadborough
Wadebridge
Wadhurst
Wainfleet
Wakerley and Barrowden
Walker
Walsingham
Walthamstow
Wanstead Park
Wantage Road
Warmley
Washford
Washington
Watchet
Waterfoot for Newchurch
Watergate Halt
Waterloo (Lancs)
Watford North
Watford West
Wath North
Watton (Norfolk)
Wednesbury Town

Welford and Kilworth
Wellingborough London Road
Wellington (Somerset)
Wellow
Wells-next-the-Sea
Welshampton
Wem
Wennington
West End Lane
West Grinstead
West Hallam
Westhouses and Blackwell
West Leigh and Bedford
West Mill
West Moors
Weston-under-Penyard Halt
West Pennard
West Timperley
Wetheral
Wetherby
Weybourne
Whaley Bridge
Whatstandwell
Wheathampstead
Whimple
Whitby Town
Whitchurch North (Hants)
Whitedale
Whitefield
White Notley
Whitley Bridge
Whitstone and Bridgerule
Whitwell
Wickham Bishops
Wickham Market
Wickwar
Widford
Widnes Central
Wigan Central
Wighton Halt
Wigston Glen Parva

Wigston Magna
Willenhall Bilston Street
Willesden Junction High Level
Willington (Durham)
Willington Quay
Williton
Willoughby
Wilmington
Wilton South
Wimblington
Wimborne
Wincanton
Winchelsea Halt
Windmill End Halt
Wingfield
Winslow
Winston
Witham (Somerset)
Withernsea
Withyham
Wiveliscombe
Woburn Sands
Woodborough
Woodbridge
Woodford Halse
Woodgrange Park
Woodhall Junction
Woodlands Road
Woodlesford
Woodley
Wootton Bassett
Wootton Rivers Halt
Worsley
Wrafton
Wrenbury
Wressle
Wretham and Hockham
Wroxall (Isle of Wight)
Wylam
Wyre Halt
Wyrley and Cheslyn Hay

Yarde Halt
Yarmouth South Town
Yate
Yelvertoft and Stanford Park
Yeoford
Yeo Mill Halt
Yeovil Pen Mill
Yeovil Town
Yetminster
Yorton

Scotland

Abbeyhill
Aberfeldy
Aberlour
Abington
Aboyne
Achanalt
Ach-na-Cloich
Achnasheen
Achnashellach
Achterneed
Addiewell
Advie
Allafearn
Altnabreac
Alves
Alyth Junction
Anstruther
Appin
Ardrossan Montgomerie Pier
Ardrossan Town
Arnage
Attadale Halt
Auchengray
Auchindachy
Auchinleck
Auchnagatt

331

Back o'Loch Halt
Baillieston
Balado
Ballachulish
Ballachulish Ferry
Ballater
Ballifurth Farm Halt
Ballindalloch
Ballinluig
Balloch Pier
Balnaguard Halt
Balquhidder
Banavie
Banchory
Banff
Barassie
Barcaldine Halt
Barleith
Barrhead
Barrhill
Beasdale
Belses
Benderloch
Bishopbriggs
Blacksboat
Blackwood (Lanark)
Boat of Garten
Bogside Race Course
Bonar Bridge
Bonnybridge High
Borrobol Halt
Bowling
Breich
Bridgefoot Halt
Bridge of Allan
Bridge of Dun
Bridge of Earn
Bridge of Weir
Bridgeton Cross
Brodie
Broomhill (Inverness)

Brora
Brucklay
Buckie
Busby

Cairnbulg
Cairnie Junction
Calcots
Callander
Cambus O'May Halt
Canonbie
Carfin Halt
Carmyle
Carnwath
Carr Bridge
Carron
Castlecary
Castle Douglas
Castle Kennedy
Clarkston and Stamperland
Cleghorn
Cleland
Clydebank Riverside
Coalburn
Cobbinshaw
Comrie
Corkerhill
Cornhill
Coupar Angus
Cowlairs
Craigellachie
Crail
Crathes
Crawford
Creagan
Creetown
Crianlarich Lower
Crieff
Cromdale
Crook of Devon
Crookston

Crosshouse
Crossmichael
Crossmyloof
Croy
Cullen
Culloden Moor
Culrain
Culter
Cults
Cumberland Street
Cumbernauld
Cumnock

Dailly
Dailuaine Halt
Dalbeattie
Dalcross
Dalguise
Dalmarnock
Dalmellington
Dalmuir Riverside
Dalnaspidal
Dalvey Farm Halt
Dalwhinnie
Darvel
Dava
Daviot
Dee Street Halt
Dess
Dingwall
Dinnet
Dollar
Douglas West
Doune
Dreghorn
Drummuir
Drumpark
Drybridge
Dufftown
Duirinish
Dullatur

Duncraig Halt
Dundee West
Dunlop
Dunphail
Dunragit
Dunrobin Private Halt
Duror
Dyce

East Fortune
Easthaven
East Kilbride
East Linton
Eastriggs
Edinburgh Princes Street
Eglinton Street
Elderslie
Elie
Elliot Junction
Ellon
Elvanfoot
Eskbank and Dalkeith

Falkirk Camelon
Falls of Cruachan Halt
Fauldhouse North
Fearn
Findochty
Flemington
Forfar
Forsinard
Fountainhall Junction
Fraserburgh

Gailes
Galashiels
Galston
Garmouth
Gartly
Garve
Gatehead

Gatehouse of Fleet
Georgemas Junction
Giffnock
Gilbey's Cottages Halt
Gilnockie
Girvan
Glasgow Buchanan Street
Glasgow Cross
Glasgow St. Enoch
Glassel
Glenbarry
Glencarron Halt
Glen Douglas Halt
Glenfarg
Glenluce
Glenwhilly
Golf Club House Halt
Gollanfield
Golspie
Gorebridge
Grandtully
Grange (Banffshire)
Grantown-on-Spey East
Grantown-on-Spey West
Grantshouse
Greenhill
Greenock Princes Pier
Gretna Green
Guard Bridge

Hairmyres
Happendon
Harburn
Hartwood
Hassendean
Hawick
Hawkhead
Helmsdale
Heriot
Highlandman
Hollybush

Holytown
Houston and Crosslee
Hoy Halt

Imperial Cottages Halt
Inches
Insch
Inveresk
Invergordon
Invershin
Inverugie
Inverurie

Joppa

Keith Town
Kelvin Hall
Kennethmont
Kennishead
Kentallen
Kershope Foot
Kilbarchan
Kilbirnie
Kilbowie
Kilconquhar
Kildonan
Kilkerran
Killiecrankie
Killin
Killin Junction
Kilmacolm
Kilmaurs
Kinaldie
Kinbrace
Kincraig
Kingshouse Halt
Kingskettle
Kingsknowe
Kinloss
Kintore
Kirkconnel

Kirkcowan
Kirkcudbright
Kirkintilloch
Kirkton Bridge Halt
Kittybrewster
Knock
Knockando
Knockando House Halt
Kyle of Lochalsh

Ladysbridge
Lairg
Lamington
Langholm
Langloan
Largo
Larkhall Central
Laurencekirk
Law Junction
Lesmahagow
Lhanbryde
Loch Awe
Locheilside
Lochluichart
Lochskerrow
Lochwinnoch
Logierieve
Longmorn
Longside
Lonmay
Lossiemouth
Lugton
Luib
Lumphanan
Lundin Links

Manuel
Maryhill Central
Mauchline
Maud Junction
Mawcarse

Maybole
Melrose
Merchiston
Midcalder
Milliken Park
Milnathort
Mintlaw
Mormond Halt
Mosspark West
Moy
Muirkirk
Mulben
Murthly
Musselburgh
Muthill

Neilston Low
Nethy Bridge
Newcastleton
New Cumnock
New Galloway
New Luce
Newmachar
Newmilns
Newseat Halt
Newtongrange
Newton Stewart
Nitshill
North Connel Halt

Old Kilpatrick
Orbliston
Ordens Halt
Orton
Oyne

Paisley Canal
Paisley West
Park
Parkhead Stadium
Partick West

Parton
Patna
Penton
Perth Princes Street
Peterhead
Philorth Bridge Halt
Philorth Halt
Piershill
Pinmore
Pinwherry
Pitcaple
Pitmedden
Pittenweem
Pittenzie Halt
Plockton
Pollokshaws West
Ponfeigh
Portessie
Portgordon
Portknockie
Portsoy
Possil

Racks
Rathen
Reston
Rhu Halt
Riccarton Junction
Riddings Junction
Rogart Halt
Rothes
Rothiemay
Rumbling Bridge
Ruthwell

St Boswells
St Combs
St Fort
St Monance
Salzcraggie
Sandilands

Sanquhar
Scotscalder
Scotstoun East
Scotstoun West
Shandon
Shankend
Shields Road
Shotts
Slateford
Southwick
Spey Bay
Springfield
Springside
Steele Road
Stewarton
Stobs
Stonehouse
Stow
Stragheath Halt
Stranraer Harbour
Stranraer Town
Strathaven Central
Strathcarron
Strathyre
Strichen
Stromeferry
Struan
Symington

Tain
Tarff
Tauchers Halt
Thankerton
Thornhill
Thornliebank
Thorntonhall
Throsk
Thurso
Tillicoultry
Tillynaught
Tollcross

Tomatin
Torphins
Towiemore Halt
Tullibardine
Tynehead

Udny
Uplawmoor for Caldwell
Urquhart

Waterside
West Calder
West Ferry
Whifflet Upper
Whistlefield Halt
Whiteinch Riverside
Wick

Yoker Ferry

Wales

Aberaman
Aberdare Low Level
Abergele
Abermule
Aberthaw
Abertridwr
Acrefair
Alltddu Halt
Amlwch
Arddleen Halt
Arthog

Bagillt
Bala
Bala Junction
Beavers' Hill Halt
Berwyn Halt
Bettisfield

Bettws-y-Coed
Birchgrove Halt
Blaenau Ffestiniog
Blaengwynfi
Blaenrhondda
Bodorgan
Bontnewydd
Bonwm Halt
Bow Street
Briton Ferry
Bronwydd Arms
Bryngwyn
Brynkir
Bryn Teify
Buckley Junction

Caerau
Caergwrle Castle and Wells
Caernarvon
Caersws
Caldicot Halt
Caradog Falls Halt
Cardiff Clarence Road
Carno
Carreghofa Halt
Carrog
Cefn-y-bedd
Cemmes Road
Chwilog
Clarbeston Road
Clynderwen
Cockett
Commins Coch Halt
Connah's Quay
Conway
Conwil
Corwen
Coryton Halt (Glam)
Cymmer Afan
Cynwyd

337

Deganwy
Derry Ormond
Dolgarrog
Dolgellau
Dolwyddelen
Drws-y-Nant
Duffryn Rhondda Halt

Felindyffryn Halt
Fenn's Bank
Ferndale
Ferryside
Fishguard and Goodwick
Flint
Forden

Gaerwen
Garneddwen Halt
Gileston
Glan Conway
Glandyfi
Glan Llyn Halt
Glyndyfrdwy
Gowerton North
Groeslon

Hawarden
Hawarden Bridge
Heath Halt Low Level
Holywell Junction
Hope Village

Jordanston Halt

Kidwelly
Kilgetty

Lampeter
Lamphey
Landore
Llanbrynmair
Llandderfel

Llandow Halt
Llandow Wick Road Halt
Llandre
Llandrillo
Llanerchymedd
Llanfair
Llanfairfechan
Llanfechain
Llanfyllin
Llangefni
Llangollen
Llangower Halt
Llangwyllog
Llangybi (Caern)
Llangybi (Card)
Llangynwyd
Llanharan
Llanilar
Llanpumpsaint
Llanrhystyd Road
Llanrwst and Trefriw
Llansamlet North
Llansantffraid
Llantrisant
Llantwit Major
Llanuwchllyn
Llanwnda
Llanybyther
Llys Halt

Maerdy
Maesteg Castle Street
Maesycrugiau
Magor
Manorbier
Mathry Road
Matthewstown Halt
Menai Bridge
Montgomery
Mostyn
Mountain Ash Oxford Street

Nantyffyllon

Olmarch Halt

Pembrey and Burry Port
Penally
Pencader
Pencarreg Halt
Pencoed
Penmaenmawr
Penmaenpool
Penrhiwceiber Low Level
Penyffordd
Penygroes
Penyrheol
Peterston
Pontcynon Halt
Pontdolgoch
Pont Llanio
Pont-y-Pant
Pool Quay
Portskewett
Prestatyn
Pyle

Queensferry

Rhiwbina Halt
Rhoose
Rhosgoch
Rhosneigr
Roman Bridge

St Athan
St Clears

Sarnau
Saundersfoot
Sealand
Senghenydd
Shotton High Level
Shotton Low Level
Skewen
Strata Florida

Talacre
Talerddig
Tal-y-Cafn and Eglwysbach
Templeton
Tondu
Trawscoed
Tregaron
Trevor
Troedyrhiew Garth
Ty Cross
Tylorstown

Undy Halt

Valley

Welsh Hook Halt
Whitchurch (Glam)
Wnion Halt
Wolf's Castle Halt

Ynys
Ynyshir
Ynyslas

Requiescant in pace

ACKNOWLEDGEMENTS

I wish to thank my editor, Helen, and my agent, Rachel, for all their help, support and friendship; thanks also to my beta readers Lesli, Gwen and Lisa.

A NOTE ON THE AUTHOR

Malcolm Pryce was born in the UK and has spent much of his life working and travelling abroad. He has been a BMW assembly-line worker, a hotel washer-up, a deck hand on a yacht sailing the South Seas, an advertising copywriter and the world's worst aluminium salesman. He is the author of the bestselling *Aberystwyth* novels. He lives in Oxford.

@exogamist
www.malcolmpryce.com